Flashman at the Alamo

Robert Brightwell

Published in 2019 by FeedARead.com Publishing

A CIP catalogue record for this title is available from the British
Library.

Introduction

When other men might be looking forward to a well-earned retirement to enjoy their ill-gotten gains, Flashman finds himself once more facing overwhelming odds and ruthless enemies, while standing (reluctantly) shoulder to shoulder with some of America's greatest heroes.

A trip abroad to avoid a scandal at home leaves him bored and restless. They say 'the devil makes work for idle hands' and Lucifer surpassed himself this time as Thomas is persuaded to visit the newly independent country of Texas. Little does he realise that this fledgling state is about to face its biggest challenge – one that will threaten its very existence.

Flashman joins the desperate fight of a new nation against a pitiless tyrant, who gives no quarter to those who stand against him. Drunkards, hunters, farmers, lawyers, adventurers and one English coward all come together to fight and win their liberty.

This is the ninth book in the Thomas Flashman series. As always, if you have not already read them, the memoirs of Thomas' more famous nephew, Harry Flashman, edited by George MacDonald Fraser, are strongly recommended.

Robert Brightwell

Chapter 1

The night of the fifth of March 1836 left a lot of time for thinking, especially if you spent it in an improvised stronghold just outside the town of San Antonio in the country of Texas. It was the first night without bombardment we had enjoyed in nearly two weeks and most of my comrades had just slumped in exhaustion. But try as I might, for me sleep would not come. Far from it; my guts were gripped by the familiar icy fingers of fear. God knows I have been in some tight spots in my long and ignoble career: a hill fort surrounded by Pindaree bandits; the British ridge at Waterloo facing the Old Guard or defending McCarthy Hill against the Ashanti spring to mind. They had all seemed utterly hopeless positions and this did not appear a whit better.

At dusk Mexican forces had been seen closing around us, a clear sign that they were preparing for a dawn assault. There were two thousand infantry, some damn handy looking cavalry and we knew all too well that they had batteries of guns covering every wall. All we had to meet the expected onslaught was around a hundred and sixty men and battered defences with more holes than my well-worn trousers.

The previous afternoon, when it had been obvious that all was lost, Travis our young *beau sabreur* commander, had given all of us the opportunity to try and slide out without recrimination. I was sorely tempted – this was not my fight. The only thing that deterred me was the red flag flying from the church in San Antonio, which signified that no quarter was to be given to our gallant band of defenders. Well, that and their lancers, who looked more than ready to chase down and impale anyone who tried to run. In the event, only one man chose to leave, an old veteran called Rose, who slipped away in the dead of night. I was still contemplating following his example when a bloodcurdling shriek from outside indicated that, for a while at least, I might be safer *inside* the walls. So instead, I sat there in the darkness, trying to work out how the hell I had ended up in this mess.

There are two great villains in this tale. One of them, you might have guessed, is Antonio López de Santa Anna, the Mexican president and general. For him a special place should be reserved in the foulest pit of hell – although knowing that devious bastard he would find some way to grease his way out of it. We will come to him presently. The second is an Englishman, George Norton. Without him, I would have instead spent that fretful night sleeping without a care in the world, tucked up in my bed in Leicestershire.

Norton was a rogue and a scoundrel and as I share those properties, I would have to say that there is nothing wrong in that. But he was also a cruel and vindictive man, not to mention a wifebeater and a blackmailer. Worse than that, he had tried to sink his hooks into me.

I had first come across him almost exactly a year before. He had married a young woman called Caroline Sheridan, nearly half his age, a society beauty full of wit and charm. The attractions of the match for George were obvious. As he was the brother of Lord Grantley and a Member of Parliament, the penniless Sheridan family must have worried at their ability to attract better suitors. Caroline soon became a successful author and leading society hostess, notwithstanding the fact that her husband was often a drunk and spiteful bore at many of her gatherings. Despite gossip that Norton regularly beat and punched his wife, she delivered for him three children, while he failed at a career as a barrister and lost his seat in parliament.

The first I knew of their problems was when Norton had the damned impertinence to invite me to call on him at his London home one evening. His note explained that it was regarding a matter of our mutual interest, but I doubted that. When strangers leave a missive like that for you at your London house or club, it invariably leads to trouble. Usually it is some hare-brained scheme to try and part me from my bank balance or worse, accusations that I have been sleeping with their wives! I should have listened to my instincts that morning to be sure, for I would never have been in this pickle if I had. Instead, boredom and the prospect of being introduced to the delectable Caroline drew me to his threshold.

"Is Mrs Norton at home?" I enquired as I was shown inside. Norton had answered the door himself, which was deuced odd. I thought perhaps he had given the maid a day off, but as we moved into his study, the layers of dust visible told me that she had been away for considerably longer.

"No, she is not," Norton informed me gruffly as he showed me to a chair opposite his desk. "Nor is she likely to be at any time soon. Can I offer you a glass of madeira?"

"That is most kind…" I started to accept the offer until I saw the dirty glasses on the silver tray and the half inch of wine at the bottom of the decanter. It was probably thick with sediment if it had not been decanted properly. "But no, I am in no need of refreshment. I had hoped to ask Mrs Norton to inscribe her latest work for my wife, who is most fond of it." I patted the volume in my pocket. "As that is not possible, perhaps we can get to whatever matter brings me here."

Norton studied me with cold dispassionate eyes, like a Spanish inquisitor considering some poor wretch tied to the rack. There was an air of viciousness about him. His features reminded me of a boy at school who had dipped a cat's tail in lamp oil and set it alight. I decided that I would sooner trust a cockney cracksman than this cove and was preparing to decline whatever offer he was about to make. Which made his next statement all the more surprising.

"Caroline has left me," Norton replied curtly. His face flushed with either anger, embarrassment or perhaps both, before he continued, "She has gone to live with her family after I took the children." He gave me a calculating look and added, "I think that she is having an affair, that is why I wanted to speak to you."

"What?" I replied, astonished that he was divulging such personal details to someone he barely knew. Then the import of his final sentence hit home. "Hang on, you surely don't think she is having an affair with *me*, do you? You must be mad! I have not even been introduced to the woman." I got to my feet, anxious to leave before the matter escalated further. I was fifty-three for heaven's sake, too long in the tooth to start fighting duels at the crack of dawn over my honour.

6

"Damn your impertinence, sir," I snarled at him, "I will take my leave." And with that I strode for the door.

"No please, wait." Norton had risen too and was holding out his hands in supplication. "You don't understand, I am not accusing you. Far from it. I believe that we have both been wronged by the same man."

"What do you mean?" I asked, turning, and I am sure my eyes narrowed in suspicion. If he was alluding to what I thought he might be, then the last thing I needed was him raking up old wounds. My worst fears were confirmed by his next words.

"I believe that my wife is having an affair with Lord Melbourne," he announced primly. "I remember, why it must be over twenty years ago now, that there were rumours that Charles Lamb, as he was then, had an affair with your wife too. I recall that there were stories that you had tried to scalp him with a tomahawk."

"Let me be very clear with you, Mr Norton," I replied sternly. "Whatever passed between my wife, myself and Lord Melbourne is a private matter and will remain so." I suppressed a grin at the memory of that infamous encounter. I had come bloody close to killing the bastard when, roaring drunk, I had flung the tomahawk at a target drawn on a door. It had missed his head by a fraction of an inch. He was convinced that my aim was deliberate and had steered clear of me ever since. That was just the way I liked it. As far as I knew, over the intervening two decades, he had steered clear of my wife as well, although I had been out of the country for much of that time. Louisa and I enjoyed a happy marriage in our own way and she would be appalled to have this scandal dragged into the light again. Mind you, so would Melbourne – the man had just been appointed Prime Minister.

"Please, sir," implored Norton, "I need your help. We must act against a man who has wronged us both." It was a forlorn appeal and I did not waste any time in dashing it.

"Your grievance, sir, is with Lord Melbourne. I suggest that you take it up directly with him. I imagine that he will be most anxious to avoid any political embarrassment given his new office. Now good day to you."

"I already have. He told me that he was not having an affair with Caroline and that I could go to the devil as he was not paying me a penny."

I turned back from the door in surprise. It was an unusually robust response from Melbourne, who was notorious for seeking compromise over every issue. "Were you asking for money?" I asked.

"Yes, I wanted him to pay for the shame he has caused me, but he insisted he would not consider giving money to a man who beat his wife and deprived her of her children." Norton slammed his fist down on the desk in exasperation. "Damn him, I am entitled to beat my wife if she is in the wrong and she will never lay eyes on our children until I am paid."

The reaction confirmed my suspicions: he might be a wronged man, but he was *definitely* a thoroughly nasty piece of work. I glanced around the study; it was clear that he needed the money too. The room was sparsely furnished and there were marks in the rugs showing where furniture had once stood, presumably before it was sold. "Do you not have an income?"

"Caroline persuaded Melbourne when he was Home Secretary to make me a police magistrate, but I am no longer being called to the bench. They have ruined me," the man whined, "and I want to make them both pay. I am going to sue Melbourne for having a criminal conversation with my wife."

I smiled at the polite legal term used in court for adultery. There would be a huge scandal if he followed through with his threat, which could easily bring down Melbourne and his Whig government. But then Wellington, leading the Tories in opposition, was no admirer of blackmailers. His response of 'Publish and be damned' to one former mistress was well known. He might choose not to take advantage of the situation. It was certainly not an affair I wanted to get involved with. Many leading politicians would support the Prime Minister as well as much of society, particularly those who had enjoyed Caroline's company or heard the rumours about her husband.

I had no wish to be associated with Norton at all and told him, "Well if you think I am joining you as a plaintiff you will be disappointed. My issue with Melbourne has been settled and I have no wish to raise the matter again."

"No, that is not why I asked you to call." Norton smiled at me but there was no warmth in it. "I am confident of winning the case. You will doubtless have heard the same stories as I of him beating and indulging his basest pleasures on those poor unfortunate orphan girls that he has given shelter to in his home." He paused, licking his lips and I sensed that we were about to come to the nub of the matter. "But to do so, I may have to consider calling you and perhaps your wife as a witness…"

"That is outrageous," I interrupted. "If you expect me to help you in this sordid matter then you can think again."

He held up a hand to stop me. "I already have a statement from someone who saw you throw the axe at His Lordship and many people saw your wife with Lamb while you were overseas in Spain and Canada. You can hardly deny that you at least suspected foul play."

"I damn well can, and I will," I fumed. The thought of being dragged into this squalid mess was beyond endurance. Any association with Norton would see me shunned by people of influence, my name would become a laughing-stock in the London clubs and Louisa would be humiliated in society. I would have to do whatever it took to keep us out of it. As if reading my mind, Norton spoke again.

"There is of course another way we could proceed." He held out his hands in a gesture of appeal, like some Bedouin trader assuring you that his knock-kneed, broken-down hack of a camel is a prime runner. "The court case will be an expensive affair. If you were to make a contribution to cover some of the costs, discreetly of course, then I think I could guarantee that you and your wife's name would not be mentioned."

So, there we had it: blackmail. Where he had failed with Melbourne, he hoped he could succeed with me. My first reaction was to regret that I had handed in my cane at the door, for I would have dearly loved to have thrashed the importuning wretch with it. But while that would have been eminently satisfying, it would not have solved the problem. So, I took a deep breath to calm myself while I pretended to consider his offer. "And how much would it cost to keep our names out of this affair?"

He sagged slightly in relief; perhaps he had half expected me to come at *him* with a tomahawk too. I guessed that he had a pistol in one of his desk drawers in case things turned ugly. "Two thousand guineas," he announced, "and I give you my word that you will never hear from me again."

"Hmmm," I gave him a doubtful glare for I have never met a blackmailer yet who took just one bite of the cherry. I knew full well that if I was foolish enough to pay him, he would be back for more and he would keep returning until the case was over. Even then, he could still drag our names through the mud. No, paying him was out of the question, but I played along as though I was considering it. "Well you will understand that I need to discuss the matter with my wife. It is a sizeable sum and she manages the income from the estate."

"Of course, of course." Norton was all smiles now as he showed me back out into the hall. As he handed me my hat, coat and cane he must have been calculating how much he could take me for. Certainly, as I looked around, there were more signs that money was in short supply. There had once been more furniture in here too, while above the fireplace, marks on the wall showed where a large portrait had been replaced by a smaller one of an angry fortune-teller. I was about to leave when my eye was drawn back to the canvas. There was something familiar about it. Then I realised. It was not a painting of a woman, as I had first thought, but of a man and one I had known well.

"Isn't that John Norton?" I asked pointing at the painting. "But wait a minute, he cannot be a relation of yours, for I know that his father was a Cherokee Indian."

"Oh, that is the son of my uncle's tame savage. He trained an Indian boy as an orderly when he was serving in North America. The lad adopted our family name when he came to England with the regiment. He ended up in Scotland and that is one of his children." He gave me a curious look, "Do you know John then? If you do, I would be happy to consider an offer for his portrait."

"I served with him in Canada and he certainly was not 'tame' then. For the money you are asking, the least you can do is throw in the portrait for nothing." I had not thought of John Norton for years and it was strange to see those familiar features staring down at me, even if the artist had painted a ridiculously romantic impression of what an Iroquois war chief might wear. "I have not heard from him for nearly ten years – I was not sure he was even alive. He must be near seventy now."

"The last letter he sent us was from a place called Laredo I think, in Northern Mexico." Norton smiled ingratiatingly again, "Alright, as you know the man, I will include the painting in our deal. I look forward to hearing from you."

Chapter 2

In the end I did not mention my meeting with Norton to Louisa. At first it was because I was considering options that she definitely would *not* approve of. I knew several former soldiers who would happily slide a blade between Norton's ribs if I asked and bury his body in some road mender's trench. At length I decided that I could not take the risk; he was a former Member of Parliament and questions would be asked about his disappearance. His brother, Lord Grantley, would see to that. If His Lordship was aware that Norton had been trying to blackmail me, then they were bound to come knocking at my door. Melbourne had people in power who would protect him, whereas I did not. Indeed, after the tomahawk incident, our noble Prime Minister would no doubt be quietly satisfied to see me scragged at the end of a hangman's noose.

The other reason I did not tell Louisa was that I knew she would feel duty bound to warn Melbourne. Then we would be inextricably drawn into the unseemly mess, for I could hardly pay off Norton then, even if I was minded to. In the end a better solution presented itself. Many years before, in Queenston Canada, I had saved the life of a young American called William Vanderbilt. He had tracked me down during the intervening time and offered a standing invitation to visit him in New York. The lad had prospered, although not nearly as well as his cousin Cornelius, who, according to my friend's correspondence, was one of the biggest employers in the city. As his latest letter arrived, it occurred to me that now might be the perfect time to take up his offer of hospitality.

I had long wanted to visit the United States again and Louisa too was fond of travel. Long ago she had followed me all the way to India, when such a journey for a society lady was almost unthinkable. With both of us out of the country and therefore unreachable, Norton could not call on us to support his action in court and the villain could damn well whistle for his money. If he tried to drag our names into the case with evidence from other witnesses, it would be dismissed as hearsay.

I spent the next two weeks stringing Norton along that payment would be forthcoming, while also arranging our passage. It had not been hard to persuade Louisa to come on the journey; she wanted to visit Washington and New York and I promised her the spectacle of Niagara Falls. She had heard all of my Canadian tales many times and while there I also hoped she would meet Black Eagle, my former Iroquois companion. I was looking forward to introducing her to the old warrior and perhaps joining him on a hunt or two. It would be a fine old adventure, I thought, and we had not had one of those for a while.

If you have read my previous memoirs, you will know that most foreign travel invariably ends up with me in the thick of some military action or on the run from a bunch of murderous heathens, or both. How many times have I sworn vehemently on a stack of Bibles that I would never leave the shores of old Albion again? But on this occasion, it was staying at home that carried a risk, to my and Louisa's reputation. In contrast, for once there did not seem any untoward danger in our journey. We booked a passage on one of the new packet ships to New York, a fine new seaworthy vessel offering ample comfort, at least to first-class passengers. But most importantly, both the United States and Canada were blissfully at peace. Apart from some Indian fighting in the frontier lands, which I had no intention of going near, all the talk was of growing and prosperous cities, invention and trade.

We sailed from London at the end of March 1835 and I am bound to say that it was a very pleasant voyage. There were only a few first-class passengers and the stewards attended to our every need. But for most of the souls aboard there were fewer comforts. The holds had been converted into space for steerage travellers. They came from all over the Old World. I could hear English and Irish accents, people speaking in French, Spanish and Russian, not to mention a vast array of tongues I could not understand or identify. But wherever they came from, they had one dream: to become an 'American'.

There were single men, couples, young families, all living cheek by jowl in the bowels of the ship, where they even had to share bunks as there were not enough for one each. Yet the only grumbling I heard came from two old grandfathers, who both moaned that no good would come of the journey and that it would see them ruined. The rest went about their chores on the deck, the women washing clothes in seawater as children ran about playing to keep warm. Men would often be found playing dice with what little capital they had gathered for the voyage, while those who had already lost their stake looked on enviously. Each evening through the planking of the ship you could hear some of them singing. Sometimes it was sad and plaintive songs of their old countries, but on other occasions jolly jigs and from the thump of clogs on the decking, they must have even managed to dance a little through the tightly confined space.

When the shoreline of New York appeared on the horizon, we joined these adventurers at the rail of the ship. While we were pleased to see the end of our voyage, the excitement of those around us was palpable. Bright eyes full of hope and expectation stared at the distant land, most imagining the opportunities of a new life that it would offer. Even a biting wind that blew across the cold grey water and through the threadbare clothes that many of them wore did little to cool their enthusiasm. Only the grandfathers showed any sign of trepidation. Old homes had been abandoned, jobs, friends and often wives and families had been left behind while they struck out on the gamble of a better life.

At bottom, those people were by their very nature greater risk-takers than those of us still anchored to the Old World. They were more willing to take a chance and if it paid off then they were likely to take another. They had all come with dreams to fulfil and if I was in any doubt of this fact, it would become all too apparent in the months ahead. Looking back, I should have paid more attention to that mood, for the ambition of my fellow travellers and their kind nearly dragged me to disaster. But equally, that fierce spirit for survival brought me deliverance too.

As our fellow passengers were directed off the ship to the customs shed on the quay, we were intercepted by a smiling middle-aged man.

"Tom, you have hardly changed a bit," he called grinning with his hand extended in greeting. I could not say the same about him, in fact for a moment I did not recognise him at all. Then I remembered that I only had one American friend who had assumed the familiarity to call me 'Tom'.

"William," I called, gripping Vanderbilt's hand. "Well you've certainly aged since I last saw *you*," I laughed. "Mind, when we last met you were just a teenager, covered in muck and grime and pale from the pain of your broken leg."

"I am near forty now, but I am afraid that I am doing a poor job of looking after the scalp you saved for me." He reached up and patted his balding pate before turning to Louisa. "But where are my manners, introduce me to your delightful wife."

Vanderbilt was a charming host for the next few weeks while we stayed in his large mansion in the city. He enjoyed showing us the sights and was relieved to take a break from his family duties. Headed by cousin Cornelius, the Vanderbilt clan were deeply involved in shipping and had just branched into railroads. They were ruthless in their determination to beat their competitors and were tough negotiators. I met Cornelius once, but he did not seem to approve of me, perhaps because I was distracting William from his work. He was soon encouraging me to head north into Canada.

It was late spring when I saw the Niagara Falls again. They still impressed with their awesome power and Louisa thought that they alone justified the trip. As they were close by, I took her to see the sights of my previous adventures on the Queenston Heights and Lundy's Lane, before heading on to the village where I had lived with John Norton and Black Eagle. Everything there had changed, though; most of my old friends had either died or headed out west. We went on to the newly named Toronto and then took a leisurely tour, travelling across Lake Erie and down to Washington, then up to Philadelphia before finally returning to New York.

The whole trip took over six months. It was what foreign travel should always be: no hint of danger, just comfortable lodgings, interesting sights and lots of good people to meet. The only moment of alarm came for Louisa when we happened across an Iroquoian hunting party, who melted out from some nearby trees. They were impressed when I managed to speak to them haltingly in their own tongue. Soon we were guests in their lodge, enjoying drinks made from fermented maple syrup.

When we returned to the Vanderbilt house, I eagerly inspected the letters waiting for us. I had greatly enjoyed our visit to North America, but now I was ready to go home. My London lawyer had sent a series of missives updating me on the progress of the Norton affair, but the wheels of British justice turn slowly. After arranging a series of anonymous articles in the press condemning Melbourne for having an affair, Norton had finally broken cover and issued his claim of criminal conversation. As I had half expected, Wellington had refused to use the case to attack the government, but they were in no rush to bring the case to trial. Perhaps they were expecting Norton to go bankrupt first. By then it was October, and my lawyer expected the case to be heard the following summer.

It felt as though I was in temporary exile from my own country and for the next few days I strolled around the city in an increasing mood of irritation. While I kicked my heels with nothing to do, all around me lay a scene of commerce and industry. Manufacturers of every conceivable commodity advertised in the newspapers and while many newly arrived immigrants were in New York looking for work, most were intent on pressing into the west of the country, where rumour had it there was land for all.

There were offices of various land agents selling huge acreages for much less than you would pay for a small paddock at home. I spoke to one of them who explained that land was so cheap because there was so much of it. Most was former wilderness which would need to be cleared before it could be put into production. But there was often valuable timber on the properties and that would go a long way to cover the cost of purchase if it could be got to a mill. I looked at some of the lots the agent had available and admitted I was surprised that he did not have farmers queuing out of the door. He laughed and told me that many of the new farmers were now going to Mexico where good prairie land was even cheaper.

I thought no more about the conversation until I mentioned it to Vanderbilt over dinner that evening.

"They are all going to the Mexican province of Texas," he told me. "By the saints, there will be some money to be made down there," he declared, his eyes gleaming with avarice. "I spoke to a seaman who had come from Mexico and he told me that he had sold his pencil for two dollars, two dollars!" he exclaimed again slapping the table. "Something you can buy here for just a few cents. I have been thinking of going there myself."

"Why on earth would you do that?" I asked. "Your family are well set up here and farming is no easy life. It will take years to clear the land and it will never show the profit that your shipping business does."

"Oh heaven," he exclaimed, laughing. "I don't want to farm – I am no homesteader. But the first people down there with trade goods will make a killing." He gave me a canny look and added, "You were just saying that you do not know what to do now. You must have some capital to invest, why don't you come in with me? We will both be rich."

For a moment I was tempted, but then I hesitated and Louisa guessed why. "My husband has an uncanny knack of finding himself involved in wars and conflicts when he travels," she explained. "In fact, I think that this is the first trip he has been on when someone has not tried to kill him."

"You know, I think it is," I agreed. "Let's not ruin my run of good fortune now. The Mexicans can't be happy with all these emigrants pouring into the country."

"There will be no great war in Mexico," Vanderbilt blithely assured me. They only got their independence from Spain a few years ago and the country is far too large for them to manage."

"So, it is all peaceful there?" I persisted.

"Well there was a scuffle last month between a group of settlers and the Mexican army. There are calls for the Texian province to become a separate country and I dare say that is the way it will go in time. Their army does not seem to have the strength to stop it. Twenty settlers forced over a hundred soldiers to back down. The old Spanish army cannot have trained them well – they don't have nearly enough men to protect their large borders."

I well remembered the catastrophic defeats of the Spanish army when I was fighting in Spain. Ragged peasant soldiers led by aristocratic officers who were completely ignorant of any military principles and inclined to abandon their men if attacked. I recalled that they had missed one assault when their whole army had overslept. If these inept fools had been responsible for training the Mexican army, I could easily imagine that it could be routed by a smaller more determined force. Yet I certainly was not taking Vanderbilt's assurances at face value. Neither of us had been to the place and his news was at least a month old. But to humour him, I got him to show me a map so that I could see where this Texas province was. The eastern side of the United States was full of towns and cities, but further south and west the names of towns were much more sparsely scattered on either side of the big Mississippi River and its tributaries. The territory of Mexico began just to the west of the state called Louisiana. It was the start of a huge tract of land that disappeared south off the map towards the central American isthmus and stretched all the way to the Pacific coast and up along it, almost as far as Canada. It was a vast country and I could now understand why they might not put up much of a fight to lose a small part of it.

"There," Vanderbilt jabbed his finger at the north-eastern corner of this land where the words *Provincia de Texas* could be read.

"But that must be fifteen hundred miles away from here," I protested. "And look at all those rivers you would have to cross, not to mention the risk of being robbed by various villains along the way. I know I said I had a few months to kill, but I will be damned if I spend it on some uncomfortable wagon train crawling through all that wilderness."

"You don't understand," Vanderbilt smiled. "We will not be going by wagon train – that I agree would be madness. We are in the largest port in America, my cousin can help me get a ship and down there is a port called Copano. The nearby towns will be full of settlers and merchants needing supplies. We will travel safely and comfortably by sea, no dangerous river crossings, no risk of Indian attack or robbery. We will surely be able to get a two hundred percent profit on the goods we bring and possibly much more. I promise you, Tom, we will make a handsome return from this venture and it will be more fun than you sitting bored around here."

"But what if the Mexicans do decide to put up a fight for this province?" I cautioned.

"They have no navy to speak of and their enemy would be the Texian settlers, not us. My cousin will lend us a ship registered here in New York that flies the stars and stripes. There is not a chance that the Mexicans will want to risk a war with the United States by interfering with our vessel."

I had to admit this made sense. While I have been tempted more than once into jeopardy by some appealing proposal, I struggled to see a danger here. We could sell our wares on the quayside and be quickly away if there was any sign of trouble. I was warming to the scheme and then I looked at the map again and saw something that for me was the decider. "There," I pointed to a town marked in Mexico. "That place called Laredo, how far away from the port do you think it is?"

"It cannot be more than a hundred miles." Vanderbilt looked at me curiously. "Why, surely you have not heard of the place?"

"I have," I grinned at him. "The last I heard, a friend lives there. You know him too; he was the commander of the Iroquois warriors at Queenston."

My companion shuddered at the memory of what was to him an awful day on the Canadian border. "It is not that giant fellow who nearly did for me, is it?" He looked aghast at the thought and I suspected he might call the whole venture off if it was.

"That was Black Eagle. I looked for him in Canada but he has gone west, according to people there. No, my friend is John Norton, although he has not written for a while. He could be dead by now."

"I remember the name. He was a wanted man for a while, wasn't he?" Vanderbilt paused as he had probably remembered that due to some bragging lies, I had been a wanted man too. "At least," he added hurriedly, "if he is still alive the locals are likely to remember a white man claiming to be an Iroquois war chief."

Louisa was happy to see me go on what seemed a safe and lucrative jaunt. She knew I was bored and there were plenty of society events she could enjoy without my brooding presence. It took just a few days to get the scheme started. Cornelius provided the ship and, I suspected, some of William's capital. I invested five hundred dollars in the venture, which brought an inordinate amount of stock. William knew plenty of local contacts and soon there was a steady stream of loaded carts coming down to the wharf where the ship was berthed. As well as pencils, there was paper, knives, shovels, saws, axes, powder, ammunition and more than a few guns. There were also cases of whisky and other spirits. I saw some brandy come aboard and while the labels claimed that it had originated in France, the gum on the back of them was still wet where they had just been stuck on. It was no more French than I was.

Cornelius was doubtless impressed to learn that we were almost in profit before we had weighed anchor, for as well as cargo we discovered a very ready market for passengers. They were the same type of bright-eyed adventurers as I had shared the passage across the Atlantic with, but on this trip the conditions were even worse. As most of the holds were full of merchandise, a fair number of the emigrants were living in makeshift shelters on deck. They did not seem to mind, though as they were all convinced that such a passage would be easier and quicker than the overland route. One young farmer from Denmark explained to me the deal that awaited them once they reached their destination. Every settler would have one league of land for grazing, which he told me was nearly four and a half *thousand* acres, plus a plot of nearly two hundred acres for crops. The cost for all this land was just thirty dollars and that was not payable for four years and not subject to taxes for six. As a new Mexican citizen, they were expected to observe the Catholic religion, but this was not strictly enforced. It was an astonishingly generous deal and if I had been a penniless clod-thumper I would have happily slept on deck to get my hands on it too.

Chapter 3

The journey down the coast took nearly eight weeks. It was a two thousand-mile trip by sea and often against the prevailing trade winds. For much of it we hugged the coast and we had some rough weather off the state they call Florida. It looked a green and pleasant shore, but I knew that there had been fighting there between settlers and the Seminole Indian tribe. Another old acquaintance from my time in Canada, Winfield Scott, who I had met in Washington, was on his way to command the US army troops there. He had told me that the Indians were proficient fighters in the swampy, alligator-infested forests. I certainly had no wish to land in that region and was glad when we rounded the bottom of the peninsula and headed west into the Gulf of Mexico.

William clearly had the Vanderbilt talent for trade as he managed to sell a good part of the cargo to our passengers. Held captive on our decks, they struggled to resist his assurances that they would need exactly the type of shovel or axe that we carried to carve out their future in the wilderness. Few of them barely had two dollars to rub together when on the eighth of January 1836 we finally made landfall at our destination, the port of Copano Bay.

I had been expecting it to be a bustling harbour, full of other adventurers, but I was to be disappointed. Most emigrants evidently came the overland route rather than by sea. Copano Bay was little more than a small fishing settlement, with a couple of warehouses to store cargo and a dozen shrimp boats. There was no sign of any Mexican authorities, the customs post was empty and either the officials stationed there were very untidy or it had been ransacked. The water was too shallow to tie up at the wooden jetty and the few swarthy villagers watched the growing band of white men being rowed ashore with suspicion. As I was the only one in our party who spoke Spanish, I was deputed to go forward and parley with them. What I learned at first horrified and then delighted me.

While we had been sailing peaceably down the coast, the province of Texas had burst into war and rebellion. A Mexican army of five hundred men had landed in that very port the previous September. We must have just missed news of its arrival when we departed New York. It was commanded by a General Cos, whose orders were to stamp out any flames of rebellion in the province and restore central control from Mexico City. Things had not gone well for the Mexicans. After some initial skirmishes, Cos found himself besieged in the town of San Antonio by a mixture of 'Texians', who I learned were what the white settlers were called and 'Tejanos' who were citizens of Mexican descent. Neither group was keen on the increasingly centralised government of Santa Anna.

At first I was aghast at learning that my worst fears had been well founded: once again I had inadvertently found myself in the heart of a war. But before I could determine to have myself rowed straight back to the ship, the locals told me that the conflict was already over. General Cos had been forced to surrender the previous month. Apart from some wounded men, all Mexican forces had been evacuated from the province of Texas. A local governor and council had been appointed to administer the state and instead of fearing another attack from the Mexicans, forces from Texas were planning to invade an adjoining territory to foment rebellion there. I remember laughing in relief – given my career this seemed a most unlikely occurrence. For once a war really had happened without me. Perhaps my fortunes had changed at last.

The farmers were much less sanguine about my news; with no Mexican authorities their land deal might have gone. But they reasoned that the land was still there and the province of Texas would continue to want settlers. In fact, they might have been better off, as we learned that during the rebellion the Mexicans were trying to stop more *norteamericanos* from entering the country.

The villagers had assumed that we were soldiers rather than settlers. It was an understandable mistake as most of the farmers owned a rifle or musket for hunting and protecting their new land. They told us that the Texas forces were gathered forty miles inland at the town of Goliad where there was a large fort. There was no alternative but for all of us to travel there. William and I needed to find carts and a ready market for our cargo, while the settlers had to establish what terms for land were now available. I quickly hired the only two mules available in the village. William and I rode them, with our regiment of farmers marching along behind.

The journey took a leisurely two days, much of it along the meandering San Antonio River, and I had to agree with the farmers that it looked good fertile land. Virtually all of it was untouched by any kind of plough, while acres of rolling grass cried out for grazing cattle. I thought you would have to be a particularly lazy or incompetent farmer to fail to make a good living here. The only surprise was the cold. Being close to the central part of the Americas, I had expected it to be warmer, but there was a frost on the grass when we awoke that first morning.

Goliad, when we reached it next day, was a small bustling town, with a stone fort on the outskirts. It was full of militia and soldiers although hardly any wore uniforms and certainly none that matched. We had hoped to find someone in charge who could help us make arrangements for the cargo and tell the farmers about any new land deal. The problem we encountered, however, was that there were rather *too many* people in charge – and they rarely agreed with each other.

The new governor, a man called Smith, and his council had already fallen out over plans to capture the town of Matamoros in the neighbouring province. While the governor had appointed a commander-in-chief of the army, the more hawkish council had appointed two men of their own, who both claimed to be in command. The day we arrived, the council published a proclamation in the town calling all to arms to defend liberty and fight tyranny. Excited men were cheering and shouting while firing guns into the air. A local doctor, who also claimed some authority over the army, was encouraging them and assuring all who would listen that they would 'light the torch of rebellion' in Mexico. At the sight of us new arrivals, men crowded round and assured the farmers that if they joined one band of militia or another then they would be certain of a land grant. Some did join up, but the various recruiting officers promised differing land grants on enlistment, while a few just seemed to be making up offers on the spot. It was a bewildering display and most of the farmers stood cautiously back, wary about joining a war that they did not yet understand.

As you would expect, your correspondent easily resisted all entreaties to fight. I was just an English merchant, I explained, eager to return to his ship once his goods had been landed and sold. It was not just my natural cowardice that held me back, but a well-honed sense of imminent disaster. By God, I have been in a few of those and this venture had catastrophe written all over it. If I have to go to war, I want a cool and experienced hand in charge, one who knows what he is up against and has organised supplies to keep the army going. These poor devils had none of that. Give it a week, I thought, and the rations will have run out. They will be stuck in the middle of nowhere thinking more about a haunch of meat over a fire than the 'torch of rebellion'.

There was a large hardware store on the corner of the street that looked to have precious little left in it. "I'm going to try over there," shouted Vanderbilt above the noise. "Why don't you try to find the quartermaster for the garrison."

As I stood amidst the hubbub in the town square I stared about me and spied some gentlemen coolly appraising the goings on from a balcony above a tavern. Businessmen, I thought, rather than soldiers would have a much better idea of the commercial opportunities available. I strolled across and having bought myself a bottle, I went upstairs to the balcony.

"Gentlemen, can I offer you a drink? My partner and I have landed at Copano with a cargo of goods. Are any of you involved in trade?"

There was half a dozen of them and although they introduced themselves, few of their names stuck in my memory. They were more interested in belligerent local politics than trade, enlightening me on the dispute between the governor and his council. Governor Smith had dismissed the expedition to Matamoros as lunacy, saying anyone who supported it was either a fool or a traitor. As I learned more of the circumstances it was an opinion I came to share. The men on the

25

rooftop looked to one called James as their leader. There was an easy air of authority about him and he looked a proper gentleman, apart from a huge knife hanging from his hip. He explained that the doctor we had seen haranguing the men to go to war was a Doctor Grant, whose enthusiasm for capturing Matamoros was not entirely unconnected with the fact that he owned a huge parcel of land there, which he no longer had access to.

"It took us weeks to drive five hundred men from San Antonio," James growled. "The Mexicans will employ a darn sight more to defend Matamoros." He gestured over the rail, "They are kickin' at a hornets' nest, when they should be defendin' what we have already taken."

"Do you think the Mexicans will come back, then?" I asked with a growing sense of alarm. "I thought that the war was over."

"General Cos, the man we whipped at San Antonio, is the Mexican president, Santa Anna's, brother-in-law. He won't take well to an insult to his family."

"Nope," stated another man. "When the Mexican province of Zacatecas rebelled, Santa Anna captured over two thousand of their menfolk and let his soldiers rape and loot their way through the city for two days."

"In that case," I replied, "we should unload our cargo without delay. We certainly have a ready market for the guns and ammunition, but it might be a while before we can sell the spades and ploughs."

I was thinking that we would have to sell those to a local merchant and hightail it out of there, but the man with the big knife spoke up again. "There's no rush. It's nearly a thousand miles from here to Mexico City. Much of it is rough country and there is often snow on the high ground at this time of the year. It is a long way to bring an army in winter, especially if the Comanche and Apache raid the column. I doubt the Mexicans would set off before the spring or they will lose too many men on the way."

I relaxed a little then. His mention of the Indians reminded me of one of my reasons for the visit. "I don't suppose you have heard of a white man who might be living with an Indian tribe near here? It may have been a year or two back as we have not heard from him for a while."

"Sam Houston lived with the Cherokee for a good while," called one of the other men. "Even took one of their women for a wife. They say his Injun name was 'Man who falls down drunk!'" Most of them guffawed at that but the man with the big knife slammed his glass down on the table to curtail the merriment.

"Sam Houston is a good man and a friend of mine." There was a slight air of menace in the way that he spoke and the laughter died immediately. He turned to look at me and explained, "Houston is who the governor has appointed as commander-in-chief of the army. Men like Grant," he nodded over the rail at the doctor, still preaching to the crowds, "have set themselves up as his rival."

"Well it is not Houston I am looking for," I explained. "I am searching for a man called John Norton. He would be around seventy now, if he is still with us."

"There was an old man called Norton living with the Coushatta," said one grizzled old-timer. I had just been thinking that my enquiry was nothing more than a wild goose chase and I was wasting my time, but now my hopes soared.

"That sounds like him. Where will I find these Coushatta? Are they friendly?"

"The Coushatta are friendlier than most Injuns," stated the veteran. "But they are all over the place. Some of us do trade with them for meat and supplies. If I remember right, this Norton did some trade with Señor Menchaca in San Antonio. He might know where your man is, or you could put a message in our new newspaper if the editor has not run off to fight. Injuns don't read it, but farmers who trade with them might."

"Thank you, I will do that." My sudden optimism dipped. I would try the paper but even if the editor had not run off south, most of his readers had. I did not hold out much hope on that idea. While I would dearly have liked to catch up with Norton again, I was not riding along a hundred miles or more into the depths of the province of Texas, not when some of the less friendly Indians or other banditry could be roaming about. For all I knew, Norton could have died months if not years ago.

I was about to take my leave when a nagging thought occurred. "You mentioned that Santa Anna and his men would have to travel a thousand miles over rough country to get here. But are you not worried that they might just come by sea? There are no soldiers or guns at Copano to stop him. He could land there at dawn and have his cavalry surrounding this town by the end of the day. These plains are good country for horsemen."

The man with the big knife fixed me with a piercing glare and then his gaze dropped to my waist, taking in my own lack of weaponry. "You a military man, mister?" he asked quietly.

"Yes, I was a major in the British army and a captain in the Brazilian navy for that matter. I know that if I was in charge here, I would sleep a lot better if I had a battery of guns at Copano."

He nodded slowly. "I reckon you're right. We could have done with you at San Antonio last month, someone who knows how to fight. Thing is, though, we don't have a battery of guns. Apart from a handful in the fort here, only San Antonio has a lot of cannon." He frowned and turned to the veteran, "Didn't Fannin send a company of men to guard Copano?"

"Yes he did," agreed the grizzled man. "But they would not have wanted to miss out on any booty in Matamoros. I'll bet they just elected themselves a new captain and followed the rest of the army."

I took my leave then, shaking my head in wonder at the idea of soldiers electing new officers when they received orders they did not like. It was cock-eyed madness and I would not have bet two farthings on the forces of Texas beating the Mexicans. The army had no discipline, while its government and commanders were too busy fighting with each other to consider a sensible strategy.

From what I had seen, I agreed with the governor that the invasion of the neighbouring province with just three hundred disorganised militia was like pulling on the tail of a snake. It was bound to end in disaster. I would have been even more convinced had I been aware

28

then that instead of waiting for the spring, Santa Anna was at that very moment amassing a huge army of some seven thousand men.

Chapter 4

I put an advertisement for news of John Norton in the local paper, even though the editor was not sure when the next issue would be printed, given that most of his readership was marching out of town. Then William and I set to work on finding wagons and getting our goods from the ship into town. It took a day to hire six men with carts and get them down the track to the vessel. Another day passed in loading them and getting the wagons back into town, but they only contained a fraction of our cargo. Given what we had heard of the Mexicans, I was happy to sell at a smaller margin to merchants, but my business partner was not a Vanderbilt for nothing. He was keen to avoid the middlemen and keep as much profit as we could for ourselves.

When we got into town after the first trip, there was quite a commotion going on. Men were jeering at a drunk horseman riding down the main street, clutching a stone spirits jar to his chest with the desperation of a parting lover. From the taunts I deduced in astonishment that this was none other than Sam Houston, the friend of the man with the big knife. Heaven knew what the governor was thinking when he appointed Houston to command an army, for the fellow looked more like a well-armed liquor salesman than a general. There was no hint of a uniform, just a brace of pistols stuck in a belt that secured a greasy pair of buckskin trousers. Over his shoulders he wore an old blanket covered in a variety of clashing colours. Topping this ensemble was a hat that was so battered his horse might have trampled it. A few men cheered him, but they were as drunk as he was; most shouted in scorn and derision yet he was oblivious to both. Swaying drunkenly, he only just managed to stay in the saddle, while glassy and unfocused eyes were fixed on the street ahead. My first impression of the man selected to defend Texas only confirmed my view that it would soon be time to leave.

I thought no more about Houston for the next two days as we made a second run with the carts to the ship. It was on the evening of our return that I saw him again. I had insisted on a rest after days of being a virtual bloody stevedore. How my life as a gentleman had come to this I could not say, but I put my foot down and insisted that I was spending the evening in the saloon. Somehow, I was prevailed upon to try and sell a case of our fake brandy while I was there. I was just negotiating with a bar-keep, who could have given haggling tips to an Arab costermonger, when into the establishment walked General Houston. He was accompanied by my recent acquaintance with the large knife, who nodded in greeting to me. They made their way to a corner table, its occupants hastily vacating at their approach.

"If you know Jim Bowie," declared the bar-keep, "then I think we can agree a better price." He reached into a drawer under the counter and started counting out bills until I had five dollars more than I was expecting.

"That is good of you," I declared. "You have yourself a bargain, the finest brandy from the Cognac region of France. I will mention your generosity to Jim next time I talk to him." I stuffed the notes quickly into my pocket and stared curiously at the man with the big knife across the room. I was sure he had called himself James when we had first met. "So, er, James – or Jim as you called him. He told me he was an investor in land when he introduced himself, but he is clearly an influential man around here."

The bar-keep gave me a shrewd look and then grinned. "You don't know Jim Bowie much at all, do yer. Land investment," he snorted in derision. "He did that sure enough. He had the papers for hundreds of miles of land in Louisiana and Arkansas. He cleared off squatters and sold it to farmers."

"So, he must be a rich man, then." I was confused as to why the bar-keep was so scornful of his wealthy customer.

"He would have been," the man agreed, "if he had not written all the land deeds himself."

"He is a forger," I whispered, astounded. "Do you think your General Houston knows?" I nodded to where the two men were huddled together in deep conversation.

"Everyone knows about the Bowie land grants," laughed my host, "but you would be a fool to challenge him about it." I must have looked puzzled, for he continued. "See that big knife he carries? He

31

stuck that into the chest of a man back on the Mississippi. He got into a brawl and was shot twice and then two fellas set about him with sword canes, but he still grabbed the man he wanted and pushed that big blade into him. The lyin' skunk had shot Bowie in a bar-fight the previous year."

"I don't understand. If he is a fraudster and a murderer, why is he not in jail or hanged, instead of drinking with your general?"

"He did not murder anyone," protested the bar-keep. "That man had it coming; Bowie was unarmed when the man shot at him before. If'n you don't buy land off him he'll treat you fair and he's been a good man for Texas. Last year the Mexicans tried to arrest him an' he escaped. He used twenty men to trick two hundred Mexicans into surrenderin'. Then he captured their armoury and despatches that showed they was planning to arrest some of our leaders. They made him a colonel in our militia for that. Then during the fighting for San Antonio, he led ninety men who saw off four hundred Mexicans with cavalry and artillery. They only lost one man but he was a damn fool running about in the open."

They were impressive achievements and I looked at Bowie with renewed respect. He was clearly an effective commander of men as well as someone it would not be wise to cross. I noticed that there was not yet a bottle on their table. There was no harm in toadying up to some clearly influential men – and God knows when we would get all the goods from the ship sold. "Would you send them a bottle of that brandy, with my complements?"

"Do you want a bottle yourself?" asked the barman. I had tasted the brandy before, it was not the roughest liquor I had drunk, not by a long chalk, but it was not good either.

"No, I'll have whisky, if you please, and do you have a copy of the latest newspaper?" I settled myself at a table near the door and swiftly discovered that the local spirit was little better than the brandy. Certainly, neither Bowie nor Houston were discerning drinkers as they were soon slugging my gift back in gulps that barely touched the sides. The newspaper was a week old – clearly no new edition had yet gone out. It was full of wildly optimistic articles about the mission to

Matamoros. The place had a population of over ten thousand and was two hundred miles away. That would be a hard ten-day slog for good infantry, but longer for men not used to marching in column with their supplies on their backs. Despite this, the editorial was still confident that once the Texas forces had arrived, the locals would throw off their shackles to the oppressive Santa Anna dictatorship. I remembered what Bowie's friend had said about the reprisals in the rebellious province of Zacatecas. If the Mexican leader had a brutal army of thousands of men, then I suspected that the good people of Matamoros would need rather more security than three hundred disorganised men from Texas to inspire a revolt.

Vanderbilt joined me a while later and we spent a pleasant hour drinking and talking about the money we had made so far and where we could sell our remaining stock. I did not want to spend more than a month in Texas and William too was keen to move on, although he already had plans to return. "We need more leather goods, saddles, harnesses that sort of thing. And if this war goes on, then there will be big money to be made from selling arms and ammunition."

"I am not coming back," I told him, "and you need to be careful. If the Mexicans come through here, they will just seize everything you have." I would have said more but a shadow fell across the table.

You must be Thomas's business partner, growled the new arrival standing alone beside us. "I'm James Bowie."

William leapt to his feet, nearly knocking over the drinks as he took the proffered hand. "William Vanderbilt. It is an honour to meet you, sir."

"So, Thomas," Bowie continued fixing me with a steady gaze. "Have you found your Indian friend?"

"Not yet," I admitted and I gestured to the paper. "My advertisement has not been published yet."

"Thought not, but I can help you." He sat down and leaned forward on the table. I noticed a smile twitch across his lips when he spotted that we had not been drinking our own spirits. "Do you remember when we spoke before, my friend Jared told you that your man was known to José Menchaca in San Antonio. I am leaving for there in the morning with thirty men. Why don't you come with me? I know Menchaca well and can introduce you."

"Well that is very kind of you," I started, "but I would not want to put you to any trouble." I did not like the idea of travelling nearly another hundred miles away from the coast. I might have an escort of thirty men going to San Antonio, but who knew how easy it would be to get back.

"It is no trouble," he insisted. "Houston has asked me to go there to dismantle the defences. You remember I told you that San Antonio is the only place with plenty of cannon? You bein' an army man, and I think you told us a navy man too, well I would like you to look at them and tell me the best cannon to bring back to Copano. You see, we are goin' to take your advice."

"Well that is good to hear," I blustered. There was an air of menace about Bowie that I could not quite put my finger on, but it did not make me feel comfortable. Perhaps it was the lethal knife hanging by his hip or the pistol stuck in his belt, but you got the distinct impression that few people said no to James Bowie. Nevertheless, I thought I would attempt a tactful decline. "I would suggest smaller six-pounder cannon would be sufficient. They would also be the easiest to get to the coast. But I really think I should stay with my partner here; we still have a lot of stock to sell."

"Do you have any gunpowder?" Bowie glanced again at the whiskey bottle and added, "*good quality* powder?"

"Oh yes," interrupted Vanderbilt, "barrels of prime grade Du Pont powder. It will punch a hole in a barn door at three hundred yards," he promised.

"Well now," replied Bowie smoothly. "If'n you don't mind me borrowin' your business associate for a few days, I will buy four kegs and cover the cost of the mules to carry it to San Antonio. Is that agreeable to you?"

"Oh yes, Mr Bowie, I'm sure that Tom will be in very safe hands with you." Vanderbilt beamed nervously at the big man, like some swot handing over his lunch money to the school bully.

34

"Well, that is settled, then," announced Bowie getting to his feet. "Send Houston an invoice for the powder and mules, he will see it is paid." He turned to me with a wry grin, as I tried and failed to think of another excuse to get out of this venture. He knew full well that I did not want to go, but I would be useful to him in his task and so I do not think he gave a damn about that. "Tom, you don't mind if I call you Tom do you?" he asked. Without waiting for a reply he continued, "I will meet you outside here at dawn tomorrow. I'll bring you a horse." He glanced down again at my belt and added, "But get yourself a gun, you might need it if we run into Injuns." With that he strolled out of the door, leaving me with a nasty feeling of apprehension.

"Why the hell did you sell me out like that?" I rounded on Vanderbilt as soon as we were alone. "You could see that I did not want to go. Heaven knows when I will be able to get back to the ship now."

"Have you not heard the stories about Bowie?" whispered William. "He once killed a man with that big knife and they say he has shot plenty more."

"I have just been hearing them from the bar-keep," I hissed. "Which is why I did not want to roam around the countryside with a murderous villain and his gang of cronies. If the Indians don't get me, one of them probably will."

"I doubt the Indians will get you, not if they know Bowie is in your group. Did you not hear about his fight with them when he was searching for the legendary San Saba silver mine? It was in the papers back home, but that might have been before you arrived." He went on to relate how Bowie and a party of eleven others had been ambushed by a band of over a hundred and twenty Indians. The warriors had surrounded them in a grove and after launching numerous attacks, tried to burn them out. But Bowie and his men had put up a ferocious resistance which had killed or wounded half of the Indians while their losses were merely one man killed and three wounded. "He also seems to be a close friend of General Houston," Vanderbilt concluded. "If you can build a good relationship with him, we should be able to sell a fortune of guns and ammunition to the Texas army. You said yourself that they would need them."

I had told William that I did not think the war would go well for Texas, which was all the more reason not to get involved with it. On reflection I had to agree that Bowie would be a very capable bodyguard for getting into San Antonio. I just had to hope that I could quickly come back to Copano with the guns – which were also likely to have a good escort. The problem was that I had come across characters like James Bowie before. They were impulsive men of action who were fixated on goals such as winning wars, gaining wealth or both. They did not let anything stand in their way. I knew from long and painful experience that they were damn dangerous people to be about.

Chapter 5

I stood shivering at dawn the next morning, standing outside the saloon with a new pistol in my belt and a short-barrelled carbine musket slung over one shoulder. Over my other shoulder was a satchel containing powder, ammunition, strips of dried beef, some spare clothes and, nestled in those, another bottle of brandy. In my hands were the reins of two mules, each carrying a pair of barrels that contained enough gunpowder to blow up half the town. Vanderbilt was not lying about that; it was good quality stuff.

The previous day the square had been packed with excitable men, often firing their guns into the air. I was glad it was eerily quiet now, as one stray shot would send us all to kingdom come. The sun was well up on the horizon and I began to hope that Bowie would not appear. One mule took a piss near my feet and the warm vapour in the cold air swirled up around me. I took a step to one side and decided that I would give it five more minutes before going back to my lodgings. According to my watch, four and a half minutes later hooves could be heard drumming towards me down the main street.

Bowie gave me a curt nod of greeting as he passed over the reins of a chestnut mare. He called for two of his men to take the mules and I was glad to put some distance between them and me. "We should get to San Antonio by nightfall," he predicted. I was taken aback. It was an eighty-mile ride and I had assumed we would camp overnight on the way. I must have shown my surprise, for he grinned, "That's why I brought you a strong horse. We will need to keep up a good pace, but you will spend tonight in a comfortable bed." With that he kicked back his heels and we set off at a steady canter.

I fell in with the group and as we rode I took in the men about me. Most were in their twenties and thirties, a mixture of white Texians and Hispanic Tejanos. They had the appearance of men recently roused from their blankets, with some still half asleep. On closer inspection, I saw that most of them were armed to the teeth, invariably with a brace of pistols; some had tomahawks stuffed in their belts too, along with a few big knives. One of the Tejanos even had a lance resting in a cup on his stirrup. They would certainly be a formidable band should we run into trouble.

I tried talking to the dour cove riding alongside and at first I thought he was ignoring me. Another man eased his mount forward to ride on my other side, "That is Deaf Smith," he called pointing at my other companion. "You have to shout."

With the noise of the thundering hooves beneath us it was easier to talk to this second rider. "Have you ridden with Bowie for long?" I asked.

"I was in his company when we fought to capture San Antonio," he replied. He nodded to where our leader rode on his own ahead of our band, "He is a tough fighter, but he knows what he is doing."

My riding companion seemed a bright and sensible fellow and so I asked the question uppermost in my mind. "Aren't you worried that the Mexicans will try to retake Texas? You will be hopelessly outnumbered if they do."

"Not while I've got this," he cried patting the stock of a long hunting rifle that was slung on his back. "We can kill them at two hundred yards with this, but their muskets rarely hit anything." He laughed, "Most of them were firing from the hip; we kept them pinned down and they barely got a shot on us."

"But their horsemen are good, *señor*." I looked around at the new voice and found the Tejano with the lance riding just behind me. "They have lots of lancers and dragoons that are very well trained and fearless." He grinned and gestured to his own weapon, "I know, because I used to be one."

"Yet now you fight for an independent Texas?"

"No, *señor*, I want Texas to stay part of Mexico, but under the old Constitution whereby we rule ourselves. That is what our governing council voted for by a big majority in October."

"Well that was before we spilt blood fightin' Santa Anna," insisted the first man. "I want an independent Texas. When this war is over I just want to be left to farm my land without *any* government tellin' me what to do."

38

I looked around at the rolling prairie land, perfect for cavalry to cut up disorganised infantry. I doubted very much whether the Texas men knew what an infantry square was, never mind how to form one. Bowie's men might be able to ambush the enemy from cover, but if they were caught in the open, they would not stand much of a chance. I doubted that either of my companions would see their wishes fulfilled.

We stopped mid-morning for a rest and to water the horses. We were by a bend in the meandering San Antonio River which ran from the town of the same name to Goliad and then on to the sea. The men took care of their horses first, like good cavalry troopers should, and then sat around on the grass chewing whatever food they had brought with them. No sentries were posted but then, apart from one homestead, we had not seen another living soul all morning, just miles of open prairie.

Bowie strolled among the troops, a word of greeting here and there, a joke with another group, checking men had food to eat. He was a good officer, I will say that for him. He certainly commanded their respect, which only made him harder to understand. This 'Colonel Bowie' was the same man who had carefully forged hundreds of land grants and forced men off property he knew he had no right to. He had got involved in murderous brawls, survived Indian ambushes and more than once led his men successfully against much larger forces of Mexican soldiers. I must have been staring, trying to make up my mind about him, when like the fighter he was, he sensed my gaze. Steely blue eyes met mine and he came over to where I was sitting on the ground, massaging my stiff legs.

"What made you bring a carbine?" he asked, nodding at the weapon lying on the grass beside me.

"It is what our cavalry carry," I admitted. "So I thought it would be the most useful."

"Not here," Bowie stated flatly. "For short range you would have been better with a shotgun, but most of us have rifles. We prefer to kill the enemy before they are close enough to kill us."

"I heard that you commanded ninety men who managed to drive off four hundred Mexicans including cavalry and artillery. Did you do that with your rifles?"

"Aye," agreed Bowie and he looked at me coolly. Perhaps he was wondering what other tales about him I had heard. Then he smiled and sat down beside me. "It was in a bend in the river like this. There was no cover to be had and so I ordered the men to stand behind the river bank, our feet just inches above the stream, so that we could fire at the enemy from at least two sides."

"You mean you had your backs to the water?" I asked, surprised.

"Oh, I know that is probably something that they teach you not to do at West Point or whatever military school you have in England. But it worked. It was a foggy morning and they came on well into the neck of land before we opened fire. We were hard to see, never mind shoot, but they went tumbling down. We even managed to capture one of their cannon before they were forced to pull back"

"You were lucky that they did not cross the river and attack you from behind," I told him. "There would have been no escape then."

"True," admitted Bowie, "but there would have been no escape if they had caught us in the open either. Now, do you have something to eat?"

"Yes, I have some dried beef," I replied pulling some from my open satchel. He nodded in approval and then he must have noticed the brandy poking out of my bundle of clothes.

"Could I trouble you for a nip from that bottle? You are better prepared for this journey than me." I passed the spirit across and he took two deep gulps. "Ah, that is better." He glanced around at his command and added, "I know that they are not the kind of soldiers you are used to, but they are good men and they mostly shoot straight."

"I did not go to military school, I learned my trade on the battlefield," I told him and took a perverse pleasure in watching him nod approvingly. It was true as far as it went, but my 'trade' was not fighting. Instead, it was desperately trying to avoid the scene of the action, but he was not to know that. For some reason I still don't quite understand, I felt the need to impress this man. "They are bristling with well-used weapons, which out here will be far more useful than any parade ground drill."

"That they are," Bowie agreed, smiling again. He watched as I winced, flexing a stiff thigh muscle as I was not used to such hard riding. "I will make sure you have a comfortable room to rest in tonight. I just hope it will be warm. We fought house to house to retake San Antonio – the Mexicans used my place as a bastion. They knocked loopholes through the walls for them to shoot through, but the housekeeper should have had them all blocked off again by now."

"I did not realise that you lived in San Antonio."

"Yes, I am a Mexican citizen, officially a Catholic too. Hell, I even supported Santa Anna in his election as back then he was promoting a federal agenda. The snake told us what we wanted to hear, but soon changed his mind once he was in power."

"You must have a big house if the Mexicans used it as a stronghold."

A look of sadness crossed Bowie's face. "It belonged to my father-in-law, a wealthy man and briefly a governor of the province. Now," he said suddenly brisk and getting to his feet, "we had better get a move on or we will not be there before nightfall."

He strolled off back to his horse, shouting at the men to mount up while I wearily got to my feet. Straightening up, I found the man known as Deaf Smith glaring at me. "Did you mention his wife?" he uttered. It was intended as a whisper but came out much louder, although I noticed that the men around us were pointedly not paying any attention.

"No, I didn't."

"Well don't," replied Smith in another whisper that must have been heard by anyone, including Bowie, within thirty yards of us. "He gets real cut up if someone mentions his wife." With that he stomped off leaving me more than a little confused. By then I had heard a fair few stories about Bowie, but not one had mentioned a wife. Several of the troopers were glaring at me as the reason their rest had been curtailed – clearly they did not believe my denial. I started to wonder what had happened between Bowie and his wife. After all, if people were happy to talk about Bowie's land thefts and gutting a man with that big blade, but kept quiet about his spouse, it must have been something bad. I struggled to imagine someone as tough as Bowie getting romantic. Perhaps he had murdered a rival for her affections or even killed the woman herself in a fit of jealous rage that he now regretted.

There was plenty of time to ponder the possibilities as we cantered on through the countryside. We stopped again at a small settlement mid-afternoon and then climbed back in the saddle. It was dark when we finally reached San Antonio; we had travelled the last few miles by torchlight. Most of the men peeled off to camp elsewhere but Bowie led me on to his house. I was so stiff by then that I needed his help to dismount. Bowie was going back to his men, but he got a woman to show me to a very comfortably appointed room with a large four-poster bed. She returned a short while later with a pot of coffee and a tray of small cakes, but I was too weary to get up and soon fell asleep.

I awoke next morning still fully dressed and lying over the coverlet of the bed. Light glinted in through the window shutters and, throwing them open, I found that the room faced on to a central courtyard in the middle of the house. It must have been a cool shady spot in the hot summers, but it was too cold to dally there early on a January morning. As I was turning away, I saw a woman wave at me from a room across the space. She held up a coffee pot and gestured for me to come around. I waved back and turned to get my coat. Seeing the room in daylight for the first time, I noticed the loopholes that had been dug through the wall that had now been roughly repaired. It was hard to imagine such a comfortable chamber full of Mexican soldiers shooting through these embrasures to keep the Texas forces at bay.

I strolled across the courtyard to the room opposite to find two young women fussing around a stove, preparing coffee and pancakes. "Good morning, ladies, Thomas Flashman." I introduced myself, feeling the day brighten already.

"We met last night," one of the women smiled. "I brought coffee and cake to your room. I am Mrs Juana Alsbury." Despite her English surname, Juana only spoke the language haltingly and looked relieved when I replied to her in fluent Spanish.

"My thanks, I was a little tired when we arrived."

"You looked exhausted. This is my sister Gertrudis."

"A pleasure to meet you, miss," I replied automatically while reflecting that Gertrudis was possibly the ugliest name I had yet come across. It contrasted strongly with its owner, who was a peach and, I judged, the younger of the two. "That is an unusual name, I don't think I have come across a Gertrudis before, not even in Spain."

"James thinks so too, he calls her Gert," announced Juana to a dig in the ribs from her sibling.

I laughed, "I don't think that I can call you Gert. I have a gardener on my estate at home known as Gert. I could not use that without picturing an old, grey-whiskered cove planting onions. If you don't mind, I think I will call you Trudy instead." She smiled with pleasure at the compromise and I added, "Is Colonel Bowie about?"

"No," replied Juana. "James is at the mission buildings. He asked if you could join him after breakfast." She turned back to the stove and a moment later I was being presented with a plate of pancakes while Trudy poured me a cup of coffee. At the clatter of plates, a small and evidently hungry boy ran into the room. "This is my son Alejo," Juana announced, lifting him up onto her lap so that he could grab some pancake from a plate.

I studied my hosts over the rim of my cup. They were both, I judged, in their early twenties. While Trudy was the prettiest, her sister was no slouch – Mr Alsbury had done well for himself. "Is your husband here too?" I asked Juana.

"No, he has been away for several weeks helping the Texas army."

"Well then, you have done an excellent job of repairing the house," I complimented them, "given it was in the middle of a battle, what, just over a month ago. That room was very comfortable."

"It was James and Ursula's room," explained Trudy, "the best in the house, but James does not like to use it now. It has too many memories."

"Ursula?" I prompted guessing that this was Bowie's mysterious wife.

"She was our cousin," Trudy replied, "but we were all brought up together in this house, so she was more like a sister." She paused as I continued to look at her expectantly. "She died two years ago," Trudy continued, now in a hushed tone. "There was an outbreak of cholera in San Antonio. We were away but Ursula and her parents decided to travel to Monclova to escape the infection, but they left it too late. Our aunt died first on the journey, then our uncle and finally our two cousins Santiago and Ursula. None were spared."

"James was ill with malaria in Louisiana at the time," Juana added, picking up the tale. "News of their deaths nearly killed him too." She gave me a canny look before continuing, "I am guessing that you have heard some of the many stories about James, but he was a devoted husband. When they were together, they were the happiest couple I know and yet since her death we rarely see James smile."

Well, that was a whole new aspect to his character: forger, fighter, prospector for silver mines, soldier and successful commander and now devoted husband. I found out later that he had pursued some legal land transactions in Texas. He also had an interest in engineering, as he had tried to set up a steam-powered cotton mill. He seemed to be a tough character who could turn his hand to anything. No wonder men followed him. As I finished my coffee I remembered that I was due in his company too. "Where exactly are these mission buildings?" I asked.

Chapter 6

Trudy offered to take me to Bowie. Soon we were setting off down the street, her arm through mine. "Everybody hates my name," my companion complained. "Juana has had two husbands. Her first, Alejo's father, also died of the cholera two years ago, then James's friend Horace soon came calling on her. But apart from the silly village boys, no one comes calling on me at all, not even with all those soldiers at the mission. I think it is because they cannot imagine declaring their passion for a girl called Gertrudis or introducing 'Gertrudis' to their friends."

I laughed. "I imagine that any reluctance from the soldiers has more to do with the fact that you are James Bowie's cousin by marriage. They are worried that he will take that big knife to them." I ran my eye over her, taking in the flawless complexion and curvaceous figure and then assured her, "Trust me, you have ample compensations to counter any disadvantage in your name."

"And do you like my *compensations*," she asked, casting me a sideways glance.

"You are a very beautiful woman," I confirmed, grinning. But I did not want Bowie taking that big blade to me either and so I deftly changed the subject, "How far away is this mission?"

In daylight I saw that the town was a sizeable place. Its streets were in a grid with roughly half a dozen in each direction plus some more filling a bend in the river. Bowie's house was on the river side of town and my companion led me to a bridge over the water. She pointed towards a cluster of buildings just a few hundred yards beyond. "There," she announced, "that is the mission."

She explained that the place had been named after a company of Mexican soldiers who had previously been stationed there. They had come from Alamo de Parras, but now the roughly fortified mission buildings were known simply as the 'Alamo'. The place had been the last bastion of General Cos and his Mexican troops the previous month and still showed signs of that struggle.

It was not a fort; there were no great walls or massive defences. It was just a collection of buildings arranged in a rough rectangle. None of them was more than one storey tall – the highest point was the roof of an unfinished chapel in one corner. As we approached, I could see at least one cannon had been placed up there for a good field of fire. While most of the buildings made a continuous low rampart around the central compound, there was a large gap near the front of the church. The earlier Mexican defenders had tried to fill that with an earthwork and wooden palisade. In front of that they had piled tree branches to make it harder to climb over. For all their efforts, a siege gun would smash the thing to pieces in five minutes.

We walked through the gate in the south wall and found another cannon in an emplacement covering the entrance. It was then I saw that the central courtyard was divided into two by another long row of single-storey buildings. The place would take a huge number of men to defend; the interior space must have covered over two acres and the perimeter was nearly a quarter of a mile long. Trudy explained that when the Mexicans had held the place, most of the fighting had taken place in the town. When the Texians finally drove their enemy out of the streets the Mexicans' General Cos decided that he could not defend the Alamo with the several hundred men he had left and so had surrendered.

We found a few of the wounded survivors of his garrison sitting in the shade and playing a game of dice. They were dressed in rags but looked little better than some of the Texas garrison, who were building a mud ramp to get another cannon onto the roof of one of the buildings.

"I thought we were supposed to be dismantling this place," I said. "But they are still building it up."

"Dismantling it?" queried Trudy. "That will come as a surprise to Colonel Neill who commands here. He has been improving the defences ever since the Mexicans withdrew."

I gestured to the men working on the ramp, "I know your soldiers do not have uniforms, but I have seen Bengali dung-shovellers better dressed than that. Are you not getting supplies here?"

"They had supplies and around three hundred men. Colonel Neill wanted them to stay but captains at Goliad were promising riches and glory if men marched south with them. Most of the garrison went off to join the Matamoros expedition and they took nearly all the stores with them as well as most of the horses."

Before she could say more, a voice called out from above, "Tom, up here." I turned and there was Bowie standing on the roof of one of the perimeter buildings. I thanked Trudy for guiding me to the mission and then walked up the new mud ramp to join him. "This is our largest gun," he called as I reached him, slapping the long bronze barrel.

"An eighteen-pounder," says I staring about me. We were on the west side of the mission and the gun faced out over the river to the town. "It must have taken some effort to haul that beast up here."

"Yes, but the Spanish did that," I was treated to one of Bowie's rare smiles. "Back when they were here and we were fighting to get in over there," he pointed over his shoulder at San Antonio. "Do you think it would be a good gun to take to Copano?"

I looked at the wheels of the gun carriage. There were deep cracks from prolonged exposure to hot summers and cold winters. I doubted that they would take the jolts of hitting rocks on the trail back. "I would dismantle it and put it on a cart," I advised, "but you would need a team of eight horses trained in the harness and more to carry powder and ammunition. It would be better to take several smaller calibre cannon. Three six-pounders would fire three balls a minute between them with good crews. This beast would only fire once every two minutes. You stand much more chance of hitting a ship with the smaller guns and what's more, the higher number of guns firing at him would also do more to deter a Mexican captain."

Bowie nodded, "That sounds like good advice. I will introduce you to Jameson, the engineer. He will show you what cannon they have. Make a note of the ones you would want to take but don't tell him why yet."

"I take it that they do not know we are abandoning the place. They are not building that new ramp next to a gun, so they must be planning to get another one up on the walls."

"No," Bowie admitted. "This is the biggest collection of cannon west of the Mississippi and the army of Texas fought hard to take it. Houston does not have the authority to abandon San Antonio; he needs permission from the governor or his council, preferably both. He has written to them and asked them to send the order here. Anyway, Colonel Neill is away until this evening, I should discuss it with him first. Tell Jameson the council has asked you to list all the guns we have captured."

I found Jameson a while later on the ramparts and he proved to be an enthusiastic guide. Given that the garrison had been stripped of supplies and largely abandoned for the last month, you could have forgiven him for being bitter and cynical to an apparent representative of the Texas council, but not a bit of it. In fact he seemed to think that Bowie's arrival portended a new energetic leadership. There were twenty-one cannon in the Alamo, ranging from the big eighteen-pounder I had seen to some small two-pounders. They were a mixture of bronze and iron and while a handful were dangerously corroded most could still be fired. There were at least three six-pounders, including one that my guide informed me had fired the first shot in the Texas Revolution. Jameson had managed to mount nearly all the usable guns on the walls and was very proud of his defences.

"We have guns covering every side," he told me. "And those on the chapel roof can be turned to fire wherever the attack is strongest." He gestured out over the featureless prairie around us, "There is damn all cover out there. I reckon with a proper garrison to man the guns and riflemen on the walls, we could beat back odds of ten to one."

I was glad that I did not have to tell him that we were going to dismantle his defences. "What about ammunition?" I asked.

"We have solid shot, some hollow shells and charges of canister all left behind by the Mexicans. I would judge there to be some twelve hundred rounds in all." He gave a grunt of disgust as he led the way down some steps from the roof to the room beneath. "The powder is poor, though. I think we will need to increase the charges. We keep that in a magazine near the chapel. We also have these," he added, throwing open a door.

48

I stepped inside, blinking to adjust to the sudden gloom. There were what looked, initially, like piles of lumber all around me. Then I realised that the wood I could see were the stocks of guns. I picked one up and took it back out into the light. It was a musket and I could see from the marks on the lock that it had once been British army issue. "How many of these do you have in there?"

"Over four hundred," Jameson replied, "and there are crates with at least another sixteen thousand rounds of ammunition for them. But those cartridges must be ancient; the powder in them is bad, little better than ground charcoal."

"Well, you needn't worry on that score," I told him. "We brought four kegs of prime grade Du Pont powder with us."

Jameson beamed with delight, "With that in our rifles and these muskets, we should be able to keep any enemy at bay." He took me to the chapel to see the magazine. He was right, the cartridges were almost useless. You would need a double charge of that powder to fire a ball any distance and the grains that did not burn would soon foul up the barrel.

"It seems that you have far more guns than men to fire them," I pointed out. "How many men are left in the garrison now?"

"You are right there," admitted Jameson. "In our last roll there were a hundred and fourteen men present, but only eighty were fit for duty. And some of those have to care for the fifty wounded Mexican soldiers we still have here. We are well supplied with guns but little else." He gestured to one of the men working on the ramp with a blanket tied around his shoulders, "We have seen no pay for over a month and our clothes are ragged and worn out. Some have traded their personal possessions for supplies, but the local merchants are reluctant to accept notes drawn on the governor or the council in case the Mexicans come back."

"Does the town not support the garrison, then?"

"Some do. Half the garrison lives in the town and the rest here. Many farmers and others help us out with food and supplies. Most of the Tejanos want a return to the old Constitution that allowed Texas to govern itself as part of Mexico. A few worry that if the *norteamericanos* dominate or Texas gets its independence, then they will suffer. Many of them have families who have lived here for over a hundred years and some don't like the way it is changing. You can hardly blame them – a lot of the houses were badly damaged in the fighting last month."

I gave my report to Bowie: there were ample guns we could choose from to defend Copano, but we needed the draught animals to get them and the ammunition and powder there. There were no cart horses in the stables, we would need to get them and the carts from elsewhere. Then I reminded him about his offer to introduce me to Señor Menchaca in the hope of finding Norton. Bowie insisted on taking me to his friend's house and ensuring that I got the help I needed.

José Menchaca did remember Norton, but had not seen him for over a year. He was a wealthy merchant in the town and had contacts with various traders and suppliers and with several Indian groups, including the Coushatta. With Bowie beside me watching on, Menchaca was keen to do all he could to help. He promised to send riders to all of the Coushatta settlements he knew to let them know that I was in San Antonio and looking for Norton. If my old friend was alive and able to travel they would bring him to me, otherwise they would come back and guide me to him.

"I will have news or Norton himself for you within the week," he promised, beaming at both of us. I could not have asked for more than that and realised that Bowie was a very useful ally to have.

Chapter 7

Thinking back, I must have met Menchaca around the eighteenth of January. I spent the next week relaxing around San Antonio while I waited for news of my friend. Bowie was waiting too, for orders from the town of San Felipe, where the governor and his council were based. He did not spend much time in his house, but I often saw him wandering around with men from the mission. Colonel Neill had returned and I remember them arguing quite passionately in heated whispers one evening in a tavern. On another occasion, when I was taking him a message from Juana, I found him lost in thought, pacing slowly around the ramparts of the Alamo. I was not entirely surprised for while he had received no orders, there had been other news from San Felipe.

A few days after we had arrived the first messenger came. The despatch was from the governor and addressed to Colonel Neill. I had expected it to contain confirmation that the dismantling of the fort could go ahead, but instead it announced that due to them reaching irreconcilable differences, the governor was disbanding his council. In this army where men elected their own officers, Neill was quick to write back to ask if the garrison could have a vote and provide a delegate for a future council. No sooner had that messenger departed than a new one arrived. This one came from the council in San Felipe. It informed us that not only had they refused to be dissolved, but they were also seeking the impeachment of the governor.

I shook my head in dismay at the news. Whether Texas was to become a self-ruling state within Mexico or an independent country, now more than ever it needed clear military and civil leadership. Instead it had several men all claiming to be commander-in-chief of the army and now its government officials were far more interested in fighting each other than making important decisions.

At least, I thought, that they would have a few weeks to sort themselves out before the Mexican government reacted to General Cos' defeat. The weather was colder than ever with the water trough frozen over most mornings and a thick frost often on the prairie. There had been little campaigning during the winter in Spain. As the Spanish had trained the Mexicans, I thought that Santa Anna was bound to wait until the spring to march. Illness and a lack of food for both men and animals would ravage an army if he came in winter, not to mention Indian raids on supply wagons. Anyway, there was no reason to rush, quite the reverse. The way things were going, the forces of Texas were likely to be fighting each other by the summer. All the Mexicans had to do was wait and then mop up the winner.

I was not unduly concerned; I would be long gone before any of that happened. Instead I spent a very pleasant couple of days riding with Trudy out on the prairie. Once we went to see a ranch owned by a friend of theirs, Juan Seguín, who was a leader amongst the Tejano defenders of the mission. The second ride was to the countryside around the San Pedro Springs. Trudy was a fun-loving companion who laughed and flirted often. She would kiss me occasionally on the cheek but never more than that. She was a good Catholic girl living in a small community, where our liaison was doubtless already causing gossip among the matrons of the town.

Ever mindful of that big blade at Bowie's hip, I did not make a more serious play for her attention. I even escorted both sisters to Mass, listening to old Father Garza chanting on in Latin. Afterwards in a gathering of parishioners in the town square I was introduced to other leading Tejanos in the town, including the mayor or *alcalde*, Francisco Ruiz. I took the opportunity to ask him what the Tejanos in the town thought of the idea of an independent Texas. He flailed his hands around ineffectually and broke into a sweat as he explained that Señor Bowie had discussed this with him at length. Perhaps fearful of Bowie and knowing where I was staying, he told me what he thought I wanted to hear.

He stated he was sure that most of the citizens of San Antonio supported the garrison and the fight for independence. He was a poor liar. I noted several dark looks in his direction from others nearby. They were all farmers, traders or craftsmen, or people of property in the town and their prime concern was hanging on to whatever they and their families had built up in this far-flung outpost. Some perhaps did

52

support independence, but others did not. It was not surprising that they were divided – so was the Alamo garrison. Juan Seguín, for example, still preferred to remain in Mexico under their 1824 Constitution.

The garrison were, however, all united in opposing the centralist regime of Santa Anna, even if they disagreed on what should replace it. His name was a byword for treachery and deceit. Initially a Spanish soldier, he had changed sides and joined the Mexicans. Then he betrayed various leaders, including those who had promoted him, until he had secured power for himself. He was utterly ruthless; the good citizens of San Antonio were bound to be mindful of the fate that befell the other Mexican province to rebel, Zacatecas, which was pillaged by Santa Anna's troops. I would have been surprised if *el Presidente* did not still have a few supporters in the town, even if only motivated by fear or intimidation.

True to his word, seven days after my meeting with Menchaca, he sent news of Norton. It came via Bowie as we sat down to dinner with his cousins and Colonel Neill, who had joined us for the evening.

"Menchaca has found your friend Norton," Bowie announced. "He was in Laredo, but he is travelling north to meet you. Menchaca says that he is old and not in the best of health. It might take him a couple of weeks to get here."

"Laredo, that was where his last letter was from." I remembered the place on Vanderbilt's map, it was only around a hundred and fifty miles away. "Perhaps I can ride down and meet him."

"You can't do that," replied Neill bluntly. "There is an army of well over a thousand Mexicans in Laredo."

"What? They are that close already?" I looked at Bowie just in time to see him give a glare of annoyance at his fellow colonel. "Why the hell didn't you tell me that the Mexicans are already advancing on us?"

"Because we don't want to spread alarm," snarled Bowie irritably. "Anyway, they're not advancing. The ones at Laredo are stopped, have been for over a week." Neill shot him a glance and I realised that there was more they were not telling me.

"If they are stopped then they are waiting for something, what is it?"

Bowie gave a heavy sigh, "There are all sorts of rumours, but there is talk that Santa Anna is bringing up another army of over three thousand men. They might be at Saltillo."

"How far away is that?" I demanded.

"Around three hundred and fifty miles off," admitted Neill. "But they are coming on slow now, they might be running out of supplies. February will be a cold month on those exposed slopes and they will have snow if this winter keeps up. They are not going to be here any time soon.

"Do you think that they are coming here?" asked Juana pulling her young son up onto her lap.

"We don't know," conceded Bowie. "There are two roads they could come. They might march up through here and drive the Texas army back over the border into Louisiana. On the other hand, they could come up the coast. Destroy any force trying to hold Matamoros and then head north up through Goliad. Once they have Copano, they can move troops by ship with far fewer losses than the land route. They would also be close to San Felipe then and our people would be forced to pull back or be trapped. If they were cut off from Louisiana, their only retreat would be west into other Mexican territory or north. Either way, Indians will consider columns of people carrying their possessions and driving livestock as ripe for raiding."

"Well then, you have no choice," I insisted. "You cannot wait for orders from San Felipe, you must destroy the fort now and pull back."

"We are not abandoning those guns," stated Neill hotly. "Enough men died to take them; we are not giving them back.

"You can hide the guns," I insisted. "Drag the barrels off in the dead of night and bury them. The iron ones might rust a bit, but the bronze ones will be fine."

Neill snorted in derision. "And you don't think that one of those bastards," he gestured to the town and then remembered himself. "Pardon, ma'am," he muttered to the sisters, "…will not tell Santa Anna where they have seen freshly dug earth when the guns went missing? They will all be desperate to prove their loyalty if he arrives with thousands of soldiers."

I could hardly blame the townspeople for that – this Santa Anna did not seem the forgiving sort. But I did not see that they had a choice. "Well, you can't stay here, so what are you going to do?" I asked.

"We *are* going to stay here," stated Bowie quietly.

"But you can't," I repeated, astounded. "You have less than a hundred men fit to fight and if Santa Anna comes, he will have thousands.

"*If* he comes," repeated Bowie. He looked at his colleague and continued, "Colonel Neill and I have been considering the options. With the cannon we have more chance of stopping the Mexicans here than at Goliad. But you are right, we will need more men. I have written to Governor Smith asking him to send us all the reinforcements he can."

"If we have just five hundred," interrupted Neill, "that would be enough to man all the guns and have a strong defence of riflemen on the walls. Jameson is sure that we can beat odds of ten to one."

"Yes, he told me that too," I protested. "But your perimeter is just too long for five hundred men to protect, you will be overwhelmed."

"I know you have seen more battles than us, Mr Flashman," Neill countered, "but you have not seen Texians fight. With our rifles and cannon we will pin down and kill the enemy long before they get near our walls. The cannon loaded with cannister will gut any large attack and our riflemen can deal with any survivors. They can kill at two hundred yards and we can move them around the walls to face any new attack."

"More importantly," added Bowie, "I think that they will attack up the coast and not here. You said yourself that Copano will be a tempting target for them. The Matamoros expedition will also be a thorn in their side that they will be keen to remove."

"You may be right," I agreed. I sat back from the table and considered things. The recent revelations had given me a nasty turn. I had thought any chance of a Mexican attack was months away but now it seemed more certain and only in a matter of a few weeks. It was true

I had not seen the Texians fight, nor the Mexicans for that matter. They might be as bad as the Spanish infantry at Talavera who were routed by my flatulent horse. On the other hand, they might be half decent and I struggled to believe that *every* Texian was some kind of dead-eye-dick marksman. Those walls, where there were any, were bloody long, made of mud bricks rather than stone and only a single storey high. Even with reinforcements, it would be a damn chancy affair trying to defend them. I had a bad feeling about the whole affair and suddenly felt a strong urge to get away.

"Well if we are not going to move any guns, then there really is no need for me to be here. I would be best returning to the coast. My business partner will be wanting to sail if he hears the Mexicans are approaching."

"There is no rush," replied Bowie, "as we said, most of their army is still over three hundred miles away. Loaded with supplies, it might take them at least a month to get here."

"And you can't leave now," interjected Trudy. "Your friend Norton is on his way to meet you."

I had a sudden vision of an old half-Indian man wincing in pain as he was dragged on a litter over rough ground. Then the look of disappointment on Norton's features when he discovered that despite his ordeal, I had left without seeing him. A pitiful image, you will agree, but I would be a liar if I claimed that was what stopped me leaving. No, it was not an imagined face that persuaded me to stay, but a real one. Trudy stared at me with a trusting innocence shared only by those who do not know me well. I had told her some favourable tales of my past and it must have been inconceivable to her that I would run out on my old comrade in arms. I glanced at the others; the two colonels watched me with hard, questioning faces while even Juana looked surprised that I had apparently forgotten the purpose of my visit. "Well, yes, of course I can wait a few days." I interjected. "If Norton is well enough and wants to go, I might take him on to the coast with me."

Chapter 8

For the next few days I spent my time working with the garrison to improve the fort's defences. For all of Bowie's efforts to avoid spreading alarm, news of the gathering enemy force had spread around the defenders. There was now an increased urgency to our efforts, though none showed any sign of wanting to leave.

"Where would I go?" Deaf Smith had half shouted at me when I asked him. "My land is here, my wife and her family are here. Everything I have is here." It was a view shared by the others, even those without family in the area. They had all fought the previous year to capture San Antonio and the Alamo, losing friends in the process. Then they had spent weeks of backbreaking work in the cold and rain to strengthen the fortifications. The fact that a huge army could now be marching towards them did not seem to dishearten them at all.

"I'm glad they're comin'," claimed another man working on the parapet. "Damn well better after I've dug all these ramps."

I spent much of my time with a Lieutenant Dickinson, who oversaw the guns. He had come to Texas a few years before to receive his league of land. Originally a blacksmith by trade, he was now a gunner and had his wife and infant daughter staying with him in the town. It was a poignant reminder of how much the men had invested in this venture.

This was not only true of the Texian defenders; the Tejanos too had lands that they were bound to forfeit if Santa Anna was victorious. They were good horsemen and many of them would ride scouting missions for several days to the south. There they would try and evade Mexican cavalry and see if the army was moving and in what direction. The Tejanos would often visit their own homesteads on the way. I asked them to look out for signs of Norton on their travels.

As well as our scouts, many other Tejanos were travelling up and down the main road from the south that led through the town. They were traders, farmers and travellers and we did not doubt that the Mexicans would be pressing them for information when they reached places like Laredo. San Antonio was the hub for several roads in the region; two that led southwest to the Rio Grande and beyond, one that went east to the town of Gonzales and another that led northeast from where there were trails to San Felipe and Governor Smith and his fractious council. Increasingly, eyes were turned to this north-eastern road, *el camino real* or royal road, in the hope of seeing the first of our reinforcements.

Days passed and the road remained as empty as a tinker's promise. Both Bowie and Neill took to writing more letters to Smith to emphasise the urgency of the situation. They updated him on the force building at Laredo and the rumours of the army beyond that. Bowie reiterated his determination that the Alamo should be held and why – with its guns, it was the best place to stop the Mexicans. It was all starting to sound increasingly desperate. While the others looked northeast, my gaze was fixed to the south for any sign of Norton.

Finally, as January was replaced by February, things began to change. One evening after dark we were visited by Father Garza. He was anxious not to be seen by his flock, for he came with information. "If they know I am talking to you they might tell me less," he warned. Once plied with spirits and given a warm seat by the fire he began to divulge what he had learned, not, he stressed from the confessional but by casual interrogation, particularly of those travelling from the south.

"They don't all say the same," he warned, "but most think that the main army will head to the coast to try and beat the largest part of the Texas army. They say that only a few hundred cavalry will come our way, to keep us bottled up here until Santa Anna has dealt with the main force."

"When will this cavalry force arrive?" I asked.

"Not for a while yet," replied the cleric. "There are still no soldiers north of Laredo." I began to wonder if heading for the coast was the right course of action; if I mistimed things, then I might ride straight into the main Mexican army. Vanderbilt would leave without me if Copano looked likely to fall and then I could head to Louisiana instead. I was certain to find a ship bound for New York in New Orleans. Yet the priest's news sounded just a bit too convenient...

"Do you think we can trust him?" I asked Bowie after the old man had gone.

"Yes," stated Bowie unequivocally. "He is a good man. He did my catechism to join the Catholic church before my marriage and he married us." He paused, considering, "Mind you, people around here know he is a friend of mine. They might be tellin' him what they want *me* to hear."

"Are you going to tell Governor Smith this news?"

"Not until we are certain. Anyways, I have not heard anythin' from Smith these past two weeks. For all I know he has been replaced by the council, not that they are writin' to me either."

At this critical juncture for the fledgling state of Texas, its government was completely distracted with its own internal strife to make any sensible decisions. Unbeknown to us, however, Smith had already taken action. He had ordered a hundred reinforcements to San Antonio under an ambitious young officer. But that man could only persuade twenty-six to come. He was none too keen himself, taking over a week to make a journey that should have been no more than two or three days.

It was mid-morning on the third of February when we saw the single rider coming in from the east, on the road from Gonzales. I was with Neill inspecting a new gun emplacement when he appeared. "Looks like we have a visitor," he muttered. "Let's hope he can tell us what the hell is going on."

We watched the man trot his horse down the slope; if he was a messenger, he was certainly in no hurry. He paused and pulled out a telescope to study the town for a while as Neill twitched with impatience. Eventually, the stranger kicked back his heels and his horse walked in through the gate. Even then the man did not rush, merely stared about him, and from his expression he was clearly not impressed with what he had found.

Neill could contain himself no longer, "You, sir," he roared. "What is your purpose here?"

"I am looking for Colonel Neill," the newcomer announced as he dismounted and walked towards us. He was a young man, twenty-six as I found out later, clean-shaven and wearing attire that was a mixture of soldier and planter: a new officer's coat with some gold braid at the collar, a wide-brimmed straw hat, blue denim trousers and boots.

"You've found him," barked Neill, holding out his hand for the expected despatch, but to his evident surprise the stranger grasped it in greeting.

"Lieutenant Colonel William Travis, sir, commander of the new Texas Mounted Legion."

"Are you bringing us reinforcements?" asked Neill, suddenly shaking the hand more enthusiastically and beaming at this pleasant surprise.

"I have come ahead of my troop," replied Travis. "They should be here tomorrow or the day after at the latest. They are still gathering supplies."

"How many men do you have?" Neill asked.

"There should be at least twenty-six troopers." Travis had the grace to look slightly embarrassed at the paltry size of his command. "I have already lost two to desertion," he admitted.

"Twenty-six!" I repeated, astonished. "But surely you have more coming on? How many are in this new legion?" Twenty-six men would barely merit the command of a cornet in the British cavalry, never mind a lieutenant colonel.

"And you are, sir?" Travis drew himself up stiffly at my challenge.

"This is Mr Flashman, a… er military adviser," explained Neill before immediately returning to the point. "Tell me, Colonel, *are* there more reinforcements coming?"

"The governor authorised me to raise a hundred men, sir," Travis explained. "But that was impossible. Anyone inclined to volunteer has already done so and most of those are at Goliad. I had to beg, bribe and almost press into service the men I have now and even then, some of them have slipped away."

"But has the governor not received my despatches? Does he not know what a desperate situation we face here?" demanded Neill.

"Oh yes, sir," replied Travis. "One of your letters has been published in the newspaper, but the discord within our government and

60

between some of our commanders has sown dissent amongst the men. There are few supplies to be had and while I am authorised to offer eight hundred acres of land to volunteers, they know it will only be forthcoming if we are victorious."

Neill turned away and looked out across the yard at the guns on the far wall. He was obviously lost for words. He must have envisioned the governor raising whole regiments of volunteers or ordering men from Goliad to help him man his defences. Instead he had been sent a wretched twenty-six. To add insult to injury, they were cavalrymen, who would be precious little use defending a fort. He needed riflemen and gunners. I watched as he took a deep breath to control himself. He must have known that it was not Travis' fault – the young man had done his best to raise some men. As he faced our visitor again he even managed to force a smile, "Well, you are very welcome. I will ask Mr Flashman to show you into town. You will best get lodging there."

There are some men that you take an instant dislike to and I'll admit that Travis was one of those for me. Partly, to be honest, it was due to his age and rank. I had spent years toiling away in the British army facing, reluctantly, all manner of dangers. A career of being shot at, lanced, of spying, dodging, lying and toadying had brought me the rank of major and I could get no further. Yet this young snirp had introduced himself as a lieutenant colonel.

As we walked back into town I probed as to his military experience, which largely consisted of a few cavalry patrols that had captured some Mexican horses. He was a lawyer by trade, he told me, as well as a newspaper editor and had been a firebrand for Texas independence for years. He had led revolts against Mexican authorities that had seen arrest warrants issued for him more than once and he had spent a spell in a Mexican jail.

"Well you have kicked the hornet's nest now," I told him. "When you were raising hell, did you not think about how Santa Anna might react?"

He gave a snort of scorn, "You are from the old world, you are used to your kings and tyrants, but we have been brought up within the call of the bell of liberty. We will not stand to be oppressed."

61

He sometimes spoke as though he was reading from one of his old rabble-rousing editorials and perhaps he *was* reciting them, but he did not impress me. "We got rid of our tyrant in 1649," I retorted, impressing myself with the date of King Charles' execution that I dragged from a distant schoolroom memory. "Since then we have been ruled by a parliament and your bell of liberty is going to be of precious little use when thousands of Mexicans march up that road." I gestured to the trail leading southwest to Laredo.

"You wait and see," he scoffed. "The men of Texas will be roused; they will not be denied their freedom.

I did not reply for we both knew that he had only managed to rouse twenty-six of them. Given the chaos in their government and army, I could not see how the country could be roused at all. We continued on our walk to his lodgings in silence.

His troop arrived two days later, bringing in a few supplies. They still numbered twenty-six; at least no more had deserted. They too settled in the town and began to ride patrols around the area, yet they did not go as far as the Tejanos cavalry led by Seguín, who were much more skilled and experienced horsemen.

Deaf Smith had ridden with Travis in November. "He is eager enough," the man had shouted at me, "but he has little idea on how to manage men." Fortunately for Travis, his legion was part of a new regular army and so his troopers could not vote for their own officers like the militia.

The weather turned colder in February and we had the first flurries of snow. Men shivered as they worked or, increasingly, huddled inside barrack blocks around fires that barely did more than take the edge off the chill. I continued to scan the southern horizon, anxious for any sign of Norton. One of Seguín's patrols claimed that they had seen a group of Indians that could have included him, but they were still a week away. I was increasingly anxious to leave and I was not the only one. Morale in the garrison had plummeted since Travis's arrival, not due to anything he had done, but because the garrison had apparently been forgotten. They had fought and lost friends to capture the place and then toiled relentlessly to build their defences. They had done it all in anticipation of hundreds joining them, so that they could be the rock that broke the Mexican wave. Now it seemed that all their effort had been wasted – all that Texas could send them was a pitiful twenty-six men. I heard some whispering that the cause was lost and a trickle of men began to drift away, many of whom were volunteers with families and land. They would wait until dusk and then quietly ride or walk away to the north.

Colonel Neill felt a heavy responsibility over our predicament. He roamed sullenly around the fort as though the weight of the world hung from his shoulders. Bowie at least still had a determined set to his jaw, but even he was quieter than usual. Then on the eighth of February, three days after Travis's troop had arrived, the mood changed again.

At first it appeared nothing remarkable, five men spotted riding into town from the east. Some more welcome reinforcements, we thought, but nothing more than that. As Colonel Neill did not seem interested, Bowie got a horse and rode off to greet them and escort them into town. It took several hours but eventually, news of who the new arrivals were reached the garrison: Davy Crockett was in San Antonio.

I might not have known the name Jim Bowie before I arrived in Texas, but even I had heard of Davy Crockett. The man was famous all over the United States; various books had been written about him and by him. I had read one, which described him as, 'half horse, half alligator, a little touched with snapping turtle.' He was a frontier legend, who would wrestle wolves and shoot a bear before breakfast. Yet he had been pressed to enter politics and had served Tennessee as a congressman for several terms. He had scorned political convention and fought for the common man, at least according to his memoirs, which were full of country homilies and anecdotes. At one point he was talked about as a potential presidential candidate, but he had fallen foul of President Jackson. His enemies had done all they could to ensure Crockett had lost his most recent election.

As news of his arrival spread, men dropped their tools and laughed with delight. He was popular, like any man who tweaks the noses of politicians, but it was more than that. His fame made it certain that they would not be forgotten. If Crockett was to stand with them, then people would notice and others would come too. The mood was jubilant; there would be no more work done that day and the whole garrison streamed out through the gate and down into town to see the great man. I went too, curious to see the legendary character who boasted of shooting a hundred bears in one season. I remembered how Louisa and I had laughed at the rustic expressions in his memoirs, his childish spellings and the feeling that he almost took pride in his ignorance. We had wondered how such a backwoodsman could have hoped to survive Congress, where the wolves were just as dangerous but wore sharp suits.

I got into the main square just as he climbed up on some crates to address the huge crowd of the garrison and curious citizens of the town that filled the plaza. He was greeted by a rousing cheer and was surprised and delighted by his reception. The man looked exactly as I had imagined, a fur hat with some animal tail dangling down his back and a buckskin shirt and leggings. He had a tomahawk stuck in one side of his belt and a hunting knife on the other. Over his shoulder hung his powder horn and ammunition pouch and in one arm he cradled his long hunting rifle. I grinned, he could have come straight from the old Iroquois village I used to live in or from some cabin deep in the wilderness. He nodded at one of his Tennessee companions in the crowd and held up his hands for silence. As a hush fell he started to speak, with a voice that carried surprisingly well to me at the back of the crowd.

"Well now, fellas, you're probably wonderin' what I'm doin' here," he began in a confidential tone as men grinned at him expectantly. "You might have heard that there was a 'lection a while back an' I stood to serve the people of my district as faithfully as I have these past eight years. Well my enemies told lies about me and those who want to punish the common man did all they could to make sure I lost." He paused and now grinned back at them and began to raise his voice, "So when my district voted me out, I told them that they could go to hell, and I would go to Texas!"

There was cheering and laughter at that. This was not how they expected politicians to speak and they loved him all the more for it. He said he led a band of men known as the Tennessee Mounted Volunteers and most would be following him in the next day or two. He told some anecdotes of his journey south, how one of his men had his best skinning knife stolen by a raccoon, while another had nearly sat on a snake in the prairie. In between these tales he dealt with comments from the crowd with polished ease that had them all chuckling again. Then once more he stopped and looked about them, gauging his audience, and became serious again. "You know this here Texas has got some of the finest land I ever did see. If'n you're left to govern yourselves I can't see why it would not be some fine rich country someday. Now some of you may know that I have a sayin' that I use to guide me, it is this: be always sure you are right, then go ahead. Well I think that what you are doin' is right, and I would be right proud if you would let us join your company."

There was more cheering at that and someone near the front shouted out something. I did not catch it, but they had evidently suggested he take command. "No, no," Crockett shouted back. "Me and my Tennessee boys have come to help Texas just as privates and with your help we will try and do our duty. Now, who will join me in this inn for a horn of ale?" With that he stepped down from the crate to more cheering and back slapping all round, as he slowly made his way through the press of bodies towards the tavern.

I stood back and grinned, for I understood now how Davy Crockett had been such a successful politician. He had held that crowd in the palm of his hand from the moment that he stepped up on the crate, and he knew it too. He was nothing like the simple backwoodsman that he pretended; he could judge the mood of an audience and play on it like a conductor with an orchestra. All the stories, the praise for this new land and then the humble appeal, they had lapped it up. I did not doubt that the morale of the garrison would soar and desertions would fall off now. I just hoped that he had brought a good number of men from Tennessee with him.

Chapter 9

Colonel Neill announced he was planning to leave San Antonio the next day. He claimed he had received worrying news from home that he must attend to. That might have been true, but I think his spirit had also been broken by the lack of support from all those in San Felipe. He must have felt that with Crockett's appearance, morale in the fort would be in good hands.

I finally got to meet the great man the day after his arrival. There had been more snow overnight and he was wearing a thick woollen coat and trousers with only his fur hat giving away his identity. It was just after dawn and he was strolling over the ramparts with Bowie as I stood on top of the main gate, staring south in the forlorn hope of spotting Norton. As they approached Bowie introduced me, "This is Mr Flashman, an Englishman. He has served in the British army and Brazilian navy. He is helping with our defences while he waits for an old Indian friend to visit."

"David Crockett," he held out his hand in greeting, "You are a long way from home, Mr Flashman. I hope your Indian friend appreciates your patience."

"He damn well better," I grunted, "I am freezing my bloody balls off waiting for him." Close to I saw that Crockett was wearing a woollen shirt under his coat if not two and I grinned, "I see you are not in costume today."

For a moment Crockett seemed taken aback, not sure how to react to my jibe, but then he grinned in return. "Well you have to give the people what they expect, or they will be disappointed," he conceded. "But it is too cold for that today."

"I read your book while I was in New York," I told him. "You have led an interesting life. Did you really kill a hundred bears in a season? I lived with the Iroquois in Canada a few years back and a whole village of hunters never came remotely close to that figure."

He laughed and then admitted, "Well between you and me the real number was closer to seventy – I think the publisher rounded it up –

but I got plenty of wolves that season too. Got paid a bounty of three dollars a pelt for those, which kept us goin' through that winter."

"Well your book was a very good read," I complimented him, but he looked a little embarrassed at the praise.

"You know I did not get schoolin' as a boy, but as a young man I did chores for a schoolmaster and he taught me to read and write and do my numbers. I lost count of the piles of wood I must have chopped for those lessons. Then when I wrote my book they told me that my spellin' was too good. So the publisher put more mistakes *in* 'cause they thought it would sound more like me." He laughed and added, "I could have saved myself a whole parcel of wood choppin' if I had known that."

After inviting me to join him for a horn of ale sometime, he went on his way. I assumed that he was lying about a publisher adding mistakes into his manuscript as that sounded absurd. A publisher was supposed to remove errors, not add to them. I thought that perhaps knowing that I was an English gentleman, he was embarrassed about his level of literacy and had come up with the story to explain it, but I was wrong. A number of his Tennessee boys drifted in over the next few days and while conversing with one of them, I learned that Crockett had written and introduced a bill in his first month in office as a congressman. That was not the act of a man who struggled with his letters.

I realised that all the books that had been written about him were a blessing as well as a curse. They had brought his exploits to the attention of a huge audience across the country, but they had also fixed an exaggerated image in the minds of the public, which he now felt obliged to fulfil.

The following night a celebration, or 'fandango', was held, in part to see off Colonel Neill but more to welcome Crockett and the dozen men he had brought with him. The whole town and garrison mixed in the central square. Sides of beef were roasted to feed the hungry and various spirits and ales were on hand for the thirsty with coin still in their pocket. I had brought Trudy and Bowie had taken Juana, although he was out of sorts and later abandoned her to the care of

Seguín and a group of the leading Tejanos. A local band were playing music and we danced, after a fashion, between gangs of stamping rowdies hooting and hollering. Clearly the men still had enough money to get thoroughly drunk and at length a call went up for Crockett to play them a tune. He was undoubtedly a man of many talents –extraordinary marksmanship being one of them. Despite what he thought, however, it turned out he was certainly not a great musician. In my humble opinion, what followed could only be called a musical obscenity.

Readers of my earlier memoirs will be aware that I am not overly partial to the sound of bagpipes. Until that night I had thought that no sound was worse, but that evening I learned that I was wrong. A far more awful din can be made with bagpipes when accompanied by a drunken man with a fiddle.

I had not imagined that there was a set of pipes within a hundred miles, but those damned Scots will insist on travelling with them. To my horror a man called MacGregor now produced some and to yells of encouragement issued a challenge to Crockett. The frontiersman was half pushed up onto some packing cases that formed an improvised stage and was handed a violin from the band. To start with it was not too bad, Crockett played a jaunty jig that had most of us tapping our feet. Then for no good reason, the bagpipes joined in. I groaned as the two players started competing on who could play notes the fastest. A string snapped on the fiddle but Crockett did not pause, scratching and sawing away on the damn thing as though his life depended on it. Not to be outdone, MacGregor, red-faced, blew into his pipes as though fit to burst, a godawful screeching, droning and wailing the result.

"Let's get out of here," I yelled at Trudy as a crowd of men surged forward, shouting their appreciation and stamping their boots on the frozen earth. If they could detect any kind of rhythm, they were doing better than me. We were across the river and walking towards the mission before the racket was quiet enough to talk comfortably.

"You did not enjoy the music, then?" asked Trudy, laughing. "You should have seen your face when MacGregor started playing."

"Christ, if you think that is music, you should go to the cattle pens when they are gelding the bullocks. You will hear a concerto."

She smiled and hooked her arm through mine as we walked along the river bank towards another bridge that led back into a quieter part of town. The moonlight showed the vapour of her breath and we strolled without talking for a while. Apart from the distant strains of the fandango, the only noise was the crackle of the frosty prairie grass under our feet and the occasional howl of a distant coyote. She was, I thought, a very beautiful woman. I felt her body shiver against me and she pressed closer for warmth. "Forgive me, you must be freezing out here in that thin coat. Here, have mine." I shrugged off the thick army greatcoat I had been wearing and wrapped it around her shoulders.

She smiled gratefully and slid her arms into the sleeves. Then she turned to face me and for a moment I thought we might kiss. Instead she looked me in the eye and asked quietly, "Is it true that you have a wife waiting for you in New York?"

"Yes," I admitted, surprised and not a little disappointed that this news had got out, for I had just been considering making a play for her after all. "How the devil do you know that?"

"James told me. He asked about you before you left Goliad. He likes to know about the people he is dealing with."

I cursed his inquisitive nature. "Why do you ask?"

"Because you are an interesting man. A soldier, a sailor, and you have told me about some of the places around the world you have visited and the people you have met. You must be important in your country. You have a big ranch, or estate I think you call it in England, or at least you did. James said that you have come to America to escape lawyers in London, but he does not know what crime you have committed."

Aha, I thought, that is what she really wants to know. So I told her all about the George Norton affair and how that had led me to try and track down my old comrade in arms.

If anything, she was even more impressed. "So your wife was unfaithful, but you have come halfway around the world to protect her reputation. You must really love her."

She was clearly imagining my life as some great romantic novel. "Well, I suppose I do. But if she has been unfaithful, well I have not been exactly blameless in that department myself. Yet you must understand that while we have been together on and off for nearly thirty years, we have had to spend much of that time apart."

"Like now," she spoke softly in almost a whisper. She opened her mouth to say something else, but changed her mind. Letting go of my arm she ran forward over the little bridge back to the town. "Come on," she shouted. "Juana will be back home and I need some coffee to warm me up."

Hello, thinks I, you old dog, you. Maybe there is running in this young filly yet. I was just picturing her naked and inviting on my bed when in my imagination the door to the room crashed open and there was Bowie, his nine-inch blade in his hand and a murderous look in his eye. My ardour was suddenly as cool as the frost underfoot.

When we got to the house we could hear Bowie and Juana arguing in the main room. A plate smashed and we rushed in to see what was happening.

"What the hell do you want?" snarled Bowie, looking almost as angry as he had in my recent imaginings, although this time the blade was, mercifully, still in its sheath. He glared at me and added, "S'pose you have been payin' your respects to our new commander."

"No, he has been with me," started Trudy defensively. "What is the matter with you? Why are you smashing things?"

"He's drunk," responded her sister. "He wanted me to get him another bottle and I refused. You know how he gets when he has been drinking. Come away with me and we will leave Thomas to try and talk some sense into him." With that the two women hurried from the room. Trudy shot me an anxious glance over her shoulder as she went through the door, while Bowie surveyed me with naked malevolence.

"What is the matter?" I asked hesitantly as I sat further down the table, well out of range of a punch or a slash of his knife. "Who is this new commander you are talking about?"

"Like you don't know," he scoffed and then his unfocused eyes went past me to the sideboard behind. "Fetch me that bottle," he demanded.

I got up and obeyed. He was already at the fighting drunk stage; the sooner he swigged enough to make him insensible the safer I would feel. I passed the bottle across the table and, as I resumed my seat, assured him that I had no idea what he was talking about.

He half emptied another glass and then nodded, apparently believing me at last. "Tell me, Tom, if there are two colonels in the British army commanding a garrison, which one is in charge?"

"Well, all other things being equal, it would be the one with the seniority in rank." Bowie frowned at me and so I explained again. "The one who had been colonel the longest."

"Damn right!" he agreed slamming his glass down on the table and spilling much of what was left in it. "I am not having some boy barely off his mother's teat tellin' me what to do."

"What? You mean Neill has left young Travis in command? All he has done is round up a few horses."

"The yellow cur resigned his commission too when things got tough fightin' around here in November. He fled back to San Felipe like a whipped dog," added Bowie, pouring himself another glass.

"But why?" I asked, astonished. "The men are never going to follow him."

"Neill insisted he had to," slurred my inebriated companion. "Travis has a commission in the regular army, while mine is just in the militia and most of that company is not even here," he explained.

"Well at least half of the men here are still volunteers. Are they not able to elect their own officers? Most of those that are here would vote for you if you asked them," I pointed out.

Bowie's brow furrowed as he cudgelled his whisky-soaked wits into order and considered what I had said. Then a slow smile spread across his features, "You know, Tom, you are right. That is what I am gonna do. I'll show the boy who is the man around here." He got unsteadily to his feet and announced, "You are a good friend, Tom, but now I'm goin' to bed."

I watched him stagger off and felt quite pleased with myself. I truly believed Bowie would command much more respect from the garrison than Travis. After all, he had been one of the men to decide to make a stand here in the first place. I poured myself a drink and considered further. Helping to calm him and save face would be another feather in my cap for Trudy too. If Bowie was busy running the garrison, he would have less time to keep an eye on us. She would, I thought, need only a little more encouragement to climb into that big old fourposter bed with me. I could not afford to take too long, though, as surely Norton would arrive any day now. I knocked back the last of my whisky and went to my room, smiling in anticipation. A moment later I paused in the doorway to discover that there was someone already on my bed. It was Bowie, lying face down across the coverlet and snoring like an old sow drowning in a swamp,

I awoke early the next morning with a stiff back having spent the night on a bench seat. I made myself some breakfast and slipped out of the house to the fort. I wanted to get there before Bowie, to see how my advice had been received. I needn't have rushed, for the place was virtually deserted. Santa Anna could have taken the fort that morning with just a dozen men; there were no sentries and judging from the noise in the barracks, those inside were still sleeping off the night before. When Travis's Mounted Legion had arrived, their number had included a slave called Joe, who served as their commander's valet. He at least was awake in the officers' quarters and soon I had a cup of steaming coffee. Fortified with that, I took a turn around the ramparts and was surprised to see Crockett and some of his Tennessee boys coming up the track from the town. He waved and they came up the steps to join me.

"It is good to see that at least our English friend is still sober enough to stand guard," he greeted me. He nodded down to the barrack blocks where there was barely any sign of movement and added to his companions, "These Texas boys would never win a girl in Tennessee, fellas." The others chuckled at the idea and one said that the father would not waste a jug on them.

"Is hard drinking part of the courtship in Tennessee, then?" I asked.

"Pretty much," agreed Crockett, grinning. "If a fella wanted to get hitched, he would send his friends to the bride's house with an empty jug. If the father filled it with strong liquor for them then the boy would know his suit had been accepted. Then he would appear and the jug would get drunk by all present and refilled a good few times. That is what happened the first time I got hitched." He laughed, "Not that I remember much about it."

We fell to talking about his time in Tennessee and local politics. It turned out electioneering there was a lot more colourful than in England. Crockett was a natural storyteller and even though they must have heard them many times before, his men egged him on to repeat their favourite tales. He told how on one campaign he and his opponent were both bored with their speeches and decided that they would join with their supporters in a squirrel-hunting competition, with the losing candidate paying for dinner. Not surprisingly, after an afternoon ridding the forest of tree-borne rodents, Crockett and his men had a free meal. On another campaign a well-educated lawyer was standing against him and looked down on the backwoodsman, who prided himself on being a man of the people. Crockett bided his time and got his revenge. "He gave the same speech in his whiny little voice in every town," he explained. "Soon I knew it as well as he did and I reckon he knew mine too. We used to take it in turns to go first and when we got to this town, he went into a tavern for an ale rather than hear my speech again. So I told the crowd that I was goin' to save them some time and I gave both speeches, mine and his. Did his in his whiny voice too, then when I finished I went into the tavern and he came out. He never did understand why everyone laughed at him as he repeated every word I had said."

He told other tales too, of his hunting exploits and his hard life as a boy in frontier country. The morning passed with the garrison starting to come to life and several gathered around to listen. It must have been nearly eleven when I looked up to see Bowie striding into the fort. His jaw was clenched shut and there was a dangerous glint in those steely-grey eyes as he ignored any greetings and strode purposefully towards the officers' quarters. A moment after the door opened there was a shout from Bowie and Joe came scurrying out, the door slamming behind him. Bowie and Travis were to be alone when they had their confrontation.

By now everyone in the mission realised something was afoot and eyes were locked on the door, some perhaps expecting a gunshot from inside or a shriek as a long blade was pulled. Instead the two men talked for around ten minutes. Travis emerged first, looking a little ashen-faced as he strolled to a tin plate hanging outside the cook house and started to hit it with a pistol barrel. The noise normally summoned men for food but this time the garrison was being called to a special meeting. Gradually the courtyard began to fill, some men staggering from the barrack block and a few running up the path from town. They all looked up expectantly as Bowie and Travis strolled silently up some steps to stand on the ramparts looking down at them.

"Gentlemen," announced Travis, glancing nervously about. "As some of you know Colonel Neill appointed me garrison commander when he left yesterday." There was a growl of discontent at this, which was clearly news for some who had been celebrating too much the night before and hadn't yet heard. Travis held up his hand to still the noise. "The volunteers among you are entitled to vote for your own officer and Colonel Bowie has offered to stand as a second choice." He glanced at Bowie who glared down at his electorate, as though daring them to vote for someone else. "Does anyone else want to put their name forward for election?" asked Travis, with, I thought, a note of hope in his voice.

"Davy is a colonel of Lawrence County Militia of Tennessee," called out one of Crockett's companions.

"Colonel Crockett do you want to stand?" asked Travis eagerly.

"No, sir," Crockett drawled. "I have not been in Texas long enough to be considered for such an honour. You already have two good candidates."

"So be it," called Travis. "Volunteers in the garrison, can I have a show of hands for all those who would like Colonel Bowie to be your commander." The result was a forgone conclusion – a sea of hands went up, not just the volunteers. A few of Travis' own men voted against him even though it was not their ballot. The only vote the young commander could be sure of was that of Joe, his slave, and even then, perhaps not in a secret ballot. There was no need to call a show of hands for Travis as he had clearly lost and he stepped back giving the floor to his opponent.

"My volunteers," Bowie growled at them, "we are goin' back into town to get drunk."

Chapter 10

The next two days were not the finest for the reputation of the Alamo garrison. Bowie and his volunteers spent most of it drunk in town, during which time things came close to a riot. When one of them was locked up in the jail, the rest broke in and released *all* of the prisoners, to furious complaints from the town officials. There were fights and threats to the regular soldiers under Travis, who gave up on gaining any control of the garrison as a whole. In the end he took his men away and set up a new camp several miles out of town to stop his men being drawn into the excesses of the volunteers.

Even some of Bowie's men tired of the disorder, while others had run out of funds to purchase drink. I saw at least one trying to trade their rifle for whisky. Their new commander was in no state to set them a better example, for he was drinking heavily and was certainly not himself. He had taken back his old room and when I looked in there one morning, I found several of his wife's dresses strewn across the bed and a strong smell of what I guessed was her perfume.

Eventually, on the fourteenth of February, Bowie sobered up, I think due to Juana as much as anyone. As she had entered his room that morning, he had thrown the wash jug at her. I had gone to help when I heard it smash, but before I reached the room I heard her start a tirade at him. She clearly had a Latin temper and she let him have it with both barrels. Reminding him that the jug had been one of Ursula's favourites, she asked what his dear wife would make of him now. Without waiting for an answer, she told him. Her cousin would be ashamed and disgusted at the way he was behaving and would have demanded that he sort himself out. I shrank back as she stormed past me, still looking furious. From Bowie's room there was not a sound.

Two hours later a shamefaced James Bowie strode out of the house for the stables. He rode out to Travis' encampment and while I don't know what he said, the regular troops were back in the town by nightfall. It was not just Juana's efforts, for news then from our scouts also had a sobering effect, not just on Bowie but on all of us. They reported that there were now two thousand Mexican troops at Laredo on the Rio Grande, including a large contingent of cavalry. Behind them at Saltillo were another two thousand five hundred men, personally led by Santa Anna. The only good news was that they were struggling to make progress as, in some places, there was a foot of snow on the ground. Travis called on Bowie at the house that evening and I made sure that I was on hand. While the charms of Trudy were considerable, they did not outweigh the need to avoid four and a half thousand Mexican soldiers bent on revenge.

"I think that they are coming to San Antonio," declared Travis. "Both towns are on the road that leads right here. I have written to the governor and insisted that we must be reinforced or Texas will be lost." He put a copy of his letter on the table. Instead of a detailed military report it was written in the high-blown language of a rabble-rousing broadsheet. It predicted that if we were not supported there would be the thunder of enemy cannon, burning buildings, the rape of wives and daughters and the cries of famished children. He had vowed to the governor that we would hold the mission for as long as there was a man left alive, as the garrison preferred death to disgrace – well he was certainly not speaking for all of us there.

Bowie tossed it aside and pointed out, "They might all be on their way here, but there is nothing to stop them then moving across the plains to the coast. They can keep us bottled up here with cavalry and capture Goliad easily. With that big garrison it would not take long to starve them out and then they could push on up the coast, free up Copano and threaten San Felipe and beyond. That is what Father Garza is hearing from those that have been down south."

I stood then, and looked at the map and I will admit that I thought that Bowie and Father Garza were right. What they were proposing was the strategically better thing to do. Santa Anna, I had learned, described himself as the Napoleon of the West. He clearly believed he was a military genius. To feint for San Antonio and then go to the coast would leave the Texas forces wrong-footed. The garrison at Goliad had few cannon to fight back with if besieged and with so many mouths to feed, I doubt that they would last more than a week or two at the most. Meanwhile, with Santa Anna's cavalry out of range of our guns, but stopping us from escaping, the Alamo could be mopped up when the rest of Texas had been subdued, if it did not surrender first. If the Napoleon of the West played his hand well, he could have a series of easy victories with very few losses.

Travis looked petulant that he might not have a central role to play in the defence of his fledgling nation. He would also look a fool if all his Jeremiah forecasts were wrong on where the Mexicans were going. He was not going to give up that easily, though. "Well wherever Santa Anna attacks, it makes sense to have as much of the Texas army as we can here. Unless we get the draught animals to move the guns, this is where we will be the hardest to beat. We will then have our walls and cannon fully manned and he will have to attack us eventually. Then we will show him how Texas can fight."

That, I had to admit, made some sense, at least for them, but where did it leave me? No scout had spotted Norton's party for days, although they might have been lying low at the sight of unknown cavalry patrols. I was ready to give up on my friend and make a run for it – but where? Should I gamble on Santa Anna coming here and ride for the coast? The news from the scouts was already four or five days old; I might reach Goliad just in time to face a flying column of Mexican cavalry. What would I do if Vanderbilt had heard of the Mexicans approaching and already sailed? Riding northeast for New Orleans did seem the safest route and perhaps Vanderbilt and the ship would wait for me there. But looking at the map, it was five to six hundred miles away and some of that looked to be swampland. It was not a journey I would want to make alone. As I pondered my predicament, Trudy brought in a tray of refreshment, shooting me a dazzling smile as she did so. I grinned back, for I had my solution.

When the Mexicans approached, the gallant Flashy would offer to take the ladies to safety. Bowie would undoubtedly want them out of harm's way. I was sure that he would give me a capable guide such as Deaf Smith and perhaps a few other men as escort, particularly if we had been reinforced by then from elsewhere. Yes, I thought, that would serve me well. I was a British visitor, no one would expect me to join their fight. If I could not find a time to get more closely acquainted with Trudy during that two-week journey, well I would be losing my touch. I watched Trudy's lithe young body moving under her dress as she put out food, glasses and a large pitcher of water to avoid any relapse into drunkenness, and I grinned. Fool that I was, I imagined that my trip to the Alamo could end very well for me indeed.

Bowie and Travis had agreed to share command of the garrison and with them united again, work resumed on strengthening the fortifications. Wherever Santa Anna went first, he would end up at San Antonio eventually. By then the garrison stood at around a hundred and fifty men with all but three of the cannon mounted on the walls. Bowie and Travis jointly signed another letter to San Felipe calling for reinforcements. Then at last, a couple of days later, they got a reply.

Once more the dinner plate was beaten and the garrison summoned to the central courtyard under an ominous grey cloud. Travis stood again on the ramparts and shouted that he had heard from the governor. He announced that Smith had promised help for the garrison and that it would arrive soon. The first raindrops fell as he finished, but they did not stop a rousing cheer from over a hundred throats. It was a relief to think that we had not been forgotten after all. Weary men returned to the hard work of building defences for a much greater garrison, now confident that their efforts would not go to waste.

Bowie moved into a room in the Alamo, leaving me to return to my former lodging. He used his local contacts and personal funds to secure more food and supplies for the garrison and made a point of introducing Travis to some of the influential local officials. To keep the garrison occupied, work now started on digging some ditches in the frozen ground outside the fort. The hope was that they would be filled with new riflemen reinforcements to increase defences as our cannon fired over their heads.

Having mounted all the guns that were serviceable, the engineer Jameson started to dig a well in the courtyard so that the garrison would have a supply of fresh water if they could not reach the river. Travis sent out more scouts, including Deaf Smith, rumoured to be the best in that line of work. Some went for information and others to recruit reinforcements, even if only one or two men, and some to do both. I even explored twenty miles south myself in a forlorn effort to find Norton.

Throughout it all Crockett and his men good-humouredly helped wherever they were required. The weather fluctuated from freezing cold to pleasantly warm and Crocket's dress varied accordingly. Digging the well on a sunny day he wore his hunting shirt and buckskin trousers. Yet riding out to hunt for the pot on a freezing morning he could be seen wrapped in a thick coat with only his fur hat to identify him.

Rumours swirled around the garrison. Some had heard from townspeople that the Mexican army was on its way, others that it was heading to the coast and yet more that it was still on the Rio Grande, starving and on the brink of collapse. One day we waited in readiness for a raid of two hundred Comanche Indians that some traders swore they had seen coming our way.

After that tale had been proved false, I tentatively suggested to Bowie that given all the conflicting speculation, it might be wise to move his cousins further up country for safety. I then generously offered my services for this purpose, while suggesting that a guide or two would also be helpful. He thanked me for the offer, but immediately dismissed the idea. They could not spare the men until reinforcements arrived. Anyway, he was sure that Horace Alsbury would come for his wife if there was any danger. But, he added, I was most welcome to join Horace in escorting the ladies upcountry. I thought that might suit my purposes well. The long-absent Mr Alsbury would doubtless be too busy renewing relations with his spouse to pay much attention to what I was doing with her sister.

One of Travis' scouts rode in from Goliad to report that the Matamoros expedition had largely collapsed. Houston had followed the men and had evidently stayed sober long enough to persuade many of them that it was doomed to fail. Only around seventy had stayed loyal to Doctor Grant and they were thought to be holed up in a town halfway between Goliad and Matamoros. That left around four hundred men who had either stayed at Goliad or returned from the expedition. Houston had returned to the governor while at Goliad a new commander had taken charge, a man called Fannin, who had at least trained for a while at West Point and had some military experience. Fannin seemed to be getting the same conflicting rumours that we were and was unwilling to move without orders from San Felipe. He was also reluctant to abandon Doctor Grant to the Mexicans. As the council had encouraged Grant to go, I suspected that they felt the same.

Then one Saturday came new rumours. Seguín reported that one of his cousins had seen the Mexican army advancing towards us over the Rio Grande. The scout had ridden hard for three days to warn us with this news, but some of the garrison's officers were still doubtful. Bowie had known Seguín for a long time and trusted his friend, yet Travis disagreed. He reminded them of the other rumours we had heard; of the Mexicans struggling to get supplies in the snow and being far from ready to go on the offensive. The younger colonel was sure that the Mexicans could not arrive any earlier than the end of March. The Tejanos in the garrison clearly did not share his view and, sure enough, that evening Seguín was back with a request: some of his men had ranches in the path of the Mexican advance. He wanted permission to release them to gather their families and take them to safety.

Travis could scarcely spare the men, but he understood that the Tejanos and any other member of the garrison would want to safeguard their wives and children first. The next morning a dozen of the Tejanos rode south. They were good scouts and knew the country well. Seguín and Bowie stood in the courtyard to wish them well and urged them to come back as soon as they could. I noticed that Bowie was not taking his life of increased sobriety well. He looked ill despite having an occasional drink. He also was leaning heavily on his long rifle.

Another day passed, which I spent helping Dickinson sort out the muskets in the store so that the best ones were to hand when the reinforcements arrived. It was hoped that most would bring their own rifles but if not, we would be ready with supplies. It was strange to feel the familiar weapon in my hands again. We test fired a few and found

81

that the Mexican cartridges were very poor. Fortunately, with some of the Du Pont powder as a charge, the muskets shot far and straight. It was over a week now since we had received the governor's promise of help and there was a slowly increasing anxiety in the garrison each day when it did not appear. They had seen the Tejanos ride off and knew the reason that had prompted the exodus. Not all of them were as sanguine as our young commander about the Mexicans' ability to arrive before the end of the month.

A Tejano trader arriving in the town swore that he had seen no sign of the Mexican army on his way north and that, I recall, gave us some comfort. Yet I had been in more than my fair share of disasters over the years and I still felt a sense of unease. Our best scouts had ridden south for their families and the report of the Mexican army crossing over the Rio Grande was now nearly a week old. On top of that, there were no further messages or support from San Felipe. It seemed to me then that it would be a close-run thing which would arrive first: the Mexicans or Governor Smith's reinforcements. It was not a race that I particularly relished seeing the result of.

I had waited in San Antonio too long already. Norton should have arrived by now. He must have either abandoned the journey or been halted by the Mexicans. The only thing that stopped me leaving the fort there and then was the report of the Tejano trader, although he looked a damned shifty fellow. I decided to wait until the end of the week and then I would go.

I thought if I offered her my company, there was a good chance that Trudy might come with me anyway and leave her sister to wait for her husband if she wished. We were bound to find people along the way who could give us directions if necessary. I had looked at the map and identified plenty of towns and settlements to the east of the province. We would stay ahead of the Mexicans, whether they came up the royal road or along the coast. Bowie had told me once that New Orleans was a very liberal place where a man could enjoy himself; he had spent many of his winters there as a single man. It seemed an ideal location to spend some time with Trudy while things were resolved in Texas.

If I had been worried before about Bowie and his large knife stopping us, well that was now less of a concern. After I had guided him over securing joint command, he had seen me as more of a friend. Even so, I doubted he would approve of me ravishing his cousin. Yet if he did oppose our leaving, I could not see him pursuing me. He had spent much of the last two days resting in his quarters. He had suffered malaria in the past and I knew, from having seen it happen in India and Africa, that sufferers often experienced repeat attacks years later. Invariably they pulled through unless they were already in a weakened state. And there were few men tougher than James Bowie.

The next day, Monday, the twenty second of February, turned out to be George Washington's birthday. To distract the men from the continued absence of reinforcements, Travis permitted another fandango, or party, to celebrate. Once again the garrison and townspeople filled the main squares with music, food and celebration. Bowie came for a while to watch but then returned to his house with Juana, while Trudy and I stayed to enjoy the dancing. Mercifully, MacGregor left his bagpipes back in the fort and as a consequence Crockett's turn on the fiddle was far more tuneful. I had hoped to steal rather more than the few kisses I got from Trudy that night, but Father Garza was there safeguarding the souls of his flock. He was assisted by a gaggle of Tejano matrons, who muttered darkly at any of the local girls getting too friendly with the soldiers.

We returned to Bowie's house and once more I slept alone. It was well past dawn when I awoke. The sounds of the house were familiar to me now – the clatter of plates in the distant kitchen, little Alejo playing in his room – but this morning there was more noise in the street outside. I could hear people talking just the other side of a blocked-up loophole; a woman was calling for her husband to hurry and bring the pots and pans. I heard a clatter as they were dropped onto something wooden just the other side of the wall. There was urgent whispering I could not make out and then the screech of a badly greased axle as a cart moved off.

I had thought little of it at the time and got dressed and moved around the courtyard. Going past the gateway to the street, I happened to glance through to see another overloaded cart being pulled down the road, followed by a family also burdened with possessions. Curious now I went outside. The Bowie house was on a corner and looking in both directions I saw a third cart being loaded, while at a further house were two mules that were being piled high with furniture.

The Tejanos, at least a good many of them, appeared to be leaving. The obvious thought was: What did they know that we didn't? As there was only one way to find out, I went across to the nearest and asked them.

"Please, *señor*," the man replied, glancing nervously up and down the street to see if anyone else was watching our exchange, "we are going to my cousin's farm. He needs some help planting crops."

"But you are a cobbler, I have seen you in your shop. Can your cousin not get some farm labourer to help him?"

"No, *señor*, and it is most urgent, I must go now, he is waiting. Good day to you, *señor*." With that the man hit the rump of the donkey attached to his cart and hurried up the street. He was lying there was no doubt about that. Apart from anything else the ground was too frozen to plant crops, but he evidently was not going to tell the truth to a known friend of Colonel Bowie.

I went back inside the house and told the girls what I had discovered and what the cobbler had said.

"That is ridiculous," replied Trudy. "He has not got a cousin who owns a farm."

"Well something has alarmed them," I insisted. "There are at least four families leaving town right now and that is just from our part of town."

"I know someone who will tell us." Juana put down her mixing bowl and took off her apron. "Leave it to me, I will be back in a few minutes." She put on a coat and hurried out of the door. We sat and waited, watching as yet another family hurried down the street behind a large wagon with a load covered in sacking.

Half an hour came and went as did two more families past the door, before finally Juana reappeared. "I went to see Juanita Músquiz," she explained.

"But I heard her husband is with Santa Anna's men," Trudy protested. "Can you trust her?"

"Ramón is with Santa Anna," Juana admitted, "but Juanita has had someone else in her bed while he was away. She does not dare lie to me or I will tell Ramón."

"Never mind Juanita's infidelities, why are they leaving?" I asked impatiently.

"There are rumours that the Mexicans are just a few hours away," Juana explained, looking surprisingly calm at this calamitous news.

"What?" I exclaimed. "Well come on, we must tell James and Travis at once and then we need to get you two ladies away." I gave Trudy a meaningful glance and added, "I have already agreed with James that I will escort you."

"Wait," laughed Juana. "They are claiming that Santa Anna was seen at the fandango last night. At least two people have sworn that they recognised him and that such an audacious act is typical of the great leader, but it is nonsense. Even Juanita does not believe it, although she is happy to spread the story to cause alarm."

"Well I still think we should tell Travis and James," I insisted. "Of course Santa Anna was not at the fandango, but when these rumours start there is rarely smoke without fire. Perhaps he is closer than we think."

We went together to the fort and on learning our news Travis immediately ordered the arrest of Juanita Músquiz. One of his officers talked him out of it – she was pregnant, although the identity of the father was anyone's guess. Bowie gave him the names of several friendly Tejanos in the town they could ask for news instead. One eventually came forward to say that he had heard a rumour that the Mexicans were at Leon Creek, no more than five miles from San Antonio. That was enough to get me saddling the horses for a quick departure, but Bowie argued that if they were that close they would have attacked at dawn when they could have caught us completely by surprise. Lookouts were sent to the top of the church belfry, which had a commanding view of the surrounding area. They reported that no Mexican soldiers could be seen.

Yet more of the townspeople were leaving, but there was still no sign of a force that could have easily covered five miles in a couple of hours, indeed much more quickly if they were horsemen. The whole morning passed without the lookouts spotting a thing. One or two citizens began to drift back to their homes as it appeared that the earlier panic had been a false alarm. The girls, Bowie and I went back to the house for lunch and the afternoon passed in a similarly peaceful manner. One o'clock came and went and then two and three. Gradually, we all relaxed. I was just carving a wooden toy for Alejo when suddenly there was the clang of church bells.

Chapter 11

At the first ring our heads all shot up like hounds at the bark of a fox. I reached for my watch, but I was sure it was too early for the chimes of four o'clock. Before I had even opened the cover there was more clanging, not giving the ordered march of time, but urgent, calling an alarm. We were all up then and despite his illness, Bowie moved quickly for the door.

"We need to get up that tower and see what is happening," he called over his shoulder. To hell with that, I thought, we need to get some horses and ride out of here without delay. Then he added something else which stopped me in my tracks. "Maybe they have already corralled us; instead of attacking this morning they might have surrounded the town."

I felt my guts lurch with fear then: was I already trapped? I followed him out of the door and across the square towards the big church. I could see Travis ahead of us, racing to the door to the church tower steps. The bell was still ringing, its noise drowning out the shouts of the lookouts who were pointing out of town to the south. I passed Bowie by the tower door. He might have been tough as teak and ten years younger, but his illness meant he was blown, puffing and wheezing from the exertion. I ran on ahead, breathing heavily myself by the time I emerged through the trap door at the top. I had half expected to see wheeling squadrons of cavalry and columns of infantry marching in all directions, but instead there was nothing.

"There were hundreds of them," the lookout was insisting, "but they turned off the road down there and went into that mesquite grove."

Travis stared at the empty countryside dubiously. "Are you sure that they were soldiers and not some ranchers?" He caught sight of me and added, "Thomas here is expecting some Indian friends to visit, could they have been them?"

"They were flamin' soldiers!" shouted the lookout indignantly. "They wore uniforms with helmets and they all had lances with flags at the top."

We looked again at the mesquite grove, but could see no sign of the little pennon flags at the top of lances among the trees. "They might be working their way around us," gasped a voice. We turned to see Bowie leaning heavily against the rail at the top of the stairs. He was sweating profusely and looked like the climb up the tower had half killed him. "We need to send a rider out there to have a look." Crockett was the obvious choice for a scout, there was none better by all accounts, but at that moment two horsemen from the Alamo trotted into the square below the church.

"Do you want us to ride out?" Doc Sutherland called. The sawbones was accompanied by a red-headed man who was already checking the priming on his rifle in case they met trouble.

"That would be good of you," called back Travis. "We will watch you from up here. If you see any Mexicans just wave and ride straight back. That will be our signal you have made contact the enemy."

The doctor wheeled his horse around and the pair of them started to canter down the road towards Leon Creek. They passed the point where the lookout claimed to have seen the Mexican cavalry, but did not stop. They occasionally stood in the stirrups to see further yet were finding nothing. They were soon a mile out of town and still giving no cause for alarm.

"Well I'm sure I see'd them," muttered the lookout to the questioning glance of Travis. But then as the horsemen reached the crest of a low rise, about a mile and a quarter out of town, they suddenly wheeled about.

"God damn, they've found them," muttered Bowie as the two riders flattened themselves low over their saddles and spurred their horses to race back into town. Sutherland was also trying to wave his hat in the air, but he needn't have bothered as a score of Mexican soldiers appeared on the path behind him and levelled their weapons. There was the distant crackle of a volley. At first I thought they had missed, but then Sutherland's horse went down, its rider going over the head of the mount. He must have screamed when the horse landed on top of his legs. His red-headed companion wheeled his own steed around to help, despite the soldiers now advancing down the path behind him.

He was a cool character, for he grabbed the reins of Sutherland's horse as it regained its footing and then helped the doctor back into the saddle. There was another fusillade of fire from the Mexicans, which must have sent balls buzzing around them, yet the red-headed man did not mount up again until his comrade was securely in the saddle.

It had all happened in just a few seconds, but already Travis was shouting orders. "Everyone to the Alamo!" he bellowed from the top of the tower, before disappearing down the steps. As I looked down on to the town I could see men, women and children running in all directions, like a disturbed ant's nest. A few men had watched Sutherland and his companion ride up the road and while they had not seen the action a mile away, they would have heard the ripple of gunfire and could guess what it meant. Those who had been nervous following the departure of the Tejanos, needed little encouragement to panic now.

"We must get the women and Alejo into the fort," growled Bowie. "Tom, you go, you will be quicker, I will meet you on the way."

"Should we not get them mounted up and away while we still have a chance?" I demanded, staring at the surrounding countryside. I could still see no sign of Mexican troops, apart from those on the road south, but that did not mean that they were not there. We knew that the cavalry the lookout had spotted earlier were around somewhere. Already a crowd of people were running down the streets towards the Alamo, but more than a few were also streaming down the roads north out of town. Most of them were Tejano civilians but I thought I caught a glimpse of a few *norteamericanos* amongst them, including two on horseback.

"It may already be too late for that," replied Bowie. "They have been working their way around us, that is why the men that the lookout spotted did not intercept Sutherland. They have us trapped." I looked again at the countryside surrounding the town. There were various undulating hills and mesquite groves that could hide men, particularly to the northwest where there was good cover around the San Pedro Springs. Cavalry there could easily cut off anyone trying to flee north to safety.

There was no time to stand around and debate our chances. I ran down the tower steps a damn sight faster than I had gone up them. As I emerged onto the street an old woman who had been heading into the church grabbed my arm. "Run away," she urged in Spanish. "Run or they will kill you all." I shook her off, but I had a growing feeling she was right, for at ground level the chaos in the streets was even worse than it had looked from above. Women were shouting for their children, shopkeepers were hurriedly closing their shutters and everyone was dashing about in a frenzy.

As I turned into the next street I found a Texian wrestling with a Tejano tavern-keeper over a long-barrelled rifle. "I know I sold it to you," the Texian shouted as he finally wrestled the weapon from his opponent's grip. "But now I need it. You can have it back when we have beaten the Mexicans." With that, he ran off with his gun towards the Alamo. He went past a grim-faced Crockett, who was riding away from the fort and south in the direction Doc Sutherland had taken. The frontiersman had his rifle securely in the crook of his arm. I guessed that if the Mexicans were still in pursuit of our earlier scouts, they would soon start tumbling down like squirrels at one of his election shoots.

Well the man who had taken back his rifle had more confidence in our success than I. Judging from the angry look of the tavern-keeper, I was not the only one who doubted our victory. I needed to decide quickly whether to try and make a run for it and hope to escape the Mexican encirclement, or to join the others in the Alamo and wait for reinforcements. It did not take me long to decide. Fannin only had around four hundred men to reinforce the fort while the Mexicans had thousands of soldiers that were either here already or on their way. The old lady who had grabbed my arm was right: it was time to go. As I approached Bowie's house I heard more gunfire, this time to the north of the town. Damnation, they were trying to surround us. Thank God Bowie had given me a good horse. I would try to make it to the road to Gonzales that ran northeast. Hopefully I would be down it before Mexican forces from the south or those shooting in the north could cut it off.

As I ran into the central courtyard of the Bowie house, I had a pang of regret as I saw the two sisters. They were rushing about and packing two bags with clothes while Alejo was crying at being told off for getting in the way. If it had just been Trudy I would have risked taking her with me on the back of my horse. She would not have slowed it down too much, at least not for the first few miles, which was all I needed to get through the cordon. But she would not leave without Juana and she in turn would not go without her son. I could not get the whole bloody family on the back of a single mount. They were the nieces of a former Mexican governor of the province, surely that would see them well treated. At least, I tried to convince myself of that fact. Then looking across the yard, I saw that the stable door on the far side was wide open and the stall empty.

"Where's my damn horse?" I shouted. I whirled about, staring in disbelief as though the wretched creature could have been hiding in the wash house.

"Captain Dimmit took it," shouted Juana as she gave Alejo a bundle of clothes to hold. "He could not find another and said he had to ride a reconnaissance." I cursed the yellow-bellied bastard for doing exactly what I had planned to do and kicked a pail across the yard in my temper. Hell, the times I had left men high and dry when I was fleeing danger and now someone had done it to me!

"What is the matter?" asked Juana and then her hand shot to her mouth in alarm., "Are they in the town already?"

"No, but they will be soon. Hurry up." I ran back out into the street. The only animal I could see was an ox slowly pulling a cart full of crying children and hurriedly piled possessions. A man was whipping the lumbering beast to go faster while a woman ran after it, clutching another box of belongings that she did not want to leave behind. I knew I would not get another horse now; I would wager that every single mount from the town was now on the roads north and northwest. Most had left earlier that morning; mine must have been one of the few horses left, which was why that thieving swine Dimmit had stolen it. There were some more at the Alamo but by the time we reached them, the Mexican net around us would be closing in. I swore

91

vehemently again when I thought of all the time I had sat around with a fresh horse in the stable, when I should have been running. Hell, I had spent most of the day sitting in Bowie's house doing nothing, when all the while the Mexicans were closing in around the town. Now it was too late, I was trapped. I felt a familiar lurch of fear. There was another smattering of shots from the north and I turned to hurry the women on, only to see them running out through the gate.

"Here, I found your spare clothes," muttered Trudy pushing my satchel of possessions into my arms. She had another bundle of her own and was holding an old sword, while Juana had a sack of belongings in one hand and young Alejo holding the other.

"What on earth are you doing with that?" I asked gesturing to the sword, which looked old enough to date back to the days of the Armada.

"It was our uncle's," Trudy explained. "It has been in the family for generations, I did not want them to get it." She nodded south in the direction we expected the Mexican army to come as we hurried back down into the main square.

The plaza was a hive of noise and activity. A shopkeeper was trying to load his most valuable stock into another ox cart while also serving several members of the garrison with last minutes supplies. Judging from the grins on their faces as they watched the merchant try to convert as much as possible into ready money, it was a buyers' market.

Half the garrison had been living in the town and they were now running to and from their lodgings for their possessions and other necessaries for the expected siege. Despite my apprehension, there did not seem any great fear amongst them. Two were laughing as they rolled a large barrel through the town towards the fort. From the branding on one end, I saw that it was full of whisky. They were clearly determined that spirits of all kinds would be high. Others had more stoic expressions – perhaps they had been in the battle that had taken the town the year before. They at least knew that a tough struggle was ahead. But unlike me, they showed no great sense of fear. I had been planning to leave well before Santa Anna and his men arrived, but they had been waiting and preparing for this moment for weeks. If the Mexicans had appeared with little warning and before their reinforcements, it did not seem to disconcert them.

Well it flaming well disconcerted me. This was not my war and I wanted out… Fast. I looked across the river at the Alamo and spotted several men on horseback riding out from the walls. At first I thought they were making a run for it too. Then I saw that they were helping to round up a small herd of cattle and drive it into a coral on the east side of the fort. Perhaps if we got there quickly, I thought, I could still grab a horse and get away. I turned hopefully at the sound of hooves coming down the street behind me. It was Dickinson the gunner. He had his infant daughter in his lap and his wife sitting astride behind him, holding his waist. For a moment I seriously considered grabbing hold of his boot and tipping the entire family into the dirt so that I could take the mare. I liked Dickinson but that wasn't the reason I let him ride past unmolested. It was not even the look of shock and disgust from the sisters that such an act would earn – well perhaps it was, just a little. The mount meant a much better chance of escape, but there were too many damn riflemen around. A pair of Crockett's Tennesseans stood across the square waiting for their leader to return. I did not doubt that they would reward such a base act with a ball between the shoulder blades as I tried to ride away.

I hurried the women over the bridge and up the track to the fort. Nearly everyone was heading in that direction, but a small ragged group was heading the other way. Some were being carried and others helped along by their comrades. On closer inspection I saw that they were the Mexican prisoners from the previous siege, who were now being released. There was no jubilation on their faces, more apprehension as they must have feared being pitched straight back into a new conflict,

There was the sound of more horsemen behind us and I turned to see Doctor Sutherland, his red-headed companion and Crockett.

"There's thousands of them," gasped the sawbones. He was wincing in pain, his leg extended at an unnatural angle. With his remaining good limb he kicked his horse on. As Juana urged Alejo to run, I stared over at the road from the south but there was no one to be seen coming through the trees.

Crockett's horse had not moved and he spoke in calm, measured tones. "Well now, we only *sighted* a company of men," he drawled, "but I don't doubt that there are a parcel more of them. But as to thousands, I could not say. Perhaps these here are just an advance party to see how we stand."

I was about to tell him that the lookout had spotted more cavalry, but a movement caught my eye. "Look!" I shouted, pointing. "They are already in town. That is the Mexican flag being raised on the church roof." I expected at least the women to break into a run and I was turning to do the same, when Trudy caught my arm.

"That is *our* flag," she explained. "See, it has the two stars in the middle, one for Texas and one for the province of Coahuila. It is the one we used under the 1824 Constitution." I looked again and saw she was right. The Mexican flag was an almost identical red, white and green tricolour, but with an eagle in the middle instead of the stars. Still, it did not make me feel any more comfortable and I hurried them on to the fort.

We went through the gate to a scene of pandemonium. Nearly everyone was running about, shouting and arguing. The only calm ones were Crockett and a man standing by the cannon covering the gateway. That fellow was called Ward. He was usually drunk, but now he hunched over his gun, smouldering linstock in his hand, as he squinted malevolently through the gateway waiting for someone he could blow to oblivion. Bowie remained outside supervising a chain of men carrying sacks of grain into the stores, although he was now far too weak to carry any himself. Doc Sutherland stayed on his horse, loudly declaring to all who would listen that he had seen a thousand Mexicans and that they had done for his leg.

As the sisters went off to join other Tejano women in the fort, I hesitated between running up to the west wall to see if there was any sign of the enemy in that direction, or going straight to the coral to take a horse. As I looked on, young Travis came running from his office and handed Sutherland a note. After a brief conversation the doctor tucked the paper into his coat and trotted his horse back out of the gate. Our young commander saw me watching and nodded after the sawbones, "He is a brave man," he declared.

"Why?" I asked. "Is he taking a message to the Mexicans?"

"No, he is going to try and take a message to Gonzales and then on to San Felipe if he can manage it. We need to tell as many as possible that the Mexicans are here and that we need help."

It was on the tip of my tongue to offer myself as another courier to Goliad, or anywhere that got me a horse and out of this mess. Then I remembered that Travis had talked of Sutherland's courage. "Why do you think him brave? Because of his leg, you mean?"

"Partly," agreed Travis, staring after the doctor as he rode out of sight. "He knows that will render him of little use as a defender. But he is going even though our men have seen lancers out in the groves to the west, ready to intercept any messengers."

"Lancers," I repeated. I felt a sudden chill that had nothing to do with the cold February day. I still bore a scar on my thigh from the point of a Polish lancer in Spain. I remembered the Tejanos telling me on the ride to San Antonio that the Mexican lancers were their finest cavalry. They were mounted on fast, light horses and once they had spotted an enemy horseman, it was only a matter of time before the poor bastard felt one of their steel points in the small of his back. Suddenly the prospect of fleeing on horseback was a whole lot less appealing.

I climbed up on the west wall to watch Sutherland's progress. He cantered into a thick Mesquite grove. If he kept in cover he might stand a chance, but if he rode out in the open I thought he would be dead for certain. I caught a glimpse of movement in the trees a few hundred yards to his right. Then I heard shouting from the south wall, the one that faced San Antonio and turned in that direction. The head of a column of Mexican troops could be seen marching into the main plaza of the town. With them were at least a dozen mounted officers, several of them glistening with gold braid and decorations. The Mexican army had most definitely arrived.

Chapter 12

There was an air of finality as we watched the gates of the Alamo slam shut. I imagine every man and woman in the place stood there, wondering if they would walk through that portal again. Most of the garrison were up on the walls, manning the cannon and staring apprehensively at the growing number of Mexican soldiers in the town. Their families stood in the courtyard below, along with other Tejano citizens of San Antonio who had decided to throw in their lot with the garrison. More than a few were staring around anxiously, evidently wondering if they had made the right decision.

I watched the Mexicans fill the town plaza and then begin to spread out along the riverbank. I could see at least five hundred infantry. They did look a ramshackle lot. Their blue coats were often torn and patched in a myriad of colours; some sported cloth caps instead of tall shako helmets and their white trousers were at best a mud-stained grey. Many of those were patched too or replaced entirely with new garments of homespun brown cloth or harder wearing buckskins. I noted, however, that for all the evident hardships of the journey they had all kept their muskets and were moving steadily in well-ordered lines and files.

"What do you make of them?" a voice behind me asked. I turned to find Bowie's steely blue, but slightly bloodshot eyes fixed on mine.

"They look handy enough," I admitted. "There must be at least one regiment here and I saw horsemen to the west when Sutherland left."

"There are more horsemen to the north," grunted Bowie and then he lapsed into silence. We stood together watching the Mexican lines move out around the edge of town. So far the infantry had stayed on their side of the river, where buildings in the town would provide cover if we opened fire. Teams of mules hauling four small cannon and carts for ammunition could now be seen heading towards us on the road.

Eventually, I asked the question that I thought was on both of our minds. "Do you think this is their main army or are they trying to keep us bottled up here while Santa Anna attacks the coast?"

96

Bowie did not reply, instead he looked along the wall where his fellow commander was working his way around the perimeter. Travis had evidently decided that the men's morale would benefit from his jovial encouragement.

"The Mexicans have fallen into our trap," he announced, when to most of his listeners it felt very much the other way around. "Soon they will be caught between our guns and the reinforcements that Governor Smith has already ordered to come to our support." There was no cheering, just a sense of grim resolve from those men on the rooftops. Some stared east, knowing that even if Fannin brought his entire four hundred-men garrison, they would need to fight their way through lancers and whatever other Mexican forces were out there to reach us. We all must have wondered if there would be enough survivors to help us repel a siege.

As if to answer Travis' breezy optimism, there was a sudden movement in San Antonio as a large red flag appeared at the top of the church tower. Several pointed to it and asked what it meant. Our two commanders exchanged a glance, but neither knew. I had a nasty feeling that it could not be anything good. This was confirmed when one of the Tejanos explained its significance to the man beside him.

"It means 'no quarter'," he said, loud enough for those standing nearby to hear. "They will not take prisoners – they mean to kill us all."

There was a shocked silence for a moment as this sank in. The men who had gambled on standing with Texas to protect their new lands and possessions realised that they had now put all their stake on the table. It was victory or death and right then victory looked long odds. Some went pale, others straightened up and tilted their chin defiantly at the enemy. One in particular, bowels churning anxiously, determined to slide out at the first opportunity.

"How in God's name has this happened to me again?" I exploded. "Christ on a stick, what have I done to upset the Almighty that he keeps putting me in pickles like this. It is just not bloody fair. Why can't I die an old man in the arms of a pretty woman>"

Several men about me chuckled at my exasperation, even though I must have been expressing sentiments dear to their own hearts. Bowie looked up curiously, "You been in a mess like this before?" he queried.

"More times than I care to remember," I growled.

"What, surrounded in a fort? How d'ye get out of that?"

"Well there was a time in India that was pretty much the same. I escaped down a well that was joined by an underground tunnel to a pond outside the walls."

Bowie looked at the well that Jameson had dug, with a few feet of muddy water swirling at the bottom. "Well, that ain't gonna serve here."

Travis sensed the unease in the crowd and shouted at the men around the large eighteen-pounder that overlooked the town. "Fire a shot at the church tower. Let's see if we can knock that flag back into the dirt."

Orders were yelled and men went running for powder charges from the magazine, while others argued over which was the roundest ball from the small stack kept near the gun. Lieutenant Dickinson took charge of the loading, adding extra powder to take account of the fact that the barrel was cold, but he was used to poorer charges than the finely ground grains from Du Pont. The cannon fired with a roar and I suspect that the ball must have landed half a mile beyond the town. The gunners clamoured for another go but Travis stopped them. He had made his show of defiance and was mindful that we only had a few balls for the big gun. "We have shown them that we are not afraid of their threats," he announced. "We will never allow tyranny to succeed here." With that he strolled down the ramp and headed off towards the officers' quarters, apparently satisfied that his work was done.

I turned back to the town and studied the group of officers watching us from the other side of the river. Was the tyrant in question amongst them, I wondered. If he was, he did not take long in sending his reply. We watched as the Mexican battery set their guns and fired a salvo in return. Fortunately, their gunners were as accurate as ours and all the shots missed.

Bowie was leaning heavily on his rifle; he did not look well at all and I noticed that his hand was shaking. Unlike me, though, he did not duck when one of the Mexican balls whirred over our heads. He too was staring at the Mexican officers and seemed lost in thought. "What are we going to do?" I asked him. "We cannot just sit here waiting for them to overwhelm us."

"Well, first we need to know how many of 'em are out there." He spoke softly so that the men nearby could not overhear. "If Father Garza is right and they are just a holding force then things will be a lot easier than if it's their whole army. We need to get someone to talk to them."

I nodded over my shoulder, "Travis does not seem to be in the mood for talking."

"The boy is a fool," he grinned. "When those cannon fired, I thought I heard one of their horns blow callin' for a parley. Surely you heard it too?"

"No," I replied, puzzled. Bowie raised one eyebrow as he waited for me to catch on. "Oh, I see what you mean. Yes, I did hear it, now you ask."

Juan Seguín was summoned and he wrote down in Spanish a message that Bowie dictated. It was a formal enquiry to see if the Mexicans wanted to talk. Seguín signed it off with the words, 'God and the Mexican Federation', but when he went to sign it, Bowie crossed that out and wrote, 'God and Texas'. Jameson was summoned to take the message, which was a relief as I thought he was going to give it to me. The engineer was told to try and engage the Mexicans in conversation and find out as much as he could.

The gate creaked open once more and our emissary, clutching a white flag, made his way to one of the bridges over the river. The conversation with a Mexican officer sent to meet him did not take long and soon Jameson was heading back.

"I think Santa Anna is there," he announced, "but they would not let me meet him."

"What did they say?" asked Bowie.

"They insisted that they would not discuss terms with rebellious foreigners and our only hope is to surrender to the mercy of the supreme government."

"So, no guarantee of safe conduct," mused Bowie. "The bastard would probably want to execute at least some of us as an example to the rest."

"What did you expect?" came a new voice and we turned to find Travis standing behind us and looking furious. "I am astonished that you took it upon yourself to conduct negotiations with the enemy before consulting with me first," he continued. "We cannot show any doubt in our resolve to hold out at all costs." He then launched into some wild speech, waving his arms about and describing the Alamo as the 'crucible in which the nation of Texas would be forged', or some such nonsense. You could tell he was a lawyer, for he spoke as though appealing to a jury or writing one of his editorials. It was an overblown tirade and I doubt Bowie had ever allowed anyone to talk to him like that before, certainly not some young whippersnapper like Travis. I half expected the notorious hardman to reach for his big knife and gut the fellow on the spot, or at the very least push the windbag off the roof. He did neither. Instead he just leaned back against the nearest cannon. Sweat had broken out on his brow and it was clear that the events of the day were taking their toll on him.

"We need to know what we are up against," gasped Bowie when Travis paused at last for breath. "Is this their main force or not?"

"I am certain it is their main force," insisted Travis. "They know this is where they must break us, or they will lose Texas. I have told Sutherland to spread the word that the entire Mexican army is here and that every true Texian should rush to our aide." With that he turned and walked back down the ramp, calling for one of the men to join him in his office.

"The impertinent wretch," I fumed behind his back, but Bowie reached out and grabbed my hand.

"Help me down to my room, Tom," he whispered. "I don't want the men to see me like this." He put his arm around my shoulders and I carefully guided him down the nearest ramp and into his quarters. Despite entreaties from Juana and Trudy, who were sharing his room, he refused to go to bed. Instead he sat in a chair and allowed them to wrap him with blankets to help fight his fever. I stayed with them for a while but then heard shouting from the courtyard and stepped outside. Travis was calling the garrison to muster again. I found Jameson and asked him what was going on.

He grinned. "After complaining that I had been sent to speak to the Mexicans, Colonel Travis decided that as he is joint commander, he should send his own representative to speak to them too. Al Martin went, but he got no further than I did." I groaned, for instead of getting information from the Mexicans, we had just demonstrated how hopelessly divided our command was. Jameson looked up as our young Caesar launched into another of his impassioned orations.

To be fair, he told them straight up that the Mexicans had refused to negotiate and were demanding our surrender. "They are insisting that we throw ourselves down on their mercy and beg for our lives," he shouted. He must have seen the looks of concern in the faces of some of his audience as the harsh reality of their situation hit them. Yet if there was one man in the Alamo who could fire them up again, it was William B. Travis.

"Are we going to go down on our knees to these devils like beaten curs?" he asked. A half-hearted rumble of voices indicated that they would not. "Are we going to let the forces of tyranny steal our lands, our property and murder or ravish our womenfolk?" he demanded, to a louder denial. "Or, with men from all over Texas coming to our aid, are we going to stand firm and show Santa Anna that we whipped his boys once and we will do it again?" There was a rousing cheer this time and Travis had to hold up a hand to silence the crowd before he could continue. "I swear to you that I will never surrender. I will fight to my last breath to show them that the flame of liberty burns in Texas. Who's with me?" At this there was a roar of acclaim.

I looked at the faces in the crowd. Many were in their twenties and thirties, young men burning with a passion to make their way in the world, much like their ambitious leader. They had much in common with those gambling on a new life with whom I had shared the journey to America and then down to this new land. One turned to me and grinned, "We're gonna show them and then make this the best country there has ever been." Another slapped him on the back and declared that he was, "Damn right." Some of the older men looked more thoughtful; they had the experience to guess at the challenges ahead, but like Crockett standing at the edge of the throng, they were nodding their approval. The great frontiersman had already decided, in his own words, "what was right" and now nothing would stop him going ahead.

Chapter 13

Though Travis had promised that reinforcements were coming, he clearly was not confident that they were. Various despatches had been sent to San Felipe over the previous weeks, but he remembered how hard it had been to gather recruits for his new mounted legion. The only sizeable force that already existed was the one under Fannin at Goliad. He must have hoped that the governor had given Fannin orders to come to his assistance, but with the dispute between the governor and the council still raging, he could not be sure. So, a short while after he gave his speech to the men, he called on Bowie again. He had drafted a direct appeal to Fannin, explaining the forces that they were up against and how it was vital that the Goliad garrison marched to their aid as soon as they could. Both Bowie and Travis signed it and that night another courier eased out of the gate and crept away to the west.

"I hope to God he gets through," muttered Travis to me as we watched the man disappear into the darkness. "Captain Dimmit has not returned from the reconnaissance I sent him on today. For all we know the good doctor is also lying in a ditch with a lance wound in his back."

I shuddered at the thought, for if the Mexicans did have a tight cordon then I could well have been killed too had Dimmit not stolen my horse. "Even if our couriers do not get through," I reassured Travis, "the Tejanos who fled San Antonio before Santa Anna's men got here will spread the word of his arrival. The news is bound to reach San Felipe in a day or two." The young colonel did not hold much comfort from that. He was probably wondering how long it would take the news to reach Goliad if his man was killed. He went back to his quarters, leaving me alone to consider my own options.

It seemed to me that the Alamo garrison was doomed. We were outnumbered by more than ten to one by the Mexicans and if our scouts were right, more of the devils were on the way. I had seen Fannin's army in Goliad and I did not fancy their chances of reaching us either. The land I had ridden across from the coast to reach San

Antonio had been miles of rolling open prairie, with very little cover. It would be easy for the Mexicans to pin down a long straggling column of the Texian fighters. They could stay out of rifle range and use artillery to stop them. Then the much-vaunted Mexican cavalry could attack any groups that tried to break away. A few Texians might manage to escape under cover of darkness, but nothing like the numbers we would need to defend the fort.

On the other hand, such an attempt might give me my best chance to escape. If the Mexican cavalry really was as good as they said, and we had seen them patrolling around the Alamo, then making a run for it now was a deuced risky venture. But if Fannin and his men approached, the 'Napoleon of the West' was bound to divert most of his horsemen to head them off and that would give me my opportunity. If I set off at nightfall and carefully skirted my way around the fires of the pickets, with luck I could be five or six miles north of the Alamo by daybreak. I would take water and food and make my way northeast. At worst it would be a hard walk for a few days, but I had done that before. If I was fortunate, I would find a Texian patrol or be able to borrow or steal a horse that would help me get to Gonzales or carry me on to San Felipe.

The first full day of the siege was something of an anti-climax. The garrison stood to at dawn in case the Mexicans were preparing an attack, but most had sensibly stayed in their beds. The cold drizzle blown in on a northerly wind soon chilled the bones and left clothes damp. Men stood and shivered as they watched a few of the enemy building a new gun battery by the river, some three hundred and fifty yards off. Eventually, the cannon that had fired on us the day before opened up a sporadic barrage, joined later that afternoon by the new battery. The Mexican gunners were woeful. They didn't fire frequently enough to keep their barrels warm and their aim was all over the place. As one grizzled rifleman put it when a ball missed the fort by fifty yards, "Darnation, I reckon that boy misses when he pisses up a wall."

They did manage to hit the fort a few times and even put a large crack in one of the walls, but that was soon shored up from our side. The only excitement of the day came when a group of generals and senior officers rode out on an inspection around the Alamo. One in particular pointed things out animatedly to the others and we speculated that this was Santa Anna himself. At one stage he got within two hundred yards of the walls, an extreme range for a rifle but Crockett thought it was worth a shot. He carefully loaded his percussion cap rifle that he called Plain Betsy. It was a stripped-down version of a presentation weapon he had been given a year or two before. "You should have seen the silver on that one," he told us. "The sun would shine on it and frighten bears away for miles."

Men watched expectantly as he used a wooden tool to check the roundness of his ball before wrapping it and ramming it home. He stood for a moment silently sniffing the air and watching his prey before he lowered himself to lie prone on a rooftop. The generals had already begun to walk their horses away as the frontiersman cocked the weapon. Then the shot rang out. There was a disappointed groan as Crockett's target remained in his saddle, but the ball must have whizzed about their ears for they spurred their horses away, looking over their shoulders.

Crockett grinned as coins were exchanged by those who had wagered on the outcome. "I'll try and get your money back next time, boys," he promised those who had put faith and dollars on his marksmanship. The former senator provided easy and natural leadership to the men in contrast to our remaining commanding officer.

Travis, very conscious of his youth and inexperience was often stiffly formal in his dealings with his subordinates. He had spent most of that day doing what he did best: writing fervent appeals for help. That evening he summoned his former emissary to the Mexicans, Albert Martin, and this time sent him off as a courier with a despatch Travis had written addressed to, 'The People of Texas and all the Americans in the World'. In it he begged for assistance and promised to hold the Alamo at all costs, finishing with the words: 'Victory or death'. It was a good job I did not know about the contents of this letter until much later, or I might have added a postscript or two of my own to show we were not all of the same mind. We still had no idea if any of the couriers were getting through. As I watched Martin disappear into the night gloom, I wondered if we were just surrendering or killing our own men piecemeal.

After Crockett had demonstrated the range of our rifles, I thought that the Mexicans might give us a wide berth for a while until they had battered us with their guns. Yet to our surprise the next morning, we saw over two hundred of their infantry crossing the river and marching towards the southwest corner of the fort. They took shelter amongst some abandoned wooden huts and started to open a steady fire on the defenders. If they were there to test our resolve, they had placed themselves at a serious disadvantage, for they were just at the limit of the range of their muskets, but well within the killing distance of our more accurate rifles. A steady fusillade of fire began from the huts, answered by a slower, sharper crack of guns from the walls. Dozens of our men lying prone, took careful aim before rolling into cover to reload. One by one the Mexicans began to fall, while our men took no injuries at all. Crockett took an occasional shot himself yet for the most part he roamed along the rooftop, careless of the danger, offering words of encouragement as well as pointers to improve marksmanship. My musketry had been taught in the British army where rate of fire was valued above accuracy. He grinned when he saw my efforts and had me hold the stock closer to my cheek. When he congratulated the farm boy to my right on a good shot, the lad's face split into a grin of pride that stretched from ear to ear.

The result of this first confrontation of arms was almost inevitable – after some two hours of very one-sided fighting the Mexicans were forced to withdraw, taking their dead and injured with them. A cheer rose up from our ranks: the first victory had gone to Texas.

That evening Travis decided to send yet another despatch to San Felipe. I wasn't sure if this was to be a daily occurrence, but at this rate I wondered if we would have any men left in the fort when the Mexicans finally made their assault. He asked for a volunteer to carry the message and I did seriously consider it. I decided that even if some of the early couriers had managed to escape the cordon, the Mexicans must have at least heard them. By then they would have tightened their lines even further. The risk was too great for me and I let Juan Seguín carry Travis' latest scribblings instead.

If I thought our fate was grim, for some it was even worse. Bowie had been getting steadily weaker and had been delirious for much of the first two days of the siege. Juana was convinced that it was not malaria and instead he was suffering from typhoid. In one of his more lucid moments, James agreed. As it was contagious, he insisted on being placed into isolation and forbade Juana from visiting him. The tough fighter's body was much lighter than I expected when we lifted his bed and carried it and its occupant across the courtyard and into a small room to one side of the main gate. Around half of those who caught typhoid survived it. Given the injuries Bowie had recovered from in the past, few would have wagered on him not coming back from this, provided the Mexicans gave him the chance. One of the Tejana women who had survived the disease before offered to look after him. I had come through more than my share of exotic fevers myself, especially in India and Africa. Most evenings I would tie a neckerchief across my face and carry into his chamber some broth or food that Juana had prepared.

Over the next few days we settled into some form of routine. The Mexican infantry did not dare come close to our walls again but, to be certain, Travis sent men out to burn down the sheds that they had used as cover before. Instead, the enemy concentrated on building artillery emplacements all around the Alamo until each wall was covered by several guns. We watched as teams of men and horses dragged gun limbers and wagons of powder and cannon balls. Even though we had more guns, we did not have enough Du Pont powder to disrupt these preparations. Travis had banned the gunners from firing without his permission as he wanted to save our fire to destroy any infantry assault. Slowly the level of the Mexican bombardment increased as more guns opened fire and then the early batteries were gradually moved forward.

I was surprised that the enemy gunners did not concentrate on a particular point to create a breach, as British gunners would have done in preparation for an attack. Instead they were content to spray balls all over the place and so did little serious damage. Not one of the defenders was killed or even injured, yet all felt their nerve gradually worn down. The Mexicans would often save their explosive shells to fire at night to ensure that we got little sleep. Increasingly, members of the garrison could be seen on our northern and eastern walls, staring out in hope of any sign of reinforcements coming to our aid. The suspicion that all the couriers had been killed or captured began to grow, as did the thought that the Alamo had been forgotten or its rescue abandoned.

Travis tried once again to raise morale with assurances that Texas would rise to our aid. He made little speeches about how we were forging a nation, but they increasingly rang as empty as the horizon. Everyone knew it was ages since he had last received a message from San Felipe and even that had been more about the division in the government rather than reinforcements. It was the man who had claimed he just wanted to be a 'humble private' in this army who did more to keep men's spirits up. Colonel David Crockett told stories rather than gave speeches. He did so to small groups of men as he roamed around the walls, taking the occasional pot-shot at any Mexican who misjudged how far away from the walls was safe. He talked about the tight spots he had been in before, such as how he nearly drowned on a boat in the Mississippi, or when he escaped mauling from a wounded bear, or his time fighting the Creek Indians. There was a calm confidence in him that was infectious. We were doing the right thing, he assured them and we just needed to stay the course. The chests of these farmers would swell with pride when the great man told them how proud he was to be fighting among them and calling them his comrades.

Well that soft soap might wash with turf thumpers and cattle drovers, but it did not work with me. I remember one evening sitting up on the north wall and trying to judge the largest distance between the picket fires. We had seen some horsemen and soldiers move out to the east in the afternoon, causing some speculation that Fannin may at last be on his way. This, I thought, was possibly my opportunity to slip away into the darkness. They could fight on for their Texas if they wanted, but my precious hide had been in peril long enough. I heard someone come up behind me and grunt as he lowered himself down so that his legs dangled over the edge of the wall like mine. I did not look up but the long percussion cap rifle resting on the man's knees gave away his identity; it was the only gun of its type in the fort, possibly in Texas.

"It won't be easy for someone makin' their way in through those," Crockett's voice spoke quietly beside me.

"No," I agreed, although I had been planning a journey in the opposite direction.

"Tell me, Tom," he continued, "you used to be a soldier, do you think Fannin and his boys will get here soon?"

I looked across at him then. It was too dark to see those steely blue eyes, but I knew they were boring into me and the politician in him was trying to weigh me up. I decided for once to be honest. "No," I told him bluntly. Then I proceeded to explain how vulnerable Fannin's men would be on the open prairie when the Mexicans had artillery and skilled cavalry.

"But when you were marching in the British army, you must have faced French horsemen. Surely you did not let them beat you?"

"No, infantry can form a square against cavalry and be perfectly safe, but they need to be well trained and disciplined. It only takes a few to get out of position and then the horsemen are inside and it becomes a slaughter. But in a tightly packed square you are more vulnerable to artillery, I saw squares torn to bloody ruin at Waterloo. We should be glad that they won't even attempt it. A handful might fight their way through, especially at night, but that I think is all we can expect."

He did not reply. Instead he just sat silently beside me staring out into the darkness, lost in his thoughts. A minute passed and then two before he finally spoke again. "I think you are wrong," he stated quietly. He held up his hand to still any objection before continuing. "Oh I know you have more experience of soldierin' than me. I might not have been in Texas long, but I know what kind of man builds himself a life in a new land. I have been with them all my life in

Tennessee and they are the same here. They are strong, independent people and when they set their mind to do somethin' they never give up. They'll succeed or die tryin'. Whether it is buildin' a farm or a country, I guess it is the same. Those men will not submit to a man like Santa Anna. So, if they are settled to come here, then that is what they will do an' I reckon they will whip those Mexicans too." He gestured into the darkness, "I don't know about their horsemen, but I've seen their soldiers and they get driven around like sheep. There is no great fight in them." He paused as a distant cannon boomed out. We waited to hear the thud of a ball landing somewhere in the quarter acre compound behind us, but there was silence. He chuckled, "Their gunners can't shoot straighter than a coon can spit either."

I kept my silence and instead sat there considering if the great man could be right. I'll admit that I decided he was deluded, an opinion I was certain of the following week. Yet, much later when I looked back, I was not so sure. Crockett must have sensed that I disagreed with him and reached out and gripped my shoulder. "You're a good man, Tom, and I'm right proud to call you a true friend. You gave me a straight honest answer to my question and did not tell me something that you thought I wanted to hear. I could have done with some folks like you in Congress." As I looked across at him, I saw his eyes glint at me in the moonlight and he held out his hand in friendship. I shook it. He grunted again as he got to his feet. "Yes, sir," he added. "With a few fellas like you in Congress we could have got through a month's jawing in an afternoon and really got things done." He strolled off into the darkness still chuckling to himself at the thought of a productive government. Perhaps I did fall for the Crockett charm after all, for I did not run that night, even though it was probably my best chance.

The next morning men climbed up onto the roof of the eastern buildings and stared out. They remembered some of the Mexican forces had moved in that direction the previous evening and many were sure it was to try and block Fannin and his men. Most were certain that our reinforcements would break through and the Alamo would be full of men by lunchtime. Instead, the eastern horizon remained as empty as a drunkard's purse. The disappointment was palpable, hopes had been raised and then dashed. Disconsolate men wondered once more if they had been forgotten or abandoned. In some ways I was relieved as the sight of a handful of survivors struggling towards us would indicate that the Goliad garrison had been destroyed. We would have heard a battle but the night had been silent, which could only mean that they were still out there somewhere.

As I had lived with them in San Antonio, so I shared Bowie's former quarters with Juana, Trudy and little Alejo. The women had worried that they had lost their protector when James had been carried into isolation. They thought that some of the Texians would view them as too close to the people of San Antonio, who now supported their enemy. I told them that they had little to fear. Some of the garrison knew Horace Alsbury but even if he was at death's door, Bowie was still a powerful guardian. Only a fool would insult the family of the victor of the San Saba silver mines battle with the Indians or the brawl where he killed a man having been attacked with swords and pistols. Trudy joked that I could be their protector instead and of course I agreed, while privately thinking it would only be until I could drop over the wall. Then they would be on their own.

It is not that I did not want to take them, but it would be hard enough for one man to slip stealthily through the Mexican lines. I tried to reassure myself that the red flag flying from the San Antonio church would not apply to women and children, but I knew all too well that terrible butchery could take place when an army's blood is up. Then, the day after I talked with Crockett a solution to this dilemma presented itself.

Heaven knows how the news got into the fort – I suspected that some of the Tejano defenders went over the wall occasionally and talked to relatives from the town who crept up at night. In any event, the word spread that an amnesty was offered by Santa Anna to the Tejanos. He was a wily bastard, I will say that about *el Presidente.* Having kept us awake night after night, he had now found a way to whittle down our numbers and sour our ranks with division and resentment. We heard of it on the twenty-ninth of February. I remember it well as I had been trying to explain to Alejo why this date

111

only occurred every four years, when Trudy came in with the news. Santa Anna had given the Tejanos three days to respond.

"You should go," I told them. "No one will blame two women and a child for leaving a place like this." But Juana would not hear of it.

"Everyone knows we are kin to James. They would keep us as hostages and what would my husband think if he fights his way here and finds that we have gone over to his enemy? No, we will stay and when the forces of Texas win, we will go back into town as a family, God willing with James recovered and among us." She could not be moved; she had spent too much time with men who had been talking to Travis and Crockett to see reason.

Other Tejanos were more amenable to the proposal. Some like Señor Menchaca, who had helped me contact Norton, asked for an interview with Bowie to get his opinion. This time James asked to see Travis first so that the two commanders were aligned in their views. Bowie advised Menchaca to leave. He was a merchant, not a fighter. Many of the Tejanos had brought their families with them, having made a rushed decision to flee with the garrison to the fort when the Mexicans had first appeared. Since then they had been given plenty of time to consider the folly of that headlong rush from the town over the river. Soon the gate opened and a steady flow of men, women and children began to depart. It was a flow that continued over the next day too. As the garrison dwindled, hope of victory receded further and those that were wavering decided to leave too before it was too late.

That day, the first of March, was I think the worst for morale in the Alamo. We had been besieged for a week, still had no word from the outside world and the early optimism for a relief force had long since faded. I suspect that if Santa Anna had offered an amnesty for the garrison who were not Tejanos then, some might have taken it. I know one who definitely would have. In fact, I had been wondering if I could leave in disguise and speaking Spanish, but I was too well known in town as Bowie's friend. We had seen the mayor and several army officers meet those who returned. I was sure someone would turn me in.

Trudy and I rowed that night. She thought I was angry because they had refused to leave, but I was just bitter at how fate had turned on me once more. Then, in the middle of the night, everything changed again.

Chapter 14

I had just drifted back to sleep after a shell had exploded in the courtyard when I was awoken by more shouting outside. I swore softly in the darkness and tried to turn over under my blanket before I realised that men were cheering. Then I heard horses galloping and braying. I got up, threw the blanket around my shoulders for warmth and stepped into the courtyard. I was just in time to see the gate thrown open as a group of riders trotted in, past sentries that were still shouting for joy. At least that proved that the new arrivals were on our side. More of the garrison were now stumbling, half asleep, out of their barracks to stare in bewilderment at the newcomers. The horsemen were whooping and hollering that help was at hand, although there was barely more than half a troop of them. Then I saw in the light of the brazier that one of their number was Albert Martin. With relief I knew now that at least one of the couriers had got out with news of our predicament. Although what in the name of holy heaven possessed the damn fool to come back to this death trap was beyond me.

Travis appeared then and Martin shouted the news so that all could hear. He had made it to Gonzales from where other couriers had taken the colonel's despatch on to San Felipe and beyond. Martin had stayed and helped to organise a relief force from Gonzales and the farms around it. They had gathered over sixty men and he had brought thirty-two with him. There was doubt as to whether they would all get through the Mexican lines and so the rest had ridden east where they were expecting to rendezvous with Fannin. Martin announced that Juan Seguín had also made it through the Mexican lines and that he was organising reinforcements from among the Tejanos. They too would try to join Fannin as he got close.

"So they are coming?" Travis asked, hanging on to Martin's bridle. "The men at Goliad are definitely marching to our aid?" For all of his earlier assurances and bold statements, it was clear that Travis had been suffering from the same doubts as the rest of us.

"Oh yes, sir," assured Martin. "From what I have heard he should have set off already – he could be here at any time." He grinned, "There are bound to be more coming from San Felipe and all over once they have seen your message."

I have rarely seen the mood of a body of people change so quickly. The day before some had been close to despair, watching with increasing bitterness as the Tejanos left us for safety. Men who had pledged to make a stand for this new land had begun to wonder if they were risking their lives on a futile gesture, as their fellow citizens did not seem to know or care what happened to them. That all changed with Martin's arrival. Whatever happened, all Texas would now know, if they did not already, that the men of the Alamo were holding out against a merciless tyrant, who was determined to steal their liberty. But more importantly, the defenders understood that their fellow Texians did indeed care and more than a few would be marching in their direction.

No one slept any more that night and as the sun rose so did the optimism of the garrison as they speculated on how many might come. As well as the four hundred from Goliad, thirty-two from Gonzales and perhaps a similar number with Seguín, they argued over how many would be bound to come from other towns. Many insisted that the men from their own communities would come en masse. They started to imagine that the garrison might rise to as many as a thousand. Still fewer than the Mexicans, but no one doubted that we could beat them now. Travis had the men dig trenches outside the walls from where these new men would fight, so that we could have deadly riflemen firing from sheltered positions at the bottom of the walls as well as the top.

By noon we saw some of the Mexican cavalry and infantry return, those who had marched away east two days before. Common thinking was that they had evidently been driven off by Fannin and our reinforcements. Some went as far as to believe that news of the host marching to our relief would cause the Mexicans to lift the siege entirely and return south. As you can imagine, your correspondent was far too long in the tooth to believe such nonsense. I still doubted

Fannin would get through at all, but it was obvious I was alone in that opinion. Men dug ditches or stared hopefully at the eastern horizon and barely noticed the few cannon balls the Mexicans fired in our direction. Their effectiveness remained woeful – still not a single member of the garrison had even been wounded. In celebration of the arrival of the Gonzales men, Travis authorised our gunners to return fire. Two balls were fired at a building in town thought to be Santa Anna's headquarters. The second demolished part of it. While Mexicans were sent fleeing from falling timbers and masonry, we soon learned that its supposed prime occupant was not inside.

In the afternoon as the air of celebration continued, men went to check on Bowie. As he was conscious and lucid, he was carried outside so that he could see the new arrivals. Propped up on his cot, he congratulated them on getting through and Martin for doing it twice. Bowie knew several of the new men and had fought with some of them before. He assured them that he would soon be well again and told them to save him a place in one of the ditches. Temporarily out of his isolation, Juana and Trudy spent some time with him too and he tried to give them the same reassurances about his recovery. This forced bonhomie must have exhausted him, though. I saw that his hands were shaking as his head sank back into the pillow. As if he had not suffered enough, someone prevailed on MacGregor to get his pipes and a fiddle was pressed into Crockett's fist. Soon the bugles in the Mexican camp and a couple of rounds from their cannon had to compete for noise with a terrible din coming from our yard. I did the decent thing and had my friend carried back into his room. Then I tore some small strips of cloth from a sheet that we could both stuff in our ears.

By dusk Fannin's men had still not been spotted, although my comrades in arms were even more certain that they must arrive on the morrow. One force which had been seen, however, was a Mexican company that had taken advantage of a gully to get within a hundred yards or so of the walls. That evening Travis organised a sally of his own to ambush these men and drive them off. A crackle of well-aimed rifle fire rent the night followed by the sound of the enemy withdrawing at some haste. It was another small victory for the men of the Alamo, but it was to be their last, as events began to turn once more.

The next morning saw the garrison back digging the ditches while also keeping a ready eye out on the eastern horizon. At eleven o'clock a lookout reported movement in that direction. Glasses were trained to reveal a single horseman riding towards us. We scanned the horizon for any sign that more were following but there were none. Instead this lone rider galloped on and managed to pass unmolested through the Mexican lines until he was up at our gate. I had seen him before. His name was Bonham; he had been sent by Travis as a courier to San Felipe just before the Mexicans had arrived. His old comrades welcomed him warmly and asked whether he had seen Fannin, but he had not. Instead of shouting out his news like Martin had done, he handed Travis three letters and accompanied him into the colonel's quarters.

It was half an hour before we heard any news about the content of the despatches. Travis appeared, standing on the barracks roof and the tin plate was bashed to summon the garrison for an announcement. "I have here a letter from Three-Legged Willie Williamson," he announced. I swear that was the name he used and I was too much of a gentleman to ask how he had earned such an epithet. "He writes," continued Travis, "that Colonel Fannin left Goliad four days ago on the twenty-eighth of February. He has three hundred men with him and four cannon. Willie says that three hundred more men were due in San Felipe by nightfall on the first of March, the day he wrote this letter. They will follow swiftly this despatch as well as another sixty volunteers already on the way. Boys, we could have near a thousand men here by the end of the week." There was a huge cheer at that and I feared that the wretched bagpipes might reappear.

"How far away is San Felipe?" I asked Jameson, who stood nearby.

"About a hundred and fifty miles. It will be hard riding to get here by Sunday, especially if they have travelled some distance already."

"And about ten days' march if some are on foot," I cautioned. It seemed to me that Travis was being too optimistic. I was also

117

surprised that Bonham had not seen any sign of Fannin if that force had set off on the twenty-eighth. Goliad was ninety miles off and if they were marching hard, as they should be, they should be at least two-thirds of the way towards us, perhaps just thirty miles away. Travis handed down Three-Legged Willie's letter so the men could read it for themselves. I noticed he had not mentioned the other two letters Bonham had given him. They might have been private correspondence, but I wondered if they contained other news. My suspicions deepened at the next order from Travis.

"Santa Anna will soon learn that men are coming to our aid and he may try to attack before they get here," he shouted.

"Let him try!" came a voice from the crowd, with several others yelling their agreement.

Travis held up his hand for silence. "We need to be prepared for an assault. I want double the lookouts at night and we should prepare the central barrack building as a redoubt in case we need to fall back from the walls. I want loopholes knocked in the walls every six feet."

"Damn, it's cold enough in there already," shouted a man standing behind me.

"It'll be a sight hotter if we have to fight from there," claimed his mate. "We will be surrounded by our own cannon. They can turn them and blow us to pieces."

"I am sure that the colonel knows what he is doing." Jameson turned and reprimanded the men behind us. Then he grinned and added, "But yes, it would be better if we fight them off from the walls."

I stared around at the men in the crowd. Most still looked belligerently confident that they could fight off any Mexican attack, but I could see that more than a few were quietly recalculating the odds. Some, like me, must have been wondering if they could take the assurances from a man going under the moniker of 'Three-Legged Willie' as reliable. Others, also like me, were realising that even if they were true, they might not necessarily mean our salvation. Travis was right, they could force the Mexicans to pre-empt their attack. If Santa Anna took the Alamo before Fannin arrived and added his cannon to the ones already here, then it would form a formidable stronghold. The Mexicans did not seem to suffer from our shortage of powder. They had enough men to properly defend the walls and their roving cavalry patrols could help get supplies in when necessary.

It was a sobering thought. We had all been pinning our hopes on reinforcements, but now I saw that it might not be the deliverance we expected. And what if these extra men did not come or if Mexican cavalry destroyed them on the way as I had first feared? Well, the garrison was still trapped in the Alamo, with that damned red flag flying from the church tower.

That afternoon, men began, reluctantly, to knock loopholes in the central barracks. It was a long, low single-storey building that stretched from the north wall to the south, effectively dividing the central courtyard in two. The men behind us had been right; it would be an impossible place to defend if the perimeter was taken. I resolved to go over the walls instead if necessary. I would rather take my chances out in the open than in a building that looked like it would soon become a rubble tomb for its defenders. In fact, I thought that a trip over the ramparts was already long overdue and resolved to try and slide out that very night.

By late afternoon a row of loopholes was visible in the central barracks. You had to look carefully for some as most had already been refilled with loose stones, bundles of old socks and other items to keep out the draughts for those still living inside the building. Looking beyond it, I could see half a dozen men braving the chill wind and occasional sleet to keep a lookout eastward. I thought they were hoping in vain for reinforcements to arrive that day, but it turned out I was wrong. Another thousand men did arrive, but unfortunately for us they came from the west and they were Mexican soldiers.

We watched with dismay an endless column of men marching up the road to San Antonio. They had at least two more cannon with them along with wagons full of supplies. As soon as they were in town, the guns and many of the soldiers were sent across the river to strengthen the cordon around the fort. We stood quietly and stared as new tents and shelters were erected and campfires lit.

"God damn, they are out there thicker than fleas on a skunk," opined the man beside me and he was not wrong. I had a sickening feeling that I had left it just too late to attempt my escape. It would have been hard before but now, even at night, it seemed impossible, especially for a man on foot. I did not fancy my chances even on horseback now that the cavalry was back in position. I cursed myself for listening to bloody Crockett when I had the chance before.

It was hard to judge how many Mexicans in total were out there, especially as several hundred horsemen often lingered out in the scrub beyond our direct line of sight. Travis was sure that there must be at least three thousand, while Crockett judged the number to be closer to two thousand. For my part, I guessed at somewhere between those two numbers, whereas the garrison was around a hundred and eighty men. It was a hopeless imbalance and if no help was coming then surely Travis, for all his fine words, would have to sue for terms. I tried to convince myself that the red flag was just a means of intimidation. Surely they would not kill us all if we surrendered? We had seen Santa Anna riding regularly – though out of rifle range – to inspect his batteries. He was energetically managing the siege himself. If he emulated Bonaparte with his 'Napoleon of the West' claim, then he must consider himself a civilised man. Certainly, my old adversary at Waterloo did not routinely kill prisoners. But then again, Santa Anna had allowed his troops to rape and pillage their way through that rebellious province. So perhaps his fine uniform was just a front to his savagery after all.

I could not sleep that night and not just because a Mexican howitzer kept lobbing shells into the courtyard. I tossed and turned on the bed, weighing up the near certainty of getting killed trying to escape through an army of murderous Mexicans, against the alternative of being butchered as they stormed the fort. In the end I got up and sat with Juana and Trudy around the small fire, watching little Alejo enjoy a careless slumber in some rugs at our feet. None of us said much – we did not want to wake the boy and we were all lost in thoughts about our imminent futures. Eventually Juana fell asleep or at least pretended to and Trudy reached out and held my hand

120

"What will we do?" she whispered.

"I don't think we have a choice any more," I told her. "The amnesty is over, but if they do attack then at least the women and children should be spared."

"Juana says it will depend on how many of their soldiers our men kill in the attack. If we shoot many of them, then they will kill everyone when they finally get inside." The sister was probably right, although there did not seem any point in admitting it and so I stayed quiet. "What about you?" she continued. "What will you do?"

I struggled to put my thoughts into words. In the past I might have ranted and raved about the injustice of it all and run around in a blue funk, but it all felt unreal. We had not yet lost a man to enemy fire and in my heart, I still believed that somehow I would come through. I had not entirely given up on the idea of trying to get away and leaving them to their fate. Not, of course, that I was going to admit that to Trudy. "Well, old girl," I whispered, "I rather think that I will die, but there will be no nobler cause than defending the lives of you and your sister and the lad here."

Her eyes welled with tears and she squeezed my hand harder. "I don't want you to die for me."

"Well I will try to give a good account of myself. I am not as young as some of these fellows, you know, but the old dog knows a few tricks. Mind you," I paused, pretending to think, "if Fannin does appear and draws some of our guards away, I might try to slip out to give him news of our position. I gather he did not finish at West Point and I have more than a little experience of fighting. So don't be surprised if I am not here when you wake one morning."

She wiped her now wet cheeks and gave me a sad smile. "You and James must be the two bravest men I know."

Chapter 15

I must have dozed a little that night for we awoke the next morning to a crash of gunfire and the sound of cannonballs hitting our walls. Trudy gave a little scream of alarm, but I assured her that all was well as I hurriedly put on my coat and went out to check. The Mexicans had built a new battery overnight, some two hundred and fifty yards from our north wall. Looking around, I counted that there were now at least ten guns, two each in five batteries that circled the Alamo. Two of these gun emplacements were aimed at the north wall and soon the cannon fired again. The rate of fire was much faster than before. I guessed that the wagons we had seen arriving the previous day included supplies of gunpowder. Already a large crack had appeared in the wall and Jameson was calling for men to come and help shore it up.

It was going to be a busy day for the garrison of the Alamo as the Mexican guns kept up their fire. Clearly the gunners were getting their eye in, as the walls were soon battered and, in several places, broken. The north wall took the worst punishment and most of us were quickly employed in digging dirt or carrying wooden beams from elsewhere to help strengthen it. Jameson put timbers in front of the worst damage to act as revetments to protect the wall behind. We then filled the space between the wood and the wall with earth. It was crude but effective, yet the rough timbers now made the wall much easier to climb from the outside. By lunchtime I was exhausted from the digging and carrying of dirt. The other walls had taken less damage, but the views from their tops were equally disconcerting. Santa Anna had evidently decided to step up preparations for an attack; soldiers could be seen gathering branches from trees. It was soon obvious that they were using them to build scaling ladders to help them over our walls. The siege, one way or another, would not last much longer.

Some speculated as to whether this meant that our reinforcements were closing in, but the eastern horizon, from what we could see through the scrub, was empty. I discovered that while I had been with the girls the previous night, Travis had sent out yet another courier although, as before, he had no idea if the man had managed to get through. At noon he gave orders for one of the cannon to be fired. Sensing that the end might be near, he had told the last courier that he would fire the gun three times a day to signal that we were still holding out. It was a sombre moment as the cannon boomed, for by then everyone knew what it was signalling. There was not a man or woman in the place who was not wondering how many more times it would fire. No one was shouting, 'Let the Mexicans come!' now, but equally there was no croaking either. In fact, there was little talk at all as men, with just one exception, faced what could be an all too brief future with a quiet stoicism.

My guts were starting to churn now. I had always felt that something would turn up to save us, but it hadn't and there was now little time left for it to appear. Not for the first time in my ignoble career, I was suddenly looking at the prospect of my own imminent death. My first thought was to speak to Travis. The idea that we could defend the Alamo against the huge force now rallied against us was patently nonsense. We had made our gesture, but it was now time to think of the women and children, not to mention my own precious skin, and seek terms. I had prepared a little speech about having made a noble defence, now stepping down with honour, and went to find him. He was up on the ramparts, but I saw at once it was not a runner. He was sitting on a barrel talking to three other men about how *if*, mark you, *if* we were beaten, we would make our defeat so costly for the Mexicans that they would think twice about taking on the forces of Texas again. He was getting himself all worked up into his usual overblown passion. I can hear him now: "I would rather die a free man fighting for my liberty than live as a slave under the heel of some tyrant."

The men he was talking to were absolutely nodding in agreement. I turned away in disgust. That was fine for him to say, the Mexicans would probably have shot him anyway, but what about the rest of us? I was not ready to die; this was not my fight. I did not care two figs who ruled in Mexico or its provinces. I would happily have sworn allegiance to any Constitution Santa Anna demanded, but at this rate I was not going to get a chance. If reason would not work then that left only one, long-overdue course of action, I would drop over the walls that night.

I went back to our quarters and began to prepare. I made sure I had a full canteen and some strips of dried meat in case I had to travel some distance before I found friendly forces. With the frequent rain, I would not need to worry about water, but it was cold at night and so I gathered my warmest clothes. I was just cleaning my pistol when Trudy walked in. She saw the weapon in my hand and smiled sadly.

"You think that they will come soon, then?" she asked.

"It pays to be prepared," I replied, trying to look nonchalant. I wondered how she'd feel when she discovered I had disappeared in the morning. Would she realise that I had run out on them all or would she believe that I was trying to reach our reinforcements, even though we had no idea where they were?

She took my hand and led me over to the small window that looked out to the west. We had blocked the windows with wooden planks, but she pulled the shutter free with ease – I guessed she had done it before. "If you stand here you can see the top of our house, look over there." She pointed and pulled me towards her so that we could both see through the small opening. She was right, it was visible over the river and just to the right of a battery of Mexican guns. "I have spent nearly all my life over there," she murmured. "Juana has had two husbands and Alejo and I have done nothing." She pressed against me, I realised that she had put on scent for this encounter, and whispered, "I wish you did not have a wife."

By George, there was no doubt what was on offer now. "I doubt she will care about infidelities if she finds she is a widow," I whispered feeling a long-repressed lust rising in me. I realised that there was nothing to stop us now. It would be a miracle if we both lived long enough for Bowie to take issue with me seducing his wife's cousin. I bent down and kissed her and she responded greedily, her arms wrapping around the back of my neck. To hell with caution, I thought. If I was looking death in the eye then this prime and willing piece was the least I deserved. I gave a growl of desire and then… the door to the room banged open and little Alejo came running in to show us a toy that one of the men had made for him. We stepped apart as his mother followed him in with a bowl of beef stew from the cook house.

"They killed two steers," she announced, oblivious to the scene she had interrupted. "So there is plenty of meat today."

"Well I had better get back out there and help shore up those walls," I replied.

"Help me with this shutter first," asked Trudy. As our hands touched over the rough wooden planks she whispered, "Meet me in the storeroom at eight o'clock tonight."

At five to eight that evening I was standing on the eastern ramparts and watched as Trudy slipped out of our quarters and into the storeroom next door. She was carrying a small lantern and a bundle of blankets. My mouth went dry as I imagined her making a comfortable bed among the sacks, perhaps lying naked to await my visit; her slim, lithe body, ripe breasts and pouting lips all desperate for Flashy's attention. I am proud to say I did not hesitate: I picked up my bag and headed away in the opposite direction.

Oh, she was a fine woman and normally I would have been on her like an old ram on a shearling, but she was, after all, just a woman. I was not sure that Santa Anna would give me another night to chance my escape. If I was still here when his men stormed the walls, my goose would be properly cooked.

I had spent the evening studying the terrain. There were gaps between the batteries and soldiers' camps to the east, but they were much narrower than they had been before. Getting through would be a damn dicey business. I had spotted a shallow gulley running southeast from near the chapel that looked like an old stream bed and would provide some shelter for the first hundred yards or so. Eventually, though, I would need to crawl slowly on my belly from bush to bush for perhaps five hundred yards before I was clear of the Mexican lines. Even then I would have to be deuced careful as their cavalry patrols were still out and about looking for couriers. They would spit a running man on their lance points in a moment.

125

In front of the chapel was the earth embankment that made up the weakest point in our lines. It was guarded by Crockett and his Tennesseans, which made it a much more formidable obstacle. Most of them were gathered around a fire and they took little notice of me as I walked past and strolled casually up on the bank. A single sentry nodded companionably in greeting. He was smoking a pipe, his long rifle resting up against one of the branches stuck in the front of the bank and his hands thrust deep in his pockets for warmth. Gesturing up at the dark night sky where just a few stars were visible, he grunted, "Looks like it will be another cold one."

"Yes," I agreed looking down at the front of the bank. The Mexicans had originally built it and then lined the outward face with stakes and the tops of trees to make it harder to get through. Recent Mexican cannon fire had enhanced the splintered effect while the Tennessee boys had added to it with wood from the smashed sheds, although I saw some of that was now being burned on their campfire. It still looked an impenetrable obstacle. I was just wondering if it would be easier to lower myself over the eastern wall instead, when the guard spoke again.

"You lookin' for the path?"

"Er, yes," I replied, not realising that there was one.

"Slide down next to that log with a rag tied on the top," he pointed to it.

"That is very kind of you, most obliged," I answered. Strolling to the rag I saw a groove in the mud forming the bottom of a tunnel that disappeared under an arch of branches down the side of the bank. I had thought that I was the only person to make a run for it, but perhaps there had been more. I glanced into the darkness and prayed that they did not alert the Mexicans until I was through the lines. I hitched the satchel I was carrying over my shoulder and lowered myself down. A moment of slithering down the slope and I was on the ground outside the Alamo, the bank looming in the darkness behind me. After so long behind the walls, I felt strangely exposed. I crawled forwards on my hands and knees until I found the shallow gulley. It was a little more than a foot deep in some places and so I had to stay low. The ground was wet and cold, but I would have to get used to that, for I had a long way to go.

Soon I was away from the dark shadow of the fort and more likely to be spotted by a vigilant sentry. I must have crawled and wriggled forward some fifty yards when I heard the first voice ahead. It was a loud laugh a good distance off, reminding me that I was not alone. I had to hold my nerve and keep going; my fate if I went back did not bear thinking about. Another fifty yards on and, looking back, the Alamo suddenly looked very small, a slight glow from the torches in the courtyard lighting the night sky. I wondered if Trudy was still waiting impatiently for me to join her. I grinned ruefully at the missed opportunity and turned to go on my way.

Another twenty yards and the gulley bent to the right towards the San Antonio River, while I wanted to go straight or to the left. I crawled slowly up the side and looked at the terrain I would have to cover. There were no fewer than six campfires flickering between me and relative safety. Men were moving in front of the flames and, straining my ears, I could hear a rumble of conversation, even if I could not make out the words. The ground between me and the fires and the groups of men was light scrub, small plants, rocks and grass. Damn, I thought, it would be hard going getting through that lot and to safety before the sun came up in the morning. I was just in the act of lifting my leg and easing myself over the lip of the gully when a voice spoke quietly behind me.

"I wouldn't do that. There is another gulley further on with some Mexicans in it."

Well they must have been asleep if they did not hear my stifled gasp or see me half leap in the air as I twisted round, my hand scrabbling for the blade at my belt. I could just make out two dark figures sitting around the bend in the gulley.

The nearest to me did not move a fraction of an inch as I turned towards him, but he spoke again, his voice familiar. "Keep quiet now. Does Jim Bowie know you have his knife?"

"Crockett, is that you?" I whispered back, astonished. "What the hell are you doing here?" I put the knife back in its scabbard. I had

127

found it when I was looking for things to take. It would kill a man more quietly than a pistol and I doubted my friend would ever be well enough again to use it.

There was a long silence before Crockett spoke again. He gave a heavy sigh, "Like you I guess, I get mighty hemmed in by them walls. Some nights I just like to come out here and sit in the open. What are you doin' here? You takin' a stroll like some English gentleman?"

"Something like that," I muttered. "I wanted to get away from the walls too, but I was wondering if I could work my way east. Try and find Fannin and hurry him along."

Crockett was quiet again for a while and I had a strong suspicion that he knew exactly what I was really trying to do. "Well," he said at last, "there is Mexicans at the other end of this gulley and over there to the east," he pointed in the direction I wanted to go, "is another gulley full of their soldiers." He gestured at his companion, "Guerrero here has listened to them an' tells me they are mighty keen on visitin' us soon. They are boastin' about the plunder they will find." He chuckled, "They think I have a gun made of solid silver and I would not let them find you with Jim's knife. A lot of them think they have a score to settle with him from when they were fightin' here before."

I shuddered at the thought. "But there must be some way around that other gulley and between the fires," I protested.

"I was scoutin' out there last night an' I tell you those Mexicans are lyin' out there thicker than the freckles on ginger Henry. They ain't got the wood for a lot of fires, but they are out there all right, campin' between 'em." He shrugged and then uttered something that will always get my undivided attention, "You can try if you want, but I'll guarantee you'll be dead by dawn."

I slumped down in resignation. It seemed there would be no escape this way after all. "I suppose we had better make our way back to the fort after all then."

"There's no rush, we can relish our freedom a mite longer. Do you want some chaw?" He held out a leather pouch but I declined. I have never liked chewing tobacco and I had long since run out of cigars. The realisation that I was finally trapped hit me hard. The chance to get through the Mexican lines had perhaps been a slim one, but while there was hope it was something to hang on to. Now the future looked very bleak and I asked my next question more to ease my sense of despair than with any expectation.

"Do you think there is any chance that Fannin will get through?"

"Bonham says not, when I asked him privately," Crockett told me. "Seems Fannin is worried about Mexicans comin' up the coast." He gave a heavy sigh before adding, "If the others have heard that then they are probably not coming either, 'specially as Travis has told them we have the whole Mexican army here."

"There is no hope then," I replied gloomily before another thought occurred. "Wait, that means that Bonham came back even though he knew we did not stand a chance." Crockett did not respond and so I added, "I'll wager you wish you had not come here now too."

He managed a hollow chuckle, "Well I confess that I am a bit disappointed in my fellow Texians, leaving us alone like this. But as my Polly used to say, when you have made your bed you must lie in it." Then he reached out and gripped my shoulder, "We've both seen some sights in our time, you bein' at Waterloo an' all and me goin' from cowhand to congressman. We've got to meet our maker sometime and if it is here, then we will be in right good company. If'n we fight and die well then they are sure to remember us for a parcel of years to come."

It was strange, but that simple speech, spoken with calm determination gave me more of a sense of backbone than all the wild imploring I had heard from countless commanders over the years. That is not to say I was ready to die, no, that spark for life will stay with me until I breathe my last, but at least it calmed my guts a little. We stayed there for a couple of hours talking about our lives. Guerrero joined in; he had deserted the Mexican army some years before and told us that the men in the gully opposite were some of Santa Anna's best troops. They did not hear us whispering in the dark, although Crockett confessed that he did not care if they did, as he preferred to die in the open. In the same way as you share a special intimacy with your fellow man if you get drunk together, so you do if you think you are going to die together. I came as close as I ever did to declaring my true nature that night. Only the thought of disappointing Crockett stopped me, although I was not sure he hadn't already guessed.

It was past midnight when we all crawled through the gap in the branches to return to the Alamo. The Mexican howitzer was still firing through the night and we arrived just in time to duck as a shell landed in the courtyard. It went off with a dull thud and I moved swiftly across the yard to my quarters before they could fire another. I found the door stuck with something jammed behind it. It was not surprising that Trudy had felt angry and slighted when I did not appear. I turned and walked into the storeroom where I lay down on a pile of sacks. I could still faintly detect her scent in the air.

Chapter 16

Trudy found me in the storeroom the next morning. She called me a very rude Spanish name and complained that she had waited for me for two hours. "If you did not want to be with me, you could have said," she shouted, tears now showing in her eyes.

"Of course I wanted to be with you," I insisted. "But Colonel Crockett needed me to go on a scout with him up close to the Mexican lines. You can ask his Tennesseans up on the embankment if you don't believe me. They will tell you I was out with Crockett until the small hours of the morning."

"I thought you did not find me attractive," she whispered as she threw herself into my arms.

"You silly thing, you are the prettiest girl in the fort by a country mile, in all of San Antonio even. I promise I will come to you tonight." I meant it too, for she was a stunner. I just hoped that Santa Anna would give me the time to keep my word.

That day passed much like the one before. The Mexicans continued their heavy bombardment of our walls, while we worked under fire to patch up the damage as fast as it appeared. It was a miracle that still no one had been injured, for sometimes several cannon balls would be fired at us within a minute. Then half an hour might pass, so that we were busy fixing their breaches in our walls before they fired again. In return we fired a single gun at the appointed hours, to show that for now the Alamo still stood. When I had a moment to look, I saw that their soldiers were building yet more ladders. They were also engaged in digging large trenches for their assault troops just beyond rifle fire range. A few men continued their lookout at the eastern horizon, but now it was more in hope than expectation.

I remembered what Crockett had told me about being found with Bowie's knife and so that afternoon I went and visited my friend. He was going downhill fast, shaking and sweating, unable to even lift his head from the pillow. I did not care about catching typhoid now. I sat with him a while and told him what was happening, although it was hard to say if he understood. Then I left him, with the big blade on the blanket beside him.

As I looked again over the walls, I could see columns of troops now marching over the bridges to our side of the river. They were not coming towards us, but starting to circle around. In town I could see yet more regiments being mustered, it looked very much like the preparations for an attack. A short while later Bowie's fellow commander clattered a spoon on the tin plate to call the garrison for one final muster. This time there were no impassioned speeches or cheering, just a quiet acceptance of the inevitable truth.

"Men, I have to tell you that I do not think that any more help is coming." Travis spoke quietly but his voice carried across the courtyard as now even the Mexicans had stopped shooting. The garrison greeted this news with silence as they must have all reached the same conclusion themselves. "I am going to try and send out another message tonight," continued Travis, "to let them know that we still stand. Can I have a volunteer for a rider?"

I hesitated a moment, wondering if I should volunteer, although I doubted any man would stand a chance of getting through the increased lines that surrounded us. "Send Jim Allen," suggested a voice and faces turned to the sixteen-year-old boy who must have been the youngest amongst us. He looked reluctant to go, but the man next to him whispered fiercely in his ear. He must have been explaining to the lad that it was his only chance. Then the man addressed Travis, "He is light for a horse to carry and we'll give him the fastest mount."

"Agreed," said Travis and then he smiled at this reluctant volunteer. "Thank you, Jim, come and see me after nightfall for the despatches and we all wish you Godspeed." There was a murmur of agreement at that and then Travis turned back to the matter in hand. "It looks like the enemy will attack us soon and so we must decide our course of action. Our choice is to surrender and hope that despite that red flag," he pointed at it, "they show some of us quarter. Alternatively, we can try to escape or to fight it out. For my part, I am pledged to fight until my last breath to defend Texas. Even if we are beaten, we can make the Mexicans pay dearly and delay their march north. But you can see

132

the odds against us and I will not order you to stand beside me. If any of you want to leave, you can do so with my blessing."

There was a rumble of voices as men talked to their neighbours. In reality, there was little choice at all and had not been since the Mexicans first arrived. You could surrender and probably get shot, try and escape and get butchered by the surrounding soldiery or stand and fight, maybe kill a few Mexicans, before getting killed yourself. With those bleak chances even an inveterate coward like myself was tempted to stand. There was always the chance that the attack would be mismanaged and fail or perhaps Santa Anna would get too close and Crockett would get lucky.

"Does anyone want to leave?" asked Travis.

"I'll go," called out a voice. Heads turned to a bearded old ruffian, who stuck his chin up defiantly. "I've seen enough war. I'll take my chances over the wall tonight." There was no resentment as the odds for him were almost as slim as for the rest of us. A few patted him on the back and wished him well. His name was Louis Rose and he claimed to be one of Bonaparte's veterans, but I doubted that. I had had to call out to him once as he was about to put his boot out to stop a spinning cannonball shot into the courtyard. If he had really been a soldier, he would have known that such an action was a quick way to lose a foot.

There was sobbing now from a few of the women at the back of the group as their fears for imminent widowhood were confirmed. A couple of men led their wives away to comfort them and I looked around for Trudy. She was standing to one side, – she too was weeping with her sister's comforting arm around her shoulder. Juana caught my eye and gave me a sad smile before leading Trudy away back to our quarters.

My attention was drawn back to Travis now as he brusquely planned our defence. Every man was to have at least four firearms at his post, so that we could deliver a good rate of fire at least for the first minute or so of the attack. He hoped that the cannon and rifles would force the Mexicans to keep their distance, but there were far too many of the enemy for that. Then he reminded us of the central barrack block as our final redoubt. He told the women left in the crowd that they and the children were to stay in the sacristy of the chapel when the Mexicans came. While there was still a little light, he urged us to help repair the walls and prepare our positions for the coming fight.

I walked away from that meeting feeling as though I were in a daze. Looking at the men about me, I am sure many felt the same. Travis had told us nothing we did not already know, but to hear him talk calmly about fighting as long as we could and 'last stands' made it all too real now. For all my hopes of miraculous redemption, I knew I was trapped and condemned. I was nauseous at the thought of it. Men were quiet and ashen-faced and at least one ran into the corner to vomit, but none joined Louis Rose in his preparations to leave. Instinctively, we knew that we were all dead men anyway and even *I* would rather go down fighting than being hanged as a rebel.

At dusk we saw more Mexican troops coming across the bridges. I was sure that they were getting in position for a dawn attack. Santa Anna would not risk a night assault as they would lose too many men to fire from their own soldiers in the confusion. Travis' signal gun boomed out once more for what we were certain was the final time. I remember looking over at the setting sun. Like countless men in condemned cells before me, I wondered if I would ever see it high in the sky again. I'll admit that a tear of self-pity ran down my cheek then and I felt a hand on my arm. Looking round I found Guerrero. He did not say a word, he simply held out a half-full bottle of whisky. I drank deeply and that steadied me for a while. I handed the bottle back and remembered that people had been trying to kill me for over thirty years. I had been in tight spots before and if my luck ran out, well I had enjoyed a good innings. My mind was suddenly filled with a memory of young Price-Thomas, an ensign under my command in Spain. That poor brave lad had been killed at just fifteen. I comforted myself that, compared to him, I had done bloody well and I was not dead yet.

With my new whisky-fired resolve I strolled to the armoury to arm myself for the challenges ahead. I was given four of the muskets, a small sack of old Mexican cartridges and a large cup of the Du Pont powder that I had brought to San Antonio with Bowie. I took it all back to my quarters and started to make new cartridges using the Mexican ball and American powder. I made enough to charge the guns with a dozen spare loads, although I very much doubted I would be given the chance to fire them all. As I worked, Juana and Trudy sat silently by the fire, the only sound coming from little Alejo, who was singing a song to himself as he played with two carved wooden toys.

When I had finished Juana got up to serve some stew that had been cooking over the fire. As she did so, she put down a metal object that she had been holding in her hand and I saw it was a watch. "It is Colonel Travis' watch," she explained when she saw me staring at it. "He asked me to look after it." She took a deep trembling breath and then looked me in the eye. "Is there anything that *you* want me to look after?" That brought me up sharp and no error. After a moment's consideration, I pulled forward a small ink pot and paper and wrote down Vanderbilt's address in New York.

"If you can, let my wife know what happened to me." I found that I could say the words in barely more than a whisper.

The stew was served but none of us ate much, we were all lost in our own thoughts. Then Juana gave me a bowl to take to James. I strolled across the courtyard, past the gun emplacement covering the gate to the small room in the wall nearby. The place was as black as pitch, the candle had gone out, but I felt for another and went outside for a flame to light it. When I returned, Bowie's eyes glinted back at me from the gloom. For a moment I thought he was dead but then he blinked and gave a grunt of greeting.

"The Mexicans will probably attack at dawn," I told him quietly. "Do you understand?" He gave a slight nod and I sat down on the cot beside him and tried to spoon some stew into his mouth. He was so weak that I thought lumps of meat might get stuck in his throat and so I fed him with the rich gravy instead. He had half a dozen spoonfuls before he turned his head slightly away to indicate he was finished. While he ate, I had told him news of the fort and about the numbers we had seen gathering outside. His expression did not change as I talked. It was only when I got up that he made another sound. It was only a

135

grunt, but I followed his gaze to the big blade I had left lying on his blanket during my previous visit. It was a few inches from his fingertips, but he did not have the strength to reach down for it. I picked up the knife and put the hilt in his hand. Slowly the fingers curled around the wooden handle until his knuckles whitened to show that he had a tight grip. I patted his shoulder, which was now painfully thin, and said my goodbye. As I reached the door I turned back a final time; he was watching me calmly but now there was a grimace of determination on his face. If the Mexicans came, I was doubtful he had the strength to wield his knife, but I was pretty sure that they would have to kill him to get the weapon out of his hand.

As I made my way back, I saw Trudy standing outside our quarters. She looked cold and had a shawl pulled up around her shoulders. When she saw that I had seen her, she moved slowly along the row of buildings and entered the storeroom where she had waited for me the night before.

"Here, put my coat on, you look frozen," I told her as I entered. I wrapped it about her shoulders as she rushed towards me, hugging me around the waist and crying softly into my chest.

"I don't want you to die," she gasped between sobs.

"Steady on, old girl," I chided her, trying to sound cheerful. "You never know, we might win in the morning. Crockett might shoot Santa Anna off his horse and our cannon and guns will send the rest packing."

My bonhomie did not have the desired effect as she cried all the louder at this ridiculous optimism. Then suddenly she grabbed my hand and placed it against her breast. "I want to be yours tonight," she whispered. I felt her warm yielding flesh through the thin fabric of her blouse and for a moment I did not care about the Mexicans, Bowie, Texas or any of it. The whole world retreated into that small storeroom and the pretty girl in my arms. I kissed her and then we were pawing at each other's clothes with a desperate hunger to sate. We did not care about the cold; we were soon naked on top of the sacks of grain as I took her gently for the first time. There was a crash against the outside wall as it was struck by enemy cannon. Dust, mud and straw rained

136

down on us from the roof, but we did not care. I doubt we would have stopped if the wall had cracked and a whole company of Mexican infantry had charged in through the breach. Lying on top of such a pretty girl would be a damn fine way to go.

Eventually, passion spent, we lay quietly together in each other's arms covered with my coat. The Mexican guns had stopped. I think I even managed to sleep a little. I awoke to the sound of someone shouting outside. I stiffened, listening in case it was a warning of an attack, but it was just one of the garrison who had sought courage in a bottle.

I had no idea of the time and was just thinking of getting up, when Trudy's hand reached out and took hold of something that persuaded me to stay. Well it would be rude to refuse the request of a lady. This time we made love more urgently, both knowing that our time together was limited.

I emerged from that storeroom with a warm glow of satisfaction, feeling strangely jubilant in the circumstances. There was still no sign of light in the eastern sky, but I went and got my muskets and ammunition and then climbed up to the north wall. Torches burned in the courtyard, but there was no light on the walls so as to avoid illuminating the defenders. I saw a few dark shadows moving around the nearest cannon and heard a call of greeting from two men sitting on the northwest corner.

"Has there been any movement?" I asked them.

"No, all quiet," one replied. I knew that Travis had put some lookouts in the newly dug ditches that surrounded the walls. Provided they had not fallen asleep, we should have some warning if the Mexicans tried to approach by stealth. I stared out into the night to where I knew from the evening before, hundreds of men were waiting to storm the Alamo. They must have been whispering and talking among themselves, but we could not hear it. The only clue to their existence was the occasional clink of metal, which carried further in the cold night air.

"I'm tired," muttered one of my new companions.

"Don't worry," responded his mate. "You'll be able to sleep as long as you want later."

It was so dark that you could only see a few feet in the gloom and once more my thoughts turned to escape. "Do you know if Rose left?" I asked. "Did he get away?"

"He left," said a voice, "but I doubt he got away. We heard some shouts and screams around ten minutes after he dropped down into the ditch."

So that was that, I thought. I am stuck here until the end. I slumped down next to my companions and pondered on the cruel twists of fate that had brought me to this far-flung outpost on this fatal night. And here we are, where I began this tale, the night of the fifth of March, or by then early on the sixth. The howls of distant wolves and coyotes sounded like they were grieving for us already, especially as they were joined by the mournful call of a bird I was told was a whip-poor-will. My earlier warmth and good humour were slowly replaced by the chill of the night and a strong sense of foreboding.

Chapter 17

"Viva Santa Anna!" The call rang out from the west, followed by some more shouting, including the order, *"Silencio"* from some officer trying to quieten his men. The noise had started me from a doze, and I looked around at the eastern sky. There was a hint of a dull grey light, but it was still well before dawn.

"They're coming!" called out one of the young gunners on the nearby cannon but I disagreed.

"No, it's too soon, just some jumpy sentry," I shouted. "They have waited this long; they will wait until dawn so that they can see what they are doing." Perhaps that had been the original plan, but as I spoke, I heard more soldiers acclaiming *el Presidente* and suddenly I wasn't so certain. There was a rising clamour of voices from out in the darkness and then came the rising notes of a bugle. The sound was spreading: first it came from the north but now I could hear distant shouting and answering bugle calls in the east too. A cannon boomed, whether it was one of ours or theirs I could not say, but it was enough to trigger the attack.

It does not matter what race or nationality, but when men launch themselves into an attack they roar. No soldier runs meekly silent into the maw of death. They will yell, "Chaaarge!" or *"Viva Santa Anna!"* or in my case, "Oh dear God, please let me live." It did not matter, really, for when you are on the receiving end it all sounded the same: an angry roar of humanity. "Crikey, they *are* coming," I remember shouting when I heard it. Then the cannon in the centre of the north wall fired; they must have aimed it at the enemy trenches the evening before – there were screams in the distance as the shot struck home. More cannon were firing, men were shouting, calling to those dozing in the barracks, and as if all that noise were not enough, some fool was banging the tin plate to call the garrison to its posts.

I prepared myself for the coming fight. I was down on one knee, there was no point in standing to make a bigger target. I had one musket in my hand and the other three in a neat row on the roof beside me. Others were doing the same as the gun crew now frantically reloaded.

I heard feet running up the nearby ramp behind the gun and then two shadows appeared beside me. "What's happening?" gasped Travis. His slave, Joe, was standing behind him holding his master's four guns and was doubtless to be his loader.

"They're coming," I stated simply as the first Mexicans running towards the north wall opened fire. From the prickles of light we saw along their line I guessed that they were still two hundred yards off. A ridiculous range for a musket, especially from a running man and I took a shred of comfort that these were clearly inexperienced troops.

"But from which direction?" demanded Travis impatiently. We both looked around beyond the walls of the Alamo, his question answered by various patches of muzzle flashes in the darkness.

"From *every* direction," I answered grimly. More men were running up the ramp behind us now and spreading out along the line of rooftops. When I looked into the central courtyard, from the torchlight I could see the rest of the garrison that had been trying to sleep now streaming out of the barracks and heading for their places on the walls.

"I see them!" called a voice nearby and I turned to look. For a second I could see nothing, my eyes taking a moment to adjust to the darkness, but then there they were, a moving shadow on the dark grey of the ground. They were no more than fifty yards off and as I put my first musket to my shoulder, I heard the crackle of musket and rifle fire ring out from all around our ramparts. Then the cannon all along the north wall fired. The muzzle flashes illuminated the enemy coming towards us and for the first time I saw that there were hundreds of the bastards.

As the light died away I just caught a glimpse of dozens of them falling. We had been short of cannister shot, but had improvised with sacks of musket balls gathered from the old Mexican cartridges. At short range they had a devastating effect. We could hear the screams and yells of the wounded in the renewed darkness and I fired my first musket into the middle of where I remembered the mass of soldiers to be. The gunners were back at their reloading, but I doubted that they would be able to depress their muzzles low enough to hit the Mexicans again, for some were already at the ramparts. I saw the top of the first ladder appear against the wall. Travis saw it too and grabbed a shotgun from Joe before striding to the edge of the parapet. Standing in full view of the enemy, he aimed his gun down at the soldiers around the ladder and gave them both barrels. I shouted at him to get back, but it was too late. Travis toppled backwards, making no effort to break his fall as he hit the rooftop, a neat hole right in the middle of his forehead. The commander of the Alamo was one of its first to die. Joe stood there staring dumbly at his master, clearly unsure what to do.

"Put those guns down," I told him, "and reload this musket." I held out my spent weapon but after a moment's hesitation he dropped the muskets he had been carrying and turned and ran. "Come back, you cowardly knave!" I roared after him as he fled down the ramp, but he was not stopping. I turned back round just in time to see a head appear over the rooftop as someone climbed the ladder that Travis had shot at. I snatched up my second gun and shot him dead, watching with satisfaction as he fell backwards, taking the ladder with him.

I am not sure how long the next phase of the battle lasted, probably just a few minutes but it felt longer. I know I fired off all of my muskets and those left behind by Joe. The gunners had joined in with small arms now as their cannon were useless with enemies right up against the walls. One of the artillerymen had found some explosive shells and was busy lighting the fuses and throwing them out into the throng. Only when they exploded did we get a good view of the enemy, although the eastern sky was getting slowly brighter. By some miracle we were holding the Mexicans off. Any that tried to mount a ladder up against our walls were soon shot down. Flashes from the shells revealed hundreds of them milling about. When they did shoot, I noticed that they often did so from the hip, with predictably poor accuracy. Apart from Travis, a couple of others had been wounded, but stealing a glance around the compound confirmed that the rest of our men were defending all the walls.

The canon on top of the chapel was still firing towards troops coming from the east. By the light of their campfire, I could see

Crockett and his Tennesseans up on the embankment by the chapel, the sharper crack of their rifles indicating that they were also keeping the enemy at bay.

For a brief moment I began to entertain the hope that we might win through after all. I was more confident when another force of men loomed out of the darkness to my left and the Mexicans attacking our wall turned and began to open fire on them. I quickly reloaded one of my guns as I squinted through the gloom, trying to make out who these new arrivals were. There were lots of them, over a hundred judging from the size of the shadow and the muzzle flashes. Had Fannin, by some miracle, arrived at just the right time?

"They're firin' on their own men," shouted a voice from the far end of the wall. Alas, about the same time we realised that, so did the Mexicans. The fire between them died out and the next shell revealed even more men in front of us, with others working their way around to the western wall. Still we held on, desperately now, as our numbers were starting to diminish. There was a shout as one of the gunners was hit. Looking around my section of the wall I saw at least half a dozen men dead or wounded. I kept away from the edge – I would not be making the same mistake as Travis. I saved my shots for when another of the devils tried to climb a ladder, for once they had a foothold on the wall we would be lost. I had just reloaded a second musket when they made a concerted attack. Several ladders appeared at once. I aimed the gun and fired as soon as the head appeared and watched as the impact of the ball snatched him off the rungs. The second man up kept his head low and tried to fire his gun over the parapet, but he was shooting blind and his ball went wildly into the night. Gingerly, he too now started to climb, but I had time to grab my last loaded gun. I fired and plucked a second man from the ladder. As yet another appeared, I had no choice but to run forward. Swinging the butt of the gun, I caught him in the face. The Mexican and his ladder went falling back into the mass of men below, but not before a fusillade of shots came my way. The musket was torn from my hand as it was struck by a ball and then something struck me a glancing blow to the side of the head…

The next thing I remember, I was down on my hands and knees, a ringing noise in my ears and a wetness on my cheek. I looked up, disorientated. The battle noise seemed quieter or perhaps I could hear less of it over the ringing, yet men about me were fighting just as fiercely. A Mexican soldier had climbed onto the parapet near one of the cannon and was fencing bayonet to cannon ramrod with one of our gunners. Another of the defenders was lying on the ground a few yards away. It was the young lad who had complained he was tired. He would certainly sleep now, for half of his head had been shot away. Fearfully, I reached up to my own skull – I felt a deep cut and a stabbing pain, but at least the bone underneath was intact.

The noise of battle was coming back. I reached for a musket before remembering it was not loaded, but that I still had my pistol stuck in my belt. There was a shriek as the gunner with the ramrod was bayoneted by a second soldier, who had come at him from behind. Then as I staggered back to my feet and stepped back from the edge of the wall, new gunfire erupted behind me. I turned just in time to see Mexican soldiers streaming out from one of the rooms that made up the western wall of the Alamo. Rather than go over it, they must have managed to smash their way in through one of the blocked windows. Already they were turning to fire into the backs of the defenders on that side.

"Christ, they are through," I shouted. A quick glance showed that there were now more men climbing up our wall than we had defenders left to stop them. It was only a matter of time before they were through here too. Men from the western wall were already running towards the chapel and the earth embankment. Crockett and his men were still fighting there and that, I thought, was also the place for me. It was a smaller space to defend and had the benefit of a gap out into the open. It was still barely light; I would take my chances out there. "They're behind us," I shouted again. "Save yourselves," I added, setting a sterling example as I started to stagger to the ramp leading down to the courtyard.

The slope to the ground gave me some momentum, but I was stumbling rather than running, my legs unsteady. I tried to summon the

143

energy to sprint, but my head was still groggy and the best I could manage was a shambling run. Younger, fitter men streamed past me, a few heading for Travis' last redoubt, the central barrack block, and yet more ran past it trying to get to the embankment. Mexicans were now running along the western wall flushing out the last of its defenders and firing on those retreating.

The flickering light from braziers and torches that illuminated the courtyard suddenly revealed a sickening sight: another stream of Mexicans was pouring over the south west corner of the fort. There were dozens of them and they were quickly sprinting forward to try and cut off those running to Crockett's corner. With despair, I realised that they would easily get between me and that embankment. I looked around with mounting panic to see that they were also coming over the north wall behind me, through the west wall to my right and would soon be across my front. The only brief sanctuary was the wretched central barrack block, a place I was sure would soon be a death-trap. I had no choice: it was either die there in a few minutes or drop dead now.

Already shots were whistling about and as I staggered to the door, I saw one Mexican soldier running straight towards me, bayonet outstretched on the end of his musket. He was shrieking some sort of challenge, his face contorted into a mask of rage. I did not have the strength to outrun him or fight him, but I had my pistol, even if my vision was a little blurry. I forced myself to stand calmly though every part of my body screamed at me to run. I only had one shot and could not afford to miss. I cocked the weapon and waited until he was just ten yards away before I raised it. He tried to launch himself at me, but too late. I aimed for low down in his chest and fired. His body jerked with the impact of the ball, but I did not wait to see him fall as several of his comrades were already turning in my direction. As his musket clattered around my feet I backed away and hurried for the door of the barracks.

Thank God I had the sense to shout out as I entered, for the inside of the barracks was almost completely dark. "It's a friend," I called as I peered around the doorway, "I'm Flashman."

"*Who* are you?" queried a voice from the gloom. I could make out three or four dim silhouettes of men standing in front of the nearest loopholes, which, apart from the door, were the only sources of the dull pre-dawn light outside.

"Colonel Bowie's English friend," I explained irritably, realising that I had not spent a lot of time mixing with the garrison. I glanced back outside the door. At least six Mexican soldiers were running across the courtyard to avenge their fallen comrade. I pressed on inside, only to bark my shins against some unseen obstacle. "Damn, what the hell is this?" I demanded, feeling a pile of timber in front of me.

"A barricade of beds," explained a voice that sounded familiar. "Go to the back wall, there is a gap... Now steady, boys, fire!" I saw four faces briefly illuminated by the flash of musket primings, among them Albert Martin's, who I realised had been speaking. As men exclaimed over their shots, I pressed myself against the back wall and worked my way along it. I was anxious to get away from the door and the vengeful survivors of their volley who would soon enter it. I heard ramrods rattling in barrels as some reloaded. "Are there more coming?" asked Martin. "Did you see Colonel Travis?"

"Travis is dead," I explained simply as I backed hurriedly into the far corner of the room from the door. "I saw him shot myself and no I don't think—"

I got no further, for at that moment the faint light from the door was blocked by more shadows. *"Viva Santa Anna!"* called a cacophony of voices, swiftly followed by the volley of half a dozen muskets. Their muzzle flashes briefly lit the room before the confined space was filled with sulphurous gunpowder smoke. Your correspondent might have been struggling to move quickly up to now, but I managed to drop to the floor with the speed of a shot whippet. I stayed down as balls cracked into the walls above me. Men screamed and cursed as they stumbled, smashed through the barricade and then wrestled and fought in the darkness. I was wounded and more importantly, I had no weapon. They could battle without me, I thought, as I cowered in the corner of the room. I listened as men struggled, shrieked and died, but

I had no idea who was winning. Then I heard a boot scrape the earth near me. I desperately tried to move out of the way, only to feel a kick in my side. As I twisted, the man toppled on top of me.

"Who is it?" I hissed as I felt a musket barrel across my chest and putrid, sour breath in my face.

"Viva Santa Anna!" shouted a triumphant response. I felt spittle on my cheek as he wrenched the musket up and across my throat. My left hand managed to grip the gun stock above my neck while my right grabbed the muzzle of the gun and tried to lever it away. My arms shook with the exertion, but my strength was failing me again as my assailant was much younger and stronger. However, in the midst of blind panic, age and experience has its benefits.

"Get off me, you damn fool," I gasped in Spanish, "I am one of us." The pressure on the gun eased momentarily as my opponent experienced a moment of doubt. He had heard me speak English, but now I was speaking Spanish. Was he trying to kill a comrade?

"Who are you?" He demanded suspiciously.

Thank God the Mexicans were using British muskets, for I did not need to see the bayonet socket to remember how the blade slotted onto the weapon. "Who am I?" I repeated loudly and indignantly in Spanish, pushing against the barrel slightly to distract him from the noise and feel of seventeen inches of Sheffield's finest steel being removed. "I'll tell you who I am," I added as I brought the point round, then I concluded in English, "I'm bloody Santa Anna!" I thrust the blade hard under his ribs as he emitted an almost feminine scream of agony. I wriggled out from under him as he lay face down panting and gasping in pain. I could hear scuffling and moving about on the other side of the room and so I grabbed the musket and reached down to pull the belt containing his cartridge pouch off from over his shoulders. I wanted a weapon in my hands again.

"Is that you, Flashman?" gasped Martin.

"Yes, is anyone else alive?"

"I'm still here," croaked another voice. "I have been shot but I can still take some more with me."

"Me too," grunted Martin. You could hear the pain in his voice, but as I dropped the musket ball down the barrel of my gun and raised the ramrod to push it down, I heard him doing the same. Beyond the odd groan of the wounded, it was quiet in the room now. The sound of battle was diminishing outside too, although there was still the crackle of fire coming from the south. I heard the boom of a cannon, which may have been the one at the top of the chapel. I bent down to squint through one of the loopholes. The sky was brighter and while I was looking west, I guessed that the sun was starting to rise behind me. I wondered if I would live to see it again.

The northern and western ramparts of the Alamo were now full of Mexican soldiers. When I looked to the south, I saw them searching the buildings on either side of the gate. I watched as two came out of Bowie's room. They did not have his knife, perhaps they were not the first to enter, but I thought my friend must be dead. Looking back across the courtyard, I thought it would not be long before we joined him. An officer was gathering together a score of men. As he was pointing at our building, it was not hard to guess where he was ordering them to attack.

"We have to surrender," I shouted. "They are preparing another assault. We will not stand a chance this time. Perhaps they will spare us." There was no reply from my comrades, but it was obvious that this was our only course of action now. From the grunting and gasps as they moved around, the other two sounded badly wounded already. We had no hope against over twenty fresh soldiers. I reached around and found an old sheet lying on the floor. I tore off a square and tied it to the end of my musket. I managed to push it out of the loophole just as the Mexicans began to run towards us. I saw the officer point to it. He shouted something that made his command slow to a walk. I breathed a sigh of relief – perhaps we would live after all. The sense of reprieve was shattered, however, by the crack of two guns firing just a few feet to my left. I watched in horror as two of the approaching Mexican soldiers fell, both shot in the chest. There were yells of rage and indignation from their comrades at our duplicity. I knew now that any hope for quarter had been dashed.

"You bloody fools," I railed at Martin. "That was our only chance, they will kill us now for certain."

"I'm dyin' anyway," gasped Martin, "an' Colonel Travis told us to take as many with us as we could. We gotta light the flame of liberty for Texas."

"Flame of liberty!" I repeated. I was astonished that even in such desperate straits Martin was still hanging on to the wild high-blown phrases of our erstwhile leader. I'd have roasted the villain with his flame of liberty had he not already been dead, for now his fatuous bombast was going to get me killed. I squinted back through the loophole and saw with horror how I was going to die. The Mexicans were taking no more chances with treachery and ambush. As the officer who had led the attack shouted orders at them, more enemy soldiers were slowly turning the wheels of the massive eighteen-pounder cannon in the southwest corner of the fort until it pointed in our direction. Then another movement caught my eye. From one of the rooms on the far side of the courtyard Juana, Trudy and little Alejo were being escorted out under guard. They must have stayed in their rooms when the attack started. At least they had not been butchered in the assault, although at that moment it was small comfort to me as I turned my gaze to see destruction coming my way. Wedges were being used to raise the breech of the huge gun until its black maw of death appeared to be pointing directly at me. I stepped back then, not wanting to see the final act of my obliteration. As I shrank back against the far wall of the barracks, I recall muttering a prayer, as I am wont to do when things are truly desperate.

The roar of the cannon's fire was lost in the crashing noise caused by the impact of its heavy ball. One moment I was crouched in the corner of a nearly pitch-dark room awaiting oblivion, the next I was lying on the ground, under the sky as the building's roof literally crashed down all around me. Instinctively, I raised my hands to protect my face from the cascade of tiles and pieces of wood that had been above.

Clouds of dirt and dust whirled about, but to my astonishment I did not seem to be hurt. I tried to sit up, pushing the tiles and mud off my chest, only to discover that my right foot was trapped under a beam of wood and would not budge. I looked across the room for signs of Martin and the other survivor, but all I could see was a leg poking out of a pile of rubble. Already I could hear the Mexicans cheering at their success. Even though what was left of the front wall blocked my view, I knew that the officer and his men would be running across the courtyard to avenge their losses. I was unarmed, my musket was still hanging half out of the loophole. They would find me tethered by my foot like some sacrificial goat. I would not stand a chance.

On impulse, I twisted round to look at the sun one final time, but it was still too low behind the remains of the back wall. I turned back. I may have even sobbed in despair. I knew in a moment bayonets would do for me just as surely as the one I had wielded a minute or two before. I stared at the man I had stabbed. He was lying face down just a yard away, but still alive as he was trying to raise his head. We were surely both to die in this rubble. Then I felt almost a jolt of hope as I realised that there was one more throw of the dice for life after all.

Chapter 18

There was not a second to spare. Twisting around as far as I could, I managed to grab both sleeves on the Mexican's tunic. I pulled hard and his jacket came away with ease. I tore my own garment off and laid it over the soldier before I pulled on the uniform coat. I had barely got it over my shoulders before I heard running footsteps. Taking a deep breath, I took my chance.

"Viva Santa Anna!" I shouted as the first of them vaulted over the lowest part of the wall, bayonet already raised for someone to kill. "They are all beaten!" I shouted again in Spanish. More men were climbing over the rubble now and one stabbed down on Martin's leg, which did not move. Out of the corner of my eye I saw the man I had stabbed struggle to move again. He was raising an arm and I did not doubt that he was about to denounce me. Well, I was one step ahead of him. "There is one," I shouted, pointing at the man lying beside me. He had barely started to croak a word when two blades plunged through his back. *"Viva Santa Anna,* that is the last of them, I think. Could you lift that beam off my foot?"

They helped without question. I was covered in blood, mud and dust and I doubt Louisa could have recognised me at that moment. Unlike nearly all the Texians, I spoke their language and wore their uniform. What else could I be especially as I had just helped them kill one of the enemy? I was freed and they even pulled me to my feet. Mind you, I could not afford to have them asking awkward questions. I pointed to what was left of the door that led to the next building in the row. "I think I heard someone moving in there," I lied and watched as some streamed off in that direction, while the officer, still outside, called for his men to regroup and move on.

I sat back down on a pile of rubble for a moment; the shock of being so close to death and then being reprieved at the very last minute, not to mention the earlier fight and blow to the head was catching up on me. My hands started to shake and I felt sick, even though I had not eaten since the night before. I was still dangerously exposed and so stood up to strengthen my disguise. I recovered the musket but could not find either the cartridge box or bayonet amongst the rubble. Yet there was light in the room now and near the door I had entered, I found the corpses of two Mexican soldiers who must have been killed as they rushed us the first time. I relieved one of his cross belt, bayonet and cartridge box and found a battered shako hat that fitted me on the other. Now I looked more like the soldier I pretended to be, but I was not finished yet. I remembered an old soldier I had known in Spain who had been wounded in the jaw and was unable to talk clearly. That was the kind of wound that would help me stay out of trouble. I rummaged around until I found another sheet and tore a strip from it. It was not hard to find some blood to stain it. I took my hat off and then wrapped the gore-stained cloth around my jaw and tied it over the top of my head. I pulled the cloth forward to cover as many of my features as possible. Then, replacing the shako, I took a deep breath and finally stepped out of the room that I had been so sure I would die in.

I half expected to be greeted by some grinning Mexican officer, who would lead me to a firing squad while laughing that I had hoped to get away with such a ridiculous deception. Instead, no one took any notice of me at all. I stared around at the ground, littered with the bodies of the dead and some still dying. There was the corpse of the man I had shot with the pistol just a few yards away and beyond him, the bodies of the two men shot by Martin and his companion. Looking to my right, the rooftops that made up the northern wall were piled high with bodies, while to my left at least a dozen defenders were sprawled in the mud, killed trying to make it to the southwestern corner.

I turned to go in that direction myself. The chapel and sacristy were there and I wondered if Bowie's cousins had been taken to join the other women. I had lost sight of Juana and Trudy and I hoped they were safe. As I turned the corner I stopped in shock, for if there had been bodies before, this area was carpeted in them. There were no women and children outside, but I was relieved to see that some prisoners had been taken. Six of them were sitting with their hands tied behind their backs against the bottom of the embankment. There was a

151

big tall Tennessean in his buckskins and five others, one looking little more than a boy. At least two were sporting wounds, but they were being well treated. They were guarded by a dozen soldiers, keeping back the curious who gazed at them like exhibits in a zoo. Well, I thought, if they have spared some of us, then surely they would have protected the women.

The Tennessean was not Crockett – the man had a beard and Crockett shaved every other day. I found my friend's body amongst those who had died fighting in front of the chapel. Even after everything that had happened, it was still a shock to see him dead. Having listened to many of his stories of survival in the wilderness, he had seemed indestructible. There was a crowd of men about him staring down, but it was not the former congressman that they were looking at, it was his gun. Plain Betsy was probably the first percussion rifle they had ever seen and several were discussing how it might work. Its muzzle was no more than a foot from Crockett's hand and I noticed that the rifle's butt was covered in a grisly coating of blood and hair, proving it had been used as a club at the last. Its owner was ignored – I doubt many of the Mexicans had heard of the famous frontiersman. He lay on his side, a grim expression on his features. His half-open mouth would tell no more tales. Judging from the bloodstains across his chest, he had been shot at least twice.

There was a crackle of gunfire from the other side of the embankment and I wondered if any of the defenders had managed to escape. I walked slowly in that direction, keeping away from the prisoners just in case any showed a sign of recognition. On top of the bank, I could now finally see the sun coming up over the eastern horizon. Its light turned the underside of nearby clouds a blood red, which seemed to match the day. I paused to give a silent prayer of thanks for my deliverance and then I turned to look south at those less fortunate. I could see the bodies of at least a dozen of the defenders scattered amongst the scrub, but there could have been many more out there in the bushes. It was clear how they died as some two hundred lancers were still wheeling around looking for prey. A volley of fire to my right drew my attention to six Mexican horsemen circling a large thorn bush and firing into it with their carbines, where I guessed some poor devil had been hiding.

I was distracted from the scene by shouting in the courtyard behind me. *"Viva Santa Anna!"* the men chorused. Then through the gateway came the man himself on a white horse, followed by a retinue of staff officers. They were all bedecked with braid and decorations unlike the ragged soldiers that ran dutifully to welcome their general. Santa Anna gave the briefest wave of acknowledgement before riding into the centre of the courtyard to survey his prize. Other commanders who had led the actual assault now also came forward to brief their president on his victory. As Santa Anna and his men dismounted, I saw one colonel pointing to the north wall and then at the northeast corner, he must have been explaining where the first breaches were made. Then he gestured at the central barrack block and even at the big eighteen-pounder cannon. It was not hard to guess what he was saying. Another older general came forward and pointed to the corner I was watching from, where the fiercest fighting had taken place. But instead of congratulating him on his victory, Santa Anna grew angry. Even without several strips of cloth wrapped around my ears, I would not have heard him clearly, but there was no doubt he was annoyed. The grey-haired commander had stiffened to attention and was clearly trying to explain something, but his younger *presidente* did not give him the chance. Santa Anna jabbed the man in the chest with a finger as he harangued him and then pointed at the embankment. The older officer reluctantly turned away and gave an order to a nearby soldier.

I watched with a feeling of foreboding as the soldier ran in my direction. He stopped below the embankment and spoke to one of the officers, pointing back to Santa Anna's party. Immediately orders were yelled and other men rushed forward to get the prisoners to their feet. Their hands were still bound behind their backs, but at least two were so badly wounded I doubted that they could have got up without help. Another was injured in the leg and a soldier walked alongside him, holding his arm to help him keep his weight off it.

The small party of six prisoners and their escort of a dozen soldiers slowly made their way across the courtyard, while Santa Anna paced up and down impatiently. At last the Texians were lined up in front of him. I watched as Santa Anna ranted at them as well, although I doubt many of his words were understood. Some may have guessed what was coming, but none reacted or begged for their lives. They just stood stoically, staring at the raving man before them and waiting for whatever happened next. Even now the old general tried to intervene, but Santa Anna ignored him and contemptuously screeched an order at the surrounding soldiers. I could guess what it was, but the soldiers hesitated, unsure what to do as their general still argued against the decision.

Impatiently, Santa Anna turned to his retinue of staff officers and these glittering peacocks did not falter in obeying. They drew their swords and seconds later were running the defenceless men through shouting, *"Viva Santa Anna!"* I don't recall the defenders making any noise, but perhaps it was drowned out by the yelling and then the laughter as the murderous bastards began hacking down on their victims' unprotected heads and necks. I watched one with a scar on his face grinning with delight as he swung a blade so wildly that the old general and supporting soldier both had to move sharply back to avoid being slashed at themselves.

I turned away in disgust. I had always insisted that this was not my fight, and it wasn't, but I swore then that if I ever had the chance, I would avenge those men. It was a feeling that was to grow ever stronger in the days ahead. I looked back round to see more prisoners being brought forward. One was Guerrero, who was rubbing his wrists as though they had been recently bound. On seeing Santa Anna, he threw himself down in supplication. That won't do you any good, I thought, but to my astonishment *el Presidente* helped him to his feet and was congratulating him. He allowed my old comrade to join some other soldiers and commanded the next man brought forward, who was Joe the slave. He too was spared. Santa Anna appeared to be asking him where Travis had died and soon Joe was leading him up the ramp onto the north wall to look down on the corpse of his former master. For the next half an hour the Napoleon of the West roamed around the Alamo like a traveller on a grand tour, taking in the sights. He had

Bowie's body carried out of his room just so that he could gawk at it. I saw that my friend had either been shot or bayonetted in the chest. Then he was led to Crockett's body, although he gave that barely a glance.

Finally, he had the women and children brought out of the sacristy. They came weeping and wailing. One woman was particularly distraught. From her shouting, I gathered that her two young sons had been killed. The boys had been around twelve. Another mother with a child of a similar age tried to shield him from the sight of carnage all around them, but the lad twisted away to look.

Juana and Trudy were not among them, but as the party was led out under guard to the town, I saw the sisters appear with Alejo again in the door of their old quarters. More soldiers guarded them, one chatting animatedly to Juana, who stared in horror and bewilderment at the scene around them as she tried to comfort her sister. Trudy was weeping hysterically, sure that her first lover was dead. I felt a pang of guilt that I could not let her know I was alive, but I knew that to attempt to do so would leave me among the poor devils whose blood was now soaking into the muddy centre of the courtyard.

"Which company are you with?" I turned in surprise to find a Mexican sergeant looking at me. Concern rather than suspicion was etched on his features.

I held both hands to my jaw and pretended to wince in pain as I mumbled incoherently.

"Ah, bad is it? Well there are few surgeons and those that are here will be looking after the officers. You had better get yourself into town. Perhaps there will be someone there that can help you."

I nodded in agreement. I needed to find a place to hide up. Then under cover of night I would try to make my escape. Until now few people had left the fort and a lone soldier wandering off by himself would have looked suspicious. But a steady stream of people began pouring out of the gate. Once the women, children and their escort had left, orders were passed for the bodies in the fort to be removed. I looked over the wall to see that dismounted lancers were gathering up their victims and putting them into two piles. Inside the Alamo pairs of soldiers were carrying its former garrison by the arms and legs outside to join them. The Mexican dead were also being carried out in a similar manner, but their porters were taking them in the direction of the town. With the Mexican dead went a slowly moving column of their wounded, who must have had the same idea about getting treated as the sergeant.

Chapter 19

My genuine wound throbbed. Cuts to the head always bleed badly and while the bandage had staunched some of the flow, the blood I had placed on the bandage to fake an injury to my jaw, was now overwhelmed with genuine gore seeping from my skull. I knew that the cut was full of dust and dirt from the falling barracks roof and would need to be washed out. I walked gingerly down the embankment, noticing now that Crockett's gun had gone. The surviving soldiers had already started to pillage everything that they could find.

Going through the gate that final time, I felt a weight lift from my shoulders. I had escaped the siege of the Alamo, although I was not out of the woods yet. I would not properly relax until I was safely back in the United States. It was a cold morning and pulling the flimsy uniform coat close about me, I wished I still had my greatcoat, but that was bound to be warming the back of one of our victors. Initially, I joined the throng heading to the town, but as I got closer to those familiar streets my nerve failed me.

Part of my face was caked in dried blood, but I could only cover so much of the other side with the bandage. James Bowie had been one of the most well-known men in San Antonio and for the last two months I had often been seen beside him. I noticed a small crowd of local citizens on the other side of the bridge cheering the returning soldiers. Whether they were there in genuine support or just trying to prove loyalty to their new masters, I did not care. But I did know that it would take only one observant man, woman or even child to point me out, for my story to unravel. Then there would be no doubt at all as to my fate.

So instead of crossing the planks of the bridge, I turned and walked along the river path instead. If I wanted to wash my wound, it made sense to be upstream of whatever ordure the townsfolk tipped into the river. It looked like I was just going to recover some possessions from one of the assault trenches further along the bank and that was my planned excuse if asked. But no one stopped me, in fact there were hardly any people on that part of the bank. Two hundred yards on from the northern bridge, I saw a small copse of half a dozen trees that overhung the river bank. It seemed the perfect place to hide out for the day. Plenty of cover, but close enough to town for me to get back at night and hopefully steal a horse to get away. I did not want to escape on foot now, for I had no idea how long Santa Anna would stay in San Antonio or in which direction he would march next. The last thing I wanted was to be overhauled.

Pretending to adjust my boot, I took a careful look around. No one was near or paying me any attention, although I had a curious sensation of being watched. I checked the other boot and stared around again. Satisfied that I was being unduly anxious, I got up and strolled as casually as I could into the copse. Having affirmed yet again that no one was glancing in my direction, I crawled into the thickest undergrowth overhanging the river. By Satan's tits, it hurt taking that bandage off. Blood had scabbed on the wound and soon it was bleeding again. I lowered the cloth into the cold water and pink trails washed from it as the current took the blood away. Having rinsed it out, I used the cold wet cloth to try and clean my wound. I could feel grit and splinters in it that were hard to remove. In the end, I just lowered the top of my head into the stream, gasping as the near frozen water felt like needles sticking into my scalp. I washed the muck away with my fingertips and sat up again dabbing at the wound with my wet bandage. Then I looked back down at the water and stiffened in alarm. My hand slowly reached around to the bayonet, now hanging from the webbing in my belt. Another stream of pink water had just come past me, but this was not from my wound. Someone else was bleeding just upstream

"Quién está ahí?" I called out quietly. Then I realised that a Mexican would not be hiding from a Mexican soldier and repeated the question in English, "Who is there?" There was no reply, but a branch moved just a few feet away. It had to be another survivor, but I drew the bayonet and prepared to spring forward if I was wrong. "This is Major Flashman, James Bowie's friend. Louis Rose is that you?"

I thought that perhaps Rose had made it to the river when he had tried to escape the night before. Instead a different voice answered. "No, it's Henry," the voice gasped in pain. "Henry Warnell, sir."

I crept cautiously forward and then pulled back a branch to find a young ginger-haired man's head watching me from the river. He was shivering with the cold. "What the hell are you doing in the water, you bloody fool?" I exclaimed, "You'll freeze to death." I reached out my hand and was surprised at the ease with which I was able to pull him out – he weighed barely more than a child.

"I saw you comin'. I thought you were searchin' for me an' so I hid." His thin frame trembled under his wet clothes. He was in desperate need of a warming fire, but I dared not risk one.

Get your clothes off and at least try to wring them out," I told him. "They will dry quicker then." He carefully shed his garments to reveal a deep gash in his side, the wound looking especially livid against his pale freckled skin. I gave him my Mexican coat to stop him getting any colder and hung his garments over some branches to catch the wind. "How did you get away?" I asked.

"Went over the mud wall by the church with the others," he explained. He was still gasping with the cold and spoke in short bursts. "But those horsemen were waitin' for us. Spittin' us on their lances like hogs, they were. I kept twistin' and turnin,' didn't know which direction I was goin'. One got me this here wound in my side, but then I was by the river an' I just jumped in. Wanted to get away from the town so I came up here. My friend came with me, but he hid under one of the bridges. A local woman spied him and told the soldiers. I just kept on going 'til I got here. Couldn't go no further then. Say, mister, you got any chaw?"

Some chewing tobacco would have helped stop his teeth from chattering, but I did not have any. A search of the pockets in the Mexican coat revealed nothing useful. I tore my bandage in half and we wrapped one part around his body over the gash. At least the cold immersion had stopped it bleeding too much, but the bandage was soon crimson as blood seeped into it.

159

"How many others made it?" he asked as I was tying a knot in the cloth.

"Not many," I admitted. "Mostly just the women and children. One was spared, I am not sure why, and then there are the two of us."

"That's it?" his blue eyes stared at me in astonishment. "No one else got away? What about the people they captured alive?"

"It is just us," I repeated looking him steadily back in the eye. "There were only half a dozen prisoners and Santa Anna had them killed."

It caught up with him then, I think, for he started to sob. I left him on his own and crept back into the bushes to check no one else was coming near.

We sat shivering in those wretched bushes for the rest of the day. Twice we had to hide in the undergrowth as people walked along the opposite bank, but no one noticed us. By midday Warnell's clothes were dry again, but I let him keep my coat as he was much colder than I. We spent much of that time talking about where we would go next. My initial thought was to head northwest to Gonzales, then to San Felipe and on to Louisiana. I would not feel safe until I was over the border and out of Texas. But Warnell had travelled that route in the other direction and warned me that it was three hundred miles, often over difficult country with swamps and bogs to trap the unwary.

"We should go to Goliad," he suggested. "That is less than ninety miles off and we are bound to meet Colonel Fannin on the way. We may only have to travel twenty or thirty miles before we get help."

"What if instead we meet a Mexican army that is coming up the coast?" I countered.

"No, Mr Bonham was with Colonel Fannin a few days back. He didn't say anything about any Mexican army." I remembered what Crockett had told me of his private conversation with Bonham. Clearly the courier had not shared his news with the rest of the garrison. I was on the verge of insisting that we travel northeast instead of what would be southeast to Goliad when Warnell came up with a far more convincing argument. "What about that ship you said you came here on. Do you think that she is still at Copano? That would be the sweetest way home. I got a young son in Arkansas; I would be mighty grateful if you an' your friend would give me a passage to New Orleans."

Would Vanderbilt have waited? I wondered. I had been in San Antonio for nearly six weeks, but he had been determined to stay and squeeze every last dollar of profit out of his cargo. That would have taken some time. If he had heard that we were besieged, surely he would have waited for news. I could not imagine that he would have wanted to return to New York and explain to Louisa that he had simply run out on me. After all, I had saved *his* life all those years back. I was certain he would not abandon me. If the ship was still there, then after just two or three days' riding, I would be back in my cabin and safe under the protection of the stars and stripes flag. Warnell was more than welcome to join us. We could put in at New Orleans, where I did not doubt people would be curious for news of what was happening in Texas. As possibly the only two survivors of the Alamo garrison, we would be much in demand. "You may be right," I agreed at last. I imagined being rowed back out to the ship and celebrating my return with a well-earned brandy, even if it was the cheap counterfeit variety.

By evening I was feeling quite optimistic about our prospects. Warnell told me that his wife had died in childbirth. He had left the infant in the care of relatives while he went to seek a future that would support the child. "I couldn't look at my son without thinking of my poor Ludie," he lamented. "When I get back, he will be two. I'll get myself fit again and then look for land somewhere else." In the circumstances we were perhaps letting our hopes rise too high, for late afternoon I saw first one and then two plumes of smoke rise into the air from fires set on the other side of the Alamo. I had a horrible feeling that they were the funeral pyres of our less fortunate comrades. As it got dark, I recovered my uniform coat and put my bandage back on my face and the shako on my head. It was time to go back to town to try and find a horse.

The day had never been warm, but now the sun was setting it was getting even colder. I hoped I would be able to find a coat or blanket too. As I got closer to San Antonio, there was the unmistakable sound of men celebrating their victory from across the river. There was music, thankfully no bagpipes, accompanied by loud raucous singing, the occasional squeal of a woman and laughter. As I got closer to the bridges, the two funeral fires came into view. They were burning fiercely; from the look of them the soldiers had made a pile of timber, put the bodies on top and doused the lot with lamp oil. I was mercifully upwind of them and so was spared the awful smell of roasting human flesh, yet I found myself drawn to the fires anyway. I would be lying if I said it was entirely to pay my respects. I was shivering by then and I will admit that the warmth from the flames was welcome. I doubted that the likes of Crockett and the others would object. They would be happier with me getting warm than the damn Mexicans, not that there were too many of those about.

A handful of people was watching, though. I looked carefully about just in case Juana or Trudy had been allowed to come to pay their last respects to James and, as they believed, me. It was then that I spotted one face standing apart from the rest that I *did* recognise. He stood with his head bared in a spot where he could watch both fires. I looked closely at his features, but there was no sign of triumph in them. In fact, I thought I could see a tear on his cheek reflecting the light of the flames. I moved quietly up behind him and as a precaution, I took the bayonet from my belt and held it slightly behind my back.

"So, how is it that Santa Anna spared you?" I asked quietly. He jumped, startled, and then when he saw me, his jaw dropped in astonishment as though he had seen a ghost. Perhaps for a moment he thought he had, but then Guerrero smiled as he took in the uniform I was wearing.

"When I saw all was lost," he explained, "I locked myself in a room and tied my own hands with my teeth. I told them I was a prisoner."

"That was quick thinking," I murmured suspiciously.

He shrugged, "I had planned it already, I had the rope in my pocket. I did not agree with Crockett that we could win. I have fought in the Mexican army, remember, some of them are good soldiers. I thought I would stand a chance to survive as long as there were no soldiers from my old company who knew I had deserted."

"Well it was a better plan than mine," I admitted, stepping forward past him and turning my back on the flames. There was genuine grief on his face and I was sure now he had not betrayed us. "I had to kill the bastard wearing this," I explained, pulling at the uniform coat. "Then I had a building fall on top of me, and even then, it was a damn close thing." I stood silently for a moment feeling the warmth behind me ease the shivering muscles in my back. "Have you been in town?" I continued. "Do you know what happened to Mrs Alsbury and her sister?"

"They have been taken back to their house. I heard that the officer who looks after them is a relative of Mrs Alsbury's first husband." He smiled knowingly, "You were quartered with them, weren't you?" Without waiting for an answer he continued, "The pretty sister was very upset over someone and I don't think it was James Bowie. Do you want me to get a message to her that you are alive?"

I thought about it for a moment and then shook my head. "No, I think it is better that she grieves for me and then gets on with her life." I nodded towards the dark river, "Henry Warnell is lying wounded upstream. I am trying to steal a horse and then we are going to make for Goliad. Why don't you join us?"

"No, there is something I want to do here first." Guerrero's face had darkened. His hand reached down and patted a knife hanging from his belt that was almost as big as Bowie's.

"Well do you at least know where I can easily steal a horse?"

"Santa Anna's horse and those of his murderous staff officers are outside their headquarters. You should take one of theirs."

"I am not going into town, I am too well known there. Anyway, I said *easily steal*, not from some bastard who would order cavalry to track me down."

He laughed and gestured beyond the flames. "The lancers' horses are out there somewhere. There will be few guards as everyone is celebrating in town. You will just need to find a saddle and bridle."

163

I shook hands with him and wished him well. Then I strode off past the pyres and into the darkness beyond. I soon spotted the sentries' fire. There were just three men illuminated by the flames and from the distant sound of singing, they were already drunk. As it turned out, finding a saddle and bridle was not that difficult as I literally fell over one. In fact, as I reached about me while sprawled in the dirt, I found I had fallen over a row of them. I rummaged around in the saddlebags for anything useful and found some dried meat and a few coins. I gathered two bedrolls tied to the saddles, then I went looking for a mount. The occasional snicker of a dozing horse led me in the right direction and eventually, dark equine shadows appeared in front of me. They had been hobbled for grazing and several started at the sight or smell of me. I found a nice calm mare and swiftly pulled the bridle over her head. Once saddled, I cut the hobble rope with my bayonet and was soon trotting quietly off into the night.

"Mr F-Flashman, over h-here," a shaky voice hissed out in the darkness. I had looped around the Alamo to avoid being seen, but it was hard to find the right copse of trees in the darkness. I had already stopped at two others before the familiar voice hailed me. I dismounted to find Warnell in a pitiful state. His thin frame was wracked with cold and his teeth were chattering so hard he could barely eat the dried meat I offered him. We could not afford to delay long as I wanted to be well away from the Alamo by dawn. I wrapped us each in a blanket and then we mounted up. I had to help hold Warnell in the saddle but at least, I thought, his eight stone in weight would not be too much of a burden for the horse. We rode out into the night, but when we had gone just a quarter of a mile my companion called out and pointed, "What are those big fires?"

I turned back to look at the pyres and felt an overwhelming sadness. "Do you remember Colonel Travis talking about lighting the flame of liberty? Well that is what those fires are. It is just a shame that there is only the two of us here to see them."

Chapter 20

I had hoped that we might find Fannin and his relief force the next day, but was disappointed. Nor was there any sign of the promised reinforcements. We did not find them the next day either, not that we could travel that quickly. To make matters worse, Warnell was coming down with a fever, whether as a result of his wound or immersion in the cold river, I could not say. The second night I managed to get a huge fire blazing by lighting a smaller one under an old fallen tree. I lay him near it but even wrapped in both blankets he still shivered. He needed a doctor, but as we were still in the arse end of nowhere, there was no alternative to pressing on.

On the third day we finally found a woman with two small children on a farm. She told us that Fannin had left Goliad to relieve the Alamo over a week before, but had turned back the same day. She asked if the Alamo was still resisting. When I gave her our news, she stood quietly for a moment staring at her fields and then declared it was time for them to leave.

"There is talk of another Mexican army coming up the coast," she explained, "but if Santa Anna marches to Goliad from the Alamo, we will be right in his path. My Ned is with the garrison at Goliad, has been these past two months, we'll not be safe here." She was only a young woman, yet she looked as tough as teak. She must have been, for she had been left with a farm to look after and two young children to raise out there in the wilderness. The field was freshly ploughed and there was recently shot game on the table. She gave us some food and even offered to take Warnell with her in the wagon to Goliad. She was going there first to see her husband and then they would head north. It was a generous offer as I guessed that her wagon would have to carry all the possessions that she wanted to keep from being plundered by passing armies. However, I declined; we were less than a day's ride away now and so I kept Warnell with me. By the time she arrived in town, I hoped to be aboard the ship.

Being so close to our destination, I rode hard that afternoon and was rewarded at dusk with the sight of the sprawling town. We kicked on and I was soon riding under the gate of the stone fort by the river. A painted wooden plank over the portal announced that the place was now known as Fort Defiance. Unlike the Alamo, this was a proper stone-built fortification with thick eight-foot-high walls around a central enclosure that must have covered three acres. There were stone gun emplacements in the corners and various stone and wooden buildings against the walls. Much of the central space was now taken up with tents; there were far more men in the town than I remembered. When I had been there before, many had already set off on the disastrous expedition to Matamoros but now most of them had returned. We had heard in the Alamo that Fannin had some four hundred men here and looking around I could well believe it.

As we rode through the gate, a sentry stopped us and asked where we had come from. I decided to give Fannin the courtesy of telling him my news first and so I told the sentry we had come from Gonzales.

"Have you heard any news of the Alamo?" the man asked. "Are they still holding out?"

I replied that I was not sure and then asked if they had a surgeon. Warnell by this time was barely conscious and delirious with fever. He kept muttering that he had seen the flames of liberty. The guard helped me carry him to an orderly, who promised to get a doctor to look at him. With Warnell in the sick bay, I went searching for Colonel Fannin. By then it was late in the evening and at first the man would not see me at all. He sent his aide back with a request that I come back at a more civilised hour. It was only when I announced that James Bowie had asked me to call on him that the door to his office swung open

"Do you have news from the Alamo?" asked the colonel, who had clearly been eavesdropping on my conversation with his aide.

"Yes, sir." I glanced at the aide and continued, "Perhaps we should talk in private?"

"Yes, yes, of course, come in, mister er…"

"Flashman, sir, Major Flashman, formerly of the British army." I thought I would use my military rank as Fannin was the first Texian soldier I had come across wearing any semblance of a recognisable

166

uniform. He was, I guessed, in his early thirties with already thinning dark hair and an anxious demeanour. I had hoped that he would offer me a drink, but there was not a bottle in sight.

"So, you have news from Colonel Bowie," he enquired, standing by a table covered in a large map of the region. "How go things at the Alamo?"

"How do you think they go?" I asked sharply. For this was the man that we had all relied on for our deliverance. Instead of being on the road, here he was safe and sound in his office.

"Has Colonel Bowie sent you to reprimand me?" he started querulously, "for I can assure you, Major, that I would like nothing more than to come to his aid but—"

"Colonel Bowie is dead," I cut him off. "The Alamo was captured by Santa Anna's forces three days ago."

He paled at that and then started to babble, "Oh God, were there many casualties? What about Colonel Travis? Bonham, he was going back there. Were many taken prisoner? How many of you got away?"

"They are all dead," I told him coldly. "Travis, Bonham, Bowie, Davy Crockett. There are only three survivors that I know of. Apart from me, one is probably dying in your sick bay and the other is still in San Antonio." I wanted to make the bastard feel guilty for letting us down and so I added, "The garrison knew its duty and fought to the last; only six men were taken prisoner and some of those were wounded. Santa Anna had them all executed."

"Oh God," he repeated, distraught. "I tried to come to your aid, I swear it. But the men did not bring enough food. Some of them did not even have boots and then one of the wagons broke and they insisted that we went back." He was fiddling with a pair of dividers on his map, as though measuring the distance again between Goliad and San Antonio would make it less than the ninety odd miles it was.

"How far did you get before you turned back?" I asked, disgusted at his string of excuses. He did not sound like a man in command at all, moaning that the men did not bring enough food. *He* should have been overseeing supplies or at least making sure that his officers did.

At least he had the grace to look embarrassed as he answered, "We only got a mile beyond the San Antonio River." Given that the river ran within yards of the walls of Fort Defiance, this meant that they did not even get out of sight of the town. My teeth clenched in suppressed fury as he added, "Wait, did you say Davy Crockett was in the Alamo too? Oh, they will never forgive me for this, I will be ruined." Then he added the last thing I expected to hear. "I told them I should not have been left in command."

As he paced anxiously up and down the room, I realised that this young officer was hopelessly out of his depth. At least he had the honesty to know that himself, but it was a shame whoever *they* were, had not listened. Mind you, this was no role for a novice commander. He had no clear leadership from above as the politicians in San Felipe were busy arguing among themselves. On top of that, from what I remembered of his men, who voted themselves new commanders when they had orders they did not like, getting them to follow instructions must have been like herding cats. What was needed here was a formidable presence that the men respected, a man like Bowie before he became ill. Instead they had Fannin, who made that great dithering cyclops Beresford, who had nearly killed me in Spain, look decisive.

The situation reeked of imminent disaster. I silently prayed that Vanderbilt and his ship were still waiting at Copano so that I could get away and leave all this mess behind. I had done enough. Fannin looked so hapless I could not help but give him some advice. "You need to retreat north," I told him firmly. "You cannot stay here now that the Alamo has fallen and I hear that there is a force heading up the coast."

"The Mexicans took San Patricio a few days back," he admitted. "I lost fifty men, but those that got away said that the Mexicans only have two hundred cavalry and the same number of infantry. They will have lost some of those in the fighting."

"Where is this San Patricio?" I asked, alarmed.

"Fifty miles south of here, but we can beat a force that size. I have over four hundred men and stone walls. We have gathered nine cannon here now and five hundred spare muskets. My last orders were to stay here."

"Are you some kind of bally idiot?" I exploded. "I passed a farmer's wife on the way here who had more strategic awareness than you. It is not the bloody Mexicans to the south you need to worry about, it is Santa Anna. He can march east and cut you off from the rest of the Texian forces. He has two and a half thousand men and with the guns from the Alamo he will have nearly thirty cannon. Even if they cannot smash down your stone walls, they can starve you out. How much food do you have here?"

"Some meal has just arrived and we have been busy drying beef. But we do not have enough for a long siege," he admitted. "I had to pay a ship to sail to New Orleans to buy whatever they could."

I suddenly felt my blood run cold. "What ship?" I whispered in horror, although in my heart I think I already knew the answer.

"I don't remember the name, but it was owned by a dutchman. His name was Van something."

Chapter 21

I had wanted Fannin to issue orders immediately to abandon Goliad and march north, but he refused. I'll grant that there was some stubborn steel to him, even if it was misplaced. He insisted that having failed to save the Alamo, he was not going to leave anyone else behind. San Patricio might have been lost, but halfway between there and Goliad was another settlement called Refugio, which had some Texian settlers. The Mexicans had shot some of the prisoners at San Patricio and he did not want the settlers suffering the same fate. So early the next morning he sent thirty men under an officer called King to fetch them back. With them went all the carts and draught horses to carry the settlers and their possessions.

When I wandered around the town that morning, I swiftly discovered that news of the Alamo's fall had spread around the town like wildfire. Fannin must have told King what had happened there to express to him the urgency of his mission and King had then told his men. Now everyone knew.

It did not take them long to learn that the man in the sickbay raving about the torch of liberty and his English companion were the ones who had brought the news to town. As Warnell was in no state to tell them anything sensible, I was soon besieged by those desperate for news. I remember a man called George Courtman whose brother Henry had been among the Alamo garrison. Others had friends or neighbours who had been there and they all wanted to know if I was sure that these people were dead. Many came from New Orleans where a regiment had been raised known as the New Orleans Greys, on account of the colour of their uniforms. The regiment only had two companies; one had been with me at the Alamo and the other was here at Goliad. While I remembered a few of the names and faces, there were only a handful like Travis and Martin that I had personally seen die. All I could do was describe how the fort fell and how the prisoners were dealt with. That sobered them up, for on top of the executions at San Patricio that they had also heard about, it showed what they might expect if they surrendered. I was sure that I would now not be the only one pressing Fannin to head north as soon as possible.

It would take a couple of days for King and his men to reach Refugio and get back with the settlers. I decided to use that time to ride to Copano myself. I wanted to be certain that Vanderbilt and his ship had sailed and to check that there was not some other vessel there that could carry me to safety. I had little confidence in Fannin and for all we knew, Santa Anna was already rampaging southeast towards us or east to cut off any escape. I would feel a lot happier with a wooden deck under my feet.

I borrowed a horse and rode comfortably the forty-five miles to Copano in a day. My worst fears were confirmed as I crested the last rise to find the bay as empty as a foundling's future. When I spoke to the fishermen, they told me that the ship had sailed a week before and there were no vessels in Port Lavaca up the coast either. There was nothing for it but to ride back to Goliad and hope that Fannin was now ready to depart.

It took me another day to ride back, but that should have given this King fellow plenty of time to return with the wagons and settlers from Refugio. The sky looked clear as I entered Goliad that evening and I thought the weather would be good the next day for our march north. I should have known better. When I went to Fannin's office, I found myself listening to a growing tale of catastrophe.

"What do you mean they have gone off to attack Tejanos?" I asked, bewildered. "I thought many of the Tejanos were on our side." The exasperated colonel had just told me that instead of obeying his orders to return with the settlers, Captain King had taken it upon himself to launch an attack on a group of Tejanos who he thought had sympathy with Santa Anna.

Now he shifted uncomfortably. "When we marched south to Matamoros we were set on an independent Texas, but many Mexicans were ungrateful for the liberty we were bringing them. Some of the men got resentful and so as many were also short of supplies, there was some looting of goods from the Tejanos."

171

I groaned as it was now all too clear what had happened. I remembered that the Matamoros expedition had several competing leaders and clearly none had kept any discipline. As a result, they had alienated much of the local population to the point where they were now helping Santa Anna's forces. I remembered Juan Seguín saying that he wanted a return to the old Constitution rather than independence. The locals must have seen this disorganised rabble marching south and remembered the vengeance that *el Presidente* wreaked on rebellious provinces. Even if the Texians had not insulted them and stolen their property, they would still have had doubts about joining the revolt. Now we had driven these men into the welcoming arms of our enemy.

"We cannot afford to wait any longer," I told Fannin. "The Mexicans must be closing in around Refugio now so they could be here in a day, two at the most. You have done your best to save these people, but that fool King has let you down."

"We cannot leave yet," Fannin insisted. "Apart from anything else we do not have any wagons now to bring supplies, they are all with King. I have ordered Colonel Ward and the Georgia Legion to march as quickly as they can to Refugio to bring back the settlers and the wagons and order King to return."

"But it is too late! The Mexicans will already be moving in," I protested.

"They only have two hundred infantry according to our reports and there are a hundred and twenty men in the legion. It should be enough to hold the Mexicans back while they withdraw."

The legion represented more than a quarter of Fannin's command and I had a fear that at this rate the Mexicans would capture it piece by piece. But I could see Fannin's point about the wagons; we would need those and the draught horses back if we had to march any distance. They would be necessary for food, ammunition and the wounded, not to mention helping with the elderly and children among the settlers. With that thought in mind I went to see Warnell, who was recovering now that he was getting rest and care. He was conscious and lucid, at least enough to listen to conversations of the men around him and realise that the Mexicans might be closing in on him again. He was desperate to get on board the ship I had promised him and broke down when I told him it had sailed without us.

"I don't want them bastards to catch me again," he sobbed. "You gotta get me outta here, mister."

As luck would have it, when I left him, I found the farmer's wife we had stayed with on the journey from the Alamo. She had come to say goodbye to her husband, who was talking anxiously to her about the journey ahead. She would have to cross some wild country, there had been banditry from both Tejanos and Texians, not to mention predations by local Indian tribes. Added to that, there were few settlements this far south. Her chances appeared barely better than our own, although she seemed a resourceful woman. Her husband tried to persuade her to stay and retreat with the army, but she was determined to be on her way.

"You soldiers will be too keen to fight. I don't want the children in the middle of a battle," she chided. At this she saw me watching and introduced me to her husband.

"I think I may have a solution," I told them. "My companion, who you met before, is recovering. He is well enough to fire a musket if needed and his armed presence on the wagon will be enough to deter casual thieves." They readily agreed that Warnell could join the party. As I helped him up onto the wagon I wondered if I should join them too. They would still be very vulnerable to a determined attack, but I was not sure if being in the middle of a well-armed force under Fannin's command was any safer. He still had around three hundred men in the garrison and if his spies were right, that was probably the same size as the Mexican force after any casualties they had taken further south. That should be enough men, considering many of the Texians had those long rifles, but only if the army was well managed and unfortunately there was little sign of that so far. A short while later I watched the woman, her children and their invalid escort urge the cart horse along the road into a hostile wilderness and decided that on balance I might just be safer with an army. But it was a damn close call.

The next day Fannin finally got new orders from General Houston, who was now in Gonzalez. Fannin was to abandon Goliad and take his army as swiftly as possible twenty-five miles northeast to the town of Victoria to join other reinforcements there and await further orders. Fannin's army was then the largest that Texas possessed. Houston tried to gather more volunteers to him to form another, but on their own they were far too small to do much damage to the Mexicans. He would want to combine his forces to make them a more formidable threat and possibly beat the Mexican force coming up the coast. I just hoped that Houston also had scouts watching what Santa Anna was doing, for the president was by far the bigger threat.

Having at last been given some direction, Fannin was more energised. He ordered his forty cavalry under a man called Horton to ride ahead to Victoria and return with as many carts and draught animals as he could find. He had been sending couriers south to Captain King and Colonel Ward, but the news was not good. From what we got back it appeared that the captain was refusing to obey the colonel and continuing his attacks on the Tejanos. With my precious skin on the line, I would have had the villain shot for mutiny, but Ward felt obliged to defend Refugio as Mexican forces began to close about it, while waiting for King to re-join him.

We spent the next two days lingering for the men at Refugio to return. Fannin sent at least four couriers to find out what was happening, but three did not make it back. The one who did reported that the Mexicans were in strength around the town and he could not get through. He was sure, though, that the Georgia men held the centre of the town and that they were putting up a good defence. I seethed with impatience to leave, but Fannin was loath to abandon so many of his men.

Houston had ordered him to take only the cannon he could easily carry and sink the rest in the river. Fannin, however, was conscious of the guns lost at the Alamo and knew that his cannon were pretty much the only ones Texas had left. He wanted to take them all, along with five hundred spare muskets that had recently been delivered. He knew that the Texians would be desperate for such supplies now Santa Anna and his men were roaming the countryside. His men did not argue, as most of them did not want to leave the fort at all. News from the Alamo did not intimidate them, quite the reverse; they were spoiling for a fight.

"We have plenty of men, guns, ammunition and food." one man told me. "Let them come and we will shoot them down from our walls."

I tried to explain that it was only worth allowing yourself to be besieged if there was the chance of a relief force, otherwise you would just be starved out and killed. The man did not seem to care. All he wanted was the chance to kill Mexicans. The garrison at the Alamo had included many settlers who had been in Texas for some time, together with men like Bowie and Deaf Smith, who had married Mexicans, not to mention a sizeable number of Tejanos. In contrast the men at Goliad were almost entirely new arrivals in the region. Most had come from the United States, usually in large bands organised there. They had sailed south for adventure and the promise of land. They had come to fight and had heard stories of the battles the previous year when the Mexican army had been driven out by much smaller forces from Texas. With stone walls for cover and their long rifles, they did not feel the slightest bit intimidated by their enemy.

Finally, after two days, Fannin's cavalry reappeared with some new wagons. Draught horses were in short supply, but they had brought ten yokes of oxen with them. Early that morning another scout had returned from the south. He reported that the Mexicans were in Refugio, the town was lost and there was no sign of the men that Fannin had sent to evacuate it. There was no reason to delay now. I would have had the entire garrison on the road by noon at the latest, but infuriatingly, Fannin wasted the whole day in preparations.

Time was lost in packing and repacking wagons as contradictory orders on what was to be taken flew about. Even when Mexican scouts appeared on the outskirts of Goliad, there was no great sense of urgency. Horton and his cavalry rushed out to see them off, but only succeeded in tiring their mounts as the more experienced Mexican horsemen easily evaded them. I was sure that the rest of the Mexican force had to be close by then. If Santa Anna had sent reinforcements, they would also be approaching. There was not a second to lose.

That night a mist appeared, which thickened into a fog, a perfect cover with which to make our escape. I pressed Fannin to give the order, but Horton the cavalry commander disagreed. He claimed it was so thick that our force could get separated and scattered all over the prairie by sunrise. I fumed as Fannin dithered and then eventually sided with the horseman.

Dawn the next day came and went as did around three hours of daylight before we finally set off into what was still a foggy day, with added showers of cold rain. While I had fretted at the delays of the morning, Fannin remained blithely unconcerned. He remained confident that we could see off any Mexican threat. Meanwhile many of his officers and men were complaining loudly about the need to leave the fort at all.

We had with us the nine cannon from the fort, a wagon full of ammunition and others full of muskets. With sick, injured and the elderly in some of the other vehicles, I realised that, incredibly, once again Fannin had allowed his men to set off with precious little in the way of food and water for the march. By then, I very much doubted that the man could have organised an orgy in a brothel – he clearly had not learned from his past mistakes. On the other hand, as we were only going twenty-five miles through prairie used by grazing cattle and it was pouring with rain, perhaps he felt he did not need to bring such supplies.

Almost as soon as the wagons had splashed through the river, the oxen started to play up. No one had bothered to feed them the day before and they were not happy about passing hungry through pasture. They would keep pulling their carts off the road to eat, causing loads to shift or injured occupants to shout out as they were bounced over ruts in the track. Behind us an orange glow appeared in the fog, as all that could be useful to the enemy in the fort was put to the flame. This included all the hoarded supplies of dried meat, wheat and corn. I wondered if any Mexican scouts were also watching the inferno. Even if they were not, when the fog cleared, the column of smoke would act as a beacon for miles around. It would clearly signal that the garrison had abandoned the town and was on the road. If it had not begun already, then the chase would soon be on with the Mexicans in pursuit.

Chapter 22

The retreat from Goliad was one of the worst debacles I have ever been involved in, and I have been in some corkers over the years. It reminded me of when I had taken part in the evacuation of Amherstburg in Canada during 1813. We were pursued by Americans under Harrison then and that had ended in a headlong rout. I had a nasty feeling about this withdrawal too. Although we were finally moving, our speed was barely that of a lame hen. The first wagon had broken crossing the river, forcing a dozen men to splash around in the cold water to recover a cannon barrel, while a wheelwright and others carried out running repairs. Knowing that the town would be lost, soldiers had ransacked the buildings for anything of value to take with them. I saw one man carrying a large chair, with the seat resting on his head like some Bengal porter. Two more enterprising souls were each holding the handle of a chest between them that was clearly heavily loaded with loot. We looked more like a travelling circus than a retreating army with an enemy close on our heels.

The fog and rain slowly lifted and at least Horton's scouts could not find any Mexicans tracking us that morning. Looking back over the undulating prairie, I could still see the pillar of smoke from the burning supplies in town. I wondered how long our good fortune would last. By eleven two wagons had been abandoned, one with a broken wheel and axle while the other just collapsed, rotten to the core. By then men were complaining that they were hungry and thirsty. I only saw two barrels of water in the entire convoy. Anger broke out when it was discovered that our food supplies had been burnt, but it was the hunger of the oxen that brought us to a stop again. We had been going for just over two hours and had barely covered six miles, when Fannin ordered a halt and allowed the animals time to graze. We were slap bang in the middle of a wide expanse of open prairie and strung out in a long uneven column. Even a witless child should have known that if the Mexican cavalry appeared, we would be cut to pieces. I railed at Fannin and urged him to go onward to the tree-lined Coleto Creek, which was just five miles away and would give us water and cover should the enemy approach, but he was having none of it.

"Ward and his men must have taken a terrible toll on the Mexicans," the stubborn fool assured me. "If there were only two hundred infantry and a similar number of cavalry when they attacked San Patricio, their numbers must be far less now. They do not have the men to take on a force this size." There was a bloody big *if* in that statement and I was not the only one arguing the case for continuing. One of the militia leaders, Doc Shackelford also pressed hard for him to continue. Shackelford had raised his own militia of around sixty men from his home town in Alabama and had brought them to Texas to fight. They included one of his sons, two nephews and many personal friends. He was determined not to put their lives at risk unnecessarily. It was clear, however, that we were in the minority. Most of the men welcomed a rest from carrying their burdens. A good number actually wanted the Mexicans to appear, so that they could pay them back for our earlier defeats. Little did they know they were to get their wish soon enough.

We eventually resumed our march and had covered another three miles before there was a shout of alarm from the back of the column. A large group of horsemen had appeared behind us. Horton's rear scouts must have been asleep or dead, as we had no warning of their approach. My worst fears were confirmed as they got closer: they were Mexican cavalry. We still had two miles to go before we reached Coleto Creek and a belated sense of urgency began to spread at long last down the column. Oxen were whipped to go faster and men picked up their burdens and began to hurry along to the shelter of cover ahead.

It was too late. It was a race we could never win. Squadrons of Mexican lancers and dragoons thundered down and passed on either side of us, well out of rifle range. It was soon clear that they had no intention of attacking directly; their goal was to cut us off from the creek where we could more easily make a stand. Our own horsemen, hopelessly outnumbered, were forced to withdraw.

For a while we pressed on regardless, just getting closer to the creek in the hope that there might be some way through. We left the road and pushed our way through the long grass of the prairie on a direct route to the distant trees, approaching safety yard by yard. Then there was another shout of warning from one of the wagons. More Mexicans could be seen coming up behind us, infantry this time and marching quickly. There were well over two hundred of them, which meant that the early reports of their numbers must have been wrong.

God, I wished I had gone with Warnell and the farmer's wife now, for suddenly our situation was precarious indeed. I swore vehemently at myself. All those weeks of waiting futilely in San Antonio, then not going over the wall when I had the chance and now waiting around like some prize plum in Goliad until it was too late. I was damned that if after escaping the massacre of the Alamo I was going to die here. Some of the men at the front of the column started to race ahead, for the trees around the creek were now no more than a mile in front of us, but the horsemen were ready for that. The lancers started to array themselves in a line ready for a charge across that tempting stretch of land. I knew that horsemen would easily kill a group of running men.

Slowly the Texians who had run forward were forced to retreat back to the main column, which had now finally come to a halt. Men glanced nervously over their shoulders at the approaching Mexican infantry. They knew that they would be in a fight now and it would be evenly matched. Both sides had just over three hundred men by my reckoning, but the Mexicans had far more cavalry while the Texians had their rifles and artillery. Fannin ordered two of the cannon to be set up and fired at the horsemen, while a rare old debate started amongst the men on what we should do next.

Everyone had an opinion. Some wanted to rush the horsemen again and take their chances. Others pointed out that this would leave the slow and infirm at the mercy of the Mexicans. In the end the decision was made for us when a wheel on the ammunition wagon hit a rock and broke. We were stuck where we were now, for any defence would require an ample supply of powder and ball.

Mercifully, Fannin must have remembered some of his West Point training, for he slowly organised his men into a square. It was no mean feat as the column originally stretched out nearly a quarter of a mile. He had most of the wagons brought together in the middle and at least one of his militia regiments on each side. Only one wagon was outside the square. The cart had been at the front of the column, but dragoons had shot at its oxen as they went past so that it could no longer be moved. It carried five wounded men and a driver, a medical orderly called Abel Morgan. He simply got some ammunition and prepared to defend his vehicle and its occupants where they stood.

"You have set up a good defence," I grudgingly conceded to Fannin as we stood watching the spare muskets being distributed so that each man had at least two long arms to fire. "But what are we going to do now? If we break out under cover of darkness, the chances are that only half of us will make it to the creek." I was privately considering a break out of my own, though not to the creek, for if there was a general rush to escape, that would attract Mexicans like sharks to a shipwreck. Instead I planned to go to the east. I had noticed that the soldiers were spread thinner there and if I crawled carefully through the long grass, I had a chance of getting through them. Then I could move more quickly in the darkness for three miles or so to another copse of trees to hide out. I was still wearing the old soldier's coat I had taken at the Alamo – there had been no new supplies to replace it in Goliad. I had a blanket over the top to keep me warm, but without that, I could easily be mistaken for a Mexican at a distance. Of course, if stopped and questioned, my disguise would quickly be revealed. It was a small advantage. I was not beaten yet; a resourceful man on his own could survive where several hundred could not. But I was surprised to learn that Fannin had a plan of his own to save us all.

"Horton cannot get back to us," he said pointing in the direction his own cavalry had last been seen. "But he knows that militia were gathering in Victoria. Perhaps Houston is there now himself with his men. If Horton can get to Victoria, he can bring reinforcements back here to break us out. It is only a day's march, so they should be here tomorrow."

I looked at the colonel with new respect. Firstly because of the orderly way he organised a strong defensive square from his unruly command and now for thinking about ways to get us out. Mind you, if he had not dithered for days or even the hours wasted this morning, we would not have been in this mess in the first place.

We were interrupted now by shouting at the front of the column. Looking out, I could see the dragoons lining up with the lancers as they prepared to attack. The Mexican infantry was still some distance off, breaking up into four companies so that they could cover each side of the square.

Distant bugles called and the enemy cavalry started to move towards us. Abel Morgan's wagon was right in their way and would serve like a breakwater to disrupt the waves of the horsemen. Fannin was already pushing forward to stand in the front of three ranks of men that were being hastily prepared. Muskets and cannon were loaded and as the horsemen moved from a walk to a trot, our commander shouted that no one was to shoot until he gave the order. I stood on a cart so that I could fire over the heads of the men in front and hurriedly began to load my muskets. The bugles rang out again and as one, the line of lance tips dipped to point in our direction as the horsemen broke into a gallop. I remembered the man in Bowie's troop warning me of the skill of these men. They certainly knew their trade as without any obvious orders, they began to part to make a gap around Morgan's wagon.

"Hold your fire," shouted Fannin. Rifle men could hit the lancers now as could the artillery gunners, but he evidently wanted to wait for a devastating close-range volley. We would only have one chance to stop them and we had to make the most of it. Closer they came. I could hear a rattle from a metal cup hanging from a nail on my wagon that vibrated from the distant hoofbeats. Not so distant now, a hundred yards no more and just as I withdrew the ramrod from my second musket, Fannin finally gave the order to fire. There was a thunderous roar from the guns of the men in front as a volley was fired and the two cannon blasted canister shot into the approaching cavalry. Long before I could get the first musket to my shoulder the enemy had disappeared behind a bank of gun smoke. I fired blindly in the direction that they had been and heard others doing the same. There was the sound of screams and horses whinnying in pain, but mercifully no lancers came crashing through the lines of the men in front of me. Fannin ordered the front ranks forward several paces to get in front of the smoke and see what lay beyond. He led them himself, swiftly discovering that the dragoons were covering the horsemen's retreat as he was struck by a ball from their carbines, which shot away the lock on his own musket.

As the smoke cleared we saw that the long prairie grass had hidden much of the devastation we had inflicted. Here and there a wounded horse thrashed about as it tried to stand, but the dead and wounded troopers were out of sight. The lancers had lost a third of their number. The dragoons were also falling back sharply as they knew our rifles were vastly more accurate than their carbines. A cheer went up as the men congratulated themselves on their victory. This was how they expected encounters with the Mexican army to go. Several shouted that it was revenge for the Alamo, while others pointed at some of the approaching infantry companies and beckoned for them to come on, like eager whores searching for new trade.

Fannin at least saw that we were not out of trouble yet for he had them reloading and dressing their lines into straight ranks for the next attacks to come. While we had been dealing with the cavalry attack, a company of a hundred men had drawn up opposite each of the other three sides of our square. They were very different creatures to the Texians. Judging from the way I had seen them shoot from the hip in the past, they were clearly not familiar with firearms. For the most part they were shorter, smaller men who were being manually pushed into lines by their sergeants and officers. They were conscript soldiers, who probably did not want to be there. They cannot have been encouraged by watching the treatment we had just dished out to the much-vaunted Mexican cavalry.

In contrast, the Texians were all volunteers and incentivised with promises of land and riches should they be successful in wrestling the territory of Texas from Mexico. Most had been brought up on farms and in rural communities, where hunting and using guns was a way of life. As they watched the sorry specimens being shoved into ranks by their officers, it was not surprising that the Texians felt confident. They may have felt less so, however, if they had looked to their rear and seen yet more Mexicans approaching, together with what looked like a group of Indians that they had recruited. Fannin's earlier scout reports that there were just two hundred Mexican infantry were clearly wrong. What we did not know was just how badly wrong they were.

More bugles sounded and as one, the three Mexican lines started to move towards us. Their officers stood behind, prodding the slower ones on to keep the lines straight. I saw that they marched with their bayonets already fixed, which meant that they were unlikely to stop to reload. If they were to charge it would be a brutal bloody affair as they were roughly the same number as the men facing them. If they got close enough to use those blades, the square would dissolve into hand to hand fighting. I did not doubt that the lancers and dragoons would then charge again to make the most of the confusion. The two sides were evenly matched and I would not want to have wagered on the outcome. Even if the Texas forces did win the encounter, I knew that few would be left uninjured.

The first guns fired. They came from our ranks, the sharp retorts of rifles as men made the most of the longer-range weapons. On the side I was watching, I saw four men fall, two of them officers. Then the corner cannon began to fire and another half dozen men fell. As the gunners hurriedly reloaded, more of our muskets and rifles fired. There were no crashing volleys, just a growing rumble of fire. More Mexicans tumbled into the grass, but the majority were still over a hundred yards off, too far for an accurate musket shot. One of their officers on horseback, raised his sword and shouted an order, but was almost instantly plucked from his saddle by a rifle ball. Perhaps the order came from elsewhere, for the men now broke into a run, a distant challenge being shouted at us as they charged.

The crackle of fire from our ranks grew even louder and more Mexican soldiers disappeared into the prairie. Every shot had to count. From my higher vantage point on the wagon, I could see the Mexicans clearly over the gun smoke. They withstood the first barrage of fire well. A score of men had fallen, but the rest were still running and shouting as they must have imagined their enemy reloading to give them time to reach our ranks. Then, far sooner than they expected, the second muskets flamed through the smoke and, closer now, yet more men fell. Some spare guns were even passed from those on the side not being attacked so that some men had three or even four weapons to fire. The Mexicans simply could not understand how we could send so much lead towards them. They started to fire their own guns, often shooting wildly on the run. Then our cannon fired again.

I could easily imagine their terror as they heard the scream of cannister shot blowing like a lethal hail through their line. Huge gaps appeared in their rank and it took any remaining fighting spirit right out of them. "They're breaking," I shouted as I watched the first Mexicans come to a hesitant halt. A breaking charge is more infectious than the plague. It only took a few to haul up and then those beside them stopped as well. No one wanted to reach the enemy lines to find that they had arrived on their own. Some Mexican officer must have seen that the game was up for then a bugle called and the whole body of men began to retreat, with cheering from the square chasing them up the slope.

We lost three men killed and at least a dozen injured in that attack, while I guessed that there must have been at least fifty dead or injured men lying in the long grass, not to mention more Mexican wounded that were helped away by their comrades. The Texians were jubilant – none of them had doubted the outcome. There were shouts that they would chase the Mexicans back over the Rio Grande. Some wanted to continue our march to the creek and beyond, but Fannin pointed out that we were unable to move two wagons and the Mexican cavalry were still in our way

"We beat them because we were organised and we stood firm," he explained. "If we try to make a run for it, they will chase us like coyotes, taking down the slow and the weak first." Soldiers looked guiltily at the sick and wounded men in and around the wagons and most agreed that they could not be abandoned. To emphasise the point, a shot rang out from one of the fallen Mexicans hiding in the long grass. If he had aimed at the large square he would have struggled to miss and a man in the facing rank howled with pain. That I think deterred many from suggesting a breakout, for we all knew that in the flash of flint on steel we could be one of the poor devils being left behind.

Chapter 23

Over the next few hours the Mexicans launched several more assaults on our line, their losses replaced by reinforcements that continued to arrive during the day. The Texians kept firing and repulsed them all. There was no shortage of ammunition with a wagon full of cartridges in the middle of the square. We had ended up stopping in a shallow dip in the prairie and so there was little wind to blow the musket and rifle smoke away. The acrid sulphurous smell always made my guts tighten, as it brought back awful memories I tried hard to forget. This looked set to be another one, for while we were able to stop their main attacks men increasingly began to fall to sharpshooters hiding out in the long grass. From the bodies we found, they were the Indians that the Mexicans had brought. These stealthy villains were far more used to stalking prey and accurate shooting than the soldiers. Our men would return fire, but they only had one man to hit, who if he had any sense, had already rolled away from the tell-tale puff of musket smoke that rose above the grass when he shot at us. In contrast, the enemy had a large block of men and animals to shoot at. They did not even need to aim; the marksman could just point his gun towards the sound of voices. Some of them I thought, must have been aiming, for we gradually lost more of our gunners than the more numerous militia men. Soon half a dozen oxen were down too.

There was a regular rumbling of stomachs that afternoon as men went hungry, but it was the lack of water that was harder to bear. We had spent the afternoon biting down on cartridges containing salty gunpowder which soon dried out the men's mouths. Those that had water bottles soon found them empty. The inside of my mouth felt like the skin of an elephant. The wounded too were in a pitiable need of water, especially those who had lost a lot of blood, but it was the gunners on whom our fate depended. They needed water to sponge out their guns after firing them. This removed gunpowder debris that blocked up the muzzle. More importantly, it extinguished any smouldering remains of the previous charge before another large quantity of gunpowder and a ball was pushed down the barrel. A gunner reloading an un-sponged gun was asking to lose an arm or worse if the charge ignited prematurely.

Soon enough there was simply no water to be had. They had no choice but to dry sponge their guns, usually several times in the hope of snuffing out any cinders before they could risk another charge. With the loss of gunners to sharpshooters and the lack of water, the rate of fire from our cannon dropped considerably. Fortunately, the resolve of the Mexican soldier to see home yet another attack after all the earlier ones had ended in deadly storms of shot, also diminished.

While Mexican morale might have been sinking, the mood of the Texians remained surprisingly high. Our stomachs might be grumbling and our voices hoarse and cracked through thirst, but we were still beating our enemy, even if it was getting tougher. I remember the man next to me croaking at one point that he thought he was dying of thirst. He was shaking an upturned metal flask over his outstretched tongue to gather any last drop.

"More likely it was that cheap whisky that was killin' you," gasped his mate. "I've drunk it and I'll wager you have not been shootin' straight all afternoon." They began to debate how long they might last without water. I told them of how I had survived in an open boat for two weeks on just a few sips a day. They were comforted by that and so I did not elaborate on the cannibalism of my shipmates or those that went mad drinking seawater.

Fannin was still patrolling around the square offering a forced cheery grin and a friendly word here and there as he tried to keep men's spirits up between attacks. "Do you think we are doing well keeping them at bay?" he rasped as he got to me. I had noticed that he often sought my opinion. Presumably he welcomed the view of a fellow military man, although he had not taken my advice when I had been urging him to leave Goliad sooner.

"I think that they are trying to keep us pinned down," I told him. "Even if we move the surviving oxen around, there are at least five wagons we would have to leave behind now. Nearly half of our gunners have been injured. They want us to stay here, perhaps to starve us out. Are you sure they do not have any artillery of their own?"

"Not that our scouts reported, they just saw infantry and cavalry," Fannin replied hesitantly, perhaps remembering how reliable their previous reports had been. Then he brightened, "I am damn glad I insisted on taking all our cannon with us now, we would not have wanted any of those to fall in their hands. Don't worry, Mr Flashman," the young man favoured me with a grin that looked more like a grimace, "even if they do have some reinforcements arriving tomorrow, with luck so will we. There are bound to be men waiting for us at Victoria. General Houston will not let us down."

I did not reply, for I remembered men saying the exact same thing at the Alamo. They had expected Houston to bring the promised reinforcements from San Felipe and Fannin to bring the men from Goliad. They had both let us down then and I was not putting too much hope in them now. Mind you, in the two hours before sunset, the Mexicans did launch some more concerted attacks as though they were trying to finish us off after all.

The lancers, who had stayed out on the prairie after their first abortive attack, decided to try again as infantry half-heartedly assaulted the other sides of the square. We watched as they formed line and our surviving gunners rushed to load the cannon on the corners they would be facing. Bugles rang out and once more they came roaring in, their lance points glistening in the late afternoon sun. This time we did not wait for a massed volley. First the rifles began to crack; galloping horses were a harder target to aim at, but some mounts and riders went down. Then the cannon roared out and two holes appeared in their line. Still the horsemen came thundering on while our gunners frantically tried to dry sponge the barrel in case they had to reload. Finally, the more numerous muskets started to crackle a carefully aimed fire. I remember a man called Duval rushing to the front with a huge blunderbuss he may have made himself. He had boasted that it was loaded with forty blue whistlers, whatever the hell *they* were. He had been saving it for when we were in desperate straits and this, he judged, was the moment. I watched as he took careful aim and then fired. We will never know what his 'whistlers' did to the enemy, but the recoil from his mighty weapon sent him catapulting backwards, head over heels through the two ranks standing behind him. They all picked themselves up and, like the men around them, squinted through the smoke for a target for their second musket. For some it was too late to find one as, mercifully, once more the horsemen could be seen wheeling away. They were short a fair few of their number with others hunched over or being held in the saddle by their comrades, clearly wounded.

As the sun started to go down there were still companies of Mexican infantry facing each side of our square. With reinforcements that had arrived during the day, they did not seem any smaller than those that had faced us at the start of the afternoon. Yet the screams and wails of wounded in the long grass were evidence that they had lost many of their number.

The Mexicans sent pairs of unarmed men out into the prairie to try and find and collect their wounded. We let them search in peace. Clearly, not all of those in the long grass were benign, though, as the Indians continued to take pot-shots at us. I think they caused more casualties than anyone else. The Mexican gunpowder was poor quality and their soldiers fired wildly and usually from long range. Nearly all of us had been hit by spent musket balls during the day. I had a round bruise on my shoulder from one, but had it been fired properly I may well have lost the arm. The Indians had better powder and got in close, so their shots did much more damage. Eventually they got Fannin.

I suppose it had only been a matter of time as his uniform clearly identified him as a leader of our little army. He was also continually patrolling around the ranks of his men instead of staying in the centre of the square. He was fortunate that they only managed to shoot him in the thigh, missing the bone. He was dragged ashen-faced back amongst the carts, where his wound was bandaged to stop the bleeding. He refused to stay there. With the aid of a stick he was soon back on his feet, if limping badly and once more among his men.

As evening drew on it became clear that there would be no further attacks during the night. The Mexicans had taken far more punishment than us and had marched and charged about more. Their men needed time to recover. We watched as the surrounding companies threw out a line of pickets to ensure we did not try to escape. Then the rest settled down to bivouac for the night. The surviving lancers and dragoons combined and placed themselves to cover that tantalising one-mile gap between us and Coleto Creek.

With at last some time to rest, we also began to take stock of our own position. Most of the men slumped down where they had fought. They sat largely in silence as they considered what had happened since we had left the stout walls of Fort Defiance and what the morrow might bring. During the day we had lost nine men killed and fifty-one wounded. Some of the injured, like Fannin, were still on their feet, but those with severe injuries were stretched out on or under carts. Many were gasping and groaning in pain and calling out for water. I doubt that there was a single cup of that precious liquid left within the square. We tried to ignore the unanswerable pleas for help from the loudest of the wounded and looked for things to do. Men began cleaning weapons or sharpening knives, anything to take their minds off their own thirst and hunger.

The unwounded gunners used knives and bayonets to try and scrape away at the powder deposits in their cannon. The only reason that the muskets and rifles were not similarly fouled was that soldiers had used the old trick of pissing down their barrels to clean them. But with no water and all of us now parched with thirst, this option would be less available the next day. It was going to be another cold night so a group of men succeeded in lighting a small fire, which sputtered for a few minutes before some old-timer stamped it out.

"Bloody fools," he roared at them. "The grass is covered in spilt powder and that wagon you are leaning against is full of ammunition. One spark gets in there and we are all blown to eternity."

The men glared at him resentfully, one had already started hacking at a dead ox for some meat to roast, but they could see the sense of what he said. We were all set for a hungry night. I looked inside the ammunition cart and could see that over half of the boxes of cartridges had been used. With men firing several guns at a time and numerous charges to fend off, we had got through a lot of ammunition. If there were no reinforcements the next day, we would need to be more sparing.

Surprisingly, as it got darker it became easier to drive the Indians off. In daylight they would fire and roll away. It would take a second or two for the musket smoke to appear above the prairie and often the shots fired in that direction missed their target. Yet at night the muzzle flash of the Indian guns gave them away instantly and alert riflemen in our ranks had much more success in stopping them for good.

While there was still a glimmer of light in the sky Fannin had someone help lift him onto a wagon and then he called out to his command. He explained that while he hoped for reinforcements in the morning, there was no guarantee that Horton had managed to get through to Victoria or that Houston or any of his command were there to come to our aid. "I know that a lot of you think that a break out at night is your best chance of reaching Coleto Creek and perhaps escaping beyond that," he continued. "That will mean leaving the slow and the wounded here. As I will be one of the men left behind, I don't think it is right for me to say what we should do. You should have a vote so everyone gets their say. If you decide to leave tonight, you go with my blessing."

It was a noble speech and I think genuinely meant. But these men had been garrisoned together for a while, some like Shackelford's company had all come from the same town or area. Most had friends or even relatives among the injured. You would have to be a complete heel to run out on over fifty other wounded comrades after an appeal like that. The grumbling stopped and the men voted unanimously to stay. Well, perhaps not entirely unanimously, for the said 'heel' kept quiet; he intended to desert his comrades as soon as it was dark. I had left it too late to make a run for it at the Alamo, with almost disastrous consequences. I was not making that mistake again.

If the day had been grim, the following one promised to be even worse and I could see our group slowly being whittled down to nothing. If everyone else was staying that meant that I could make directly for Coleto Creek, which was the shortest distance to cover. If I had any spit left, I would have been drooling at the prospect of sinking my face into the running water and drinking my fill. I still had to get past the pickets and the horsemen, but I fancied my chances. My days of learning to stalk with the Iroquois had not been wasted. I could move quietly and thought that I would hear the Mexicans before they had a chance to hear me. I just had to pick the right moment to make my move.

Even at night the Mexicans gave us no peace. There had been bugle calls, which at first we thought might signal the arrival of the Victoria reinforcements. I waited to see if it was necessary to escape at all until more bugles from the opposite direction revealed that the Mexicans were simply mocking us. There was still the occasional sharp shooting from the grass, which kept us awake, but from further back now as the Indians had learned their lesson about getting too close. There would be a flash of flame in the darkness, followed by the crack of a musket and a ball thudding into a wagon or whizzing overhead. Often a rifle would shoot in reply, but we knew that the sharpshooter would already be rolling away. Few men were hit now – the Indians must have been firing blindly – as most of our men were either lying or sitting in the long grass, making a smaller target. But every once in a while we would hear a sudden shout of pain.

I went to the north face of the square and stared into the darkness trying to make out the shadows of the distant trees. There was hardly any light now. Low cloud covered the sky. In fact it had just started to drizzle. It was enough to make your clothes damp, but not enough to fill buckets and give us a drink. Few paid me any attention as most were intent on trying to doze and get some rest. I looked around at their faces and wondered what would happen to them. More, I thought, would die in the morning as their defences gradually weakened. I felt sorry for them, but I did not feel any guilt as I stared back out into the prairie. I had done my bit, albeit reluctantly, for the cause back at the Alamo and I had accounted for a Mexican or two that afternoon as well. I did not want to own hundreds of acres of Texas prairie like them, I just wanted to get back to New York for Louisa and then go home to England.

193

"I think I see something out there," I murmured. With that I pulled off my blanket and stepped out into the night. Nobody paid me any attention. Perhaps they thought I was going for a shit in the grass like several before me. Ten paces and I could see nothing of the lines behind me; only the loud snoring of one soldier gave any indication that they were there at all. I was free. All I had to do now was move quietly between any infantry pickets, then avoid their cavalry and I would be safe.

Another ten paces and then twenty, my ears straining for any sound of men moving in the wet grass ahead of me. All I could hear above a gentle breeze now was the distant snoring behind me. The man sounded like a carpenter, slowly sawing wood, with the occasional grunt and snort, but for me it was a welcome beacon. I pressed on; the Mexican pickets had to be out here somewhere. I needed to know when I was through their line as then I would be able to move faster. There was a chuckle of laughter off to my left and I froze. I could barely see a hand in front of my face now, but would they somehow sense I was there? I crept cautiously forward, half crouched in the long grass. They were Mexicans all right, for now I could hear them talking quietly in Spanish. "Did you see that one Chico hit? The rebel was only winged, despite what he says."

How I did not piss myself with fright in the next moment, I will never know. For a voice replied from just inches beyond my left toe. "Lying bastards," the man growled. "He dropped faster than a man on the gallows and was just as dead when he reached the ground." Then he sniffed the air, "You smell something?"

I swallowed back the whimper of terror that had gathered in my throat. Then I thanked my stars that my muscles were already tense, so I had not jumped at the shock. I did not dare breathe, but very slowly eased my left boot back. I was close enough to hear the man rub a stubbly chin. He was still relaxed, and there was no hint of suspicion even if he had smelt me or my clothes. In fact, he yawned loudly and I used the noise to hide moving my right boot back after my left. It took me five minutes to get away from that soldier. I tried to time my movements with gusts of wind that swirled around the hollow we were in. Eventually, I was far enough away to walk normally. I dared not run yet, though, as there was still cavalry beyond the pickets. The last thing I needed now was to blunder into a lancer. I could no longer hear any snoring – perhaps he was too far away or one of his comrades had kicked him to turn him over. But there was an incline now to guide me and I knew we were at the bottom of the hill. If I kept climbing, I would be going the right way.

The drizzle was getting thicker, but I did not care, for it gave me more cover. My buckskins were soon soaked and sticking to my legs as I walked through the long, wet grass. I heard the horse when it was still some distance away and grinned with relief. It was over to my right and so I turned to my left. I had only gone a hundred yards when I heard more distant voices ahead of me. This time I went to my right, aiming between them as I continued to climb the slope. I started to count my paces, first a hundred and then two hundred. Surely I was through the Mexican lines by now?

The ground was flattening out so I thought I must be at the top of the small rise halfway between the square and Coleto Creek. My throat felt as rough as a blacksmith's file. It was painful to swallow and I felt light-headed from thirst. I could almost visualise the creek ahead of me, full of cool flowing water. I just wished I could have a drink to help me on my way. It was as I pulled my wet leggings away from my skin that I had the idea. The standing grass all about me was soaked with rain, all I needed was the means to collect it. I pulled off my large linen neckerchief. Holding it by two corners, I swept it in an arc through the grass. In a matter of seconds it was sodden. Then I put my head back and wrung out the precious water over my mouth. It was barely more than a thimble full, but that was a thimble full more water than I had sipped in many hours. I greedily unfurled the cloth and brushed it through more fresh grass. Half a cupful, I decided, would sustain me for the rest of my journey and then I would drink my fill from the creek.

I must have swept that cloth around in the grass for ten minutes until I had drunk enough to swallow without it hurting. My face was split into a grin for I had made it through Mexican lines. I was refreshed from the rain and soon I would be in the shelter of the trees. I would lie low there during the day while the enemy concentrated their attention on Fannin. It would be too dangerous to travel when the sun was up and I could not risk a cavalry patrol spotting me out on the prairie. Any scouts sent out to keep an eye on Victoria would see me in the open; I would have nowhere to run.

If the Mexicans were victorious, I would move north the following night. On the other hand, if our reinforcements did come and drove the enemy back, I could always claim I had gone out looking for them to guide our rescuers to us. For once, things were finally going my way. I believe I even ran a little down the slope towards the distant creek, just half a mile to go to safety and sustenance. Oh, I felt sorry for the poor devils I had left behind, but they had brought this situation upon themselves with their incessant delays. I did not fancy their chances the next day, for I knew what happened to people who pin their hopes on reinforcements. The Mexicans had been deliberately killing gunners and oxen. I had a nasty feeling that the Texians were not the only ones hoping for more men to join them.

There was a noise ahead – was it the bubble of the creek? I could not help it, I broke into a run, grinning in delight as I pictured my destination ahead of me. Then I heard the sound once more and I came to a stumbling stop, half in horror and half in disbelief.

"There is someone out there," called a voice in English in front of me. "Come forward or I will shoot your fool head off." Then there was that awful sound again and the voice continued, "Ned, will you lay off your damn snoring? It's worse than a bear in a bog."

Chapter 24

I still don't quite understand how I ended up back where I started. I can only assume that I lost my bearings when I was sweeping my kerchief around for water and came back down the wrong side of the slope. It was nothing short of a miracle that I had not found the Mexican pickets first, for I think I had been humming a tune some of the way and was completely careless of the need for caution. Not that I appreciated my good fortune then, of course. For as I identified myself to the sentry and staggered forward back into the square, my face must have been a picture of bewildered frustration. I had been gone for well over an hour and they thought me quite the intrepid scout. I somehow mustered a grin and with a vague reference to my stalking days with the Iroquois, I gave a report of what I had seen. I did not have the heart to try again. I had been deuced fortunate to get through the Mexican lines the first time, never mind my casual jaunt through them on the way back. I thought I would be pressing my luck to make a third attempt.

I had been up early the previous morning, thinking that we would depart at dawn. It must then have been well past midnight. I was exhausted and so settled myself down in the now flattened grass around the wagons and waited for sleep to come. It arrived more slowly for me than for the snoring Ned. I lay there listening to his growl, interspersed with the occasional cry from the wounded and wondered what the next day would bring.

I felt like I had barely slept at all before Fannin had us roused again at sun-up in case the Mexicans launched an early assault. The cold and damp during the night had caused a low mist to form in the valley bottom. We stood bleary-eyed in our lines and I felt a chill that was not entirely due to the weather. There was a nasty air of anticipation too and I began to curse my stupidity of the night before.

To the Mexicans we must have looked like rows of disembodied heads, as the fog only came up to our chests. I even considered crawling away through the fog, but already the sun was rising and I knew that its heat would soon burn off the mist. Blundering around blindly in the prairie, the chances were the fog would lift just as I was under the nose of a lancer. They had taken too many casualties yesterday to miss the chance of skewering one of their enemies. Instead I joined the men in the north face of the square, who stared hopefully in that direction for any sign of reinforcements coming from Victoria. They reminded me of the soldiers who had gravitated to the east wall at the Alamo to look for promised aid. They were to be equally disappointed.

Happily, there was no sign of a Mexican attack either. We watched the bodies of horses and their riders move like ships over the ground, their legs invisible in the mist. The heads and shakos of soldiers could also be seen, but not moving in any haste. We had not been shot at for a while. I guessed that anyone creeping through the grass would be blind as to where we were until they were right on top of us. Stomachs rumbled as men missed their breakfasts, while others complained that the powder of their cartridges would be getting damp in the fog. Both were drowned out by the sound of gunners once again scraping at the inside of the cannon barrels to remove the fouling. There was also the noise of a couple of men hammering as they tried to improve a new barricade around our square.

Evidently, while I had been running blindly about the countryside, some of my fellow defenders had been busy. The broken carts that we could no longer take with us had been dismantled along with empty ammunition boxes and anything else that could be spared. It was all piled around us to make some form of barrier, and to it the bodies of the dead oxen, which had been dragged out of the square to help fill the gaps, had been added. One group of men had even tried excavating a well, but the hole had remained stubbornly dry. Others had started to dig trenches to shoot from, piling the earth as a rampart in front of them. It was not a solid structure all around us, however, in parts there were big gaps. The barricade would do little to stop a Mexican charge, but it might give our riflemen some cover and forestall some of their sharpshooters.

A few grumbled that we should have stayed behind the three-foot-thick stone walls of the Goliad fort, but it was pointless talking about the past. We would have been just as trapped there. Our only hope had been to move north. As the sun rose, I thought it promised to be a grim day. The pitiable groaning from the wounded seemed a harbinger of what was to come. I think we all wondered how many of us would be laid out on that bloody patch of grass in the centre of the square before the day was out.

As the sun climbed into the sky and burned off the morning mist, the reason for the lack of haste among the Mexican forces was revealed. There on the top of the rise overlooking our square was a man on horseback with enough gold braid to be their general. Beside him, as he surveyed us, were two small bronze cannon and a stubby howitzer. It was the thing I had most feared seeing: while men in square can fight off horsemen and infantry, they are horribly vulnerable to cannon. A single ball can smash through the tightly packed ranks, killing and wounding many. I was appalled at the prospect as memories of being in other squares came to mind. But the situation was even worse than we feared. Beyond the guns we could see yet more fresh infantry arriving. Bloody hundreds of them.

The Mexican general was clearly in no hurry. He wanted us to see how hopeless our position was. The fresh troops were directed to take up positions around our square and I estimated that with the men already there, the Mexican force must be approaching a thousand men. Against that, we only had around two hundred and fifty men left who were fit to fight. I saw Fannin talking to our surviving gunners and could guess what they were telling him. Without water, they would only be able to fire a few balls before their guns jammed. It was also much harder to hit an enemy when firing uphill. The Mexican balls would bounce down through our ranks with ease. Once the howitzer got the range, it could lob exploding shells right into the centre of our square with devastating effect.

Our plight was now truly desperate. Fannin had no battle experience so I started to make my way across the square to stop the fool doing anything stupid, but I was too late. He had seemed worried as he turned away from his surviving gunners, but then he stared at his command, who were now looking expectantly in his direction. This, he must have thought, was the moment to demonstrate the leadership he had learned about at West Point. I saw his chin tilt up defiantly.

"We know what they did to our men at the Alamo and at San Patricio," he shouted. "They executed them without pity. I would rather die fighting than be shot like a dog." There were some rumbles of agreement.

"With respect, sir," I countered, trying to interrupt him before they all committed themselves to some suicidal action, "I rather think that we should at least explore if terms are available before we decide what to do next." I expected to be shouted down by the Texians. They had been bristling for a battle all along and had held their own the previous day. None of them could have had experience of an artillery bombardment, but to my surprise there were murmurs of support.

"We won't stand a chance if we stay and fight," agreed one of the company commanders. The man stared about him, clearly calculating the rising odds against us. "They will pulverise us with them cannon," he continued, "and we will not be able to do a thing in return. It is death for certain if we do not try to seek terms. If we save them the trouble of fighting us, they may give us an honourable surrender and keep us as prisoners or even parole us." That brought yet more agreement from the garrison of Goliad, with shouts of, "Damn right," and "you tell him." I was relieved that far fewer than I feared were in the mood for a glorious, but completely pointless death. The commander certainly got my vote, for parole would suit me very well: I had no wish to fight for Texas ever again. Whether the Mexicans would be that generous, of course, was another matter entirely.

The debate was roundly interrupted when the Mexican general ordered his guns to fire. The first ball pitched down the slope, bounced twice and then buried itself in a dead ox, releasing a malodorous stench as the beast's guts were torn open. The second whistled high over our heads to disappear in the grass while the howitzer shell landed just beyond the south side of the square, which was peppered with sods of earth from the resulting explosion. I'll swear that every single one of us must have been thinking that it would not be long before their barrels warmed up and the gunners got the right range.

200

There was quiet for a moment – I noticed that the Mexican gunners were not even reloading. The general had sent that salvo as a demonstration and I wondered if they had deliberately shot wide.

Fannin must have sensed that he had misjudged the mood of his command, for now he asked quietly, "Does anyone here *not* want me to try and seek terms?" There were a few mutters of discontent and a man near me murmured that he "did not trust those bastards one inch," but no one raised their voice to formally object. The decision was unanimous: we would all rather take our chances of quarter from the enemy than face certain death.

A white flag was soon waving over our ranks. It was immediately answered with another, raised by one of the gunners standing by the Mexican general. They had it ready, clearly expecting our decision. The general had known before we did that we really had no choice.

A few minutes later three Mexican colonels walked down the slope towards us holding the white flag. They stopped halfway down and waited patiently for our representatives to join them. Having agreed a truce, it took rather longer to decide on who would be in the parley. The militia commanders did not trust Fannin to go alone, perhaps because he had not wanted to surrender in the first place. Eventually, three company officers were selected, none of whom spoke Spanish and they then set about drawing up a list of their demands. They would insist on an honourable surrender, on keeping their personal possessions and being paroled to the United States. If they could pull all that off, I thought, it would be brandy and cigars all round, for we did not seem to be in a position of strength. Several swore that they would not settle for anything less; the known fate of prisoners at San Patricio and the Alamo was fresh in all our minds.

Suitably briefed, our party set off up the slope to meet the Mexicans. I watched them read our demands. Much discussion followed and I learned later that the parley was partly conducted in German as that was the only language that both sides had in common, with terms then being translated into Spanish and English. Twice we watched one of the Mexican colonels climb back up the hill to consult with the Mexican general and come back down with his decision.

Members of our party would also come back and update Fannin. It was clear that the negotiations were a tortuous affair.

When a colonel turned to climb the hill a third time the general lost patience. He descended the slope himself and sent the colonel to summon Fannin from our ranks. The leaders of the opposing sides were clearly going to have to resolve matters themselves. When the larger group met, I saw the Mexican general jabbing his finger at Fannin as he made his points and then gesture back at his cannon. It was clear he was spelling out the alternative to an agreement. Eventually, they reached a joint conclusion and the two commanders shook hands. We waited while a document of surrender was drawn up and watched as it was signed by both sides. As the Texian contingent returned to our ranks, everyone studied them for an indication of how closely our demands had been met. To our surprise they were all grinning and were soon shouting out what had been agreed.

"We will be treated as prisoners of war," Fannin called out. "We get to keep our private property and we will be given food and water like their own soldiers. But best of all, we will be paroled within eight days and sent to the United States. There is an American ship that has just arrived at Copano, we will likely be sent back in that." My heart leapt at the news for it was far better than I had been expecting.

"You don't know the name of this American ship, do you?" I asked, wondering if by some miracle it was Vanderbilt back already with supplies.

"No, but they are taking me to see it once we get back to Goliad." Fannin gestured at the Mexican officers climbing back up the slope, "I think General Urrea wants to get rid of us as quickly as possible."

I was entirely in agreement with him there, "You did well to get him to agree to so many demands," I told him. I still could not quite believe that the Mexicans had been so obliging when they had us trapped at their mercy. "I say, these terms they *are* all confirmed in that document the general signed, aren't they?"

For the first time Fannin began to look uneasy. "Well we have had to surrender at the Mexican government's discretion, but the general assured me that the Mexican government had never had a man shot who had trusted to its clemency."

I felt my stomach lurch in alarm, "The six surrendered men I saw Santa Anna have butchered at the Alamo might disagree," I told him, but before we could continue, we were interrupted by an eavesdropper on our conversation.

"Sir, you have not only signed your death warrant but the death warrant for all of us." It was Duval, the man with the blunderbuss, and he looked furious as he continued, "You can give up if you want, but I will never surrender." He stormed off then to harangue his fellows.

"General Urrea has given me his word that he will write to Santa Anna strongly endorsing the terms we have discussed," insisted Fannin defensively. "But he explained that he did not have the authority to grant them himself." He lowered his voice and added, "Between you and me, I think that is one of the reasons he agreed to the prompt parole arrangements. If Santa Anna spends too long considering our appeal, it will be too late for him to act – we will have already sailed." He may well have been right, but I was not sure that this gave me too much comfort. If General Urrea was an honourable man, as Fannin believed, it was clear that even he did not trust his own president to also act in an honourable manner.

The formal surrender process began. We were marched away from the square to surrender our weapons but, true to their word, the Mexicans let us keep our personal property. They even let old Abel Morgan keep his knife when he indicated that without it, he did not have enough teeth left to cut meat. Most were relieved, some even excited at having escaped almost certain death. A few, though, like Duval, were far from happy at the situation. One, a man called Johnson, decided to express his dissatisfaction in spectacular fashion. Having surrendered their weapons, a few men went back to the square where Texians were collecting their possessions in preparation for the march back to Goliad. There were Mexicans there too, exploring the defences that had so brutally rebuffed them, several of whom were smoking cigars. Johnson must have decided that he would stop the Mexicans using our American gunpowder against the remaining forces of Texas. Some saw him toss a lighted cigar into the ammunition wagon. Perhaps he thought he would have time to run before it burnt through the paper of the exposed cartridges, but he was wrong. He was killed instantly as the whole cart exploded in a sheet of flame. The grass around the cart caught fire and now there was the sound of more gunfire as various cartridges, which had been dropped in the battle the previous day exploded, sending balls flying through the air.

Apart from Johnson, several of the wounded were badly burned in the fire. While none of the Mexicans had been hurt, many were furious at the destruction of valuable property they thought had been captured. They felt it breached the goodwill of our surrender. Now instead of providing us with promised water, we were sent on our way, still thirsty and hungry.

"You will march faster to get a drink," one of the guards mocked us, but he was not wrong. While it had taken us a whole morning to get to the battle site the previous day, the thought of drinking our fill from the San Antonio River, had us cover the same distance in little over an hour. The citizens of Goliad who had remained behind crowded to the river bank to watch the spectacle of our return. Just over a day before they had seen us all set off, many spoiling for a fight and confident that they would see off any Mexican pursuers. Now we were back, unarmed, conquered and splashing into the water in our desperation for a drink.

Once we had gulped all we could and refilled our bottles and canteens, we were driven on into the town. For that first night we were kept in the small chapel. While the wounded and stragglers were still out on the prairie, there were over two hundred of us crammed into that building. There was barely room for us all to sit down, never mind stretch out. The guards were less than sympathetic and ignored requests for food. Fannin was not among us; he had been left behind with the wounded along with two of our doctors and some orderlies as well as a few men to dig graves for our dead.

The hours went by but still we were not fed. Some of the Mexican soldiers who looked in on us even tried to steal the blankets that we had brought with us. It was not a promising start to our captivity and already Urrea's assurances began to ring hollow. At least we were dry and with so many tightly packed bodies, we were warm too. It was not until the next evening that we had the first food, a broth with a piece of boiled beef, smaller than a fist, floating in it. Though the men moaned, I doubted that the Mexicans were eating much better themselves, for we had burned all the food stores before we left.

The next day we were moved out of the chapel and into the central courtyard of the fort. This meant that we were no longer warm and dry, but we had room to move. The chapel was to be used as a sickbay for both our wounded and the Mexicans. All of our doctors and orderlies were sent there while we sat out in the cold, wind and often rain. By now our attention was very much focused on the promise that we would be paroled. Many were counting down the hours to the promised eight-day deadline, although I could not see how it could be arranged at such short notice. It seemed I was wrong, for on the day we were moved into the yard, Fannin appeared briefly to announce that he was riding to Copano with a Mexican colonel who spoke English. Their goal was to secure a vessel thought to be there to take us all to the United States.

The arrival of this ship appeared a remarkable coincidence but the cynics, such as I, were soon reassured of its existence when a new group of prisoners arrived the following day. There were eighty of them from Nashville Tennessee, under a Captain Miller. Their timing on joining the war could not have been worse. Their ship had docked at Copano and the men had disembarked and were relaxing and swimming in the sea when the Mexican army arrived. With no weapons to hand, they had little choice but to surrender without a fight. I soon ascertained that the ship was not Vanderbilt's and as far as anyone knew it was still at Copano. More importantly, it was big enough to take us all back to the United States. Some would have to sleep on the decks, but that was a small price to pay

The day after Captain Miller's men arrived, we were joined by yet more prisoners. This time it was the survivors of the Georgian Legion under Colonel Ward and they had a sorry tale to tell. They had managed to escape from Refugio under cover of night and had then spent days evading the Mexicans by moving near the coast through creeks and swamps. It had been tough going with little food and they often could not light fires as the Mexicans were searching for them nearby. Ward had received a message from Fannin that he was heading to Victoria and so the colonel led his men in that direction. When they finally reached the outskirts of the town, they found not Fannin and his party or even the Texian militia that we were supposed to have joined with. Instead the town had been taken by the Mexicans. Tired and hungry they had finally been cornered and like us had chosen to surrender, being offered almost identical terms.

We consoled ourselves that our trials were nearly at an end, for surely soon we would be marched off to the ship. Then, the day after Ward arrived back in Goliad, the orderlies brought news that Fannin was back from the coast. The journey had re-opened the wound on his leg and so he stayed in the chapel. The news he sent back via the doctors was not good. The ship that had brought Miller and his men was no longer at Copano. It had weighed anchor and left before Fannin could reach it. A feeling of despondency spread over the compound as the news quickly circulated among the prisoners. The mood was not helped by a steady shower of rain. Some, however, tried to remain positive.

"General Urrea must have known the Copano ship was there when he offered us the terms," explained Colonel Ward. "That was why he agreed such a short timescale. He was not to know that the American sailors would put to sea again so quickly. There are bound to be other ships; we will just have to wait a bit longer."

He was right, but I could not help musing on what Fannin had said about Urrea wanting us out of the way quickly in case Santa Anna overruled his terms. I remembered all too well the execution of the six prisoners at the Alamo, but strangely it was the sheer number of prisoners at Goliad that gave me comfort.

With Ward and his men back, not to mention the new arrivals under Captain Miller, there were close to five hundred prisoners, nearly all of them recently arrived from the United States. Surely not even Santa Anna would consider executing such a huge number, for there would be an immense outcry from his powerful northern neighbour. Nearly five hundred American families would be left grieving. They would create a storm of anti-Mexican feeling, particularly in the southern states where most of the volunteers came from. Up until now the United States had been studious in its neutrality, refusing to allow bands supporting Texas to be raised in its territory, although a few ignored that law. Such an atrocity could see its tacit support for far more volunteers and military supplies to cross the border, for those wanting to avenge the dead.

Chapter 25

Sunday, the twenty-ninth of March 1836 is not a day I will easily forget. One of the men, a preacher, told me it was Palm Sunday, the one before Easter. That gave me a pang of homesickness as I remembered services in the little local church. The preacher had planned to hold a service himself later that day, but he was not to get the chance. The Mexicans were busier than usual, the little sally port cut within the main gate that only allowed one person in or out at the same time was continually opening and closing. We could hear orders being shouted on the other side of the wall. From what I could make out, it sounded like the Mexicans were planning some sort of parade. Then there were commands for us to form up in ranks.

I cannot recall any fear or trepidation at the time, the immediate thought that occurred to all of us was that another ship had been found. There were exclamations of, "At last!!" and men laughed and joked as they grabbed their possessions and lined up with their fellows. I was just as pleased to depart from that wretched yard as the rest of them. In fact, I was vowing to myself that I would spend the next Palm Sunday safely in Leicestershire.

First, Captain Miller's men were called forward. They were counted and then marched out of the sally port, each stooping his head under the low gateway. The rest of us shifted impatiently, waiting for our turn to leave. Instead, we were reorganised into three long ranks of equal length. While the men were being moved about a Mexican colonel arrived. We had seen him before and he spoke perfect English. He summoned the doctors from the ranks and a handful of their orderlies. There were groans at this, for we knew that the doctors spent much of their time with the Mexican wounded. It looked like they would be kept while the rest of us left. I remember the colonel repeating the name of one orderly who did not step forward. The man was not giving up his place in a ship to look after the injured. Impatiently, the colonel plucked a young Texian from the line to howls of protest and sent him with the others towards the gate as a replacement.

Our guards started to shuffle men about to make the rank lengths equal again after the departures, but I ceased to pay much attention. For coming in through the low gate was the first vision of beauty that I had seen in several weeks. She was a proud piece for she walked with her head high, another woman trailing in her wake. I nudged the man beside me and nodded at her. "Well if she is to be one of our shipmates, I don't mind sharing a berth."

He cackled back, "There will be plenty of Mexicans at the front of that queue. You'll never get near the likes of her."

I thought he was right for she appeared a passionate sort. One of the officers overseeing us had tried to get her to leave. She turned on him with such vigour that the fellow shrank back from the onslaught and allowed her to continue into the courtyard. She stood with her older companion in the middle, surveying us. As I was by chance in the front rank, I returned her inspection with interest. She was an officer's wife if I was a judge, as was the woman beside her, for they were both well dressed in expensive gowns. Her dark eyes blazed at us as she ran her gaze up and down our lines, while many of us did the same to her. Then she pointed to young Ben Hughes, a lad of just fifteen, and two soldiers pulled him from the ranks to stand beside her. There were more groans of protest as it seemed yet another of us was to be detained. "Perhaps she wants the lad to warm her bed, lucky bastard," called a voice from the ranks behind me and there were several more ribald comments.

"Do any of you speak Spanish?" The woman shouted out the question in that language and then looked for a response. I did, of course as did several others, but none of us volunteered; we all wanted to get home too. She watched us impatiently – she must have known that there were some Spanish speakers amongst us. Just then I was distracted by a disturbance at the gate. Several of the townsfolk from Goliad were looking at us through it and soldiers were shouting at them to go away. As one of the women turned to go, I distinctly saw tears on her cheek. She made the mark of the cross in our direction before crossing herself. I felt the first prickle of alarm then. I turned back to the yard to see that the pair of women were trying to detain two other young boys, but their father was with them and protesting that his sons stay with him.

Why were they trying to take the youngest men? I wondered. Even then I did not guess the truth, but I suspected that we were set for a more arduous ordeal than a short march to the coast. The gate had been shut. I looked at the other soldiers around us for some sign that my new fear was justified. Instead of their normal bored demeanour, they were tense and alert. There have been many times in my life when lust has led me astray, but this time I think it saved my life. Had she been some ugly harridan, I may not have been so quick to trust her, but now I found myself calling out, "I speak Spanish."

She looked up at that and gestured for me to step out of the line and join them. I glanced at the officer and he reluctantly agreed. As I approached, I saw the older woman urgently whispering into the younger one's ear while gesturing at me. My pretty new friend nodded in agreement. "Tell him to let his sons come with me," she commanded.

"They are worried that if they go with you, they will not board the ships," I told her. Then I looked her in the eye and added, "Are there any ships?"

"Yes, there are ships, but in different ports. These men will be marched to Matamoros, it will be a long and arduous journey. But if the man lets his sons stay with me, I will put them on the first ships to arrive at Copano or Port Lavaca."

She was a good liar, I'll say that for her. If her companion had not twitched at the explanation, I might have believed it. "Are you sure that they are not being marched all the way to incarceration in Mexico City?" I asked suspiciously, for that was my first thought. It was a journey of nearly a thousand miles and many were likely to die on the way.

"Please, *señor*," she implored me. "Help me take the boys, it will be better for them."

So I did. I took the old man aside and told him her explanation and my fear that they might be marched a whole lot further. I also told him that I thought the woman was genuine in trying to protect his sons. I

210

think he sensed that as well, for he nodded when I had finished and gave his boys a hug each before pushing them towards me.

The woman told me that the Mexicans needed carpenters and we persuaded the guards that two other slightly bewildered young men were in that trade, even though one loudly protested in English that he was a farmer. We might have got more, but an angry captain appeared through the gate and put an end to our recruitment drive. Here was an officer who was not going to be browbeaten by the woman and he kept referring to the orders of a Colonel Portilla. Initially, he wanted us all returned to the ranks, but she hissed furiously at him something I did not catch and eventually he relented. We were all marched to the gate and as I stooped under the low threshold, I was surprised to find most of General Urrea's army waiting outside. Dismounted cavalry troopers were arranged to form three huge pens while beyond them lines of Mexican infantry stretched out of sight.

"What is going on?" I asked once we were outside. "What are these orders of Colonel Portilla?"

She blanched slightly at the mention of the name and then brushed a sergeant aside who had moved forward to drive us into one of the enclosures. "They come with me," she told the man before turning in my direction. "These orders are no longer your concern," she announced, then she frowned. "Your accent is not Mexican, where did you learn Spanish?"

I told her that my mother had been Spanish and that I had also been an officer in the British army in Spain. "So why have you joined the forces invading Mexico?" she demanded.

"I came here with an American just to trade. I wanted no part of the war and certainly do not want to farm here. I have land in England." We were walking briskly through the town and I noticed several of the passers-by watching us with curiosity. "Where are we going?" I asked.

"You are joining Captain Miller's men." She stopped suddenly, grabbed me by the arm and looked into my eyes. "Whatever happens today," she urged, "you must stay with them, your life depends on it." That brought me up sharp. I remember looking back down the street to

211

the cavalry and long lines of infantry. Only then did realisation of what was going to happen sink in.

"Oh God," I gasped. "They are not marching them south, they are going to kill them, aren't they?"

Her gaze dropped and she whispered, "Nobody here wants to. General Urrea has ordered that it should not happen, but the president has overridden him. Colonel Portilla fears he will be killed himself if he disobeys. Colonel Garay and I are trying to save as many as we can."

"But how?" My mind could not get over the sheer scale of it. There were still over four hundred men left in the fortress and I was damn sure that they would not wait patiently for their turn in front of a firing squad. "Why did you not tell us back there?" I pointed back to the now ironically named Fort Defiance. "We could have rushed the gate – at least some might have got away."

"Did you not see the men guarding the gateway?" she demanded. "You would have been stopped and everyone would have been killed. This way at least some will survive." We turned a corner and I saw all of Captain Miller's men sitting out in an orchard on the edge of town. With them were the doctors and orderlies who had volunteered earlier, as well as the one fortunate replacement. Including our group, there would be close to a hundred who had been saved. The officer guarding them clearly knew the woman and smiled in greeting.

"Wait in there with them," she told me, "I must go back and see if I can find more." With that she was gone, and I realised that I did not even know her name.

As we entered the orchard, the guards gave each of us a strip of white sheet. We were told to tie it around our arms and not to take it off under any circumstances. I saw that all of Miller's men were wearing similar armbands and guessed it was the symbol to show that we were to be spared. None of my new companions had any idea what was happening. They were sitting around, talking, laughing, playing cards, apparently without a care in the world. I almost blurted out what the woman had told me, but I still could not quite believe it would happen at all. I had seen mass executions before. In Spain, General

212

Cuesta had shot forty of his soldiers for desertion, but nothing on this scale. I could not see how they could shoot four hundred men without the event turning into a pitched battle.

In the end I decided that it would not serve anything by telling them. They would find out soon enough and there was nothing we could do to stop the bloodshed. Quite the reverse; if they knew, then they were likely to rush to the aid of their comrades, which would almost certainly see more of them killed. Perhaps Colonel Portilla would then decide that no one should be excused execution at all.

I was just pondering the awful horror of it when one of Miller's men came up to me.

"I see you know our guardian angel, then."

"Eh, what's that?" I asked, distracted.

The man leaned against an apple barrel and pointed with his homemade pipe down the hill at the street I had come up. "Francita, the woman who brought you here," he elaborated before puffing on his tobacco.

"You know her?" I asked, surprised.

"I would be missing a hand now if it were not for her," he explained waving his pipe in the air again."

"How?" I asked puzzled. "Who is she?"

"Her name is Francita," he repeated. "Francita Alavez. Her husband is one of the cavalry officers who captured us at Copano." He lowered his voice and added, "The man is a cruel swine if you ask me, but his wife is an angel, pretty as one too," he grinned.

I could not disagree there, yet I was still confused. "But how did she save your hand?"

"When we were captured her husband ordered our hands roped behind our backs and he got his men to tie the knots tight. That was bad enough, but then it rained and the knots got even tighter. We were all in agony, I couldn't feel my fingers at all but Francita heard our moaning. She got her husband to loosen our cords. I think she has been looking after us ever since."

"I believe you are right," I agreed with feeling, looking around at the men sitting under the trees with no idea how fortunate they were.

"Do you think we are going to be put on this ship?" the man asked. "Some reckon as we arrived last, we will be boarded last too." Before I could reply, he looked up and gestured down the road, "Hello, that must be the first of them going."

I turned to see a procession of men headed up by twenty mounted Mexican cavalry coming down the road. Beyond the horses were three files of marching men. The middle one was made up of the Texians, and each was flanked on either side by a Mexican infantryman. It was clear that they still had no idea of their fate, for they were chatting amiably amongst themselves. The father of the two boys spotted his sons in the orchard and was shouting at them what to do if they got to New Orleans before him. Then Shackelford came out of the tent he had been sitting in and called out to the column. His company was among it. The doctor was shouting, calling out to his friends and kin, giving them messages to pass on to his wife as he was sure he would be tending to the Mexican wounded a while longer.

I watched still in partial disbelief as the column reached the road south and turned onto the Matamoros trail. Perhaps this Francita had got it wrong. Perhaps they really were being marched to the southern port. There were bound to be ships they could board there. Then as the last of the men disappeared behind the scrub lining the road, I heard more people shouting from the other side of the orchard. They were pointing north, where another identical column could be seen marching away from us, following the river northwest. While Shackelford had returned to his tent, Ward's men at last started to question and debate what on earth was going on. If the Mexicans were taking Fannin's command to a ship, why were they marching in opposite directions and, still uppermost in their thoughts, when would *they* be allowed to board a vessel too? Soon both groups had disappeared into the countryside and I stood leaning on the fence rail, waiting to see what would happen next.

Twenty minutes later, my worst fears were confirmed when there was the sound of a long stuttering volley from the south. Over half a mile away musket smoke drifted up above the mesquite trees that lined the road. Ward's men all ran to the fence to look. Mercifully, the column was out of view, but now men stared in horror as an awful realisation began to sink in.

"They can't be," gasped the man beside me, still unable to articulate the possibility. As he spoke, we suddenly glimpsed around twenty men running full tilt away from the road as distant screams and shouts carried to us on the wind. The men dashing through the scrub were just dark tiny figures to us, it was impossible to make out uniforms, but no one doubted who they were now. For close on their heels appeared Mexican cavalry. We watched as one raised a sabre above his head. When he passed, his victim had fallen into the dirt.

There were shouts and yells aplenty then, with men cursing, running about and swearing vengeance. Mexican soldiers, who must have been placed ready, rushed up to the fence to keep us in the orchard, but no one tried to leave, for it was too late. The noise was so loud that we almost did not hear a similar volley coming from the northeast where we had seen the second column go. I remember sinking my head into my hands, horrified at the scale of the slaughter. Then when I looked up again, I saw Shackelford. In all my life I don't think I have ever seen a man look more stricken. He was staring to the south where he now knew his son, two nephews and nearly sixty other friends from his town were either dead or dying. He had raised the company and brought them there. You could tell he was not only picturing the fallen, but the widows and fatherless children that had now been left behind. If ever a man was inconsolable, it was he.

Beyond him I saw Francita and the English-speaking colonel rushing into the orchard, they had with them two more of Fannin's men that they had saved. The pair had been beaten from the look of them and stared about bewildered, but at least they were alive. The colonel was immediately surrounded by angry men, demanding to know what was going on even though it was now obvious.

"Gentlemen," he shouted and waited for some silence to fall. "It is my deep regret to inform you that the men who took up arms against the forces of Mexico are being executed."

There was a roar of rage at this confirmation and then one of the orderlies pushed his way forward and shouted, "But what about the terms of our surrender? You promised to put us on a ship."

"I can assure you that the orders did not come from any officers here or from General Urrea," the colonel stated sadly. He gestured to Francita and added, "We have tried to save as many of you as we could, but the instruction came directly from President Santa Anna."

The anger dissipated immediately, for we all knew that we owed our own lives to these extraordinary individuals. At the same time, I suspect in every heart there grew a burning hatred of *el Presidente*. I know it did in mine. As you know, I do not get ardent about much beyond saving my own precious skin, but I'll admit that I gave a silent prayer that I would get the opportunity to settle the score. Not just for the Goliad men, who I had only known for a couple of weeks, but also for Crockett, Bowie, Travis, Martin, Bonham and all those other brave men at the Alamo.

As I fumed and swore vengeance, the colonel spotted Shackelford, now kneeling and weeping on the ground. The Mexican gently helped him to his feet and steered him back towards the tent. I heard him explaining to Francita that Shackelford's son was among the fallen. She threw up at that, demanding to know why he had not told her before and swearing that she would have got him out too.

If we thought that the horror of that morning was over, we were wrong. For a while later we heard more shooting, this time from the fort. It was just two or three muskets being fired at a time and only every couple of minutes. For a while we were puzzled and then one of the orderlies announced, "They must be shooting the wounded." Given the number butchered already it might sound strange, but that thought made us angrier than ever. What kind of creature could shoot a wounded man lying on a stretcher?

We sat there now in almost total silence as we pondered the twists of fate that had brought us to that green orchard surrounded in bloodshed. I noticed that as the distant shots rang out now, men would flinch as they imagined the slaughter they could not see, or perhaps thought about how their time would come. The colonel had assured us

216

all that we would be safe as long as we stayed there and wore the white armbands. Yet as one of the orderlies reminded us, "We have heard such promises before, haven't we."

That afternoon two of the doctors and the orderlies were marched back to the chapel to look after the Mexican wounded and two of Fannin's men who had miraculously survived. Shackelford was excused, they must have been worried that he would run amok and murder the lot of them. No one in that orchard would have blamed him if he had. While they were gone, a steady stream of Mexican soldiers and their camp followers walked back into town after completing their grisly work. Many of them looked shaken and I saw a couple weeping. Others did not look the slightest bit remorseful; they were laden with bundles of clothes, some still bloodstained, and other loot that they had pillaged from our dead. I well remember one old crone holding up a silver watch she had plundered and shouting to us in Spanish that we would be next.

In the evening the doctors and orderlies returned. To our surprise there were three extra orderlies including old Abel Morgan. He had seen the wounded being blindfolded and shot at close range. He owed his survival to a Mexican officer, who had spared him, as most of the other orderlies on duty that morning had been shot along with their patients. They also brought with them news of Fannin. After virtually all of his command had been executed, he too was dragged off his bed and taken out into the yard, where the corpses of the other wounded still lay. He was told that he too was to be killed. According to the man who saw it, he took the news well; he would have heard the volleys and been expecting it. He still struggled to stand and so was led to a chair in a corner of the yard. Then he was blindfolded and shot in the face. The largest army Texas possessed, had just been utterly destroyed.

Chapter 26

None of us in that orchard slept much during the night after the massacre. Some prayed, some wept and others cursed and swore vengeance. For my part, a cold anger built in my heart for the man responsible to burn in hell. The following morning, the Mexicans brought us the normal pails of beef broth and allowed us to get water, but otherwise left us alone. That suited us as emotions were still raw, with many spoiling for a fight with our captors. Now I just wanted to get away. Our little group was a powder keg, one that could blow up at any moment. The Mexicans had shown just how ruthless they were prepared to be. We had only survived due to the extraordinary goodwill of a few individuals. They could be posted away at any moment, leaving us at the mercy of others. It would only take some reckless act from one of my comrades, such as killing a sentry, for them to reconsider keeping us alive. After the number of murders they had already committed, a few more would make little difference to their conscience.

While the soldiers left us alone that first day, the same could not be said of the local populace. Many of them streamed past the orchard, staring at us like curiosities in a zoo, no doubt wondering what we had done to be still alive. There were men, women and children, even an old Indian chief. I wondered if it was his men who had been such effective killers near the Coleto Creek. Most of the townspeople were friendly. A few wept when they could not see their friends among us, or called out asking about members of the garrison. Some of the soldiers' wives came to jeer at us. Perhaps they had lost husbands in the earlier battles. One old woman from the town came to try and recover unpaid rent on her rooms. She got very short shrift from one of her former tenants!

The following day the Mexican commanders decided to put us to use. The English-speaking colonel arrived with another officer and a group of soldiers. He announced that he wanted a party of men to work in a quarry. If you will pardon the pun, his request was met with stony silence. The colonel assured us that while the men would have to work hard, they would not be shot. "You will all be back in the orchard by the end of the day," he promised.

Twenty soldiers went forward and each grabbed one of the prisoners and brought them to the corner of the orchard by the gate. Then the colonel pointed at me and called me over. His name I had discovered the previous day was Colonel Garay. Francita had introduced us and so he knew I was a translator. "I want you to go with them," he said, "so that the prisoners understand the orders of Lieutenant Montoya." He lowered his voice and added quietly, "Try and ensure that there is no trouble, or it will make life difficult for us all." Then he led me down to the lieutenant. He told the junior officer that I was his interpreter and that I used to be a major in the British army.

Garay must have revealed my old rank in an effort to get the lieutenant to treat me with respect, and indeed it worked, at least until the colonel was out of sight. Then Montoya gave me a nasty smile and revealed, "My father died in Spain because of you British." He gestured at his charges and added, "Tell them that if any of them escape I will shoot you."

I stared at my fellow prisoners. They were all from Miller's company, hard-faced Tennesseans who glared at their captors with looks of unbridled hatred. Most were in their twenties and I guessed that at least half of them had fathers who had fought against the British in the last war. I doubted that my death would prove much of a deterrent. "He says that he does not care what the colonel told you," I announced. "If any of you escape, they will shoot five prisoners." There were growls of suppressed rage at this new perfidy of the Mexicans, which grew louder as the soldiers began to grab their hands and tie them behind their backs.

"Is this really necessary?" I asked as my wrists were wrenched together by rough cord.

Montoya laughed. "Tell them that if I see them trying to escape, I will run them through with my sword," he boasted proudly patting the weapon at his hip. "But if they get away, they will soon wish that I had killed them." He pointed at the surrounding prairie. "If my men could

219

not find you then the Indians would. Then you would take days to die. You would be praying and begging for my sword through your guts then."

With that cheery image in our hearts, we set off. Twenty-one prisoners, the same number of guards and a couple of carts to carry back the stone. I was sure one of the wagons had been in the square at Coleto, for it still had a musket ball embedded in its side. Almost inevitably we had to pass the scene of one of the massacres. The men fell silent as we approached a low mound of bodies piled just a few yards off the side of the road. The Mexicans had tried to burn them, yet had made a poor effort of it. The fire had not been nearly big enough to consume the bodies. Many of the corpses were only blackened by flame and smoke. Some were contorted where muscles had contracted in the heat, but several were still clearly recognisable. It looked like a scene from Dante's Inferno. I think we all muttered a silent prayer then, for it was just by the grace of God and a couple of brave Mexicans that we were not among them.

Even Montoya had the decency to look slightly ashamed of the scene and his soldiers pointedly avoided the eye of their prisoners. Two hundred yards further down the road we found the body of another Texian soldier lying sprawled on the track. He must have tried to make a run for it and, from the look of him, had been lanced for his trouble. Already a coyote or some other creature had eaten their fill from his remains. The lieutenant's horse was skittish at the smell of blood. The officer turned and surveyed his charges. He must have been able to sense the fury rising amongst them. Perhaps he knew that even bound, they were likely to run amok if he expected them to just step around the remains of the young Texian. He looked at me. "Tell them I will untie two men and give them shovels from the cart, so that they can bury your soldier."

Montoya had allowed us to stand at the grave and one of Miller's men recited a short prayer before we moved on. It went unsaid, but we all understood that the prayer covered the larger mass back down the road too. Then the gravediggers were bound again, and once more we hit the trail. It took us more than an hour of hard marching to reach the little quarry. We were driven into its middle with guards standing all around the edge covering us, before we were untied and given picks and shovels. All day we spent hammering at rocks and carrying them to the carts. The Tennessee boys were mostly farmers and used to hard labour. Some were taking out their anger and frustration on the rocks, for they swung the picks with immense strength. I on the other hand was soon exhausted. In my defence, I was at least twenty years older than all of them. I could not remember the last time I had done anything resembling hard labour, unless you count carrying a fat German Frau up the backstairs in a Portobello brothel.

At midday one of the returning wagons brought some pails of the beef broth. While none of us had wanted to eat much the day before, now we were ravenous. But there was little time for rest and soon we were being shouted at to go back to work. A huge fellow paired himself with me in the afternoon. He grinned conspiratorially as he split most of the big rocks and left me with the small ones. Even with this help, I could barely stand by the end of the day. The carts left with the last loads of rock and then once more our hands were tied behind our backs. I could barely feel the pain in my wrists, for my back ached and the muscles across my shoulders burned. We set off with the men from Tennessee even managing a song between them, while it took all my effort to put one foot in front of the other. Soon I was falling behind the rest of the men. Eventually, even the sentry beside me realised that clouting my back with his musket butt was not going to make me go faster. Montoya rode his horse down the line of his command and laughed when he saw me flagging already a hundred yards behind the rest of the men. He must have seen instantly that I was not shamming and took delight in mocking me.

"So, the British major is defeated by a few stones," he laughed. Then he turned to the sentry and added, "Stay with him until he is back in the orchard. This is one who will not run away." As soon as his officer was out of sight and evidently not coming back, the soldier relaxed and allowed me to go at a slower pace. I tried to get him to untie my hands, but he refused, although he did give me some water from his bottle.

We talked and I discovered he was conscripted from a province I had never heard of. I gathered it was to the south as he complained bitterly of the cold in Texas. The man detested the army and could not wait to get back home. I was astonished to learn that he had been taught to shoot from the hip as part of his very rudimentary training. We chatted quite amiably as I staggered along. I deliberately did not ask if he had taken part in the massacre, for I did not want to know. He was a poor man, driven by circumstance. If he had been there, then I sensed he would not have been happy about it. He was just telling me about his son when suddenly he stopped and gave a gasp of pain. I thought he had been bitten or stung by something and I remember looking at the ground for any sign of a snake. He put out his hand and tried to say something and then pitched forward into the dirt.

I had thought I was exhausted, but it turned out I just needed the right incentive. The sight of the feathered arrow sticking out of the Mexican's back, combined with the tales of torture I had heard from Montoya, proved to be sufficient. In an instant I was hurtling off down the track, while bawling for the far distant column to come back and help me. Almost immediately one of the savages stepped out of the scrub in front of me. He was saying something, but I did not listen; all I cared about was that he was too slow to raise his musket. I barrelled into him, sending him flying. I only just managed to stay on my feet and staggered on up the path. I must have gone at least twenty yards, running in a wild blue funk, expecting the toppled man to send a musket ball into my back at any moment, when my brain finally registered what the man had said. He had called my name!

I skidded to a stop and turned around, gaping in astonishment. The man was getting to his feet, making no attempt to raise his weapon. He was only in his twenties and I was sure I had never seen him before. "Who are you?" I asked.

By way of reply he first cocked his head and then gave a strange bird call. "Quickly," he replied. "This way," he gestured into the nearby scrub. "The horseman is returning."

I had no idea who this fellow was, but I had seen what the Mexicans could do and I had no wish to stay with them. The stranger was a real Indian by the look of him and yet he had not killed me when he had had the chance. How the devil he knew my name was beyond me, but working on the adage, 'the enemy of my enemy is my friend', I decided to throw in my lot with this newcomer. I followed him into the low brush surrounding the track.

We crouched and ran twenty yards before he pulled me down to lie prone behind a bush. I sprawled in the dirt and then felt a knife at my wrists as the rope holding them was cut. I lay there aching in pain, rubbing circulation back into my hands, with my mouth open to gasp for breath as quietly as possible. Montoya came into view, glimpsed through the branches of the bushes between us. He had a pistol in one hand as his horse galloped along the trail. He reined in as he must have seen his soldier lying prone in the dirt. The arrow sticking in the back of the corpse was proof that I had not killed him. Montoya stared around for any sign of his missing prisoner. I shrank back, pressing my face into the dirt. I looked up when I heard the click of a well-oiled musket lock, to see my new companion taking aim at the Mexican's back.

"No," I whispered, reaching forward to pull the gun down. I doubted Colonel Portilla would give a fig about some poor conscript, but if he started to lose his officers then he certainly would care. The prisoners' lives were hanging by a thread as it was. With one escaped and a guard dead, I did not want to make it any harder for Colonel Garay to keep a lid on things. Montoya had one final look around. Then he must have decided that he was vulnerable on his own with Indians about. I watched as he urged his horse quickly back up the trail in the direction he had come from.

"Why did you not let me kill him?" asked my companion.

"Because there are another twenty prisoners up the track," I explained. "If their officer is dead and they think they are under Indian attack, the guards might just kill them before rushing back to the fort."

He did not look convinced, but issued another one of his strange bird calls and a moment later another Indian appeared crouching through the bushes, he had a bow in his hand and another arrow ready for use. This must have been the one that had killed the Mexican.

"Who are you? How do you know my name and what do you want?" I demanded.

"Our chief wants to see you," my companion explained simply before getting to his feet. "Come on, this way." That was all the sense I could get from them. At least that one spoke English; the other didn't. They chattered away in their native tongue as they embarked on a fast march over the rough ground. They soon realised that I could not keep up and would turn and wait for me until I reached them. Then they would charge off again. They must have been talking about me as I staggered towards them during their times of rest. Judging from their faces, they were not too impressed with what they saw. Mind you, I could not blame them, for I certainly did not look my best. I had not shaved or changed my clothes since I had been in the Alamo. Only my recent immersions in the San Antonio River had stopped me stinking. My face and clothes must have been covered in a mixture of stone dust and mud from the trail, liberally mixed with sweat from my recent exertions.

Only my desire to get away from the Mexicans kept me going at all. Twice I insisted that we stop for a rest and both times they assured me that their chief was just a short distance away. It was dark when we finally reached their camp, which was hidden in a hollow on the prairie. There must have been around a dozen shadows moving about in the light of a campfire that had been lit between two rudimentary shelters. I was led into the centre of their group and eventually saw the man who had summoned me. It was hard to make out his features in the flickering flames, but I could see he was old with a thick, grey beard.

His dark glittering eyes surveyed me and then a slight smile twitched around his lips. "Do you recognise me?" he asked in English.

"Yes I do," I told him. "You were looking into our orchard yesterday."

The grin broadened. "I was … Little Father."

I gaped at him then, scarcely believing what I had just heard. "No," I gasped, "it can't be." I had not been called 'Little Father' in over twenty years. It was a name given to me by the Iroquois in Canada.

The features widened further into a beaming grin as my new host laughed and replied, "Sit down, Flashman, before you fall down."

"How the devil...?" I started but my old friend John Norton would not answer any questions until I had been given some food and drink, for as he rightly claimed, I looked exhausted.

"You are a hard man to find, Thomas," he explained at length. "But it seems you are a hard man to kill too. The Mexicans stopped us reaching the Alamo, but we camped nearby waiting to see if the Texian forces would relieve the siege. When the place fell we thought you had died with the rest. We even did our grieving ceremony for you. We had just turned back when we came across a man who was fleeing from Goliad. He told us that the Mexicans were closing in there too, but more interestingly he said that they knew the Alamo had fallen as a British soldier had brought the news. I could not go back to my home without making sure that it was not you. So we turned again and headed to Goliad, only to discover that the garrison there had been captured and shot, too, the day before we arrived. Then we heard that there had been some survivors. That was why I went to the orchard to see if I could find you there."

"Why didn't you say something at the orchard?"

"The Mexicans were watching you all closely. The guards informed us that you would soon be put to work and so I had some of my men keep an eye on you to see if they could break you out." He was interrupted by a commotion among his young warriors. The one with the bow and arrow was running around, crouched down with his hands behind his back and yelling loudly as he shoulder-charged his friend, knocking him down. They were evidently recreating the moment of my capture and the other warriors were roaring with laughter. "They are calling you Runs-like-Buffalo," Norton informed me, smiling.

"Well their appearance was something of a surprise," I admitted, "especially when one spoke to me in English and knew my name."

"That is my son. He is called Hamish after an old friend back home."

225

"Hamish Norton," I chuckled. "Well there cannot be many Indians called that. I thought you would have been with your father's people now, the Cherokee?"

"I was for a while, but Hamish's mother is a Coushatta." He saw my puzzlement and added, "It is a much smaller tribe, but they have several settlements to the north and south of here."

"Can you help me go north?" I asked, suddenly feeling hope soaring in me again. "I need to get back into the United States, and then to New York. My wife is waiting for me there."

"Ah yes, I remember that when we were last together you had just found out that *you* had a son. He must be a grown man now."

"He is and I have a daughter too." I paused for a moment at the thought of them both. "So, could you help me travel north?"

"Of course. I did not go to all this trouble to find you, just to let the Mexicans have another go at killing you. But first you must tell me everything that has happened to you since our time in Canada. My life here is very dull and I remember that you had many stories to tell before. I suspect that you have even more now.

I grinned, "My old friend, it will be a very long night if I do that."

"Then," he said reaching into a leather bag by his side, "I will give you this to sustain you." He passed across a bottle of 'French' brandy with a very familiar label. I took a swig and it was a strange thing: after forced marches and rock breaking, escaping massacres, hopeless battles and fleeing slaughter, it did not taste nearly as bad as I remembered.

"Well," I started, "I am not sure where to begin. Have you heard of a battle called Waterloo?"

Chapter 27

While Norton claimed he had rescued me so that the Mexicans would not have another go at killing me, almost one of the first things he did was to give them another chance, although the odds were not in their favour. I had talked for much of that first night before falling asleep by the fire. The sun was high in the sky when I awoke and after the recent days it was a relief to remember that I was now at liberty again. While I had dozed, Norton had been preparing for my journey north. His son Hamish was to accompany me, for I would need a guide and Norton himself was too old to travel quickly.

"Santa Anna's army must be moving north by now," he told me. "And the Mexicans on the coast will be heading north too now that they have beaten your army. There will be nothing to stop him recapturing all of Texas."

"We heard General Houston was raising a new army," I told him. "It was supposed to be at Gonzalez. He may have a few hundred men."

Norton scoffed. "Santa Anna had at least a thousand men marching to him as reinforcements after the Alamo fell, we saw them. They boasted there were even more on the road behind. How many soldiers did he have left after the battle?"

"Well over a thousand," I admitted.

"And the general coming up the coast, he has at least a thousand men. So the Mexicans have at least three thousand to your few hundred. The Texas forces cannot win."

I was sure then that he was right, for I recalled that when we had been in San Antonio, Bowie and Travis were receiving reports that the total size of Santa Anna's army was around five thousand men. There could have been another sizeable column of them somewhere we were not even aware of. Some of them died at the Alamo and Coleto, but it was still hard to see the forces of Texas beating odds of ten to one. The Texians might have their rifles, but I doubted that they had any cannon left now. In contrast, the Mexicans had a whole park of artillery, with the guns they had brought with them as well as the ones they had captured.

I shuddered at the thought of being seized by them again. The sooner I was safely back over the border in Louisiana the better I would like it. I remembered the look of fear on the faces of the locals at Goliad when they came to see us in the orchard. Both the Tejanos and the few Texian civilians who were left there looked frightened and cowed by the recent slaughter. It was clear now what would happen to anyone who took up arms against Santa Anna. I wondered if Houston's army had stood firm or if that had melted away. I could hardly blame them if they deserted the cause, for that was my intention too, but it would be a dangerous journey. Apart from avoiding Mexican patrols and armies on the move, I would also need to be wary around civilians. There were bound to be a few willing to turn me in to prove their loyalty to the new government, or as a means of getting clemency for someone else.

From where we were, it was three hundred miles to Louisiana. To get there, I would need to get around the Mexican army and anything that was left of the Texian one. In addition I had avoid the more hostile Indians and assorted banditry on the roads and be wary of anyone else I met on the way. I thought I would be glad of Hamish's company; he seemed a resourceful young man.

"We will need horses," he announced when the venture was put to him. I was in full agreement there, as the ability to ride away from trouble would be invaluable. I might have been able to cover three hundred miles in a couple of weeks in my youth, but that was in an army with someone else looking after supplies. I doubted if I could do it in three or four weeks now, especially as we would have to detour around enemies and obstacles and find our own food. The obvious problem, though, was that Norton's band did not have any mounts at all. Hamish proposed to solve this by stealing from the Mexicans, whose cavalry was camped on the outskirts of Goliad. He thought that they could creep in there and cut some out. Having done the same at the Alamo, I was not sure it would be that easy. I had only succeeded because the troopers were too busy celebrating their victory to mount proper pickets. As it turned out, we did not need to worry, for the Mexicans brought the horses to us.

The plan had been for me to rest and recover my strength during my first full day with Norton. Hamish and some of the other warriors would steal horses overnight and we would set off the next morning. I was happy for him to take all the risk and it was good to catch up with my old friend. At worst if things went awry getting the mounts, we could travel north on foot and I could disguise myself as an Indian again. It would not be the first time I had done that. I was dozing in one of the shelters when a bird call had my new companions scurrying about.

"What is it?" I asked, yawning.

"A Mexican patrol," whispered Norton. "Lancers, they must be looking to clear any hostile Indians away so that they can get stone from the quarry again." He clapped me on the shoulder and grinned. "We just need to lure them over here and then those horses are ours."

I got up and went to see for myself. The Indian camp was in the trees next to another small creek that we were using for water. Small pockets of trees dotted the prairie but, looking for Indians, who always preferred to ambush their prey, the lancers were wisely staying well clear and keeping out in the open. There were six of them and I watched as an officer studied another grove of trees with his telescope. I suspected that as soon as they had spotted their quarry, one of the troopers would be despatched to bring some infantry and possibly a cannon, while the rest ensured that we did not make a run for it across the open ground. "Well I don't see how we are going to get them to come close," I murmured.

"That is easy," explained Norton. "We use you."

"What do you mean?" I asked feeling suddenly alarmed.

"They know you were captured by us when we killed your guard. They will think we have held you prisoner ever since. You just need to go out there and shout that you have escaped from us and ask to be taken back to Goliad."

"We should tie his hands so that he is like we found him," added Hamish.

"To hell with that!" I exploded. "I am not going out in front of lancers trussed up like some bloody fowl for the oven, they'll run me through as soon as look at me. Look, surely it would be better to stick to our original plan and go and get some horses after dark."

"No," insisted Norton. "If they ride around the other side of the creek, they will see our shelters and then we will have lost the element of surprise. It would be better for you to attract them. There are only six; we will kill them all if you can get them close enough."

Reluctantly, I agreed, we did not really have a choice. I would not let them tie my hands but had them behind my back as though they were still bound. It was then I discovered that there were only five muskets between them; two of the warriors were using bows and arrows instead. The only weapon they could spare me was a large knife that I hid in the back of my belt. As I walked out into the open prairie my throat was dry, but not due to thirst. This felt a mad venture, reliant on five men hitting each of their fast-moving and mounted targets with notoriously inaccurate muskets. It would only take one of them to miss for me to end up skewered on a twelve-foot steel-tipped pole

"Stagger about, Flashman," hissed Norton. "You have been on the run, remember?"

Obediently, I tottered about as I took a deep breath and yelled for help in Spanish. They heard my distant bellow instantly and I watched as one pointed in my direction. The officer got his glass out to study me and I duly staggered and collapsed down on my knees like an exhausted fugitive. I could hear whispering in the nearby trees as the marksmen argued over the best cover. "Come on, you bastards," I murmured to myself. I have never liked lancers and wanted to touch the scar on my thigh from when I was attacked by the Polish variety in Spain.

If we were hoping that they would trot conveniently up to where I kneeled, we were to be disappointed. Mexican lancers had not got to be their elite horsemen for nothing and they must have been used to avoiding Indian ambushes. Like a pack of wolves they separated, one pair coming straight on, while the other two approached on either flank. Even then they did not ride together; the front horseman was some ten yards in front of the other, who would give him cover. I quickly realised that stealing their mounts would be no easy task.

"Who are you?" shouted the officer who led the central pair. I weakly shouted back something that was deliberately incoherent to get him to come closer. The pair to the officer's left were closest to the trees and while the front man was studying me, his mate was looking carefully at the undergrowth. The Indians should be able to shoot them, I thought, if they were not spotted first. It was the ones to the officer's right who worried me. They were circling around so that I was between them and the Indians. It would take some exceptional shooting to miss me and hit them. "Who are you?" the officer repeated. He was now just fifty yards away, his lance lowered in readiness and this time I did not think I could avoid giving him an answer.

The trouble was I was not sure that the truth in this case would serve. If I told him that I was an escaped American, the chances were that they would just kill me out of hand anyway. I stared down, looking for some inspiration and found the answer right under my nose. I was still wearing the blue coat I had taken at the Alamo. It might be covered in mud and stone dust, but I thought it was still recognisable as Mexican army issue. Surely they would not kill one of their own?

"I am a Mexican soldier," I shouted. "I was with the president at the Alamo, but was sent with supplies to Goliad. We were ambushed by those cursed Indians on the way. Have you found any others from our column?"

I thought that finishing with that question was a convincing touch, but the officer was still suspicious. "How do I know you were at the Alamo? What regiment were you in?"

I had no idea how to answer the second question and so I concentrated on the first. "The invaders used to fire a cannon three times a day, just after dawn, at midday and just before dusk. When we beat the traitors, we piled their bodies into two huge pyres near the south wall."

At last he seemed convinced and, raising his lance point, he trotted his horse forward. "We have not seen anyone else," he told me and then he frowned as he must have remembered that I had still not answered his earlier question. "Are you with the Toluca regiment?" he enquired, casually.

He was only twenty yards off now and I glanced nervously into the trees. Why hadn't they opened fire? "Yes, that's right, I am a sergeant in the Toluca," I replied, thinking that such a rank would explain my greying hair. Too late I realised that the question was a trap. In the blink of the eye the lance was once more at the horizontal. As the officer shouted out a warning to his men, he spurred his horse forward. I was almost mesmerised by the steel lance point hurtling towards my chest. Then I threw myself to one side as everything happened at once.

Gunfire thundered out from the trees just behind me. My eyes locked on the officer charging towards me; he was hit in the chest, his body flung from the saddle while the lance stuck in the grass just a few feet from where I stood. Frantically, I glanced around. The two horsemen to my right were both down, one with his wounded horse on top of him. An Indian ran out with a tomahawk to despatch the rider. The two horsemen to my left, furthest from the ambush, were already wheeling their mounts around and heading back out into the prairie. It was the horseman following the officer who now worried me. He was not wheeling away and showed no sign of being wounded from the recent volley of shots.

Already he was lowering his weapon and he gave a roar as he spurred his mount forward. I knew that to run now would be fatal and so I dropped the knife, which would be useless, and instead picked up the fallen lance. By the time I had got the business end pointing at my assailant he was only ten yards away and closing fast. I pushed the spear out in front of me as far as I could and tried to yell a challenge of my own. It sounded more like a bear being gelded, but while it did not deter the lancer, it did his mount. Horses are not stupid; they will never charge into an infantry square lined with sharp bayonets and this one did not like the look of the lance point aimed at its chest. It whinnied in panic and tried to pull up, and when its rider dug in his heels to urge the creature on, the horse reared up in confusion. The lancer had to pull up his weapon to stay in the saddle and, seeing the opportunity, I charged forward determined to give him a taste of his own medicine. As I ran, I heard a 'zeep' noise over my head and then my prey was falling from the saddle, an arrow embedded deeply in his chest. I just had time to grab the reins of the horse and sooth the animal before it tried to bolt.

In a matter of moments four of the lancers were either dead or soon would be. One of their horses was dying too, but we still had the other three. The two surviving horsemen, having seen the fate of their fellows, wheeled about and headed back to Goliad.

Norton looked up at the sky. "I doubt that they will get any infantry here until early tomorrow, but they will send out patrols looking for you. They will guess that you are heading north. You had better be on your way."

"What about you?" I asked.

Norton grinned, "It was good of them to supply a spare horse for me so I will not slow down the rest of my band. We will head south," he gestured to the creek, "in the stream for a while so that we do not leave a trail for them to follow. We will be long gone by the time they get back." He stepped forward and shook my hand, "It was good to see you again, Thomas. Give my regards to your wife when you see her."

I realised that I had not got around to telling him about George Norton and how his namesake had driven us to leave the country, but there was no time for that now. London felt a lifetime away. Looking across at the rudimentary shelters that they had been living in when I found them, I wondered if he missed his old life. "Why don't you come with us?" I blurted out. "Come with me to Louisiana and then on to New York. I will pay for your passage home and then you can see Dunfermline again."

For a moment he looked wistful as he considered it. He stared across at where two of the women were hastily packing belongings ready to move and then shook his head. "There is nothing for me there anymore," he said quietly. "My place is here now, but look after my boy for me. He is all I have left." He took a deep breath and then

233

forced another smile across his features. "When you get home," he added, "raise a glass of good whisky to my memory."

Chapter 28

We rode hard north for the rest of that afternoon. I was anxious to put as much distance as I could between us and the scene of the ambush. Hamish appeared confident in the saddle, vigilant too.

"There," he pointed to a low ridge across the prairie, "smoke."

By then it was early evening and with the dull grey clouds beyond, I struggled to see anything unusual at first. Then a dark wisp moved on the wind and I made it out too. "Let's head for those trees," I replied, and pointed. "They will give us some cover as we crest the rise." We did not have the time for long detours as their patrols would soon be on our trail. Nevertheless, I had already decided that caution would be our watchword on this journey; by now at least two Mexican armies would be chasing the remnants of the forces of Texas. Like us, the Texians were probably retreating to the United States too. I was determined not to accidentally stumble into their pursuers.

We need not have worried, for the smoke was only coming from burnt and abandoned timbers. They had once been a farmhouse – there were still rail fences around now empty fields. Half a mile beyond the smouldering embers we found traces of who must have put it to the torch and stolen the livestock. A broad expanse of the long prairie grass was flattened where a large force had recently travelled that way. There were deep ruts in the mud where cannon or wagons had been moved and the hoofprints showed that they had been moving from west to east.

"Several hundred men," announced Hamish, but you did not have to be a great tracker to see that. There were patches of burnt ground, some with animal bones still showing where meat had been roasted and the unmistakable stench of uncovered latrines. The campfire ashes were cold and wet, the army must have passed through at least two days previously, but that did not make me feel any more comfortable. We pressed on, anxious to put a few more miles behind us before dark.

Eventually, we were forced to stop ourselves, both horses and riders were exhausted. The mounts were hobbled to graze on the rich pasture while we used the long grass to shield a small fire from any nearby prying eyes. We sat quietly together eating some dried meat. I realised I knew virtually nothing about my companion, who had barely spoken on our journey. I was just opening my mouth to ask who his mother was when he asked me a question of his own.

"Did you think my father would just leave his people to come with you?" He looked at me with suspicion, perhaps wondering why Norton had risked so much to meet someone he had probably never mentioned around their hearth in Laredo. I told him about my time with Norton in Canada and that we had also had a reunion on one of his rare visits back to Britain.

"When we were fighting together," I explained, "the British generals often thought he was too close to the Iroquois, while many of the people in the tribe thought that he was too close to the British. Is he accepted by the Coushatta as one of their people in Mexico?"

Hamish threw another piece of wood onto the fire and hesitated before answering. "We don't live in the main Coushatta territory. That is to the north, on the border of the land claimed as Texas."

"Then why do you live down south?" I pressed.

My companion shrugged, "We run a trading post there. Some Indians distrust my father because they know he is white, but it is easier for him to trade with the Americans and Mexicans."

"What about you? Are you accepted as an Indian?" I asked.

"I live with my father," he stated simply, which was the only answer I was going to get.

We did not see another living soul as we travelled across the wide-open country the next morning. Eventually, our path was blocked by a line of trees and bushes, which turned out to be the bank of a wide but shallow river. Hamish led our horses splashing through the water for a quarter of a mile upstream to try and shake off any Indians that the Mexicans might use to track us. Then we rode up the far bank. The thick pasture would soon hide the footprints of two horses and I thought anyone would struggle to follow our trail. Mind you, I kept a ready eye over my shoulder, for with such little cover we were as easy to spot as a boil on a buttock.

It was the cows we heard first, a deep agonised groan of animals in pain. The sound was coming from behind a stand of trees a quarter of a mile to our front. I felt a prickle of alarm and instinctively felt for the weapons at my belt. I had a pistol and a sword that I had taken from the corpse of the lancer. It looked a peaceful enough scene and I saw some deer grazing near the trees. Surely, they would not be there if the woods were infested with hostile soldiery? Still, there was no point taking chances. I pulled out the gun, cocked it and followed Hamish as he spurred his mount forward. Our horses trotted up the gentle slope and gradually a farmhouse came into view. In front of it was a paddock containing the two cows we had heard. From the look of them, both had udders fit to burst, which was the cause of their moaning. There were chickens and some pigs in view too but no sign of any people. I circled round to the front of the house; a line of washing was still blowing in the breeze and there was an axe embedded in a log next to a half-cut pile of lumber. It looked like a perfectly normal farm but for the absence of its owners. I stared about but could see no sign of anyone all the way to the horizon. Hamish had already dismounted and was striding to the door when it swung open before him in the wind. He took a cursory look inside and then called for me to join him.

"It is empty," he shouted. "They must have left in a hurry." When I entered I found a half-eaten meal still on the table. Judging from the plates, two adults and two children. The loaf of bread in the middle of the abandoned feast was stale on the outside, but when I cut it with the knife lying beside it, the middle was still soft.

"They have only been gone a couple of days at most," I told Hamish.

"At least we will eat well today," he grunted. "I will go and milk those cows."

The cabin had been owned and built by the Cutler family from St Stephens Alabama. I learned this from the family Bible that had been left behind in one of the cupboards of a homemade dresser. There were only two rooms in the little house and the other showed similar signs of a hasty departure: an open trunk half full of clothes and an abandoned rag doll dropped in the middle of the floor. The place was so isolated I wondered if they had even known that a war was underway in the countryside around them. I could easily imagine some public-spirited neighbour galloping out to them with the news that a Mexican army was on the way. They must have learned of the Alamo's fall and perhaps even the massacre at Goliad. The family had not even finished their meal, such was their terror of what was approaching. They seem to have taken barely more than the clothes that they had stood up in. Perhaps they thought that the Mexicans would slaughter them all. Cooking pots and pans lay by the fire, which I soon had ablaze as Hamish brought in buckets of milk and a freshly slaughtered chicken

We did eat well that day as did our horses from hay and grain we found stored in the barn. Every hour either Hamish or I would make our way out of the back of the farm to stand in the trees to the rear. We would study the terrain for any sign of pursuing patrols or the armies that had so terrified the farmer and his family. We could see a fair distance in all directions. Apart from deer, and the cows and pigs that Hamish had turned out of the paddocks to fend for themselves, not a hint of movement was to be seen. It made no sense to leave two comfortable beds unoccupied and so as darkness fell, we slept in the farmhouse.

I remember lying there in that borrowed bed, staring up at the roughly hewn timbers above my head and thinking of the couple who lived there. They must have been like the young families I had shared a ship with across the Atlantic, determined to build a new life for themselves. They had made a good start here, but I wondered if they would come back when the war was over. It looked certain then that after its brief flowering, the country of Texas was finished. I doubted that Santa Anna would make life easy for *norteamericanos* afterwards; he would not want to encourage more settlers who could cause problems again. The family, if they managed to stay ahead of the Mexicans, would probably go back to Alabama or elsewhere in the United States to try and build a new homestead.

We found the first of the refugees the next day when we continued our journey north. They were not the Cutlers; this family had brought some of their livestock with them as they were sure they would not be returning. Three women and twelve children were slowly driving half a dozen cattle on foot alongside a cart loaded with possessions and several cages of poultry. The whole menagerie had scattered at the sight of us, the women shrieking that the Mexicans were here and screaming at the children to run for their lives.

"We are not bloody Mexicans," I had roared back, but my voice was lost under a cacophony of squeals of panic, clucking and baying steers. One boy, no more than eight, came charging towards me, yelling a high-pitched challenge and holding out a sharpened stick like a bayonet. "Put that down," I yelled sternly at him, "or I will tan your backside so hard you will not be able to sit down until next week." He stuttered to a stop, dropped his weapon and promptly burst into tears. That at least convinced the womenfolk that they were not to be butchered on the spot.

It took half an hour to restore some sort of order to the group. The women roamed the prairie trying to persuade terrified children to reveal themselves and return, while Hamish and I did our best to round up the cattle. Eventually, they were settled enough to give us what news they had, not that it was worth much.

"Them Mexicans are marching north with an army of fifty thousand men," the matron in charge of the group informed us. She raised her chin defiantly and added, "They are killin' every white person they find, men, women and chil'en. They don't show no pity for anyone, the murderous heathens." Evidently disappointed in our measured reaction to this catastrophic pronouncement, her eyes narrowed and she asked suspiciously, "Where are you boys from? Why aren't you with the army?"

I was quick to allay any fear that we might have been Mexican spies, or she would have ordered her recently gathered brood back into the prairie. "I was with Colonel Fannin's force at Goliad. He sent me north to find Houston."

"Are they still holding out at Goliad?" the woman pressed. "They murdered every last one of our boys at the Alamo, everyone around here knows that."

"I don't know," I lied. It sounded as though she would be spreading panic wherever she went and news of another massacre would only make things worse. "What about your menfolk and Houston, do you know where they are?"

The woman hawked and spat over the side of the wagon in a very unladylike manner. "Houston is a yella, drunken, Indian-loving bastard," she pronounced with considerable passion. "He took off north with his army as soon as he heard about the Alamo, leavin' us women and chil'en to fend for ourselves. He won't stop until he is safely across the Sabine. I told my Dan to wait for us at Fort Jessup if we aren't all raped and murdered on the way."

"Lyra," admonished one of the other women, "don't talk like that in front of the chil'en."

"What is the Sabine?" I asked, turning to Hamish.

"It is the river marking the boundary between Texas and the United States," he told me. As the woman called Lyra continued to curse and heap scorn on the Texian commander I struggled to suppress a grin. Houston might be despised by the settlers of Texas, but to me he was doing the right thing. Twice now I had seen Texian colonels overestimate their military strength and both times it had ended in bloodshed and disaster. While Lyra's claim of a Mexican army of fifty thousand had to be a wild exaggeration, even a tenth of that figure would be more than a match for the few hundred that Houston might have been able to gather. I suspected that many of those would try to desert him when news of the Goliad massacre reached them. Headlong flight to the border was exactly the right course of action to me.

"Well, ma'am," I interrupted her diatribe on their general, "we must be on our way. Good luck to you on your journey." Hamish and I kicked our horses on into a canter but Lyra had not finished with us yet.

"You tell that no good sonofabitch," she screeched after us, "that we are gonna string him up from a tree when we get our hands on him."

Once we were out of earshot of the harpy I called to my companion, "I think we should ride to join Houston and his army." He looked surprised and so I added, "If they are riding for the United States, we would be safer to join them. Where do you think he is?"

"I don't know, but an army is easy to track. We know he started his journey in Gonzales, so we should look for a trail north of there. But he will not run away," claimed my companion firmly. "He will try to stop the Mexicans at the Colorado River."

I was not so sure. I had only seen Sam Houston twice and he had not been an impressive figure. He was so sozzled he could barely stay on his horse when he had arrived in Goliad. Later, when I saw him drinking with Bowie, he had appeared drunk too, even before he had started on the cheap brandy. If he had been at Gonzales, then clearly he had not made any effort to relieve the Alamo either. It was only seventy-five miles away, despite the fact that most of the men of the town had ridden to join us. I struggled to forgive him for that, even though I had to admit that any such attempt was likely to have ended in defeat. Surely if he was too cautious to attempt to relieve us in San Antonio, he would not stand now when the odds against him would be infinitely worse.

We found a broad trail through the grass a few hours later. It had started to rain by then, hampering visibility, but we could see that grass had been flattened by boots, hooves and wheels and churned into ankle-deep mud. The strip was fifty yards wide, much bigger than the one we had seen before. Whoever had made it was heading northwest, which Hamish told me was in the way of the Texian capital of San Felipe, on the far side of the Colorado. Looking in the other direction, they must have come from Gonzales or San Antonio. At first I thought that it had to be Houston and his army. Then Hamish called out and pointed to a rag-wrapped bundle lying half submerged in the muddy ooze. It was a dead soldier, a Mexican one. He looked to have died in the last day or two. A vulture or some other creature had already feasted on his face, but what was left of his cheeks was sunken. I guessed that he had died of some sort of fever.

"Do you think that the Mexicans are following General Houston?" asked Hamish.

"I have no idea. Santa Anna may be rushing on to capture the rebel government in its capital," I suggested. "But either way, it makes no sense for us to follow the Mexicans. Let's ride north to this Colorado River you mentioned and get across. If Houston is making a stand, he will be on the far side."

We pressed on due north but a mere ten miles further on we found the trail of yet another army. This time there were no dead bodies by the side of the road, but there were plenty of clues to indicate that this was the line of retreat for the Texians. There were trunks of clothes, a hand plough, pieces of furniture and all manner of other items that farmers and other civilians had started to flee north with. As the miles passed and the roads became muddy in the frequent rain, many had evidently decided to abandon their burdensome possessions. We followed the trail for a while and found the remains of a camp. The ground was rutted from the wheels of wagons and the grass trampled flat from hundreds more boots. It was still raining but Hamish pointed to a dark line of trees that were just visible through the downpour on the horizon.

"That will be the bank of the Colorado River. We will find Houston on the other side. He is known as a fighter among our people." As we trotted our horses on I hoped that Hamish was right. At least we knew that the Mexicans were downstream – unless they had already crossed the river and attacked Houston's camp. This was a lawless land; even two armed men were vulnerable to gangs of thieves or the more hostile Indians. I would be glad to find the safety of an army to protect us, especially if for once, it was doing what I always wanted an army I was in to do: fleeing headlong out of danger.

An hour later and we both stared in disappointment at the far bank of the river. There was no army, although we could see its trail had moved along the far bank in the direction of San Felipe. Houston must have learned of the Mexican advance and gone to defend the capital.

Of more immediate concern was the fact that he had burned the ferry before he had left. A thick hawser tied to a tree on our bank was trailing in the water. Across the river we could see the blackened timbers of the ferryman's hut and the burnt remains of his craft pulled up on the bank. At first I thought that the place was deserted, but then we saw several men moving about on the far shore. One of them was studying us with a glass. Houston must have left them to guard the crossing. I hoped that they had left a boat, for the river was some two hundred yards wide and after all the rain, the current was strong. We tried shouting at them above the noise of the water splashing over the rocks that lined the shore. Either they could not hear us or were ignoring us, for they showed no reaction. They certainly did not drag a boat from the undergrowth.

"We will have to swim the horses across," I said.

"Yes," agreed Hamish. "But we should go a distance upstream first as the flow will wash us a long way down river." In the end we went a quarter of a mile upstream before we found a shallow part of the bank from where to ride the horses out. Having secured our possessions, we guided the animals out into the water. They soon lost their footing and in the heart of the current we were swept away at some speed. I had a sudden vision of still being astride the animal in the middle of the river as we passed between the Mexican and Texian armies. I could feel the horse kicking and trying to run in the water, only its neck and head above the small waves as it struggled to make headway. Holding tightly to the saddle, I took my feet from the stirrups and began to kick against the water as well to help drive us forward.

Looking around, I could see Hamish struggling as well, when he tried to shout something, a wave broke into his face. We were, however, making progress, we were more than halfway across when we were washed past the burnt-out ferry buildings and six men, who watched us impassively. I thought the bastards could have thrown us a rope or done something to help yet they were content to leave fate to decide if we lived or drowned.

Eventually, my horse's shoulders moved up out of the water as it found purchase on the riverbed beneath. I sighed with relief, but we were not out of danger yet – we still had to get men and beasts out of the river.

"There," shouted Hamish behind me, pointing. I looked up to see that in front of us a tree had partially fallen into the river. Wood and other debris from ferry crossings had gathered in its branches forming a small dam that weakened the flow of water. With little guidance from me, my horse aimed for the small patch of calmer water. It then stood with the river now flowing just halfway up its legs, trembling from its exertion or fright. We had to dismount. Hamish used a knife to cut and snap off branches until there was a path up onto the bank. I urged the horses up it one at a time with a sharp slap on the rump and at last we were all on firm ground. Before I could even breathe out a sigh of relief, a voice called out from behind me.

"So, who the hell are you?" I turned to see four hard-faced men staring at us, all with weapons in their hands.

Before I could even answer, another one added, "Looks like a Mexican scout and a goddamn Indian guide to me."

I was cold, tired and angry, in no mood to put up with any nonsense from these devils, who had just stood by while I had nearly drowned. I knew that with my part-Spanish parentage I did look a bit Mexican and the old uniform did not help. I decided to come at them high and mighty. "Damn your eyes!" I exploded. "Do you think we would have tried to cross the river right in front of you if we were bloody spies?" I drew myself up and looked them in the eye. "I am Major Thomas Flashman, formerly of the British army, and this is my friend Hamish Norton, who is half Scottish."

"I'm an Indian," Hamish corrected me quietly. "A Coushatta, our lands are to the north."

"Well whoever the hell you are," continued the first man who had spoken, "what are you doin' here?"

"I am trying to find the Texian army," I replied. Then thinking that this would be exactly what a Mexican scout would also want to do, I added, "You can take me to General Houston. He knows me and can vouch for me." Given the state he was in when I last saw him, I was not sure that Houston would remember me at all, but I knew enough

244

about Jim Bowie to convince him that I had gone with Bowie to San Antonio. I thought that mention of their general's name would see me treated now with some respect. However, I was quickly proved wrong.

"If you are a friend of that gutless coward, p'raps we should just shoot yer now," sneered the second man.

I was astonished. "Is Houston not in command of this army?"

"By now," replied the Texian soldier, "there should be a man in charge who knows his duty and how to fight."

"General Houston knows how to fight!" Hamish declared hotly and his hand dropped down to his knife as though daring them to disagree. It was a challenge that the first soldier was happy to take up.

"Does he hell!" the man retorted. "He promised us a battle right here, then when some Mexicans appeared opposite Beason's Crossing, he swore we would fight there. We had more men than they had. Our boys begged the general to let them cross and send the devils to hell, but he would not. Then he marched us to San Felipe and vowed we would defend the capital of our country to the last man. Do you know what he did then?" We remained silent and so he continued, "He hauled up his skirts like a frightened old woman and ran away again. Some of our boys have refused to retreat another step. We are stopping the Mexicans crossing the river at San Felipe, but your precious general is all the way back at the Brazos River now. He won't stop running until he is sitting on Andrew Jackson's lap, 'cos he has been serving the United States rather than us."

It was the second scathing criticism of Houston we had heard in the last few days. He was clearly not winning many friends in Texas. Mind you, having just crossed it, I could understand why he did not want to give up a good defensive position and allow his men to charge back across the Colorado to attack Mexicans, who would doubtless be waiting for them. It was less clear, though, why he had abandoned the northern shore, for the river was a significant obstacle to the Mexican advance. Still, that was no longer my concern, I was more than happy to continue north. I grinned as I suddenly remembered the people we had passed on the way there.

245

"There are some women and children behind us on the trail," I told the men. "They are going to need your help to cross and you will be pleased to know that they share a very similar view on General Houston to yours."

Chapter 29

The soldiers gave us directions to the last point they knew about on Houston's retreat, a plantation owned by a man called Groce. We set off straight away, for despite shivering with cold and wet, Hamish still looked as though he would fight for Houston's honour and I did not want to lose my only companion. In addition, I had promised his father that I would look after the young fool. So we trudged on through the trees, until after a mile, when my muscles were aching with the cold, I allowed us to stop. We cut some wood and used the powder in a couple of cartridges to get a fire going and then built it as high as we could. Soon we were standing near naked beside it, feeling its warmth drive the chill from our bones while our clothes steamed, draped on sticks nearby.

"I still don't believe that Houston is a coward," muttered Hamish through chattering teeth. "To us he is known as Raven and we know he has fought bravely in battle. He is one of the few white men who deal fairly with our people."

"Well for what it is worth, I think he was right not to let them cross the river," I told him. "Although why he did not stay at the river to defend it, I am not sure."

"Perhaps the Mexicans have brought cannon to shoot across the water," suggested Hamish. I did not say anything, but I knew that if that were true, the Texians could have dug in on the bank to protect themselves from cannon. Their rifles would still have been able to decimate any force trying to cross the Colorado. I thought it was far more likely that Houston was worried about being outflanked. We knew a separate army was travelling up the coast; perhaps Santa Anna had divided his main army into several columns. If one of them got behind Houston's men while they were defending the river, they would be trapped between the two forces.

Whatever was on Houston's mind, he clearly did not want to share it with his men. Perhaps he did not want to scare them, or he might have been too drunk to have a coherent plan. Yet when I thought back to the great commanders I had known, they had not shared their plans either. Cochrane drove us to frustration with hare-brained schemes that he would reveal at the last minute, often to some alarm. Wellington too was notorious for keeping his intentions to himself. But both had reputations for success and were used to the discipline and order inherent in the Royal Navy and British regiments. In contrast, the Texian army was little more than an armed rabble and men came and went as they pleased. With his haughty manner, I doubted Wellington would have lasted five minutes before he was booted out and sent packing. Still, the Texian army was, albeit reluctantly, to the north of us and on our way out of danger. So it made sense to head to this Groce's plantation to see for ourselves. If Houston had been driven out and sent to the United States, I thought we might keep him company.

It was not an easy journey to the Texian camp. We were knee deep in mud and water for part of it and drenched in more showers. I had no idea what to expect when we got there. I would not have been surprised to find Houston hanging by his neck from a tree. What I did not anticipate, though, was the sight of bands of men engaged in drilling and marching. Whoever was in charge was clearly preparing his soldiers for a fight. Several hundred of them were filing about, changing direction and preparing to fire volleys. Some were even doing bayonet drill, although most did not have the long blades on their muzzles. I knew from my time at the Alamo that many preferred to use a hunting knife or a tomahawk for hand-to-hand fighting. We had not even got close before a sentry stepped out and demanded to know what we were about.

"I would like to see General Houston, or whoever is in charge," I told him, after giving our names. They had surely heard by now that Fannin's men had been captured, but I wondered if they knew that most of the prisoners had been murdered. Whether such news would stiffen the resolve of these men or cause more desertions and panic was hard to say.

The sentry looked up at the sky, it was late morning. "General Houston will be sleeping now, sir, but he should see you later this afternoon."

"Sleeping?" I repeated as I glanced at his soldiers working hard at their drilling. "Is he drunk?"

"No, sir," insisted the sentry defensively. "An' despite what some say, he is not taking no opium either. At night he roams around the camp to make sure that all the sentries are awake." He lowered his voice and added in a scandalised tone, "He ordered one he found asleep to be shot, but his officer got him reprieved."

We were allowed to pass. While Hamish attracted a few curious, if not hostile glances with his long hair and Indian beads, no one stopped us moving about. Now we were inside, we saw what must have been over a thousand soldiers in the camp, maybe more. It was hard to tell as few wore uniforms. The numbers were swelled by hundreds of civilians that had stayed with the army for protection or because their menfolk were serving in it. We found a camp kitchen where a great beef carcass was being roasted and were given food and a hot drink to warm our cold bones. As with most army cooks, our host was a large and gregarious man, full of the gossip that he had accrued from previous diners. It was a good opportunity to find out what was really going on in this army.

"From what I have heard from your soldiers at the Colorado," I told him, "I was surprised to find General Houston still in command of the army."

"There are plenty of hotheads," the man agreed, wiping a long knife on a cloth. "Colonel Travis was one of them – and look what good it did him and all those boys at the Alamo. Colonel Fannin was another and now all his men are prisoners. Say what you like about Houston, but we are still alive and free and not lost in some reckless last stand. I did not lose land like some; I am happy to go back to Louisiana and start again."

"But don't some of the officers want to replace Houston and go back and fight?" I pressed.

"Aye, some of them are proper worked up about it. Colonel Sherman is their favourite to take command." He chuckled and added, "He won't do anything about it, though, Sam Houston has got his measure."

"What do you mean?"

He nodded across the clearing towards the centre of the camp where I now saw that two freshly dug graves had been excavated. "He has issued a proclamation that the first two men to call for a ballot on a new commander will be going in those."

"So, you don't think that the Texian army will fight the Mexicans?" I probed.

"I don't know, we had two cannon delivered yesterday. Perhaps he will, but only if he thinks he can win. Why don't you ask him yourself?" he gestured back across the clearing and grinned. "He is over there now."

I stared across but all I could see were a couple of blacksmiths working at a forge. One was cutting up horseshoes, I guessed to make cannister shot for the cannon, and the other in an old leather coat was repairing a musket. I was about to turn back to the cook when I noticed something about the second man that looked familiar. As he handed the musket back to a young soldier, I realised that the second blacksmith was none other than Houston himself. "Wait here," I told Hamish, and strolled over.

My quarry was turning back to his tent when I caught up with him. "General Houston," I began. "My name is Major Flashman, formerly of the British army. I was hoping to have a word with you."

The man turned and surveyed me with all the enthusiasm he might have shown for a turd on his boot sole. A beard covered most of his features and he sighed wearily and replied, "Are you another military man sent by Burnet to tell me my duty?"

"No, sir, I have no idea who Burnet is, but we have, or should I say had, a friend in common, James Bowie. In fact, I was in the same bar the last time you saw him. You might not remember, but he talked about taking a British soldier with him to the Alamo to survey the guns. I was the soldier he took."

I had hoped that the recollection of his old friend would spark some familiarity between us, but Houston still looked singularly unimpressed. "Well, what is your business with me, sir?" he demanded.

I looked around to check that we could not be overheard, "I have news, sir, from the south."

"Well I hope it is better than your brandy," he growled, showing that he had remembered his last meeting with Bowie after all.

"I was with Fannin when he surrendered and later as a prisoner at Goliad," I whispered. "I regret to inform you that Fannin and nearly all of his command were executed. Only a few of us who could translate or serve in the hospital were spared."

I had expected the general to show some sort of reaction to this calamitous news, but he continued to survey me calmly. "Have you told anyone else this?" he demanded.

"No, sir, I thought I should tell you first."

"Good. You are not the first with this news. I would be obliged if you would keep this intelligence to yourself. It will only spread panic among the meek and encourage the rash to greater foolishness."

"Of course, sir." I stood staring at him, burning with curiosity to know what his intentions were, but if he was not going to trust his own officers, he was hardly likely to share confidences with a stranger.

"Are you sure that they are all dead? Did you see it happen?" he asked quietly.

"From a distance, we saw one of the columns shot and we heard the others. A few might have got away, as we glimpsed cavalry chasing those who had escaped the first volley, but not many. Fannin had been wounded in the leg. I heard from someone who was there that he was put in a chair and shot in the head." I gritted my teeth in a sudden fury that I had thought was past and added, "They even dragged the wounded out of the sickbay and shot them as they lay prostrate on the ground, as well as many of the orderlies."

"How did you get away?"

I gestured to Hamish still standing by the cook. "I have an old friend I fought with in Canada and who is now with the Coushatta. His people rescued me – that is his son over there." Houston nodded and turned to go, but I could not help myself from asking another question. "Tell me, sir, at the Colorado, were you worried about being outflanked?"

251

For a moment I thought he would ignore my impertinence, but then he slowly turned back to me. "Have you fought many campaigns in the British army, Major?"

"A fair few," I admitted.

He nodded and then continued, "Well now, you know General Urrea is coming up the coast and we hear his army has been reinforced. There is another army far out to the west, which in time will try to come along the Sabine Valley and cut off any forces still in Texas. Santa Anna has divided his main army into three: one part he leads himself; another under General Sesma was the column I faced across the river. A third under Santa Anna's brother-in-law, a general called Cos is also out there, God knows where. So tell me, Major, would you have stayed with an army by the river?"

"No," I admitted. "I heard that you had some men blocking their attempt to cross the Colorado near San Felipe. Are the Mexicans still on the other side of the river?"

"We hear that they have given up there and moved downstream."

He had been far more open than I had expected and so I decided to push my luck. "Are you planning to meet him downriver?" By way of reply, Houston gave a grim smile and turned away.

I watched the general disappear behind his tent flap and felt strangely comforted. Houston exuded a calmness despite the overwhelming odds that faced him and he certainly appeared sober.

"Who is Burnet?" I asked when I got back to the cookhouse.

"Burnet is the new president of Texas," announced the pot-stirrer. "An' he hates General Houston. Wrote to him, he did, and told him to fight and that the enemy were laughing him to scorn."

"And how would you know what is in a letter between the president and the general?" I asked dubiously. It sounded like more cookhouse gossip to me, but the cook did not look the least abashed.

"I know 'cos Burnet has his spies in the camp doing all they can to damage Houston and get him replaced by Burnet's friend Colonel Sherman. Now Houston has stopped drinking, they are the ones spreading rumours of opium. Burnet has made damn sure that everyone knows what was in his letter."

252

"Why would he do that?" I asked, puzzled.

"He is a goddamn politician, ain't he?" stated the cook as though it were obvious. "If Houston does fight and win Burnet will claim the credit for calling him to his duty, an' if he turns and runs Burnet will say he was right about Houston being a coward all along."

I had to concede that the man was a very shrewd judge of politicians after all.

Chapter 30

For the next few days it looked like it would be the charge of cowardice that Burnet would level at Houston, for we began to retreat once more. As news was confirmed that Santa Anna had crossed the Colorado, Houston took his army across the Brazos River, so that there was a waterway between the armies once more. At least this time there were boats to carry us across so we did not get our feet wet. Then we received news that the Mexicans had captured the Texian capital of San Felipe. Its politicians had long since left the city and they too had headed north, to the town of Harrisburg, nearer the coast and American border. The loss of the nation's capital brought fresh shame on its ramshackle army. It was not hard to find those complaining bitterly about its spineless leader. The voices of dissent were soon swelled by those who had stayed back to try and defend the Colorado crossing and who were now re-joining the army.

Once across the Brazos, Houston turned the army east, but he was as tight-lipped as ever as to our destination. I was told that a few days down the trail we were on, there was a fork in the road. Turn left and the track would take you north to Nacogdoches and beyond that the Sabine River and Louisiana. If we went straight on, then we would continue to head east and towards the enemy. Most of those with families following on with the army favoured the northern route to get them to safety. Despite me keeping quiet, rumours of executions at Goliad were beginning to circulate up and down the column. A survivor of the Goliad slaughter had reached the men defending the Colorado crossing, which had fired them up into an even greater passion.

The two different factions argued fiercely as we marched slowly over the rough terrain. You can imagine which side I favoured; the sooner I was back in the United States, the better I would like it. Anyway, it did not look as though the country of Texas would exist for much longer. We got news that Santa Anna was personally leading a flying column of his men ahead of the rest of his army to Harrisburg. Whereas before he had pursued Houston and his army, it was now clear that *el Presidente* no longer viewed the Texian army as a threat. It had fled from him for hundreds of miles and not once given a hint of offering battle. Instead, Santa Anna focused his attention on the political leaders of this rebel state. He doubtless thought that once he had them dangling from a gibbet, the rebellion would be over and the Texian army would have nothing to fight for.

The countryside was different now. Instead of wide-open prairies, the land was more wooded, interrupted by fields cleared by settlers. It was better ground for the Texians to fight on, providing more cover for their riflemen and impeding the Mexican cavalry. Of course, if Santa Anna managed to bring up several of his larger cannon, they could turn woodland into a storm of lethal splinters that would swiftly outweigh that advantage. Our newly acquired artillery would be no match for them. They were only a pair of small six-pounders, pulled along by some oxen Houston had borrowed from one of the settlers following on behind.

As we drew closer to the fork in the road, speculation in the column as to what Houston would do, rose to fever pitch. Some swore that the general was sounding out his officers about taking the road north and that we would retreat once more. Whether this was true or agitation by Burnet's men I could not say, for he did not include me. But for a man notorious for keeping his opinions to himself, it was unlikely that he would start sharing them now. Others announced that if Houston marched north, he would be instantly replaced by a new commander, who would take the army east anyway. They would trap Santa Anna's flying column against the coast and gut them like hogs, one announced. All were agreed that the murderous Santa Anna should end his days paying for his crimes by dangling from a hangman's noose.

A steady stream of scouts rode to and from Houston each day to keep him informed on what the enemy was doing. I did not pay them much attention until one shouted at me from just a few feet away.

"Hey you, I thought you were dead!" I turned to look at a face I had last seen two months before in San Antonio. Back then he had been riding out on a scouting mission before the Mexicans had arrived. It was Deaf Smith.

255

"I am hard to kill," I yelled back at him, grinning. He had always struck me as a slightly intimidating figure, but now he beamed back and dismounted to walk beside me. He demanded to know how I had survived the Alamo attack. Not wanting to yell my story to half the column, I steered him away from the marching line so that we could bellow at each other with slightly more privacy. He gave a low whistle of astonishment when he learned that I had survived the Goliad massacre as well. He had been riding on reconnaissance missions for Houston for the last few weeks and had just reported to him from his latest jaunt.

"Do you think Houston will fight?" I asked.

The man shrugged, "He won't tell me, but I don't see why he would keep sending me out if he wasn't fixin' to fight." He grinned and added, "He might get his chance too."

"What do you mean?" I was curious for any information. By way of answer, Smith showed me a roughly drawn map he carried where he marked the position of the enemy forces he found and those that other scouts and Houston had told him about. It showed the route of our march too, but only up to the fork in the road. All the pencilled lines showing the routes of the various armies were converging on the north-eastern corner of the country. He pointed at one Mexican army that was getting ahead of the rest and told me that this was the one Santa Anna was personally leading.

El Presidente was racing recklessly ahead of the rest of his forces in his determination to capture Burnet and his cabinet. Smith told me that the self-styled Napoleon of the West had only four or five hundred men with him, whereas the Texian army was double that. Mind you, there were two other Mexican columns trailing behind in Santa Anna's wake. One had only another five hundred men, but behind that was a huge force of three thousand. The map also showed that if the Texians did continue east, then we would become the pursuer. Until recently we had been the army being chased north. Now that Santa Anna had contemptuously decided that we were no threat to him and turned his attention northeast, we would be coming up *behind* his army.

"Do you think we can catch him?" I asked.

Smith shrugged again before shouting, "I would like to see that bastard pay for what he has done."

I thought back to the only time I had seen Santa Anna, when he had ordered the execution of the prisoners at the Alamo. He did not have to do that; the grey-haired general had already accepted their surrender. It was an act of vindictive spite. I remembered his annoyance when his soldiers had hesitated at butchering unarmed and bound men, then his delight when his entourage of staff officers had completed the task for him. I did not doubt that General Urrea had pleaded clemency for Fannin's men too. If he had wanted us dead, the general could easily have slaughtered us at Coleto Creek when he had us at his mercy. Instead that murderous swine had ignored his general and issued orders for us all to be killed too. My dance card would have been torn up with the rest if it had not been for that young woman who had saved us. The more I reflected on it the angrier I became. I could not rid my mind of the image of the pile of half-burned bodies on the way to the quarry and the forgotten corpse of the young soldier lying on the track.

The day after I met Smith, the army was due to pass the fork in the road. From dawn men scurried from one campfire to the next whispering about which path they would take and what they would do if Houston headed north. Hamish and I readied ourselves for the day as usual, my companion chatting about people he would meet in the Coushatta villages near the Sabine River. Our general, as he rode down the column, was as inscrutable as ever. He must have been aware of the tension building among his command, yet he did nothing to dissipate it. I wondered if he had actually made up his mind, or if his fierce glare and beard was a mask for his indecision. We set off with the army to the fore, the two cannon in its midst. A long straggling line of civilians followed to the rear, pulling their wagons and what livestock they had managed to bring with them that had not been consumed on the journey

I did not know the country, but I could tell when we were getting close to the fork. The men's pace began to quicken and a trio of pipe players at their head started up with a martial air. Men started to shout

out, "To the right," and, "To Harrisburg." Even the onset of a shower of rain did not dampen their spirits. Houston was nowhere to be seen as the head of his army reached the junction. There was no signpost, but a local man stood there calling out "The right-hand road will take you to Harrisburg just as straight as a compass." They hardly needed any encouragement, for they did not hesitate to turn in the direction he indicated. A few like Hamish and I peeled away to take the road north, although I stood in the junction for a while, watching the others pass. Rarely have I seen an army more jubilant as it splashed through the puddles, heading towards a battle. Their mood contrasted somewhat with their commander's. The army had given Houston a simple choice: he could follow them towards the enemy and stay in command, or take the road north and leave them. Without hesitation, his horse trotted down the road to Harrisburg, to a mixture of cheers and jeers from his men.

"Come on," called Hamish pulling at my sleeve. "We should get on and use the path before the carts churn it up. I turned to go with an odd feeling of reluctance. It was strange as getting out of Texas had been my ambition for weeks and now it was within my grasp. I took a final glance over my shoulder and to my surprise I saw someone else I knew. A grim-faced Juan Seguín was riding up the column, and behind him a dozen Tejanos, several of whom also looked familiar. I was sure that they were some of the men who had left the Alamo to take their families to safety.

The last time I had seen Seguín, Travis had sent him out as a courier and it had been by no means certain that he would be able to get through the Mexican lines. I was glad he had survived. I opened my mouth to call out to him, but then hesitated. As I watched him take the Harrisburg road to avenge the deaths of friends like Bowie, Crocket, the loyal Martin and even that blowhard Travis, not to mention all those that had followed Fannin, I felt what was, for me, a rare emotion: shame.

If you have read my memoirs you will know that I have run out on more than a few brave souls in my time and not thought twice about it. I would not be here now if I hadn't, but it was not the same that time.

To this day I am not quite sure why. I know that the image of Santa Anna laughing as the prisoners were butchered in the Alamo courtyard burned in my memory, as did those long lines of men at Goliad, thinking they were being marched off to ships. My hatred was not for the Mexicans at large, instead it was concentrated on just one man: *el Presidente.* I would have given a good deal to see him scragged and kicking the air under a noose.

Perhaps the difference in my feelings that day was due to the information Deaf Smith had given me: Santa Anna was racing ahead of his army and was vulnerable. There was a chance we could cut off the head of the Mexican snake, then perhaps the rest of it would wither away. Certainly, I knew that if I made it into Louisiana, only to learn that the Texians had caught and topped the villain without me, I would have been furious. The bastard had tried to kill me twice, I had a score to settle. More pertinently, the Texians had a military advantage too.

"No," I told Hamish decisively. "I am not going north. I am going to Harrisburg with the others. I want to see this through."

To my surprise, he did not try to stop me or argue at all. He just grinned and said, "My father warned me that this might happen."

Chapter 31

Three or four hundred men turned north at the fork in the road, many of whom were settlers with families in the train behind or had already gone on ahead of them. I guessed that Houston had less than a thousand men going with him on the road to Harrisburg. They were full of spirit, although one was to face a fight rather sooner than he expected.

If the Texians thought that their first adversary was to be the Mexicans, they were wrong. The column was brought to an early halt by a formidably large woman called Mrs Mann. She had ridden a horse after the men going east and then planted herself foursquare in front of the oxen pulling the two cannon. As Hamish and I were moving back to our old place in the column, we were just in time to witness the confrontation.

"Those oxen are mine," she declared. "I only lent them 'cos the general said he was taking the Nacogdoches road north."

The waggoneer driving the animals was a huge fellow in buckskin with a booming voice to match. He told her to get out of the way and clearly thought the objection was insignificant to the larger issues of state at hand. Yet as he cracked his whip to drive the animals on and force her out of the way, he suddenly found himself looking down the barrel of a large pistol the lady had pulled from her belt. I doubt anyone has ever called Mrs Mann bashful, for she now launched a stream of curses and invective on the wagoneer that the coarsest sailor would have been proud of. The man gaped at her, utterly lost for words and looked around with relief when he saw that Houston had ridden up to see what was causing the delay. If anyone thought this matron would be cowed by the commander-in-chief of the army of Texas they were soon disabused.

"You tol' me a damn lie," she spat at the general. "You tol' me you was goin' on the Nacogdoches road and here you clearly ain't. I want my oxen."

"But Mrs Mann," Houston favoured her with what he hoped was a charming smile, "you can see that we cannot spare the animals. We cannot pull our cannon without them." If he was going to appeal to her goodwill, he did not get the chance.

"I don't care a damn about your cannon, I want my oxen." With that she got down from her horse and, putting the gun back in her belt, withdrew a large hunting knife and started to cut through the traces on the beasts. The waggoneer shot the general another look that implored him to intercede again, but Houston wisely saw that it was pointless. He must have given the woman the assurance about the route and was not willing to break his word. He would have had to shoot her to keep the oxen. We all stood there silently in the rain and watched as Mrs Mann got back on her horse and started to drive the animals back down the trail. As she left, the waggoneer looked down at the muddy ground in front of the guns and gave a heavy sigh. There was only one thing left to do. "Well, boys," he declared, "we had better get some ropes and pull the damn guns ourselves."

We all pitched in hauling those wretched cannon. Even Houston would get down from his horse and put his shoulder behind one of the wheels when it got stuck. Everyone knew that speed was now of the essence if we were to catch up with Santa Anna and take him by surprise. The rain did not let up and we slipped and strained in the mud as we kept not only the guns moving, but also the horse-drawn carts of supplies and ammunition that often became bogged down in the deep muddy patches that beset the road. I was soon exhausted, but somehow I kept putting one foot in front of the other. Whenever I needed more energy, I just imagined Santa Anna's face when he realised that he was cut off from his armies and about to die. Each evening we would slump down so covered in mud that we were barely distinguishable from the ground we lay on. Hamish would normally go and get us both food as, once we stopped, I would soon be too stiff to move. That first night I fell asleep still with a half-eaten beef rib in my fist and did not wake until dawn. Then groaning with aching muscles, we would slowly stagger to our feet, still covered in mud as though we were the dead rising from our graves.

Some of the early enthusiasm had gone now; the singing and pipe playing had been replaced by a grim resolve to get the job done.

Unlike the men at Goliad who were mostly new arrivals from the United States, many of this army were settlers. They had lost homes, livelihoods and perhaps friends at the Alamo. I was not the only one burning for revenge. Seguín and his men were the only Tejanos in the camp and they usually gathered around their own fire, set apart from the rest. Others came from further afield. The ambitious Colonel Sherman, whose uniform now did not look so grand, came from Kentucky. Some of them looked on the Hispanics with suspicion, but the old hands knew of their loyalty. Most knew that Seguín had been a friend of Bowie's and had only left the Alamo because Travis had wanted him as a courier.

We covered fifty-five miles of boggy road in just two and a half days to reach Harrisburg. I had visions of falling on the rear of an unsuspecting Mexican army as it besieged the town, but the final miles were suspiciously quiet. Had we got ahead of Santa Anna or were we too late? Perhaps we would catch the Mexicans unawares after their capture of the town. The thought of interrupting *el Presidente's* siesta as we crashed into his tent to string him up kept me going that final morning. But when we caught our first glimpse of Harrisburg it was obvious that our bird had flown. The town was empty and had been put to the torch by Santa Anna's men before they left. Mind you, as I stared at the ruins, I was quite glad that they were unoccupied. We were all tired from the long march and I discovered that a river lay between us and the blackened timbers. It was called the Buffalo Bayou and I would not have fancied crossing it weary and under fire from Mexican infantry.

We sat and rested for a while, waiting for Houston to decide where to go next. Deaf Smith and another scout swam across the river to see if they could find any enemy stragglers who could tell us where the Mexicans had gone. They returned by evening with an enemy prisoner and as they came back across the water, Smith held a deerskin leather saddlebag high in the air to ensure that its contents did not get wet. Several men excitedly pointed out that the bag had the name William Barret Travis written on the outside, but it was what was *inside* that proved to be more interesting.

We knew nothing of the contents that day, for once again Houston kept his thoughts and this intelligence to himself. Instead we cleaned ourselves and our clothes in the river and queued for the first hot food we had enjoyed in several days. We knew we had to gather our strength, for the Texian politicians were running out of land to flee from if they wanted to stay near the coast and the state of Louisiana. This meant that their pursuing army would also soon be cornered. Whatever happened, this drama would be resolved near the northern tip of the Texas coastline.

The next morning Houston gathered his refreshed soldiers about him and made what may have been his only speech of the campaign. He stood in the middle of a hollow square of his men and told us a little of what he had learned from the despatches. The prisoner Smith had captured was a courier and the despatches he carried confirmed that the president was now far ahead of his army. The Texas politicians were thought to have retreated to Galveston Island to maintain a last foothold in Texas while Santa Anna was pressing on to a place called Lynchburg to trap them. General Cos with some five hundred men was hurrying to reinforce him but was still some two days away. Further back still was the largest part of the Mexican army, some three thousand men under General Filisola. Most significantly, the despatches revealed that the Mexicans thought that we were on our way to Nacogdoches.

"The army will cross the water here and we will meet the enemy," he continued. "Some of us may be killed, but trust in God, fear not and victory is certain." There was a half-hearted cheer from the men as though they felt that it was expected of them. Perhaps they did not like being reminded of the chance of death or maybe they had heard Houston promise them battles too many times before. Their general clearly felt something was lacking from his oration too and so he took a deep breath and thundered, "Remember the Alamo!"

There was a second's shock at their general shouting at them and then they considered his words. This was their chance to avenge those brave men who had laid down their lives for Texas. Heroes like Bowie and Crockett, whose unwitting sacrifice had bought the fledgling

263

republic the time to gather for this opportunity. They were not going to let them down now. Hell, I thought, *we* were not going to let them down, for at that moment I started to shout along with the rest: "Remember the Alamo! Remember Goliad!"

Weary backs were straightened and murderous glints appeared in the eyes of the men about me, as we kept shouting and promised ourselves that they had not died in vain. I remember catching the eye of Juan Seguín as he stood across the square from me. We at least could recall the faces we had left behind. We had also heard Travis' impassioned speeches about the flame of liberty. Strangely, it was not that puffed-up rhetoric that came to mind now. I suddenly recalled sitting on the wall of the Alamo with Crockett. I remembered him quietly telling me that once the frontiersmen set themselves a goal they never give up. I did not believe him at the time, but as I stood with these men roaring their determination, I thought he might have got their measure after all.

Without delay, we threw ourselves into the business of crossing the river. The carts would be left behind along with the sick and those too exhausted to fight, but anyone with an ounce of strength left wanted to go on. We marched a distance up the river until we found a good place to cross. Near it was an abandoned cabin, which we soon tore down and used its floor to make a raft to carry the guns across one at a time. A leaking boat was also discovered hidden along the bank, but most of us just waded or swam across. The Mexicans had to be nearby, for we were just a few miles from the sea. Houston wanted to make sure that we did not lose the element of surprise and so we crept into a wood to hide while our scouts fanned out to find our prey. Word was passed that we would move again as darkness fell and when we did we had to be as quiet as possible. Blades were obsessively sharpened, weapons checked and equipment muffled so that all was ready to advance. At nightfall Deaf Smith and his companions returned. We were organised into several long files to weave through the trees, each concentrating on not losing the man in front.

Out into the open we went, crossing meadows before passing once more through trees and splashing over boggy ground. Then we came to a narrow bridge over a gully with the chuckling noise of another river in the darkness below. We crept across, our nailed boots sounding deafeningly loud on the wooden planks. We had barely gone a few yards on the other side before we spotted black patches on the grass to our right. I bent down to touch one – they were the ashes of campfires. One of the men kicked at a half-burned log. Golden cinders flew up in the air like burning fireflies. The Mexicans had camped there before us and could be no more than a day's march away.

We pressed on, following their trail, which soon led down a ravine and then up the other side. We had been marching quietly for hours. Every once in a while there would be urgent whispering as men lost touch with the man in front, but nine hundred men do not move with the stealth of a single Iroquois tracking a deer. You only had to listen for a moment to hear a twig snap, a muttered curse or even the rumble of a hungry stomach. Sometime after midnight we found ourselves in another large wood and there, at last, we were allowed to stop once more. Like the others I just slumped down among the sparse grass, my head resting against a gnarled tree root, and tried to sleep. Despite the discomfort, the noise of snoring soon echoed about the woodland, probably loud enough to be heard by any alert Mexican scout within half a mile

We awoke hungry and tired at dawn after a bare three or four hours' sleep. Men who had brought food with them wanted to eat and others just wanted more rest, but Houston growled that they would have their breakfast later. "The enemy will know we are here soon enough now," he told the men about him. "We need to find some land of our choosing to fight from." Reluctantly, we stretched creaking joints and got back on our feet. We set off again, marching north, but this time I noticed that we were flattening the prairie grass as we went. The night before we had found much of it knocked to the ground already by the army which had gone before. Wherever we were going now, we were no longer following Santa Anna. Men groaned and grumbled as they went and after two hours Houston finally relented. We came across three abandoned cows grazing on the rich pasture: breakfast for those of us who had not brought enough food. I'll say one thing about

Texians, they know how to butcher cattle. Every one of them would find a job at Smithfield market in London, for in the blink of an eye, the animals had had their throats cut and were being skinned and cut into steaks. More men built fires and the smell of roasting meat soon filled the air. My mouth was watering in anticipation as the sound of galloping hooves heralded the arrival of Deaf Smith.

"Santa Anna has burned Washington on the Water," he announced to Houston. He had intended the information as a confidential report to his general, but his booming voice carried halfway across the camp. The Texians had a curious enthusiasm for naming towns after the American capital. There was another Washington on the River Brazos. I had to turn to my neighbour to find out where this other one was.

"It must be about five miles away," he told me. "It faces out to sea near where the River Jacinto flows out into the ocean."

Before I could say any more, we heard Houston ask Smith another question. While I could not hear what our general had asked, we all heard the answer clear enough. "They are heading for the ferry at Lynchburg."

"Damn them!" exclaimed Houston. "We must get there first." Men hurriedly put half-cooked meat into their packs or gnawed on cuts so raw that the blood ran down their chins. I grabbed a piece of steak myself; it would have been a shame for the cattle to have died in vain. I have campaigned too long now to leave food in an army that was supplied sporadically at best. On we went, still going north, and now glancing nervously over to our right, where we expected the Mexican army to appear.

We won the race and arrived at the Lynchburg ferry by mid-morning without seeing a single Mexican soldier. Colonel Sherman had gone ahead with some of the cavalry and had managed to capture an enemy boat full of flour to feed their army. It was a useful addition to our now long-delayed breakfast. Once more fires were lit and I left my meat impaled on a stick over one of them as I explored the battlefield that Houston had chosen. I swiftly realised that the coming engagement was one the Texians would have to win, or without doubt, their army would be lost.

The army of Texas was defending a position that was bordered on two sides by wide rivers. The San Jacinto River, with the ferry to the town of Lynchburg on the opposite shore was immediately to the north. When I faced the east, the direction the Mexicans would come from, I had a thick grove of oak trees behind me, but beyond them was the broad Buffalo River we had crossed earlier. If the Texians were routed they would be trapped in the corner of the two rivers. I was sure that those who did not drown or manage to swim across under fire, would be shot by *el Presidente* like the captured men taken before them. On the positive side the oak trees, fallen branches and other brush would give excellent cover to riflemen and those of us with muskets if the Mexicans chose to charge our position. Our pair of cannon, which had been christened the 'twin sisters', loaded with cut up horseshoes to add to the fusillade, would take a terrible toll on Santa Anna's smaller force. He was no fool, though; he would work that out for himself. I very much doubted he would be so obliging as to assault the trees if he knew the Texians were there.

Having retrieved and eaten my steak, I went out onto the prairie in front of the oak grove. With the tall grass and a slight rise in the ground it was hard to see far ahead, but when I reached the top of the small hill, I saw a sight that brought a lump to my throat. The San Jacinto River flowed into a small bay, beyond which was the wide-open ocean. It reminded me sharply of my voyage with Vanderbilt. While that was only four months ago, given all that had happened since, it felt much more distant a memory. I watched the glint of light on the waves and felt a sharp pang of homesickness. I took a deep breath trying to smell the salty sea air, but the wind was blowing in the wrong direction. The only odour I could detect was one of decay and rotting vegetation. Looking closer, I could see the bank of the San Jacinto River was lined with a deep swamp at least a hundred yards wide. It followed the river from just beyond the ferry all the way round into the bay. As far as I could tell there was a tidal marsh around the bay as well. It did not look a healthy place; in summer it would be crawling with flies and insects.

This would be the place for the army of Texas, which had retreated almost the length of the country, to finally make its stand. For a moment I regretted my impulsiveness in joining it when I could by now be well on my way to the United States. I would not want to be buried on this alien shore. Cheering myself up, I tried to imagine Santa Anna's face when he was captured and told his fate. Seeing that would be worth the last few days of hard marching. I reassured myself that I would not be killed; we outnumbered the enemy and we had the woods to fight from, which would suit our riflemen perfectly. There would be no marching about on open plains as at Coleto. We had cover and fresh water and, according to one man who knew the area well, the rivers were full of fish too. It was time to go back. I stared at the enticing sea one final time but as I turned, something else glinting in the sun attracted my attention. I ducked down so that just my head was above the waving blades of grass. There it was again, sunlight on metal, the helmet of a dragoon. I watched as half a dozen of them trotted into view from behind some trees half a mile away. The Mexican army had arrived.

Chapter 32

I watched with astonishment as the Napoleon of the West positioned his army – his namesake would have been appalled. Instead of staying southeast, which would have given him a clear line of retreat, Santa Anna placed his five hundred men around half a mile away due east of us, directly opposite the woodland. It meant that he was surrounded on two sides by swamps and marshes, boggy land that would hamper his superior cavalry. I was not sure if this was due to strategic stupidity or monumental arrogance. He was evidently not contemplating the possibility of retreat, even though his army was smaller. I estimated the Texas force at around eight hundred men hiding among the oaks. Perhaps Santa Anna did not think that the Texians had the courage to fight him, after all, they had fled from him time and time again. However, he would soon be proved wrong on that point, in fact their enthusiasm was nearly our undoing…

The Mexicans had arrived just after midday. While I had watched their placement with incredulity, most of my comrades quietly sharpened their knives and tomahawks, muttering about the scores they had to settle with those across the prairie. If they looked to their commander to inspire them with confidence, then they were disappointed. Wearing an old leather coat and a battered hat, Houston looked more like a ranch-hand than a commanding general. He paced about, staring through his glass at the enemy and muttering to himself, before patrolling through the camp and scowling at anyone who caught his eye. In contrast the pretender to his command, Colonel Sydney Sherman was resplendent in his smart uniform, which matched that of the men he had brought with him from Kentucky. He was with his usual clique of friends and other officers, most of whom had criticised Houston through every step of the retreat. It was obvious from the scornful glances they shot at their commander, that even though he had finally delivered them a situation to their advantage, they still doubted his ability to seize the opportunity.

It was mid-afternoon before the Mexican camp was finally set up. The last stragglers had arrived and the first tents appeared on the plain.

269

I was relieved to see that they had only brought one cannon with them, for a battery of guns would have made life in the trees very uncomfortable indeed. For all their effort to reach us, they did not appear to be in any hurry to begin a battle. The Texians who had initially crouched at the edge of the oak grove, rifle in hand waiting for the enemy to march towards them, had long since got bored and moved away. Many of them were familiar with the marshy terrain, it reminded some of home, and they were soon fashioning fishing poles to pass the time.

I began to wonder if Santa Anna intended to fight that day at all; perhaps he was waiting for reinforcements. Houston must have been considering that too, for I had seen him send Deaf Smith out on another scouting mission to the south. It must have been around four in the afternoon when e*l Presidente* finally decided to test his opponents' mettle. Bugles were blown and his soldiers began to form up into ranks in front of his camp. It was hard to see them through the long grass and over the slight rise, but a nimble young lad had climbed high into one of the oak trees and called out what was happening.

"They're sendin' a line of men out now, marchin' towards us," he yelled excitedly. There was a cheer from those about me as they settled themselves into position, re-checked the priming in their guns and prepared for battle.

"How many are coming?" called out the man beside me.

"Only a company, I reckons, 'bout fifty men," called down the youth.

"What is the rest of the army doing?" I asked the lookout.

"Standin' in a long line, with their horsemen on the end," he shouted back. It seemed to me obvious what Santa Anna was up to. He knew it would be near suicidal to march his men up to the oak grove and so he was trying to draw us out into the open, where his cavalry might negate his shortfall in numbers. I glanced across at Houston, but as usual he was keeping his thoughts and feelings to himself. We waited and sure enough a few minutes later a line of black dots appeared over the top of the grass.

"There is a cannon!" shouted the lookout. "It is by that copse of trees in the middle of the field. They must have hidden it there so I did not see it coming," he added accusingly. A few moments later we all could see the gun, a twelve-pounder, double the size of the twin sisters, as it was set up at the top of the rise. I watched its crew unlimbering the weapon from the team of mules that had pulled it. As the line of infantry passed to one side of it, the gunners threw themselves into its loading. There was a dull boom as it fired and at the same moment, the sound of wood splintering nearby and twigs and branches falling to the ground.

Almost immediately came the two sharper cracks of the Texian cannon. We had not had the powder to practice firing them, but one of our guns must have got close for we saw the gunners jump back as a ball must have bounced out of the long grass towards them. The Mexicans loaded again, this time with cannister shot, for I heard the unmistakable whistle of the balls coming towards us. They were aimed at our gunners, who I could not see down the line, but once more the 'twins' fired in response. This time they sent chopped up horseshoes in the opposite direction. I saw two of the mules go down and large splinters fly off one of the limbers. By now the line of skirmishers was getting close, waist high in the grass, no more than a hundred yards away. Their officer called a halt – perhaps he sensed the two or three rifles aimed at each one of his men. He must have known that it was futile to get any closer. He shouted his orders and they brought their inaccurate muskets to the shoulder. Houston let them fire, for they were unlikely to do any damage. The fools stood then to reload and our general's voice called out, "Make ready... Fire!" There was the crash of a volley and when the smoke cleared not even one of the skirmishers was to be seen.

The men about me cheered, for them war suddenly appeared very easy. They shouted in delight again a few minutes later when we saw the enemy gunners limber up their surviving mules to drag their gun back to the shelter of the copse of trees in the middle of the battlefield. Santa Anna's attempt to draw out the Texians had failed. First blood had gone to us.

"We got them on the run," shouted one excited rifleman. "Let's chase them devils into the sea." He was on his feet now all set to do just that, when I pulled him back.

"Wait here, you fool," I told him. "That is just what Santa Anna wants you to try. He can't get us in the woods and so he wants us out in the open."

The man looked puzzled for a moment and then one of his mates called out, "He's right, Abe, let them come to us. If they come like those others it will be the finest critter hunt we ever had."

The rifleman was not the only one getting carried away. When I looked to the rear, I saw several officers haranguing Houston that now was the time to launch an attack. "We have momentum," shouted Colonel Sherman. "We must not let them recover from this reverse. At the very least we should ride out and capture that gun. The sight of its loss and our men victorious again could cause their whole army to rout."

Houston flatly refused the request and turned away to a clamour of protest. I distinctly heard one of the officers decry his commander as 'yella', while another muttered about 'gutless decisions'. Houston chose to ignore them. This was not the time for a court martial, he needed to hold his fractious force together long enough to beat the enemy.

Sherman came after Houston and tried another tack. "Sir, at least let me take our cavalry forward on an armed reconnaissance. We can't see clearly what is happening over the rise. For all we know the main body of the enemy could already be in disarray."

Houston paused to consider the request. Men were crowding around him shouting that victory was theirs for the taking. Passions were so high he must have thought that they would go anyway if he refused them. "All right," he agreed at last. "But only a reconnaissance, mind. I do not want you doing anything that will bring about a general engagement."

Sherman had turned away grinning in delight before Houston had even finished speaking. You did not have to be a gypsy fortune teller to foresee that this could end in disaster. Sherman called for his horsemen to mount up, adding to all who would listen that "Now they will see how Texians fight."

"It is to be a reconnaissance only," Houston's voice boomed out after him. This admonition was half lost in yells as Sherman led his men off to where the horses were tethered. The general shook his head in dismay; I clearly was not the only one with a sense of foreboding.

There was a cheer from all along the oak grove as Sherman led out his sixty mounted riflemen. The treacherous swine even paused to acknowledge the acclaim, raising his hat and causing his horse to rear up on its hind legs. In his uniform he looked the epitome of military valour, a sharp contrast to his scruffily dressed commander scowling at him from the trees. The colonel had been campaigning to replace Houston virtually ever since he had joined the army. He clearly saw this as an opportunity to win the rest of the men over.

I am sure that Sherman never had the slightest intention of carrying out the reconnaissance as he was ordered. He led the men straight up the shallow slope and must have soon seen that just the other side of it, Santa Anna had arrayed his infantry. Others might have hesitated or perhaps tried to draw the soldiers onwards to the waiting riflemen in the woods behind, but Sherman did neither. Convinced of the superiority of Texian arms he simply sounded the charge and attacked.

Now you might be confused by the concept of mounted riflemen. I don't blame you, for I never saw them deployed in any other army, at least not in the way that Sherman used them. The main advantages of a rifle in battle is its accuracy and ability to fire from a distance. Both of these are lost if the marksman is shooting from a cantering horse and his halfwit of a commander orders him to ride full tilt at the enemy. We watched as the galloping men fired a ragged volley towards a force we could not see. I doubt if more than a dozen shots hit targets, but then the riders encountered another disadvantage of their unique military formation. The barrels of the long rifles made them impossible to reload on horseback, which meant that the poor devils had to dismount to use ramrods to push another charge and ball into their guns. Sherman had them wheel about so that they were at least beyond the musket range of the infantry. Now back in full view of the men watching from the trees, they lost all mobility as most dismounted to reload, while a few who had not yet fired circled protectively. The far more experienced Mexican cavalry did not hesitate to take advantage of the situation. To the call of bugles, a squadron of lancers appeared over the ridge, their long spears couched under their arms as they picked out their victims. I watched one ginger-haired lad, who was one of the circling guardians, take a lance in his shoulder. The force of the impact plucked him from his saddle and deposited him prone in the grass a full ten feet from his horse. There was a crackle of fire from dragoons, who, with their short-barrelled carbines could reload while mounted, although most just drew their heavy sabres and piled in among the Texians slashing about them at any they could reach. Hardly any of Sherman's men had a sword, they were reduced to swinging their precious rifles wildly about them as clubs to keep the enemy at bay.

In but a moment any sense of order was lost. We watched aghast as the mass of horsemen dissolved into a frantic melee. Lancers wheeled around the outside looking for an opening to thrust their weapon into an exposed back, sabres hacked down on rifle barrels frantically thrown up to parry and others desperately whirled their weapons around like windmills. I watched one poor devil hit in the face by a rifle butt swung by one of his comrades and knocked clean off his mount. Yet some of the Texians in the centre of the throng had managed to hurriedly reload. Now they began to fire at almost point-blank range to drive the Mexicans off. Bugles called the recall and the enemy horsemen began to pull back, but only a short distance where they regrouped to charge again.

One of the Texian cavalry used the lull to gallop back to the line of trees. "Colonel Sherman requests infantry support," he was hollering long before he reached the line of oaks. He stared about looking for his general.

"No," shouted Houston, stepping forward. "Tell him to withdraw as best he can." The trooper sat and gaped in astonishment at this refusal. Then the sound of bugles heralded the start of another attack on his beleaguered comrades.

"Sir, we can't leave them to be butchered out there," called out an officer from back in the trees. "We have to march to their assistance."

"No," repeated Houston. "Colonel Sherman did precisely what I told him not to. Santa Anna wants to draw us out from the trees and into the open. I will not lose any more men to this stupidity."

"Hell, I am going to help Sherman," called out another voice. "I ain't lettin' them boys get killed. Forward, men!" With that a company of infantry started to move out of the trees, some yelling and jeering at those about them for obeying their own general. Before I knew it a whole regiment of the Texians was advancing.

"Come back here!" Houston roared at them. "I order you to counter march at once."

"Counter march yourself," called out a voice from the insubordinate ranks. "Yes, run away, you spineless bastard!" called another.

The officers in the next regiment along were looking at each other, uncertain whether to obey their general or follow the example of their comrades. Houston helped them make up their mind. He looked furious as he tugged a pistol from his belt and threatened to shoot the next man to put a foot out of the oak grove.

"We have not come all this way to waste our advantage in some reckless folly," he yelled. Even then they were uncertain whether to obey. I was appalled. I had only joined this army because I thought that they had the benefit of numbers and were set to fight the enemy on their terms, making the most of their superior marksmanship. Now it seemed that they would throw away these advantages and hand the enemy victory through foolish bravado and indiscipline. I did not need to be reminded of our fate if we found ourselves prisoners. It was time to intervene.

"The general is right," I called out. "I was at Coleto with Fannin. Out in the open we will be beaten. We need to fight from cover, then we can shoot down their forces long before they can do us any harm. Santa Anna knows that and is trying to draw us out from the trees."

"How do we know he will march on us?" asked someone.

"Because he wants to cross the ferry and capture Lynchburg," I told him. "He can't do that with us here."

There was a murmur of agreement and the regiments started to step back into the trees. A few of the men had learned on the march that I had some military experience and so I like to think that my support of Houston helped, not that he showed any appreciation. Yet it was what was happening out on the prairie that swung things as much as anything. The infantry commanders seeing the two groups of horsemen wheeling and hacking at each other, wisely decided that it was no place for men on foot. They halted their line halfway between the oak grove and cavalry. Then the rifles started to crack and more Mexicans fell from the saddle. The lancers and dragoons began to pull back. They could see that were they to attack the exposed infantry, who were straggled out in a tempting line, they would also come within range of the more numerous riflemen in the woods. Clearly, they did not fancy their chances of surviving that encounter.

Colonel Sherman did not waste any time in leading his men back, leaving a scattering of dead men and horses lying in the grass behind him. They had pulled back at least fifty yards, when to my astonishment the young ginger-haired lad I had seen lanced earlier, staggered back to his feet, one hand holding his wounded shoulder as he tottered unsteadily towards us. His appearance was too tempting for the lancers and a pair of them wheeled about to finish the job they had started. Men shouted out warnings from our lines and one of our cavalry on a huge stallion turned to rescue the boy. The Texian came galloping in, blocking the two lancers before shooting one of them out of the saddle with a pistol. Another of the mounted riflemen came up behind and helped the lad climb up on his horse, while the man on the stallion continued to wheel about. It was a reckless move with at least a dozen lancers nearby, but instead of attacking, they actually applauded his bravery. The Texian swept off his hat and gave a low bow before finally retiring from the field.

Now you might have thought that a man who had so blatantly disregarded his orders and then got himself into such a mess that he had to be rescued by others, would be a tad shamefaced on his return. If you did, then you clearly did not know Colonel Sydney Sherman. He had lost a number of men killed or wounded while a handful of his

276

troopers were running back to our lines after having had their horses killed or injured under them. Admittedly, a number of Mexicans lay dead in the long grass too, but to listen to Sherman you would imagine that some carefully calculated strategy had been interrupted rather than a reckless charge.

"You cost me a victory," the subordinate yelled at the man in charge of the army. "If you had supported me, we would have swept the enemy from the field."

"Damn you to hell," Houston shouted back, beside himself with fury. "We will fight the enemy on our terms, not theirs." His fists were clenched tight and if Sherman had dismounted and approached him, I did not doubt that the general would have pummelled the colonel into the ground. "I'll not have some whoreson like you in charge of my cavalry a moment longer," he fumed. "You are dismissed, sir, back to your regiment." Sherman shot him a look of pure venom before turning and joining his cronies, still loudly complaining about *his* lost victory. Houston stood alone glowering at the men about him, then he turned and saw the man on the large stallion trotting into the oak grove. "You, sir," he called out, pointing at him. "What is your name?"

"Mirabeau Bonaparte Lamar, sir,"

Houston's eyebrows rose in surprise at such an ostentatious moniker, but then replied, "Well, Mister Lamar, you are now the commander of my cavalry. I hope you do a better job of obeying orders than your predecessor." It was a meteoric promotion for young Private Lamar. Mind you, he was not done there. Years later I saw his unusual name again in *The Times*, he was then President of Texas!

Chapter 33

After the excitement of that late afternoon, we all sensed that there would be no more fighting that day. Scouts who did as ordered and carried out a reconnaissance, reported that Santa Anna had withdrawn his army to their camp on the other side of the prairie, up against the marshland. Sherman's aggression must have alarmed the Mexicans, for we got reports that they were building up a rudimentary rampart in front of their tents of carts, boxes, pack saddles and other equipment, as though they anticipated an attack from us.

Another assault was evidently the last thing on Houston's mind as he allowed the men to relax, with just a few sentries and an occasional man riding to the ridge to ensure that the Mexicans had not moved. After marching through much of the previous evening, we all welcomed the rest. There was no shortage of food; some still had joints of meat from the cattle slaughtered the previous night, while others had enjoyed success with their fishing poles. Great big catfish were hauled up from the river and soon chunks of them were cooking over fires. We also had the flour that Sherman's cavalry had captured from the Mexican boat. So, with my fish that evening, I had a flatbread that had been cooked on sticks over the flames.

I wondered what the next day would bring. If the Mexicans waited for us to attack, while we sat in the woods waiting for them to assault us, then it could end in disaster. We had numbers on our side, but not time. We knew that the rest of Santa Anna's army was marching hard to catch up with their commander-in-chief. If thousands more Mexicans appeared over the horizon, we would be trapped in the junction of the two rivers. Yet I could not see it coming to that, for I could not imagine Houston's army sitting idly by.

The general had only just kept the lid on a revolt that afternoon. If he did not fight the next day, then Sherman and others would start another attack without him. I tried to imagine it: the Texian army marching across the plain, the Mexican's big twelve-pounder flaying our soldiers with cannister while the rough rampart protected their soldiers from our rifle fire. Sherman would order our men to charge, he had little imagination for tactics. Then, if Santa Anna had any sense, he would choose that moment to release his remaining cavalry. Skilled horsemen would cut through running and disorganised infantry like a hot knife through butter. I did not think that our own grandly named cavalry commander would have the experience to stop them. What had once looked an almost certain victory and a chance to get much needed revenge, was now a far more precarious prospect. I huddled up in my blanket that night and began to wish that I had gone on to the Sabine River after all.

As it had every morning, a drum called the men to stand to just before dawn. Often Houston did this himself, but not that morning. He was still sound asleep, his head resting on a coil of rope. He had left instructions not to be disturbed – evidently, he was not planning a charge at dawn. Men who had been roused reluctantly from their slumber stared at their dozing commander with open resentment. "Is the big drunk going to sleep all day?" I heard one grumble as he went past. Deaf Smith reported that the Mexicans were standing behind their ramparts and so men turned their attention to making breakfast. Coffee was soon brewing and more dough roasted over the fire. When I went to the river to wash, I saw one man hauling out a trap he had made from an old sock and some sticks. It contained a dozen creatures that looked like small lobsters, which he assured me were good eating.

I did not risk the fresh-water lobsters as Hamish had already got breakfast in hand. He had fallen in with a group of backwoodsmen, and while they had initially distrusted the Indian, he was gradually winning them over. The night before Norton Junior had managed to spear a catfish so big that it had taken two men to haul the monster ashore. We had shared it with his new friends for supper and there was still some left in the morning. Hamish already wore buckskin leggings and a tunic like the backwoodsmen, and one had given him a broadbrimmed hat. Now he looked much more like a *norteamericano*. The Texian army was a very varied bunch, with judges to squirrel-hunters all mixing together. In fact, setting a fine example to others of his station, the Texian minister of war took his duties so seriously that he too had joined the army, serving as a common soldier so that he could see the conflict first hand.

Hamish had obviously been thinking about the British part of his ancestry, for he asked me that morning what Scotland was like. "It is a ghastly place," I told him. "Always raining or covered in fog. In the few brief weeks they call the summer, the air is full of little flies from the lakes. And don't get me started on what they call music, a dreadful caterwauling din. Trust me, you would not like it there." Hamish looked disappointed. I learned later that one of his new friends had been born in the Highlands and had been waxing lyrical about the place.

While we washed and had a leisurely breakfast our general did... absolutely nothing. When I stared over at him, he was still lying where he had slept. He was awake by then – I doubt even he could have slept through the clatter of a waking camp – but he was staring idly into the sky at an eagle that was circling above us. He could not have done anything more to irritate his command, most of whom were still champing at the bit to be at the enemy.

Colonel Sherman sat a hundred yards off surrounded by a coterie of followers. I watched him rail at them like some Baptist preacher outside a liquor house. While I could not hear what was said, from the frequent jabbing of a finger in Houston's direction, I could guess that he was once more pressing home the need for a change in command. The general must have heard some of the comments, but he remained apparently oblivious to the growing mood of revolt in the camp, which was far from assuaged by what happened next.

Deaf Smith arrived in the camp mid-morning on a lathered horse and with an anxious expression. Men who were already worried that we had wasted too much time, drew near to hear the news, only to find their worst fears confirmed.

"General Cos has arrived with at least five hundred more men," Smith advised the general, in a voice that carried halfway across the camp. A hubbub of whispers, exclamations and curses spread through the grove and for the first time Houston looked rattled. The general jumped to his feet and guided Smith out onto the prairie, where they

280

could talk in private. We all watched as the guide pointed over the hill, answering questions that Houston spoke directly into his ear. Eventually, grim-faced, Smith walked off towards the lines of horses for a fresh mount. The general stood lost in thought for a moment and then turned towards the watching faces at the edge of the trees. He forced a smile across his features and announced, "Smith has been fooled by the oldest trick in the book. Santa Anna has been marching his men around a hill to give the impression of reinforcements."

He was as convincing as a recruiting sergeant promising feather beds for soldiers. There was a moment's stunned silence as men took in the absurd claim and wondered if they were just angry or insulted too. Then everyone started talking at once, as far as I could tell, not a single voice in support of the general. Predictably, Sherman pushed his way to the front and held up a hand to silence the clamour.

"Do you take us for fools?" he demanded. "If you had supported my attack yesterday, we would have had that tyrant swinging from a tree by now. Instead we have had to watch you snore while the enemy makes fools of us. They outnumber us four to three now and if General Filisola arrives too, it will be at least three to one."

"We will fight the enemy on our terms when I say we will," snapped Houston.

"Your terms!" mocked Sherman. "The only terms you know are retreat, retreat, retreat." With that he turned away to a cheer of acclaim from his supporters. Houston sat back down by his bed roll and looked a solitary figure as he stared into the flickering flames of a camp-fire. After a while he got up again and wandered off to where Juan Seguín and the Tejanos were camped.

I was not surprised to hear a short while later that men were moving around the camp spreading the rumour that Houston was planning to cross the San Jacinto River to continue his retreat north. The general was still with Seguín's men and I was pretty sure that this tale had not originated with him – it was Sherman stirring the pot once more. This time, though, it was working as the war minister joined a group of eight officers to demand a council with Houston. The minister, a man called Rusk, had until now been studious in his support of the general, but even he was now losing confidence. Houston had little choice but to agree. The officers sat in a clearing to discuss the way forward, with a crowd of men around them doing their best to eavesdrop on the discussion. I can't complain about that for I was among them, curious to learn what was likely to happen next.

Sherman started with a scathing criticism of Houston, but the war minister cut him off. "We are here to decide what to do next," he reminded the gathering, "not to talk about the past." Sherman then pressed the case for an immediate assault before any more Mexican reinforcements arrived. Others, though, disagreed. They wanted to wait for the Mexicans to attack, particularly now we were outnumbered. "Our strength is in our rifles," one insisted. "Even if Filisola does arrive with more men," he continued "we would cut them down like hay if they marched towards us over that open ground."

They talked on in that vein for some two hours and never seemed close to reaching a consensus. I did not stay for the end but instead wandered off to find Seguín. I wanted to know what Houston had been talking to him about. Perhaps that would give me a clue as to what was going on.

"He was asking if the Mexicans were likely to take a *siesta*," the Tejanos leader told me.

"A siesta?" I repeated in astonishment. "Why in God's name would he want to know that?"

Seguín grinned, "Tell me, Flashman, when do you think Santa Anna expected us to attack him today?"

I thought about it for a moment and remembered the Texians cursing at their sleeping commander. "Well, at dawn, I suppose, that would have given us the best chance of victory, before any reinforcements arrived."

"And if you were Santa Anna," prompted Seguín, "and the enemy who has retreated from you for hundreds of miles failed to attack at dawn, would you expect him to attack when he knows that you have reinforcements that outnumber him?"

"Probably not," I admitted. "So is Houston going to attack, then?"

"I told him that the Mexicans would start their *siesta* around three. General Cos' men will have marched through the night to get here and so they will also be tired and wanting to rest."

"But what about Filisola's men? If they arrive while we are attacking, we would be slaughtered out in the open."

"The general has sent Smith and some men to cut that bridge we came across the other night. If Filisola is coming that will slow him down, but Smith and the other scouts have not seen any sign of a large force this side of the Buffalo River."

"So, Houston is definitely planning an attack?" I pressed again.

By way of an answer Seguín smiled again and reached out and grasped my hand. "Fear not, my brother," he promised me, "we will have the chance to avenge our friends." Still grinning he shook his head slightly as though he still could not quite believe what he was about to say. "Do you know, Houston offered us the chance to sit out the battle. He was concerned that feelings were pretty high against the Mexicans and some of my men do not speak English. He did not want them killed by mistake. I had to remind him that their friends died in the Alamo too, including some Tejanos. We have as much a score to settle as anyone. Everyone in San Antonio knows which families supported Texas. We cannot go home until Santa Anna is beaten." He held up some pieces of card, each one of which had the word 'Texas' scrawled on it. "We will wear these in our hats to show our loyalty to our new home."

I wandered back into the main camp feeling slightly stunned. I had come with this army precisely to get my revenge in a battle like this. I had expected an easy victory over a smaller force, thinking that the Texians would use their rifles from cover. They could easily kill three or four times their number if their enemy was out in the open. I had anticipated a bloody slaughter, swiftly followed by a well-deserved execution and had rubbed my hands with glee at the prospect. Now it was very different: I was looking at the Texians being out in the open and us being outnumbered by the Mexicans. The whole thing looked a lot less appealing. From his silent brooding and inactivity, I had even begun to believe that Houston might just retreat again. Since Cos had

283

arrived with his reinforcements, I was perhaps the only man in the camp not appalled by the idea. Now it seemed that our general might have been planning his attack all along.

One thing I was sure of was that the Mexicans would not be expecting us. If Houston's own army did not believe he would attack, why on earth would his enemy anticipate an assault? What Seguín had said about *siestas* and the reinforcements resting made sense too. On the other hand, the Mexicans were trained soldiers with discipline and order, whereas the only attack I had seen the Texians make had quickly dissolved into a shambles. If they messed this up, we would not get a second chance.

Houston called his army to order at three-thirty that afternoon. There was no shouting or bugles, he just summoned his officers and gave them their orders. Some came pretty reluctantly, convinced that he was about to order them to retreat across the Buffalo. Sherman did not come at all, sending a junior instead. They might have walked dragging their feet to Houston's tent, but they ran back, bright-eyed with beaming faces to bring the news to all they met, hushing any cheering and urging men to be quick and silent.

Hundreds hurriedly rechecked that their flints were tight in the locks and priming pans had powder. Many gave wickedly sharp hunting knives and tomahawk blades one final sweep up a sharpening stone, before all made their way to where their regiments were gathered. Then quickly they marched out onto the prairie where a line was beginning to form up. The left flank was protected by the swamp that ran along the edge of the San Jacinto River. Houston sent the newly promoted Colonel Lamar with his cavalry to protect his right flank. In the middle came the twin sisters, with a group of men on the ropes pulling the two guns forward.

The general rode up and down the line on a white horse, checking all was ready. There were no heckling shouts about him being gutless now, instead men beamed with delight at the prospect before them. Like the Tejanos, many had lost all they possessed to this enemy over the hill. Years of back-breaking work taming the wilderness gone to waste, friends shot, a nationality stolen. They were proud, self-sufficient men and had felt humiliated from weeks of retreat and showing no resistance. There was a burning anger to them; damn even I felt it as I stood there among them and remembered those burial pyres. Until half an hour before, much of that fury had been directed at the man on horseback in front of them. Perhaps a few now felt some shame at that, for, like me, they realised that this would be the perfect time to catch our foe unawares.

There were perhaps five hundred yards between us and the hastily thrown up rampart in front of the Mexican camp. The long prairie grass and the slight rise in the ground in front of us would hide our approach for much of the way; but a lot would depend on the alertness of Mexican sentries and how quickly their infantry could man their defences. Houston did not make any speech to fire up his men, he must have known that it was not necessary. His soldiers were full of aggression, it was order that they lacked. He took a final glance along our double rank, gave a slow nod of satisfaction and then silently signalled the advance.

Hamish and I had placed ourselves with the frontiersmen, just to the right of the twin sisters. As we began to march, I looked up and down the long line. While I have been to war with some colourful characters in the past, the Texian army bore more of a resemblance to a travelling circus than an army. We only needed the jugglers, for I was sure we had the knife throwers and I had my suspicions about a bearded lady too. Only Sherman's regiment had the appearance of soldiers; they at least had uniforms and even a little regimental flag. The colonel, with the wind now knocked from his sails, rode in front of his men, with his one-man colour party carrying the banner beside him.

Our immediate companions, like us, were wearing buckskins and while I had a musket, the rest all had rifles. I did not doubt that they could shoot the tail off a squirrel at a hundred paces. Marching beside our group was a grim man in a frock coat and top hat holding a shot gun. Beyond him, came a planter in a wide-brimmed straw hat and canvas jacket, with pistols and a sword stuck in his belt. The variety continued all along the line, farmers, lawyers, some men who appeared to have deserted from the United States army as they still wore parts of their uniforms and the twenty Tejanos led by Seguín, all with the little white squares of card in their hat bands. We were all sporting beards – most of us had gone days if not weeks without shaving. Our clothes were covered in dirt and mud from marching and trying to sleep in fields and forests. We were without doubt a motley crew, but we had shared together so many hardships over recent weeks. I was reminded again of the settlers who I had travelled with on two ships. They had gambled everything on a new life and these poor devils had seen nearly all of their stake pass across the green baize of the gaming table to a cruel and greedy opponent. Now they had a last chance to win at least some of it back on the final turn of a card. As I looked at the resolve set in their mud-spattered faces, I began to feel my confidence grow.

That short walk across the prairie seemed to take for ever. Houston rode in front of the line, mounted on a white horse, while in long wavering ranks we followed on behind. A team of cursing and grunting men were in the middle, pulling on the ropes attached to our two cannon. It was hard going pulling the guns through the long grass and we had to keep pace with them, or we would be in front of the muzzles when they fired. As we neared the top of the rise, we caught our first glimpse of the Mexican line, a rough barricade that only stretched a hundred yards at most. Beyond were tents, laid out in neat rows like the new streets in an American town, while to the right I could see strings of horses cropping on the pasture.

"Look at that grand tent in the middle, the one with the flags." Hamish pointed at what must have been Santa Anna's campaign quarters.

"If we get in the camp, aim for that," I told him. "I want to get my hands on that villain, but if someone has beaten us to it, there is bound to be some valuable booty in there." By now we must have been visible to any vigilant Mexican sentry as at least a long row of heads above the grass, with our general even more prominent on his horse in front of us. Despite this, there was no sign that we had been spotted. The only men I could see at all in the camp were three by the barricade, who were playing cards on the top of a barrel. We marched

286

on; I could scarcely believe our luck. Seguín was clearly right about the *siesta*; if Santa Anna had roused his men at dawn in case we attacked then, his soldiers were clearly catching up on their sleep now.

We were little more than a hundred paces from their breastworks when a bugle from the cavalry lines finally signalled the alarm. As the first strident notes rang out, the card players looked up from their game. I watched as they pointed at us and shouted. Two grabbed their muskets and fired wildly in our direction, while the third ran off, squealing the alarm into the depths of the camp. More soldiers stumbled out of the nearby tents, some still rubbing their eyes and yawning, but they woke up pretty smartly when they saw us. I watched one run to a nearby stand of muskets, grab a gun and then half climb up on the barricade to get a shot at us. It was just too tempting for one of the frontiersmen we were with. He snatched his rifle to his shoulder and a second later the Mexican was dead before he had even fired his weapon.

"Hold your fire, goddamn you, hold your fire," Houston barked at us. There were more shots coming at us now and the general prancing about on a large white horse in front of us was an obvious target. The mount reared as it was struck by a ball. Then a man standing behind the animal gave a grunt of pain and went down clutching his leg. Finally, the white steed was struck a fatal blow and Houston was pitched forward onto the ground. He did not let that distract him from his command for a moment. He called for one of the cavalry horses as a replacement and I heard hooves coming up behind us. I thought it was the general's remount, but instead it was Deaf Smith.

"Vince's Bridge is down," he called. Then to encourage us on he added, "Fight for your lives!"

"Does he mean we are trapped?" asked Hamish, alarmed. I noticed the lawyer in his top hat marching nearby also looking about him anxiously.

"No," I replied, loud enough for them both to hear. "It means that the Mexicans can get no more reinforcements. We just have to beat the men in front of us."

287

That task was not looking so simple, though, for now more and more Mexicans were running to the ramparts. Some were only half dressed, but all had muskets. We were now just twenty yards away and finally Houston called a halt. The men hauling the twin sisters hurriedly pulled the already loaded weapons around to aim them at the enemy.

"Front rank, take aim," called Houston. At twenty yards even my musket was reasonably accurate. The riflemen could virtually pick the button on an enemy coat they wanted to strike. As we stood there, a sudden stampede of defenders came rushing through the gaps between the tents. There were at least a hundred of them and they had arrived at precisely the wrong moment, at least for them. I watched several nearby muzzles shift up slightly – the new arrivals were much easier to hit than those crouching behind barrels. I took aim at one soldier who had just stood up from behind cover to encourage his comrades to join him. What had possessed him to stand when eight hundred guns were aimed in his direction I will never know, but I am pretty sure that it was the last thought he had.

"Front rank, fire!" There was the crash of a volley and our view of the enemy was obscured by a bank of gun smoke. The twin sisters cracked out, sending a lethal hail of horseshoe fragments into the barricade and the men surrounding it. While we could not see the impact, we could hear it, with screams of agony coming from the men in front of us.

"Second rank, advance!" called Houston. He was clearly planning to take us forward in orderly ranks, firing volleys as we went. It gave him control, but it also gave Santa Anna time to reorganise his men. We had the momentum now and some unseen voice further down our line was determined not to lose it.

"No," he called. "Don't let them stand. Come on, boys, charge. Remember the Alamo!"

All the pent-up frustrations of the last two days broke in that moment. Without any hesitation the line surged forward yelling, "Remember the Alamo!"

Chapter 34

According to all the principles of warfare, the Texas army should have
been beaten that day. It was outnumbered, charging an enemy in a
prepared defensive position and had given away its one advantage of
ranged accurate fire. Instead, I watched as the Mexican troops
dissolved into panic. Some even started to run before the Texians were
halfway towards them. It cannot have been the appearance of their
enemy that intimidated the Mexicans, for most of the line coming
towards them had all the martial demeanour of a pack of well-armed
vagrants. It certainly was not the withering fire, for few of the running
men bothered to pause and shoot their weapons. Instead, I think it was
the noise they made as they came on. It was a guttural roar of rage,
interspersed with words that the Mexicans understood all too well:
Alamo and Goliad.

Every Mexican soldier knew what had happened at these places. I
suspect that more than a few, like the ones who had hesitated at the
order to execute the prisoners in the Alamo, felt ashamed. They knew
that they had provoked a terrible fury in their enemy and now they
could expect no quarter in return.

The whole line surged forward like a wave breaking on a shore.
When I had sat on that wall with Crockett, neither of us could have
imagined the price that would have to be paid to bring forth this
avenging horde, but I knew now that he was right. After weeks of
humiliations and retreat, the loss of property and friends, this was at
last their chance to pay back those responsible. I shouted and ran with
the rest of them, for firing volleys from the wide-open prairie against
an enemy that outnumbered you did not sound sensible to me either.
As I pushed on through the smoke, I saw that the twin sisters had torn
a large gap in the barricade. The resulting wooden splinters and metal
fragments had left a score of dead and wounded. Beyond them the
ground was littered with the bodies of Mexican soldiers who had met a
hail of well-aimed lead from our single volley. The few survivors took
one glance at the line of men hurdling over the barricade yelling their

battle cry, before turning on their heel and dashing back the way they had come.

They were wise to run, for there was no pity from their pursuers. We all knew how the Mexicans had dealt with prisoners and while no orders had been given, few were in the mood to be merciful now. As I climbed over the barricade with Hamish and the men who we had stood in line with, I saw a Mexican sitting on the ground with a shattered leg. There was terror in his face as he looked up at us. He raised his arm shouting, "Me no Alamo, Me no Alamo!" It did him no good. One of the frontiersmen stuck a huge knife into his throat with no more emotion than if he was dispatching a wounded deer.

We pressed on through a gap in the tents and there we found a Mexican officer trying to organise a line of defence. There were thirty or forty soldiers in a hastily gathered rank. They mustered around the Mexican cannon, but already several of the gunners lay dead. The men were under heavy and accurate fire and as we arrived their discipline began to dissolve. Half fired at us, many from the hip and then turned to run, while others just ran, a few even abandoning their weapons as they did so. The officer and a few men about him stood firm, determined that if they had to die, they would do so fighting. As those in front of him disappeared, I realised that the officer was the old grey-haired general who had tried to save the prisoners at the Alamo. "Don't kill that officer," I shouted, determined to try and return the favour. More of his comrades were killed or ran away but even when the old man stood alone, he would not retreat. He had his sword in his hand and was daring us to fight him. My view was suddenly blocked by a man on horseback; it was Rusk, the Texian minister for war. He too was trying to save the general, either out of respect for his courage or because he would have made a valuable prisoner. I watched him push one Texian away, but it was too late, for when the horse wheeled about, I saw another man shoot the general in the back.

We pressed on through the camp, the tents dividing the battlefield into smaller segments of revenge and destruction. Never one to be first at the enemy if I could help it, I was content to let the more bloodthirsty precede us. I paused to reload my musket. It was well to

290

be prepared for anything we might encounter. The air was filled with screams, truncated Spanish calls for mercy and above them the roaring shouts of, "Remember the Alamo!" There were no regular crashing volleys as at Coleto, but instead sporadic single shots, often, I suspected, of execution. Certainly, the ground between the canvas walls was littered with the dead and precious few wounded as we passed through it.

I was sure I had already accounted for one of the devils and was in no great hurry to kill any more. Colonel Garay and that young woman had saved my life, and there was only one more Mexican that I wanted to see dead, Santa Anna, or so I thought. We pushed on, cautiously now for you never knew what a desperate or frightened man might do. As we passed one tent, I heard a man inside reciting a prayer in Spanish over and over again. I let him be. Hamish pointed to a flag flying just beyond the next tent. We were in the centre of the camp and I knew that the flagpole had to be outside the grand marquee of *el Presidente.* I grinned with delight. I did not care if someone had killed him before us, just as long as the bastard was dead. We crept forward. It was quieter now as most of the battle had moved on, but we could hear some Texians shouting in the next avenue between the tents from us.

"He went to the right," asserted one man.

"Dang you, I'm sure he went left," called another.

Hamish reached out and grabbed my arm. He gestured to a gap between a row of tents and there I saw him. A man was crouched down next to the side of a tent, a sword in one hand and a plumed hat in the other. He was slowly backing away from the men who were searching for him. It wasn't Santa Anna, but judging from the braid on his shoulders and sleeves he was quite senior for a young man. His head turned briefly so that I got his profile and then I recognised him. There was a scar on his cheek that I had seen before: he was one of Santa Anna's peacock staff officers. I remembered all too well his laughing face as he had sabred the bound prisoners at the Alamo. I raised my musket, but as I did so the hand holding his hat found the flap of the tent. Before I could even cock the weapon, he had slipped inside. I cursed quietly but I was not blindly following him inside. We had passed a campfire a few yards back. I was just contemplating burning the devil out when I saw the side of the tent stretch. There was a rustling sound as the man crept about, probably to shift a campaign bed or chest so he could hide behind it, and then the tent wall moved again. There was the curve of a back pressed against it and if I was in any doubt, I could see the shape of a boot heel below it with a silver spur poking out underneath the canvas side.

Smiling, I crept forward and levelled the musket so that the muzzle was not more than a couple of inches from the man's spine. "This is for the prisoners at the Alamo," I whispered softly in Spanish. The canvas moved as the man jumped in surprise, but it was too late, much too late to escape his richly deserved end. I pulled the trigger and stepped back. There was the clatter of falling furniture inside and then a lump slumped against the bottom of the tent. Where I had shot, the blackened edges of the hole smouldered from the muzzle flash, but I was watching, with a grim satisfaction, the canvas below it, where a dark crimson stain was slowly soaking into the cloth.

Chapter 35

The battle now known as San Jacinto lasted no more than twenty minutes. In truth there was little of a battle at all, as few of the Mexicans made any show of resistance. Houston had lost control of his army as soon as someone had shouted our battle-cry and Santa Anna was nowhere to be seen marshalling his forces. Hamish and I entered *el Presidente's* tent to find that it had already been ransacked, a large bed upended, presumably to check that the knave was not hiding underneath it.

Unrestrained, the Texians were free to indulge in a terrible bloodlust on their enemies. As we moved forward we found the bodies of men who had been shot, clubbed, stabbed, tomahawked and one who had even been scalped. Initially, we saw no prisoners taken at all. Screams from the marsh ahead confirmed that the slaughter was continuing. Following the sound of shooting we found a large lake in the middle of the marsh beyond the camp. Mexicans were trying to swim across although only yet more swamp and the sea waited beyond. I could also see some of our army already working their way around the other side. The rest stood on the bank, firing their rifles at any of the bodies that moved on the water. It was literally like shooting fish in a barrel – there must have been at least a hundred corpses floating on the lake. Some did not even get that far. We found the bodies of Mexicans who had sunk beyond their knees in the marsh mud as they had tried to escape the vengeful Texians. They must have been stuck and helpless when they were discovered, but musket and rifle ball injuries to their heads and bodies showed that they had received little mercy.

Some of the Texian officers belatedly tried to regain control of their men. They rode around the edge of the lake and attempted to persuade their men to take some prisoners instead of killing every Mexican they saw. I spotted at least one Texian colonel be threatened with a gun himself for his trouble. To me it looked little different to the Mexican cavalry hunting down the running fugitives of the Goliad massacre. I turned away in disgust and was relieved to find at least one Texian commander had held sway over his soldiers, for a large group of some four hundred Mexican prisoners were being marched back to the camp under guard. They had surrendered en masse on the promise of being spared. Disappointingly, Santa Anna was not among them, in fact no one I spoke to knew if he was dead or alive.

Eventually, even the most bloodthirsty Texian had sated his need to avenge fallen friends, burnt farmsteads and the fear inflicted on him by the Mexican invasion of Texas as they saw it. By then the surface of the lake was covered in bodies, either shot, drowned or surviving by floating *very* still. Men at last found the time to stop and reflect on what had just happened. The army of Texas had won its battle and it was an astonishing victory. There can have been no more than thirty Texians killed or wounded that I saw. In contrast there must have been five hundred bodies of Mexican soldiers scattered throughout the camp, floating on the water or lying on the ground in between. A similar number had also been eventually taken prisoner. The Mexican cavalry had been chased away. Most had ridden to where they expected to find Vince's bridge and were then forced to ride down the near vertical sides of the ravine, before falling into the water where many drowned.

The prisoners were herded in to a circle of brightly burning fires, partly for their own protection as the Texians drank and celebrated their victory. Mexicans were still being found hiding in the camp or out on the prairie and now, more often than not, these were spared. Small groups of them would be pushed forward between the flames to join their comrades who sat and quietly speculated on their likely fate. The sound of shooting had been replaced by laughter and even drunken singing as men celebrated their victory.

For a man who had just accomplished an extraordinarily one-sided triumph against the odds, Houston was surprisingly sombre when I next saw him. He was sitting against a tree glowering at the prisoners, as though he had been beaten by them rather than as their victor.

"What is the matter with him?" I asked Seguín, gesturing at our general.

"He has been shot in the ankle," explained the Tejano. "But I rather think it is the absence of Santa Anna that is causing him more pain."

"Yes, I was hoping to have seen him get his neck stretched by now myself," I grumbled.

"Houston wanted to use Santa Anna rather than kill him," explained my friend. "He is worried about Filisola. He is out there with an army of some three thousand Mexican soldiers. Urrea too still has over a thousand. We might have had a victory, but the war is not won. Only Santa Anna can order them back and even then, they might not obey if he is held prisoner."

"You mean we might have to retreat over the San Jacinto after all?" I asked.

"If *el Presidente* makes it back to the rest of his army," explained Seguín, "then he will be even more determined than ever to crush resistance in Texas to outweigh the memory of this defeat."

Thoughts like that rather took the edge off any feeling of jubilation, at least for me. Many of my comrades in arms were not looking that far ahead as they caroused into the night. I was fairly sure that they would not take the suggestion of another retreat well. This victory had only convinced them that they were easily the match for any Mexican force that they came across. If they rushed headlong south, then I feared another Coleto Creek encounter and I resolved that they would go south without me. I was still feeling cheated that for all the days of recent marching, I had been robbed of seeing Santa Anna's well-deserved end. I was not the only one. The following morning Houston sent out search parties far and wide looking for more prisoners trying to escape south. As well as *el Presidente*, General Cos had also escaped us. Many wanted to hang him too as he had broken his parole given when they let him leave the previous year.

I was among the few Texians who had actually seen Santa Anna. Consequently, I was sent out to look at the corpses of various officers who had been gathered to see if he was among the dead. It was a grim task. The long line of broken bodies I was obliged to study included the grey-haired general, who had died with a look of fierce determination on his face. There was also the murderous bastard I had shot in the back. With his gaudy uniform, several had been convinced that the staff officer was *el Presidente*. I had to explain why I had killed him before they would believe that their quarry was still at large. In the afternoon a boat was found and men rowed about the lake turning over the floating bodies and dragging any senior officers ashore for inspection.

By the end of the afternoon it looked like our bird had either flown or was dead and lay undiscovered in the marshes. A steady stream of fugitives had been found, though, most grateful to be helped from the swamps once they understood that they would not be summarily executed. We had been obliged to widen the circle of fires to accommodate the extra prisoners. They had been fed and allowed to fetch water, and some had even been sent out to gather firewood. Most were miserable specimens who were just grateful to be alive. I doubted that they would be tempted to escape. They still looked fearfully at the men who had suddenly stopped running and had turned on them with the ferocity of fighting terriers.

I remember I was chewing on some beef as another group of Mexicans was driven into the camp from the marshes. They were wet and covered in mud, barely recognisable as human, never mind soldiers. A couple of voices called out in greeting from the prisoners and one even fetched the new arrivals a bucket so that they could start to wash the filth off. I watched them idly, hoping familiar features would be revealed, but none of them had the bearing of a man who had imperiously ordered hundreds of executions.

"Viva Santa Anna!" I had been distracted by a pretty woman sitting amongst the prisoners when I heard the shout. Immediately my gaze shot to the men by the bucket, but they like the others were craning their necks to look at the other side of the camp. There five horsemen were reining up. One had lowered a prisoner to the ground from behind his saddle. The new arrival was a bedraggled figure in a blue peasant's smock and what appeared to be red carpet slippers. As he stooped submissively before his captors I was unsure, but then he looked across at the men acclaiming him and he could not help his back stiffen with pride.

"That's him," I shouted somewhat unnecessarily, for now half of the prisoners were on their feet yelling, *"Viva Santa Anna!"* and *"El Presidente!"* I rushed forward, running around the prisoner encampment and calling for someone to fetch a rope. A quick lynching would have to wait, though, for Santa Anna had formally introduced himself to one of the Texian officers and asked to be presented to Houston.

"Keep back, we're taking him to see the general," the officer shouted, for I was not the only one with ideas on how *el Presidente* should be dealt with. The other prisoners must have been left unguarded, for I suspect that virtually the entire army followed Santa Anna across the prairie. We went to where Houston was lying under a tree with his bandaged ankle propped up over a blanket. He looked surprised, if not slightly alarmed to have his soldiers converge on him in such excitement. Wincing in pain he forced himself up into a sitting position and then stared with curiosity at the strangely dressed man thrust in front of him.

The prisoner drew himself up as tall as he could, he was much shorter than the men standing around him. Then he spoke in a loud, clear voice in Spanish. "I am General Antonio López de Santa Anna, President of Mexico, Commander-in-Chief of the Army of Operations. I place myself at the disposal of the brave General Houston."

I doubt Houston understood more than half of this little speech, but he did pick up the name of his guest and a smile of relief spread across his features. "General Santa Anna, ah indeed. Take a seat, General. I am glad to see you." He gestured towards a black box nearby for the president to sit on and beckoned a Tejano to come forward to interpret.

Santa Anna sat nervously on the box, clearly conscious of a growl of disapproval from the growing crowd of men towering over him. I was not the only one who thought that our general was being far too hospitable. The prisoner cleared his throat and spoke to the interpreter while gesturing at Houston. "That man may consider himself born to no common destiny who has conquered the Napoleon of the West. It now remains for him to be generous to the vanquished."

Houston's eyes narrowed in scorn when he heard the translation. "You should have remembered that at the Alamo," he replied. Santa Anna started to make a bland excuse about the necessities of war, but Houston did not let him finish. "What excuse is there for the massacre of Fannin's men?" he demanded.

We all cheered our approval at this line of questioning. I turned when something knocked against my leg as it was passed through the crowd. I grabbed eagerly at the coil of rope with a noose already tied at one end and threw it on the floor in front of Santa Anna and Houston. "He has no excuses, let's string the bastard up," I demanded to a cheer from those around me. Santa Anna glanced down at the rope and colour drained from his features, then he turned to look at the crowd of us towering over him on his box. Our hatred must have been visible on every face. More than a few were holding knives and tomahawks and set to do the job of the rope personally.

Santa Anna raised a hand to his cheek and unconsciously brushed at his neck. I saw that the fingers that just minutes before had waved to acknowledge the shouts of salute from his soldiers, were now trembling with fear. "I am feeling a little indisposed," he mumbled. "I wonder if I might trouble you for a piece of opium."

Houston sent someone off to fetch the drug, while he ordered us all to take a couple of paces back to give Santa Anna more room. There were shouts of protest at this but, as he often did, the general ignored the views of his men.

Suitably restored with the soothing effects of the poppy, *el Presidente* recovered some of his confidence. "You have beaten me and I am your prisoner," he admitted. "But Filisola and Urrea are not beaten and they will be here soon."

"Then you had better give me some good reason to keep you alive," Houston retorted. Gesturing to the crowd of men encircling the discussion he added, "Or you will not live to see their arrival."

"We could agree an armistice," suggested Santa Anna, "but my officers would not observe it if I was killed."

"You will give orders to your generals that they should immediately evacuate Texas," demanded Houston. "Then the government of Texas will decide your fate." There was a murmur as this ultimatum was repeated through the crowd. Some were groaning in disgust at the leniency, but others could see that a single man's life to get their country and property back may not be a bad deal.

Santa Anna's eyes flickered once more at the crowd. He can have been in little doubt what his fate would be if he refused. This master of treachery and intrigue knew he had no choice but to agree, yet still he hesitated. I could guess at what he was thinking. He studied Houston, gauging if the general was a man of his word, or if he would be swinging from a rope before the ink on the orders was dry. Houston returned his gaze with a steady glare. Perhaps Santa Anna remembered stories that indicated his captor was a man of honour. The Cherokee trusted his word and when Houston's marriage broke down within days of the nuptials, he had refused to reveal the reason to protect the lady's reputation, even though it cost him the governorship of Tennessee. Slowly the Mexican nodded. Hundreds might have died for his ambition over the previous weeks, but he would live, at least for now. He still had cards to play and if these simple Texians were foolish enough to trust *his* word, then he would let them have their country. He would bide his time and make what promises he must to get his freedom. Then, God willing, he would take it all back and make them pay for their leniency. Santa Anna summoned a smile that did not extend to his eyes and asked the translator for a pen, ink and paper to issue the necessary orders.

"You really gonna let that snake live?" demanded one of the Texians as the Mexican president was taken away under a heavy guard. It was a sentiment I shared; from what I had heard of him, I would not have trusted Santa Anna an inch. I did not care about Texas, but I did want to avenge the poor devils I had fought with and settle the score for his attempts to kill me.

Deaf Smith was to take the freshly signed orders to Fisicola. He would be accompanied by some Mexican officers who could vouch that the orders came from the Mexican president and that he was still alive. But once those couriers were over the horizon, there was nothing to stop us stringing the villain up. I was damn sure that was what Santa

Anna would do if the boot was on the other foot. I will say one thing for *el Presidente*, he was a good judge of character, for he had sensed that his opposing general was a man of rather more scruples than many of the Texian soldiers, including me.

"Are we fighting to kill Mexicans or are we fighting to win Texas?" Houston demanded. Without waiting for an answer, he gestured over his shoulder where piles of bodies still lay unburied or floating, now swollen, in the lake. "There are enough dead Mexicans over there," he growled, "I want Texas." Then he pulled an ear of corn from under his blanket and began to nibble on it to signal an end to the discussion. I'll own to feeling cheated at the time and I was not alone. Houston allowed Santa Anna to stay in his old tent although under a heavy guard of men he trusted, for there were more than a few who would have liked to cut one more Mexican throat.

A day later the Texian president Burnet arrived. For a man who had openly accused his army commander of cowardice, he was remarkably ungrateful to a general who had achieved an astounding victory. By then we were getting reports that Fisicola had stopped his advance and was now retreating in accordance with his new orders. Texas was secure, yet Burnet spurned Houston's company. He had the nerve to reprimand his general for the use of profanity. Then this back-stabbing weasel toured the scene of the victory with his friend Colonel Sherman. I did not doubt he was getting a very biased view of affairs.

The politicians confiscated every souvenir they could lay their hands on, but mindful of votes in the future, promised generous land grants to all who had taken part in the battle. Hamish had begun to look less like an Indian the longer I knew him. Now he was conflicted at the thought of having land of his own to farm like the other soldiers or continuing to live by Indian traditions. "Your father spent years trying to persuade the Iroquois to live as farmers," I told him. "You have got me to safety and I am grateful. Now I am going to get on a ship back to the United States. Why don't you speak to your father about it? He knows all about living between two cultures." I gave him my address in England and he left the next day. As it turned out he need not have worried, for the Texian government was not going to give land to Indians, whether they had fought at San Jacinto or not. A few years later he wrote to me asking if I had been given land. I had not even made a claim, but I did then. I was granted acres not just for San Jacinto but for the Alamo and Goliad too. It came to quite a holding and I gave it all to Hamish. It was the least I could do for the son of an old friend.

I easily managed to get passage on the ship that was taking the politicians back to Galveston Island. I simply mentioned my rank and gave the impression that I was an unofficial observer from the British government. I hinted that a report from me should see their nation recognised in London and a berth was swiftly provided. Houston was not so fortunate. His wound was getting worse and Doc Ewing was certain that the general should go to New Orleans for surgery. Burnet insisted the boat was full and he would have to wait, which was a wicked lie. Fortunately, the captain of the vessel refused to sail until Houston was on board. A more grateful Rusk, the secretary of war, helped carry his stretcher aboard. As revenge, Burnet then spent much of the passage regaling passengers with licentious tales of Houston's private life. It was then I heard about the end of his marriage and several colourful explanations of the cause.

On reaching Galveston, a request from Houston to travel to New Orleans on a Texian naval vessel was likewise refused. Eventually, by dropping Vanderbilt's name and promising payment on reaching our destination, I managed to secure a filthy trading schooner called the *Flora* to take us to the United States for an exorbitant fee. For seven days that damned tub rolled about in a storm. I began to doubt if Houston would survive the journey, for at times he was delirious. Finally, at noon on Sunday the twenty second of May 1836, some four and a half months since I left New York, we tied up at the levee at New Orleans.

If the politicians in Texas had not appreciated his efforts, the people of Louisiana certainly did. As word spread of our passenger, the pier was soon packed with a cheering crowd. Many had friends and relatives who had gone south to fight in the war. News of San Jacinto had come before us. Those who had been certain that the Republic of

Texas was lost, were anxious to recognise the man who had pulled off an impossible victory. They were soon swarming up the gangplank to congratulate Houston personally. Some even tried to carry him ashore, but the pain of his wound caused him to cry out and throw them off. Eventually, he insisted that he would stand and address the growing crowd from the rail. Leaning on his crutches he staggered to the side and stared down at the throng on the key. Those looking up for the Hector of this new country, found their rousing cheers dying in their throats.

Instead of a victorious general, before them stood a wild man leaning heavily on my arm. He had no hat, his coat was in tatters and his shirt was wrapped around his ankle. But above his matted beard and pale cheeks, two eyes stared fiercely at the now silent crowd before him. You could have heard a pin drop until Vanderbilt's voice called out plaintively from the shore, "I say, Flashman, is that you?"

While Houston was having twenty pieces of bone removed from his leg and nearly dying in the process, I was enjoying the finest hospitality New Orleans had to offer. I remembered James Bowie saying he often went there for the New Year celebrations and I could see why. Vanderbilt could not do enough for me when I told him of my adventures, blaming himself for bringing me to that hostile shore and persuading me to go with Bowie. I let him feel guilty too, for it was all his deuced idea anyway. While I had been suffering, he had been in New Orleans waiting for news and then consoling himself when he thought I was dead. Free from the shackles of his uncle, he had been working his way through all the best houses the French Quarter had to offer. I was about to avail myself of the same, when he announced we had to leave without delay.

"I wrote to tell Louisa that you were last heard of at the Alamo," he admitted. "If she has not already, she will hear soon what happened there and fear the worst. We must set sail tomorrow and try and outrun the news."

"But surely we can wait a day or two," I protested, eyeing a comely wench who exuded licentiousness in the same way that the smell of meat precedes the pieman.

"But no," objected Vanderbilt, handing me a sealed letter. "She has sent me this and insisted that I hand it to you the minute you return."

I reached forward and snapped the seal of the letter. What could be so urgent? I wondered. Perhaps the Norton trial was over and we could go home – now there was a thought. A few days in this delicious den of vice, a swift passage to New York and then home to Leicestershire. No wide-open prairies there or Mexican cavalry, just peaceful bucolic English countryside, relaxation and a trip to London for gaming and other mischief when required. If ever a man was more deserving of the comforts of home, I could not imagine it. I undid the letter and looked on with disbelief.

Dear Thomas, I read, noting that the letter was dated a month before.

William tells me that you are riding around looking at guns, while he sells your goods for profit. Do come back as soon as you can, for while you are enjoying yourself, I fear we are straining the hospitality of our hosts. A letter from Ben D'Urban has been forwarded on inviting us to join him in South Africa. I have accepted as it will be a delight to travel again and you must soon be bored riding around looking at old cannon.

Your loving wife, Louisa.

Historical Notes

As usual I am indebted to a range of often deliberately conflicting sources to confirm the detail in Flashman's account of the war that secured the independence of Texas. These include *Texian Iliad* by Stephen L. Hardin, *A Time to Stand* by Walter Lord, *Exodus from the Alamo* by Phillip Tucker, *Three Roads to the Alamo* by William Davis, *The Raven: A Biography of Sam Houston* by Marquis James and *A Narrative of the Life of David Crockett* by the man himself.

The term 'Texan' was not used in Flashman's time in Texas. Citizens originating from North America were referred to as Texians while those with Hispanic roots were called Tejanos. Many early Texian settlers married Tejana women and so initially there was little conflict, but tensions between the two communities grew in subsequent years.

The Norton Trial

The character of Charles Lamb/Lord Melbourne will be familiar to readers of *Flashman's Waterloo*. He was sued by George Norton for damages of £10,000 relating to 'criminal conversation' with Norton's wife, Caroline. The trial took place in June 1836. Norton bribed servants to provide salacious testimony, but the case was dismissed as his witnesses were thought unreliable. George Norton does seem to have been the repellent character that Flashman describes. When his wife left him and lived on earnings from her writing, he claimed this money as her husband. He also denied her access to their children until one died in an accident. As a result of Caroline Norton's campaigning various pieces of legislation were introduced to protect the rights of wives and women in general. There is no evidence to confirm that Norton's uncle is the forbear who gave John Norton his surname, although his uncle, Chapple Norton, was serving as an army officer in North America at the right time.

James Bowie

'Jim' Bowie is now more famous for his knife, but in Flashman's time, at least in certain states, he was more notorious for his fraudulent land dealing. He was certainly a formidable character and all the stories told to Flashman of his past exploits, such as killing a man with his huge blade after being shot and stabbed and his fight with Indians while looking for a silver mine, are all true. Bowie did seem to be genuinely in love with his wife Ursula, who was the daughter of a former governor of the province. Bowie converted to Catholicism for the marriage and had many friends among the Tejano community. He had been a pugnacious leader in the fight for Texas independence in 1835, but may well have been in pain from his illness for much of the time Flashman knew him. He certainly supported the plan to hold the Alamo, although he doubtless expected more in the way of reinforcements when he made that decision. He resented Travis, who had far less experience, being in command and did insist on a ballot that saw him elected commander of the volunteers. His illness prevented him from playing any major role in the siege and despite Hollywood depictions, he was unlikely to have been able to put up much of a fight during the final storming of the Alamo.

David Crockett

'Davy' Crockett was an expert hunter, scout and marksman, though a poor farmer and husband (he was faithful, but abandoned his wives for long periods to pursue things he wanted to do). Most of the anecdotes recounted in Flashman's account are confirmed by other sources, often Crockett's own autobiography. He was a great storyteller, could command a crowd and was a reasonably straightforward and principled politician – a rarity then and now. In short, he is probably the real historical figure in this book that readers would most like to share a 'horn of ale' with.

In the 1950s a memoir of a Mexican officer present at the Alamo was published, which claimed that Crockett was among those who had surrendered. This caused some controversy as a Walt Disney mini-series on Crockett was running at the time. However, it is highly doubtful that any Mexican officer would have recognised Crockett from the other prisoners. One of the few present who would have known him, Susanna Dickinson (wife of Lieutenant Almaron Dickinson, who died in the battle,) attested that she saw his body in front of the chapel, where Flashman found it.

William Barret Travis

Travis trained as a lawyer in Alabama and also ran a small newspaper there, but his practice did not flourish. He had taken a young wife and lived beyond his means. Eventually, his creditors sued for payment. To escape prison and humiliation, he abandoned his pregnant wife and infant son and fled south to start a new life. In Texas he set up a new law practice, which due to less competition, began to succeed. Travis then gradually became involved with Texas politics. He became a spokesperson for the rights of Texians against what he saw as oppressive Mexican authority and spent time in jail as a result. He increasingly worked for Texian local government officials and was one of the first to agitate for Texan independence. During the fighting in 1835 Travis served in the Texian army and briefly commanded a cavalry troop, but he had little military experience before he found himself in command at the Alamo. He died aged just twenty-six.

Antonio López de Santa Anna

A copper-bottomed villain who served twelve non-consecutive presidential terms in Mexico over a period of twenty-two years. It is difficult to summarise such a long career in a single paragraph, but essentially there was not a cause he faltered to betray or a back he refrained from stabbing, if it advanced his career. His many periods of disastrous rule saw Mexico lose huge swathes of territory to the United States. He also accrued vast wealth while his people languished in poverty. When he finally fell out of favour, he travelled extensively to the United States and Europe. As if his earlier crimes were not bad enough, he is also credited with introducing chewing gum to the United States – think of him next time some is stuck on your shoe. He died in Mexico City in 1876, at the ripe old age of eighty-two.

The Battle of the Alamo

Contemporary witnesses confirm that the siege and battle at the Alamo took place largely as Flashman described. In contrast to Hollywood depictions, the assault took place before dawn, possibly pre-empted by the shouting of a soldier. Initially, the defenders managed to hold the Mexicans off, but once they made their way in through the west wall, the defence quickly collapsed. While legend has it that the defenders all fought to the death at their posts, it is likely that some tried to make an escape. There is evidence from various Mexican sources of men trying to flee over the south wall, through the palisade. Other claims that virtually the entire garrison made a run for it, seem unlikely. Certainly, some made it to the central barrack block to make a final defence. Mexican accounts also confirm that at least one defender tried to surrender with a white flag through a loophole while his comrades were still shooting. This outraged the Mexicans, who did then demolish that building with the eighteen-pounder cannon.

Legend also has it that the entire garrison was slaughtered, but there is evidence of some survivors. The man known as Louis Rose certainly survived although historians are divided as to whether he left at the end of the siege as he maintained. He certainly does not seem to be the veteran French officer he claimed as that man died in France, never having visited Texas. Historians are similarly divided over the case of Henry Warnell. He was definitely at the Alamo during the siege, but some court documents claim that he escaped and died of his wounds three months later at Port Lavaca. Others suggest he died at the Alamo with the rest of the garrison as they cannot understand how such a wounded man could have escaped and travelled all the way to the coast. Flashman's account gives an explanation.

A more certain survivor is the former Mexican soldier Brigido Guerrero. His discovery by the Mexicans as an apparent prisoner of the Texians is mentioned in two contemporary diaries. Later the evidence was sufficiently clear to entitle him to a pension as an Alamo survivor.

Finally, despite Flashman's colourful assumptions, Three-legged Willie Williamson, the man who wrote to Travis with news of reinforcements, got his name as he had to use a crutch to get about.

Coleto Creek and the Goliad Massacre

The more famous siege of the Alamo has overshadowed what was a much larger massacre of Texian forces at Goliad. This is probably because Alamo defenders were, according to legend, making a noble self-sacrifice for their country while those at Goliad surrendered and trusted to the mercy of their captors. In reality, the Alamo defenders had little choice once they were trapped in the fort, as Santa Anna did not give the Texians the chance to surrender. General Urrea did offer terms at Coleto Creek, which were accepted by Fannin and his commanders, as by then their position was truly hopeless. Outnumbered, outgunned, without food or water and with substantial numbers of wounded, there was really little alternative. Fannin had led his men bravely through the battle and should not be condemned for the act of surrendering. However, his delays and prevarications in the days and hours before the battle were largely responsible for his army being caught in the first place. Captain King should also shoulder some of the blame as if he had swiftly withdrawn the Texians at Refugio as he had been ordered to by Fannin, then the Goliad garrison may well have been able to escape and join with Houston.

General Urrea does seem to have been genuine in offering terms. The only surviving copy of the surrender document makes it clear that it is at the Mexican government's discretion, but Urrea sent a strongly worded recommendation of his terms to Santa Anna. He also did his best to countermand the massacre order when he heard of it.

Francita Alavez also known as the 'Angel of Goliad' really existed and there is a statue of her in Goliad to this day. Along with Colonel Francisco Garay, they saved a number of Texians from execution. However, it seems that Miller's men owe their survival to a brave officer on Santa Anna's staff who pointed out that these volunteers had not yet taken up arms against Mexico when they were captured. As a result they were excluded from the original execution warrant.

San Jacinto

The battle of San Jacinto took place as described by Flashman, including the great disparity in the casualties. The timing of the attack took the Mexican force completely by surprise and they were not able to recover any order before the forces of Texas rampaged through their camp. The attackers were spurred on by a pent-up sense of frustration at their earlier retreats as well as anger at the atrocities suffered by their comrades.

A largely conscript army that probably did not want to be in Texas in the first place was overwhelmed by a smaller, but highly motivated assault. Beyond Houston choosing the timing of the attack, the two commanding generals played little part in the actual battle. The grey-haired general mentioned was Manuel Fernández Castrillón. Mexican accounts confirm that he did try to dissuade Santa Anna from executing the prisoners at the Alamo. He was the only senior Mexican officer who was seen to try and organise a defence at San Jacinto. He refused to retreat and while the Texian secretary of war did try to save him, the general was killed in the melee. The other Mexican general at San Jacinto and Santa Anna's brother-in-law, General Cos, was captured by the Texians two days after his president.

While Houston faced huge pressure to execute Santa Anna after the battle, he was mindful of the much larger Mexican army of Fisicola that was nearby and the leverage that holding a living president gave him in liberating Texas. Once Santa Anna issued the orders, the remaining Mexican generals and their armies in Texas began their retreat south. Texas was finally liberated.

Sam Houston

Houston is a very divisive figure amongst contemporary sources, with some claiming he was an unreliable, drunken incompetent, while others describe him as a father of the nation. For example, accounts of the council of war before the Battle of Jacinto vary wildly, some witnesses categorically claim that he proposed a retreat across the river, yet others are equally adamant, he did no such thing. My personal view is that if he had proposed another retreat, that would probably have been the final straw for most of his officers and he would have been relieved of command. Secretary of War, Rusk, had an authority to do just that, which he refrained from using.

After this book ends, Houston was called back urgently to Texas and became its next president. He did much to build the new nation, creating a new currency and developing policies that gave it a stable value. He also tried to rebuild relations with Mexico and with Native American tribes in the region. Barred by the Constitution from seeking a second term, he was succeeded by Mirabeau Bonaparte Lamar, his former cavalry commander. Lamar, working with Houston's old enemy Burnet, undid much of his good work, causing the Texas economy to crash. Houston was re-elected president in 1841and worked with his friends north of the border to have Texas annexed into the United States. This was finally achieved in February 1846, ten years after the siege of the Alamo began. Subsequently, Houston served as a United States senator and later as governor of Texas. He campaigned against Texas joining the confederacy and as a result was dismissed as governor. He died during the American Civil War in 1863, aged seventy.

Thank you for reading this book and I hoped you enjoyed it. If so I would be grateful for any positive reviews on websites that you use to choose books. As there is no major publisher promoting this book, any recommendations to friends and family that you think would enjoy it would also be appreciated.

There is now a Thomas Flashman Books Facebook page and the www.robertbrightwell.com website to keep you updated on future books in the series. They also include portraits, pictures and further information on characters and events featured in the books.

Also by this author

Flashman and the Seawolf

This first book in the Thomas Flashman series covers his adventures with Thomas Cochrane, one of the most extraordinary naval commanders of all time.

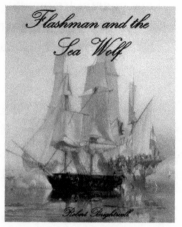

From the brothels and gambling dens of London, through political intrigues and espionage, the action moves to the Mediterranean and the real life character of Thomas Cochrane. This book covers the start of Cochrane's career including the most astounding single ship action of the Napoleonic war.

Thomas Flashman provides a unique insight as danger stalks him like a persistent bailiff through a series of adventures that prove history really is stranger than fiction.

Flashman and the Cobra

This book takes Thomas to territory familiar to readers of his nephew's adventures, India, during the second Mahratta war. It also includes an illuminating visit to Paris during the Peace of Amiens in 1802.

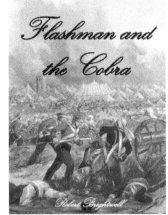

As you might expect Flashman is embroiled in treachery and scandal from the outset and, despite his very best endeavours, is often in the thick of the action. He intrigues with generals, warlords, fearless warriors, nomadic bandit tribes, highland soldiers and not least a four-foot-tall former nautch dancer, who led the only Mahratta troops to leave the battlefield of Assaye in good order.

Flashman gives an illuminating account with a unique perspective. It details feats of incredible courage (not his, obviously) reckless folly and sheer good luck that were to change the future of India and the career of a general who would later win a war in Europe.

Flashman in the Peninsula

While many people have written books
and novels on the Peninsular War,
Flashman's memoirs offer a unique
perspective. They include new accounts
of famous battles, but also incredible
incidents and characters almost forgotten
by history.

Flashman is revealed as the catalyst to
one of the greatest royal scandals of the
nineteenth century which disgraced a prince and ultimately produced
one of our greatest novelists. In Spain and Portugal he witnesses
catastrophic incompetence and incredible courage in equal measure.
He is present at an extraordinary action where a small group of men
stopped the army of a French marshal in its tracks. His flatulent horse
may well have routed a Spanish regiment, while his cowardice and
poltroonery certainly saved the British army from a French trap.

Accompanied by Lord Byron's dog, Flashman faces death from Polish
lancers and a vengeful Spanish midget, not to mention finding time to
perform a blasphemous act with the famous Maid of Zaragoza. This is
an account made more astonishing as the key facts are confirmed by
various historical sources.

Flashman's Escape

This book covers the second half of Thomas Flashman's experiences in the Peninsular War and follows on from *Flashman in the Peninsula*.

Having lost his role as a staff officer, Flashman finds himself commanding a company in an infantry battalion. In between cuckolding his soldiers and annoying his superiors, he finds himself at the heart of the two bloodiest actions of the war. With drama and disaster in equal measure, he provides a first-hand account of not only the horror of battle but also the bloody aftermath.

Hopes for a quieter life backfire horribly when he is sent behind enemy lines to help recover an important British prisoner, who also happens to be a hated rival. His adventures take him the length of Spain and all the way to Paris on one of the most audacious wartime journeys ever undertaken.

With the future of the French empire briefly placed in his quaking hands, Flashman dodges lovers, angry fathers, conspirators and ministers of state in a desperate effort to keep his cowardly carcass in one piece. It is a historical roller-coaster ride that brings together various extraordinary events, while also giving a disturbing insight into the creation of a French literary classic!

Flashman and Madison's War

This book finds Thomas, a British army officer, landing on the shores of the United States at the worst possible moment – just when the United States has declared war with Britain! Having already endured enough with his earlier adventures, he desperately wants to go home but finds himself drawn inexorably into this new conflict. He is soon dodging musket balls, arrows and tomahawks 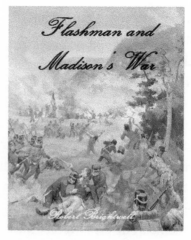 as he desperately tries to keep his scalp intact and on his head.

It is an extraordinary tale of an almost forgotten war, with inspiring leaders, incompetent commanders, a future American president, terrifying warriors (and their equally intimidating women), brave sailors, trigger-happy madams and a girl in a wet dress who could have brought a city to a standstill. Flashman plays a central role and reveals that he was responsible for the disgrace of one British general, the capture of another and for one of the biggest debacles in British military history.

Flashman's Waterloo

The first six months of 1815 were a pivotal time in European history. As a result, countless books have been written by men who were there and by those who studied it afterwards. But despite this wealth of material there are still many unanswered questions including:

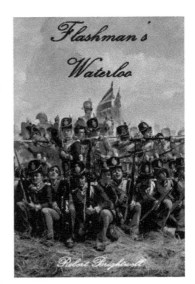

-Why did the man who promised to bring Napoleon back in an iron cage, instead join his old commander?
-Why was Wellington so convinced that the French would not attack when they did?
-Why was the French emperor ill during the height of the battle, leaving its management to the hot-headed Marshal Ney?
-What possessed Ney to launch a huge and disastrous cavalry charge in the middle of the battle?
-Why did the British Head of Intelligence always walk with a limp after the conflict?

The answer to all these questions in full or in part can be summed up in one word: Flashman.

This extraordinary tale is aligned with other historical accounts of the Waterloo campaign and reveals how Flashman's attempt to embrace the quiet diplomatic life backfires spectacularly. The memoir provides a unique insight into how Napoleon returned to power, the treachery and intrigues around his hundred-day rule and how ultimately he was robbed of victory. It includes the return of old friends and enemies from both sides of the conflict and is a fitting climax to Thomas Flashman's Napoleonic adventures.

317

Flashman and the Emperor

This seventh instalment in the memoirs of the Georgian rogue Thomas Flashman reveals that, despite his suffering through the Napoleonic Wars, he did not get to enjoy a quiet retirement. Indeed, middle age finds him acting just as disgracefully as in his youth, as old friends pull him unwittingly back into the fray.

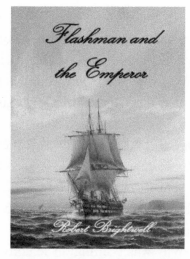

He re-joins his former comrade in arms, Thomas Cochrane, in what is intended to be a peaceful and profitable sojourn in South America. Instead, he finds himself enjoying drug-fuelled orgies in Rio, trying his hand at silver smuggling and escaping earthquakes in Chile before being reluctantly shanghaied into the Brazilian navy.

Sailing with Cochrane again, he joins the admiral in what must be one of the most extraordinary periods of his already legendary career. With a crew more interested in fighting each other than the enemy, they use Cochrane's courage, Flashman's cunning and an outrageous bluff to carve out nothing less than an empire which will stand the test of time.

Flashman and the Golden Sword

Of all the enemies that our hero has shrunk away from, there was one he feared above them all. By his own admission they gave him nightmares into his dotage. It was not the French, the Spanish, the Americans or the Mexicans. It was not even the more exotic adversaries such as the Iroquois, Mahratta or Zulus. While they could all make his guts churn anxiously, the foe that really put him off his lunch were the Ashanti.

"You could not see them coming," he complained. "They were well armed, fought with cunning and above all, there were bloody thousands of the bastards."

This eighth packet in the Thomas Flashman memoirs details his misadventures on the Gold Coast in Africa. It was a time when the British lion discovered that instead of being the king of the jungle, it was in fact a crumb on the lip of a far more ferocious beast. Our 'hero' is at the heart of this revelation after he is shipwrecked on that hostile shore. While waiting for passage home, he is soon embroiled in the plans of a naïve British governor who has hopelessly underestimated his foe. When he is not impersonating a missionary or chasing the local women, Flashman finds himself being trapped by enemy armies, risking execution and the worst kind of 'dismemberment,' not to mention escaping prisons, spies, snakes, water horses (hippopotamus) and crocodiles.

It is another rip-roaring Thomas Flashman adventure, which tells the true story of an extraordinary time in Africa that is now almost entirely forgotten.

Lightning Source UK Ltd.
Milton Keynes UK
UKHW040616121219
355254UK00002B/284/P